Praise for
STARFIST I: FIRST TO FIGHT

"CAUTION! Any book written by Dan Cragg and David Sherman is bound to be addictive, and this is the first in what promises to be a great adventure series. *First to Fight* is rousing, rugged, and just plain fun. The authors have a deep firsthand knowledge of warfare, an enthralling vision of the future, and the skill of veteran writers. Fans of military fiction, science fiction, and suspense will all get their money's worth, and the novel is so well done it will appeal to general readers as well. It's fast, realistic, moral, and a general hoot. *First to Fight* is also vivid, convincing—and hard to put down. Sherman and Cragg are a great team! I can't wait for the next one!"

—RALPH PETERS
New York Times bestselling
author of *Red Army*

By David Sherman and Dan Cragg

By David Sherman

By Dan Cragg

STEEL GAUNTLET

Starfist
Book Three

David Sherman
and
Dan Cragg

A Del Rey® Book
BALLANTINE BOOKS • NEW YORK

A Del Rey® Book
Published by The Random House Publishing Group

Copyright © 1999 by David Sherman and Dan Cragg

Published in the United States by Del Rey Books, an imprint of The Random House Publishing Group, a division of Random House, Inc., New York, and simultaneously in Canada by Random House of Canada, Limited, Toronto.

DEL REY is a registered trademark and the Del Rey colophon is a trademark of Random House, Inc.

ISBN 0-345-42526-X

Printed in the United States of America

www.delreybooks.com

First Edition: January 1999

OPM 9 8

Dedicated to:

Staff Sergeant Pichon, USMC

In peacetime his Marines hated him for being a harsh taskmaster—yet trusted him because he was fair.

In war they knew he had them well enough trained to win their fights—and that he was a good enough leader to bring them back alive.

And:

Staff Sergeant Patrick Spiker, Jr., USA, KIA, Bien Hoa Province, RVN, 15 July 1965

"No plan, no matter how well designed,
ever survives the first shot."
Old military aphorism

ACKNOWLEDGMENTS

Frank Crean for being an idea wall. Owen Lock, who asked, "How would you two guys like to . . ." Linda Lough, Dan West, his sister, Carolyn, and others at the Brick Playhouse for their constant, quiet encouragement and assistance in helping to focus on what storytelling is. J. B. Post, who was there from the beginning, or even earlier, and was more than generous with ideas. And brave readers Lee Lanning, Peter Joannides, and Hal Neeley, who at times might have found our prose as hair-raising as anything the VC/NVA ever threw at them.

PROLOGUE

"Tell me, Gunnery Sergeant Bong, is it true what they say about Marines?"

"What's that, Madame Proconsul?"

"Call me !Tang'h, Gunnery Sergeant. Well, is it true?"

"Ma'am?"

"That they're like their swords. . . ?" She smiled seductively, then looked quickly at the ceremonial sword fastened by its peace knot to his sword belt.

"A good Marine is always ready to stand tall for action, ma'am."

"Gunny, I think you should take a look at this," a small voice said in his right ear.

"Not now, Winterthur," he whispered into the throat mike concealed in the high stork collar of his dress scarlets.

"Gunny, it's *really* important."

"Excuse me for a moment," Gunnery Sergeant Bong said with some frustration. The Honorable Mistress !Tang'h looked even more ravishing than usual, Bong thought as he turned away from the Second Assistant Proconsul from Kalari'h. She'd been flirting with him for several months, and he'd finally managed to convince himself that a personal liaison on an official liaison mission might help in the successful completion of that mission. He blocked out the sounds and sights of the diplomatic reception that swirled around him.

"Take a look at what? This better be good!" he said.

"Ah, Gunny." Lance Corporal Winterthur's voice sounded nervously bemused behind the buzz of the receiver in Gunny Bong's ear. "Somebody just drove up with a bunch of tanks."

1

"What kind of tanks?" Bong asked. "Chemical? Storage? Hydroponic?"

"Don't know their model, Gunny, but they've got turrets with what look like projectile cannons and plasma guns. Looks to be sixty of them."

Bong blinked. "*Armored* vehicles?"

"That's an affirmative, Gunny."

"You sure they aren't armored personnel carriers?" Bong was already walking briskly out of the reception hall, the Honorable Mistress !Tang'h forgotten. Major Katopscu, the Confederation military liaison, watched him leave.

"They're not APCs; they look like something out of a history vid," Winterthur replied over the receiver.

"I'm on my way." As soon as Bong reached the corridor, he broke into a sprint toward the main gate, two hundred meters away. His left hand undid the peace binding that secured the hilt of his ceremonial NCO sword to the sword belt so it couldn't be drawn and shoved the binding into his trouser pocket.

Tanks? Where could anybody come up with sixty tanks? Where could they be made? Then Bong stopped wondering about the wheres and started thinking about the whys of tanks at the gate.

Throughout history, whenever someone paraded cavalry, drove up in tanks, or surrounded an embassy with infantry or artillery, it usually meant war. Three planetwide wars had already been fought on Diamunde for control of its wealth—wars big enough that the Confederation Army had to be sent in to fight along with the Marines who'd originally been dispatched to deal with the situation. The gunny hadn't fought in any of those wars himself but he'd served with plenty of Marines who had. Wars on Diamunde were tough, and just then it seemed that he and his ten Marines might be all that stood between the Confederation of Worlds and another war. He whispered a prayer to the nine Buddhas of peace that Winterthur was mistaken.

"Allah's pointed teeth," he whispered as he rounded the final corner, the Buddhas of peace forgotten and the god of a warlike people invoked. A dozen armored behemoths were arrayed under the lights outside the compound, and a lone Marine, blaster held at port arms, stood at attention in dress scarlets in front of the closed vehicle gate. One tank, probably the battalion commander's, stood five meters in front of PFC Krait. The muzzle of its main cannon pointed directly over his head. In the turret hatch the tank commander casually stood looking down at the Marine.

Bong didn't think there was a chance that none of the tankers were using night-vision devices, but he took that chance anyway and kept to the deepest shadows he could find as he rushed the last thirty meters to the gate house. "Winterthur, I've got your situation in sight," he whispered. "Be with you in about ten seconds."

"Glad to have you aboard, Gunny."

"What did they have to say?" Bong asked as he entered the cinder-block gate house through its rear door and joined the corporal. Cinder block. A nice, cheap building material. The compound's outer walls were also built of cinder block, so neither the gate house nor the walls could stand against a tank's guns or even slow down a tank if its commander decided to drive over or through them. When the embassy was built, nobody had considered the possibility of an armored assault on the embassy compound.

Winterthur shook his head. "Nothing, Gunny. Just a polite request that we open the gate for them." His mouth twisted in a wry smile. "He said," he nodded toward the tank commander looking down at Krait, "they left their invitations in their other suits."

"Right." Bong kept an eye on the lead tanker while he rummaged through the small storage areas of the gate house. "Where is it?" he asked. Winterthur pointed at a drawer. Bong pulled the drawer open, withdrew a holstered hand blaster and hastily strapped it on. A side arm wouldn't be any use against a tank, but having it would make him look more serious than the silly ceremonial sword would.

"What's *he* doing out there?" Bong asked, nodding toward Krait. If one of the two Marines on the gate was facing down the tanks, he thought, it should be Winterthur, the senior man.

Winterthur shook his head. "As soon as they arrived, Krait

said, 'I always wanted to be Horatio at the bridge,' and ran out before I could stop him."

Bong shook his head. Typical of many young Marines, Krait had more courage than common sense. And, compared to the tanks, he wasn't any better armed than Horatio had been. He dismissed the thought. "Is the guard mounted yet?" he asked as he gave his uniform and equipment a final straightening.

"I called Corporal Kovaks right after I called you," Winterthur said. He looked down the street, deeper into the compound. "I hear them coming now."

Bong touched the mike at his throat to change the transmission frequency. "Kovaks, Bong. Hold back. Get everybody out of sight." The rest of the detachment was probably in chameleons and effectively invisible to the eye. But those tanks most likely had infravision devices and could see the Marines' heat signatures. He shook his head sharply and wondered if there was any point in being out of sight. The embassy Marines could take on an infantry battalion and win, maybe even a light armor battalion, but they didn't have any weapons that would be effective against heavy armor.

Satisfied that he was as ready as he could ever be, Bong stood at attention and faced the gate-side door of the gate house. "Wish me luck," he said softly.

"Good luck, Gunny," Winterthur replied as he opened the door for him.

Bong marched outside to a position in front of PFC Krait and pivoted to face him.

Krait sharply twisted his blaster from the diagonal of port arms to the vertical of a blaster salute. "Gunnery Sergeant, Post One reports all secure," he said in a loud, firm voice.

Bong had to admire Krait; he wasn't sure he'd be that calm himself if their positions were reversed. "Post One all secure, aye," Bong responded, and returned the salute. Krait returned his weapon to port arms as sharply as he'd brought it to salute. "Who are these people behind me and why haven't they been dispersed?"

"Gunnery Sergeant, they say they are invited guests and forgot to bring their invitations." A smile flickered across Krait's lips. "I couldn't find their names on the guest list."

"Is your weapon armed?" Bong asked in a lower voice.

"You know it is," Krait answered just as softly.

Bong nodded. "I'll deal with the situation," he said loudly enough for the tank commander to hear him, then dropped his voice again. "If anything happens, take out the man in the turret first. Understand?"

PFC Krait grinned. "Got it, Gunny. He's mine."

Bong turned around, clasped his hands behind his back, and casually looked up at the commander of the lead tank.

"I am Gunnery Sergeant Bong, commander of the Marine Security Detachment. Can I help you, sir?"

The tanker leaned a little farther forward over his folded arms so he could look directly at Bong and smiled wolfishly. "We want to go to the party," he said in a voice that crackled with suppressed laughter.

"Certainly, sir. I'll be happy to admit you to the reception. May I see your invitation, please."

The tank commander barked out a laugh. "I don't have an invitation," he said, still grinning. "I want to crash the party."

"I'm sorry, sir, but the reception is by invitation only."

"I'm quite sure the omission of my name from the guest list was inadvertent," the tank commander said. He wasn't grinning anymore. "Do you know who I am, Gunnery Sergeant?"

"Nossir, I haven't had the pleasure."

"I am Major General Marston St. Cyr, commander of the Diamundian Armed Forces."

"Sir." Bong brought his right hand up in a crisp salute, but didn't hold the salute for St. Cyr to return—a very polite insult. "I'm acquainted with your name." St. Cyr's name figured prominently in dispatches about the deteriorating situation on Diamunde, but Bong had never seen an image of him. He was the head of Marketing and of Research and Development, and member of the board of directors of Tubalcain Enterprises, the largest of the corporate powers on Diamunde. "Sir, if the distinguished head of R and D will bear with me for a moment, I will place a call and attempt to secure permission to admit you."

St. Cyr gave Bong a sardonic smile and nodded. "By all means, Sergeant."

Bong snapped to attention, snapped another salute, and executed an about-face. "Give a yell if he does anything," he said to Krait in a low voice.

"Aye aye, Gunny." Krait maintained his position at attention, weapon at port arms, the beginning of a smile niggling at the corners of his mouth.

Bong resisted the impulse to shake his head. He's enjoying this, he thought. Krait really doesn't understand how wrong everything *can* go.

With a few parade-ground-sharp steps and turns, the commander of the Marine Security Detachment was back inside the gate house. He breathed a sigh of relief. So far, so good. He touched his throat mike to change frequencies again and said, "Top Cat, this is Bong. We have a situation at the main gate."

"How so?" Top Cat replied immediately. Major Katopscu, the military liaison, wasn't Bong's boss—the Marine commander reported directly to Minister Whithill, the ambassador's chief of staff—but "the situation" was in part a military matter, and Bong knew Top Cat had probably intercepted the original exchanges between him and Winterthur. Besides, Top Cat was wearing his communications set and, as a civilian, Whithill probably wasn't.

"Marston St. Cyr is here demanding admittance, sir. And he's got main battle tanks to back up his demand."

"Minister Whithill and I are on our way, we'll be with you inside two minutes."

Bong resisted the urge to fidget while he waited, because St. Cyr could see him through the gate house windows.

Top Cat was back on his comm unit almost immediately. "Whithill says to tell him he can come in. Unarmed. I don't imagine he's in dinner wear?"

"Nossir. He's wearing a jumpsuit. What if he doesn't want to come in alone?"

"He can bring his primary staff, that's it. We'll be there before that becomes an issue."

"Aye aye, sir." Bong drew himself to attention and marched back to St. Cyr and the tanks.

"Sir." Again he saluted, and again failed to hold the salute. "The ambassador regrets the oversight. You are most welcome to join the reception." His voice betrayed none of the nervousness he felt; where violence was imminent, any Marine noncommissioned officer worth his Eagle, Globe, and Starstream could outdo any diplomat.

St. Cyr straightened up from leaning on his folded arms and with one hand signaled to the tank, which immediately rumbled to life.

"Sir," Bong had to shout to be heard over the noise of the engine, "there isn't room inside for your vehicle. If you will kindly dismount. Chief-of-Staff Whithill is on his way to escort you."

St. Cyr gave Bong a surprised look, then said, "But you know how New Kimberly has gotten lately. If we leave our vehicles out here, someone will surely come along and vandalize them."

Bong made a production of looking to his right and his left, sweeping the armored vehicles with his gaze. "Sir, the invitation is for you and your primary staff. Surely you have enough men to secure your vehicles from theft or vandalism. And if your men are insufficient, my two Marines here on the gate can easily do the job." He paused to give St. Cyr a hard, pay-close-attention look. "When Marines are present, nobody in New Kimberly is foolish enough to do harm to persons or property associated with the Confederation Embassy." St. Cyr could take that last as a challenge, but it could also serve as a reminder that he was dealing with forces that were far stronger and ultimately more violent than he was.

St. Cyr glared briefly at the Marine, then threw his head back and guffawed loudly. "Gunnery Sergeant," he said when he recovered, "it appears that Confederation Marines are every bit as bold as I have heard. Perhaps more so." He looked to his sides, taking in the size and might of his tank battalion, then back at Bong and the lone PFC standing behind him. He picked up a headset and murmured into the mouthpiece, then put the headset back down. He bounded out of the tank cupola, to its side and down to the ground. Quickly, four other jumpsuited men joined him. All five men wore side arms.

"Sir, if you please." Bong made a gesture toward their pistol belts.

"But you are armed," St. Cyr said with some amusement.

"I will leave my side arm in the gate house, sir."

St. Cyr nodded. "That may be so, but you were wearing your sword inside."

"Yessir, secured with this." He pulled the peace binding from his pocket and held it up. "I will resecure my sword before I return to the reception."

"We can peace-bind our weapons as well."

"Well, well, St. Cyr," a new voice cut in. Chief-of-Staff Whithill stepped through the gate, followed closely by Major Katopscu. "I see you are as determined as ever to be a thorn in the side of civilized society." As chief of staff, he felt he wasn't always required to be as diplomatic as other members of the diplomatic mission. He didn't deign to look at the tanks.

"Whithill. So good of you to meet me." There was no humor or friendliness in St. Cyr's voice. "We are coming in. And then the Confederation will recognize Tubalcain Enterprises as the sole legitimate power on Diamunde and conduct all of its business with me."

"We will do no such thing. You may come in, but it will be on sufferance. By appearing this way, you will convince the few remaining undecideds how unfit you are as someone to deal with. Drop your weapons and follow me." He spun on his heel and began to stride back into the embassy compound.

St. Cyr glared after Whithill for a second, then raised his right arm and sharply brought it down.

Almost as one, the sixty tanks fired their main guns, then fired their engines to life and rumbled forward, crashing through the cinder-block walls. St. Cyr jumped onto his tank as it began moving forward and was climbing back into its cupola as it ran over the vehicle gate.

Almost as quickly as the tanks fired, Krait fired back, killing

one of St. Cyr's staff before the plasma gun on the lead tank
flamed him, Gunny Bong, Major Katopscu, and Minister Whithill. Lance Corporal Winterthur wasn't able to get out of the
gate house before a tank ground it to rubble. Farther back in the
compound, Corporal Kovaks realized immediately that he and
his seven Marines didn't have a chance against the heavy armor
so he hurried them to the ballroom to attempt to evacuate the reception attendees. But there were too few exits from the ballroom and from the compound. Very few of the four hundred
people inside the compound were able to flee before the tanks
broke through. None of the Marines was among those few. Nor
was the ravishing Honorable Mistress !Tang'h.

CHAPTER
ONE

Marston St. Cyr was a man of direct methods.

He had been sitting patiently in the boardroom of Tubalcain Enterprises for the last hour as his fellow executives discussed his most recent request for additional research and development funds. As vice president for both Marketing and Research and Development, St. Cyr held the fate of the company in his hands. As VP for Marketing, he had cultivated an impressive array of clients for Tubalcain's gems, ores, and by-products on dozens of worlds. Moreover, he had successfully tied major shares of those worlds' economies to Tubalcain's solvency.

But more important, as VP for R&D he was solely responsible for maintaining the corporation's technological edge over its only competitor, the Hefestus Conglomerate: The supply of natural gems and valuable ores in the crust of Diamunde and its moons would last an estimated decade longer, at the most. Tubalcain's spies at Hefestus had reported its scientists were on the verge of a breakthrough in the manufacture of synthetic gems and minerals. In the normal progress of business, whichever company was first to develop artificial substitutes for the planet's mineral wealth would survive the depletion of its reserves. The board was dubious about giving St. Cyr any more money for research that thus far had shown no results, despite his spectacular success in other areas. But very soon it would, he continued assuring them. The promised "results," however, would not be what they expected, and in just a few moments they would find that out.

Now Tubalcain's CEO, Mona Schroder, was arguing that the money St. Cyr wanted would be better spent diversifying the company's interests. If they started immediately, while they still had enormous cash reserves and a top credit rating, she was saying, glancing nervously at St. Cyr as she spoke, within five years the company would not have to depend on its mining ventures but could continue to show a comfortable profit margin from a variety of other enterprises, as well as from the low-risk loans they had been making to various entities throughout the Confederation. At that point she nodded at St. Cyr, a sterile and reluctant acknowledgment of his marketing genius; he had engineered most of the loans. He smiled back coldly. It was Schroder's plan to convert Tubalcain from a mining and industrial giant into an interplanetary banking system, and in that she was supported by most of the other members of the board. She was opposed only by St. Cyr. She thought that at long last she was in a position now to force him out of power, and her heart raced at the thought that in a few moments she would make the announcement. A small rivulet of nervous perspiration trickled down her left side as she anticipated her triumph.

St. Cyr was calm and confident. Actually, he had spent none of the money in his considerable budget developing synthetic substitutes. The board members did not know that. Schroder suspected St. Cyr had diverted the money to his own business interests but she had no positive proof. In a few moments it would make no difference, because St. Cyr was about to be dismissed. He knew it was coming. He let her rattle on for a few more moments, and then:

"Ladies and gentlemen," St. Cyr announced suddenly, cutting the CEO off in mid-sentence, "you have sat long enough." He kicked the Woo crouching at his side beneath the table. "Briefcase," he said in a low voice, and the Woo obediently held up to him the briefcase he always carried along to these meetings. St. Cyr snatched the case and slammed it on the table, kicking the Woo again, harder this time, to discourage it from looking for a reward. Smiling wryly, he drew a pistol out of his briefcase and shot the CEO where she stood.

The blaster was set on low power, and the bolt, instead of hitting Schroder square in the chest, merely vaporized her right breast and shoulder. She shrieked and stumbled away from the conference table, flailing her one good arm helplessly as the horrified board members leaped to get out of her way. She staggered back into the table, leaving gobs of singed flesh on its highly polished surface, then fell to the floor where she writhed helplessly. The room filled with the stench of vaporized flesh. Board members gagged or vomited or screamed in terror while Marston St. Cyr sat quietly in his comfortable chair, casually toying with the blaster.

The Woo at St. Cyr's feet cringed even closer to the floor, moaning "Wooooo, wooooo." It began to glow brightly, as Woos did when experiencing distress or other strong emotion. "Stop it!" St. Cyr kicked the Woo. Its glow faded immediately.

"Security! Security!" Tubalcain's VP for Human Resources shouted into his wrist communicator. The man should have been a Woo, St. Cyr had often said, always worrying about the health and welfare of the company employees. He had vigorously, if unsuccessfully, opposed St. Cyr's enormous budget, arguing that the money would better be spent on what he called "social services."

Marston smiled. "Paul, security is in my hands now." He depressed the firing lever on his weapon and the social services programs at Tubalcain vaporized along with the VP's head. His body stood upright for a few seconds before collapsing to join the CEO on the floor. St. Cyr regarded his pistol admiringly, as if congratulating himself on the shot. Meanwhile, the board broke into pandemonium. "Gentlemen, I'd hate to flame the rest of you," Marston shouted over the screaming. "It's getting a little close in here right now." Marston coughed politely. The surviving board members huddled in terror at the far end of the conference room.

A door opened and several men in black uniforms armed with blasters trooped into the room. "Major Stauffer, remove those," Marston ordered, gesturing at the smoldering corpses.

"Yes, General," Major Stauffer replied. He signed to two of his men, who grabbed the corpses by the feet and dragged them outside. "Will there be anything else, General?" the major asked, looking at the remaining executives, the beginning of a smile on his lips.

"No, Clouse," St. Cyr said, and then added, "Oh, yes, one thing: have building maintenance scrub the air supply in here, will you?" He turned his attention to the surviving executives. "Sit!" he commanded, and they began to sit, staring apprehensively at St. Cyr's blaster as they returned to their places.

"Gentlemen," he began, "briefly, I am in charge of this company now. I am going to destroy Hefestus's management team and take it over as well. Those of you who wish to join me are welcome. Those who do not may leave." He paused. Nobody said anything or even moved a finger. "Good! You have decided to go your own separate ways then. You are dismissed. Major Stauffer will see you out immediately."

A long moment of silence passed before the first shaken executive arose and stumbled out of the conference room. Then, more quickly, as if they couldn't wait to be gone, the others followed him. In the hallway outside they were met by St. Cyr's security guards, escorted to the parking garage and summarily shot. The bodies were incinerated. Teams were dispatched to the executed men's homes, and their families and servants were murdered. Using lists compiled long before, the teams then spread out to find the friends and business associates of the newly dead, and they, as well as their families and friends, were shot. Before the day was out, the entire management elite of Tubalcain, along with a substantial number of the corporation's lower-ranking management, were dead. A student of ancient Roman politics, Marston St. Cyr knew he could leave no one alive who might oppose him.

"Clouse," St. Cyr said to Major Stauffer after the doomed executives had departed, "I must change now for the embassy reception." They both laughed. "Is everything ready?"

"All is ready, General. Your commanders are waiting."

St. Cyr absently swatted the Woo crouching at his feet, his briefcase dangling from an appendage. The creature cringed and uttered a mournful sigh. Stauffer had worked for St. Cyr for forty years and was prepared to do whatever his boss demanded, but the way he treated the Woos disturbed him. Once, many years before, when Stauffer had been recovering from injuries sustained during a mining accident, St. Cyr had come to visit him in the hospital. It was the only time his boss had ever done anything so remotely human, and Stauffer had been impressed. Still woozy from painkillers, Stauffer had been bold enough to ask him why he treated the Woos so inhumanely. "Because, my dear Clouse," St. Cyr had answered, "I can't treat people that way. Yet."

Now, St. Cyr said, "Since all is ready, my dear major, let us proceed. The hors d'oeuvres will be getting cold. Oh, you are now Colonel Stauffer."

Marston St. Cyr had not spent Tubalcain's money on the synthetic gems project or even mining R&D. He had not spent it on himself. He had spent it building armored fighting vehicles.

CHAPTER
TWO

"Ladies and gentlemen," Cynthia Chang-Sturdevant said, "it is my decision, after extensive debate and a voice vote of all the members of the Congress present, having obtained a quorum of votes, that we commence military operations immediately against Diamunde and Tubalcain Enterprises." A chorus of angry shouts and denunciations rose from the floor of the Confederation Congress, but they were countered just as loudly by Madame President's supporters on the floor. Fistfights erupted. "Sergeant at arms! Sergeant at arms!" Madame President Chang-Sturdevant shouted. It was twenty minutes before the delegates could be quieted down and put back into their seats.

"Ladies and gentlemen," she began again, "I will overlook this disgraceful conduct—"

"Madame President, Madame President!" The delegate from Cinque Luna rose to his feet. "No more disgraceful than this decision of yours to make war on a member world! I demand—"

"Madame President!" the delegate from Gimel Ghayn protested. "The honorable gentleman from Cinque Luna forgets that it was our ambassador this monster murdered! We cannot let his crime go unavenged!"

"Madame!" an opposition member screamed. "If this war goes sour, we're all finished!"

There was more shouting, but this time the delegates remained seated. When they had quieted down, President Chang-Sturdevant tried again. "We have discussed this in the Council and on the open floor of this congress. We have discussed this decision endlessly. Each of you has had his turn to speak. The talking is now over. By the authority invested in me under the

Confederation Constitution, I hereby declare that a state of war now exists between our member worlds and Diamunde." She slammed her gavel on the podium, caught her breath, stepped down and out the door behind the platform into the private chamber behind the podium.

"Jesus God," she sighed, "I've never seen the bastards so riled, Marcus." Marcus Berentus, the Confederation Minister of War, smiled and handed her a towel, with which she wiped the perspiration from her face.

"This war will upset a lot of members' egg baskets, Madame. But you had a quorum. Your decision is legal and binding. We go to war. The other ministers support you one hundred percent in this, and the Combined Chiefs are unanimous that we can defeat St. Cyr quickly and with minimal casualties."

Under the Constitution, the President of the Confederation Council was empowered to make certain binding decisions on behalf of the entire Confederation, providing a quorum of votes could be obtained from the Congress. That was because even using hyperspace travel, it could take six months or longer for the delegates to obtain instructions from their home worlds. These decisions were never taken lightly, however, only in cases of the gravest emergency, because if they proved mistaken, impeachment proceedings could be initiated.

"The war you served in, Marcus, the First Silvasian?" She tossed the towel down a disposal chute, glancing briefly in a mirror and straightening her hair. There were more strands of gray. Madame Chang-Sturdevant had been a beauty in her youth and she still remained a very attractive woman, but there were crow's-feet under her eyes now, brown spots on her hands, and the beginning of wrinkles around her neck. She couldn't remember having any of them before she became President of the Council.

"Yes. I flew a Raptor." He shrugged. "It was a piece of junk, compared to what the boys fly these days, but still a good atmospheric fighter craft. I was shot up but never down."

Cynthia Chang-Sturdevant smiled wryly. She appreciated Marcus's self-deprecating sense of humor and sage advice. Of all her ministers, he truly understood the human cost of war.

She stood for a moment before a mirror and straightened her clothes. The small chamber behind the podium was equipped with a full bar and other amenities but she decided against indulging. There was just too much work to be done.

"During your administration we've intervened on Elneal and Wanderjahr, Madame," Berentus said, "for humanitarian reasons. You overcame the opposition to those operations too. St. Cyr is a threat to all of us because he can project his military force to other worlds in the Confederation. We don't know how far he's spread his coils throughout the member worlds with his loans and investments either. He can pull a lot of strings among our delegates. He attacked our embassy, for heaven's sake, killed our people. And besides that, he's a goddamned murderer! Those worthless bastards!"

"Don't talk about our—" She hesitated slightly. "—Congresspersons that way, Marcus," she murmured, leaning over and kissing her Minister of War affectionately on the cheek. "But you know, Marcus, what that delegate shouted from the floor? 'If this war goes sour, we're all finished.' It's happened before."

"I know, Madame, I know. But in the navy we used to have an expression for such things: Fuck 'em if they can't take a joke. Besides, I'm ready for retirement. There's only one thing—"

She put a hand on his shoulder. "Marcus, you old gunfighter, I don't give a damn about this job, or all the trappings of this office either. There are plenty of people out there who'd willingly take over my responsibilities, and most of them would do a better job than I ever could." She waved her minister's protest to silence with a hand. "But that 'one thing' that bothers you bothers me too. I don't want to sacrifice the lives of our fighting men needlessly." She shivered involuntarily. Madame Cynthia Chang-Sturdevant had a son and a daughter serving as ratings in the fleet. "Marcus, let's hope and pray the brass hats have it right this time."

Admiral Horatio "Seabreeze" Perry, Chairman of the Confederation Combined Chiefs of Staff, thought he had it right, as he always thought he had it right every time in his career since he'd been an ensign. The briefing he'd arranged for Madame Chang-Sturdevant the week before had gone off superbly, except for one annoying little detail.

"Madame President," Admiral Perry began, "allow me to introduce General Markham Benteen, commander of the Hefestus Conglomerate's armed forces."

A white-faced man in battle-dress uniform stood and bowed politely. President Chang-Sturdevant couldn't help noticing that the general's hand shook ever so slightly as he sat down and placed it back on the conference table. He looked exhausted; "defeated" was the word that came to her unbidden. She realized suddenly that the admiral had spoken of his command in the present tense, obviously a professional courtesy, because everyone knew his forces on Diamunde had been wiped out and he was now a political refugee, along with the few surviving members of Hefestus's management staff.

"Tell me what happened," she said.

In terse, clipped sentences the general told her how St. Cyr's forces had attacked his with a ferocity thus far unmatched in the many wars Diamunde had suffered as her corporate rulers vied for supremacy. Most of the Hefestus corporate management were killed in St. Cyr's attack on the embassy, but Benteen and his staff had managed to survive. By the time they could rally armed resistance it was already too late; St. Cyr's aircraft had demolished Benteen's air force on the ground, knocked out his headquarters complex, and heavily damaged his depots and garrison installations before the rubble at the embassy had even cooled.

"We could have resisted," General Benteen concluded, "but it was the tanks that got us."

" 'Tanks'?" Madame President asked. She thought she hadn't heard him correctly. She glanced at Berentus and Admiral Perry for confirmation. They nodded.

"Heavily armored fighting vehicles—" General Benteen said.

"Yes, ma'am," General Hanover Eastland, Chief of the Confederation Army Staff interrupted. He was afraid Benteen was on the verge of breaking down. "They have not been used in warfare for hundreds of years. I believe St. Cyr built them in secret, funneling Tubalcain's R and D money into their construction. He called them 'tractors,' and said they were to be used in the company's mining operations. We've prepared a full intelligence briefing for you."

"We couldn't stop them," Benteen went on as if he had never been interrupted. "They're monsters. They weigh up to sixty thousand kilos and move as fast as a landcar. Only concentrated plasma bolts are powerful enough to penetrate their armor, but they wouldn't stand still long enough for our gunners to hit them. Our artillery just bounced off their hulls. When they didn't blow my men apart with their guns, they just, just . . . ran over them where they stood—"

"Ma'am," Admiral Perry said hastily, cutting General Benteen off again, "I'd now like to introduce Admiral Hank Donovan, our intelligence officer. Admiral."

"Madame President, this is our enemy." An image flashed onto the vidscreen at one end of the conference room. It showed a middle-aged man of indeterminate height with close-cropped brown hair and a prominent nose. His jaw was square, with a marked cleft in the chin. His eyebrows were dark and bushy. He seemed to be staring out of the vidscreen speculatively. There was just the slightest hint of a smile on his lips—or perhaps a nervous condition that drew up the muscles on the right side of his mouth. At any rate, it gave him a somewhat sardonic expression. Overall, though, his visage was rather handsome, not the face of a megamaniacal killer.

"That is Major General Marston Moore St. Cyr," Admiral Donovan intoned.

"Excuse me, Admiral, 'Major General,' did you say?" Madame Chang-Sturdevant interrupted.

"Yes, ma'am. Oh, yes, I see. He picked that title because his idol, Oliver Cromwell, achieved early fame as a cavalry commander, and in European armies of Cromwell's day the major general commanded the cavalry. St. Cyr fancies himself a dashing cavalryman." Donovan smirked. Madame Chang-Sturdevant had the impression Admiral Donovan might be seriously underrating the man. "To continue. He was born on Diamunde eighty years ago. He has never seen military service. He was off-world, on Carhart's World, studying engineering at the University of M'Jumba, when the decisive battles took place on Diamunde that left the Hefestus Conglomerate and Tubalcain Enterprises the dominant corporations on the planet. During the many skirmishes and turf battles that have characterized business practice on Diamunde since then, St. Cyr was working his way up through the corporate management team at Tubalcain."

"Then how'd he get so damned smart about military affairs?" Madame Chang-Sturdevant asked suddenly. She was beginning to dislike Admiral Donovan.

"Well, ma'am, there's a lot of similarity between duty on a military staff and work in a corporate staff. Look at how many retired flag officers go on to head up corporations, for instance. Besides that, St. Cyr *is* a genius of sorts. It is said he has based his life on three books: his politics on Niccolo Machiavelli's *The Prince*, his personal relationships on Shakespeare's *Richard III*, and his military expertise on Heinz Guderian's *Panzer Leader*. That's probably oversimplifying it a bit, but the man is very well read and a natural, if totally ruthless, leader. There are many examples of men like him in history, ma'am, who took naturally to soldiering. Nathan Bedford Forrest and Oliver Cromwell are two such. As I mentioned earlier, St. Cyr admires Cromwell a lot. You know who they were, I presume?"

"Yes, Admiral, I do," President Chang-Sturdevant replied sarcastically. She was beginning to dislike the Admiral a lot. "I suppose like Forrest, his motto is 'Get there first with the most,' and he's fashioned his forces on Cromwell's New Model Army, prayer services and Puritan self-denial and all?"

"Ahem . . ." Donovan's face reddened. "Well, not quite, ma'am. Uh, here is another gentleman to watch," he said, rushing on. The image of Clouse Stauffer replaced that of St. Cyr. "This is St. Cyr's chief of staff." Stauffer was a strikingly handsome man with dark hair, an aquiline nose, strong chin, and intelligent eyes. "His name is Clouse Stauffer. He started out as St. Cyr's administrative officer when St. Cyr was chief of a research project at a company called Vulcan Enterprises, before Tubalcain bought them out. That was forty years ago. Nobody knows St. Cyr better than this man. We suspect he played a significant role in St. Cyr's military preparations and will continue to do so once the invasion is under way."

"If there *is* an invasion, Admiral. First I have to get the Confederation Congress to agree we need to invade. I'm going to need the support of all you gentlemen in that effort, and believe me, it's not going to be easy." Madame Chang-Sturdevant signed Admiral Donovan to continue with his briefing.

"Madame President, what you must know about St. Cyr is that for forty years he has slowly and meticulously built up a loyal following among Tubalcain's employees. He showed promise early in his career, and everyone expected that sooner or later he would rise to a position of great influence and power in the company's affairs. They were content to wait for that day, when he would reward their loyalty. You know that among the people of Diamunde company loyalty is probably stronger even than family relationships. They have never heard of representative government there and wouldn't want it if they had. The companies in turn take very good care of their people, but the bottom line on Diamunde has always been profits. Human considerations have always come second to corporate survival. And everybody there accepts that."

"What is your plan for invasion?" she asked.

"We will work out the details once the Congress gives you the go-ahead, ma'am," Admiral Perry answered. "But the Marines will go in first in divisional strength and secure a beachhead. They will be reinforced by the army. From there they'll spread out and engage St. Cyr's forces."

"We'll get 'em there on time," Admiral Jaime "Spider" Webb, Chief of Naval Operations, promised. A short, slight man with steely blue eyes and curly hair, Admiral Webb was known for his incisive wit and his ability to make quick and correct decisions. When he retired, which was expected to happen soon, he would be sorely missed.

"What about these tanks?" Berentus asked.

"He calls them 'Toyful Panthers,' " Benteen said dully.

"Uh, that's 'Teufelpanzers,' " Donovan corrected Benteen. "I believe it's Old High German for 'devil tank.' "

"Armaments? Capabilities?" Chang-Sturdevant asked.

"We are not too sure, ma'am, aside from what Admiral Donovan has already mentioned," Admiral Perry responded. "We believe St. Cyr has at least enough tanks to equip two divisions, supported by infantry. We guess their organization and tactics are based on those of the German Army during World War Two, since St. Cyr admires them so much. But General Benteen is the only person we have who's seen them in action and, uh," he nodded at the defeated general, "he had other things on his mind at the time besides, um, studying nomenclature." This was meant as a bit of levity, but neither Benteen nor Chang-Sturdevant took it that way.

"How many tanks would that be?" Madame Chang-Sturdevant answered.

"Two thousand," General Benteen answered. "I did manage to keep count," he said, looking directly at Admiral Perry. "There are fifteen tanks to a platoon in St. Cyr's army. I found that out the hard way, up very close. Since there are three platoons to a company, three companies to a battalion, three battalions to a regiment, three regiments to a division, that makes one thousand, give or take a few, for each division."

Chang-Sturdevant began to experience a sinking sensation in the pit of her stomach. "Admiral, do we have anything that can stop these things?"

"Madame President, we do," answered a heavyset man with closely cropped hair who'd remained silent up until now. The speaker was Commandant Kinsky "Kickass" Butler, Confederation Marine Corps. Commandant Kinsky was famous for his terseness. "It's called the Straight Arrow, Madame."

Madame Chang-Sturdevant looked questioningly at Admiral Perry and turned to Minister Berentus. He shrugged.

"Madame President, the Straight Arrow is old technology that was developed specifically to stop heavily armored vehicles," Admiral Donovan said. "It's a rocket-propelled explosive charge that will penetrate armor."

"How old is this technology, Admiral?" Madame Chang-Sturdevant asked suspiciously.

Admiral Donovan hesitated. "It was developed, um . . . well, about three hundred years ago, ma'am."

"Three hundred . . ." Madame Chang-Sturdevant gasped.

"Well, there was no need of them, so they were scrapped two hundred or so years ago, but now that this St. Cyr has resurrected, as it were, armored fighting vehicles, well, the army found some money in its budget to build some prototypes, and we're putting them back into production immediately, Madame." Admiral Perry added brightly, "Our next budget submission will have a line item for the continued production of these weapons." A pregnant silence descended upon the room. "Uh, we'll need them now, you see, in case somebody else gets the idea to—" Madame Chang-Sturdevant's icy stare froze him into silence.

The silence became embarrassing as Chang-Sturdevant continued staring in outrage at her Combined Chiefs. "Gentlemen," she began at last, and coughed. "Gentlemen," she began again. She felt that she was losing control of herself quickly. "H-How many of these things do we have in our inventory?"

"Well, we're rushing them into production," Admiral Perry answered. "Within a month we should have—"

"Goddamnit! I asked, how many of these things do we have right now?" Madame Chang-Sturdevant shouted.

"Well, Madame President, um, ah, we have, in our inventory, right now, that is," Admiral Perry mumbled, "I believe, eleven."

CHAPTER
THREE

He stood shivering in the rain-soaked field, not so much from the exhaustion of the last ten days' march through the French countryside or the damp chill in the morning air, as from the sight of the French host, drawn up no more than 250 yards from where Henry's army had finally taken up its battle lines. This was it. They would fight it out here at last, vastly outnumbered. His heart began to race, the chill and exhaustion forgotten.

At a spoken command from Vinetar Fletcher, the twenty men under his command pounded their wooden stakes into the ground before them. The other archers in Henry's army were doing the same. The field echoed hollowly with the sound of mallets pounding on wood, and then the chips flew everywhere as each man quickly sharpened the protruding end of his stake with the small hatchet he carried at his side. Hopefully, the stakes would impale the French cavalry.

"Lay your arrows," Fletcher commanded. Quickly, expertly, he disposed of his arrows, two sheaves of twenty-four chisel-nosed clothyard killers, each of which could penetrate one inch of solid oak at a hundred yards. He struck them points down into the ground within easy reach. Earlier, Sir Thomas Erpingham had given orders to the cenetars, each of whom commanded one hundred archers, to have the vinetars assure that each man's bow was strung before the army marched into line.

He stood behind his stake now, and notched an arrow onto his bowstring. Each man looked to Fletcher, who looked to the cenetar sitting on his horse. Evan Cooper, standing just to his right, said something, and when he looked over, Evan grinned ferociously, exposing the conspicuous gaps in his front teeth.

Incongruously, Fletcher was reminded of the old wives' tale that a gap-toothed person was sexually insatiable. Well, that was true enough in Evan's case, but the grin was reassuring just now. He grinned back.

"Draw!" Fletcher shouted, taking his command from the cenetar, who had also seen the signal to draw bows: huge bright flags that had just been raised from where King Henry and his entourage calmly sat on their warhorses. "Two hundred and fifty yards, lads!" Fletcher shouted. "Put 'em in there!"

The flags went down. "Loose arrows!" the vinetars screamed, and thousands of archers simultaneously let their arrows fly. The flags came up again. He bent and notched another arrow and drew his bow as the first volley arced one hundred feet into the air and then descended toward the French battle line. He lost sight of his own projectile almost instantly as it blended into the cloud that swarmed out to fall upon the waiting Frenchmen. The flags went down again. "Loose!" the vinetars screamed, and the second volley sped away from Henry's archers with the sound of huge, whirring wings.

Standing in the second row of his cenetar, he could see clearly and hear the arrows impacting upon the Frenchmen. The sound of thudding and spanging echoed across the wide field. Horses screamed in agony as the descending volleys found unprotected backs and flanks. Some men-at-arms were unseated as their mounts plunged madly, but protected by their steel helmets and body armor, few were disabled at that range. King Henry was hoping the volleys would goad them into charging, get them close enough so massed aimed volleys could knock them off.

And then they did charge, one thousand armored horsemen rumbling across the field. The ground beneath Henry's archers began to shake. As one, the archers stepped back six paces from the stakes to give themselves plenty of room to draw their bows once the cavalry was in range. Fletcher was very calm now, totally absorbed in what he was doing, oblivious to the destruction thundering down upon King Henry's army.

"Shoot straight, me lads!" Fletcher shouted. "Send the god-damned frogs to hell!"

Professor Jere Benjamin, dean of the M'Jumba University History Department, was suddenly and painfully called back to the twenty-fifth century by the insistent shrilling of his communications console and a sharp burning sensation in his right thigh. "Yipe!" He brushed furiously at the glowing cigar ash that had burned still another hole in his trousers.

"Jere?" Kevin Fike's face appeared on the vidscreen. "Jere, are you there? Anything wrong?" Fike's normally flushed face was even redder that morning, almost matching the color of his hair. When his face got that flushed, Benjamin knew that the president of M'Jumba University was dealing with something out of the ordinary.

"Uh, okay, Kev," Benjamin muttered, massaging the hot spot on his thigh. Carefully, he marked his place in the book he had been reading and closed its covers. "I'm fine. What's up?"

"Jere, something very important. Can you come over to my office right away?"

Two men sat in President Fike's office, one a white-haired, distinguished-looking gentleman in civilian clothes and the other a heavyset, grim-faced man in the dress red uniform of the Confederation Marine Corps assistant commandant. Professor Benjamin stood in the doorway transfixed with surprise. The civilian looked vaguely familiar.

"Come in, Jere, do come in," President Fike said, rising from behind his desk. "I'd like you to meet Secretary Berentus, whom you know by reputation, and General Boxer, Assistant Commandant of the Marine Corps. General Boxer is also chief of R and D for the Marines. Please, come in and sit down."

Slowly, Benjamin crossed the room and shook hands with the Confederation Secretary of War and the Marine assistant commandant. "Evan Boxer," the general said, shaking Benjamin's hand. He smiled, revealing conspicuous gaps in his front teeth. Evan? For a moment Benjamin did not know when he was.

"Something wrong, Professor?" Boxer asked.

Benjamin just stood there for an awkward moment, staring at the officer. "Uh, no, no," he replied quickly, recovering himself.

"You look vaguely familiar, is all," he explained, his face reddening. Then to himself: I've got to stop living in the past so much.

"Cigars?" President Fike asked brightly, offering a humidor. The cigars were imported from Old Earth, where the tobacco was grown and then hand-rolled according to an ancient technique. The several cigars in the humidor cost President Fike about a week's salary. "Fidels," he said proudly as each man gratefully took one and bit off its end.

Secretary Berentus produced a lighter and they all leaned toward him to catch the flame. As he took the light and drew on his cigar, Professor Benjamin self-consciously placed his elbow to cover the recent burn spot on his trousers. For several long moments the four were silent as they savored the delicious texture and aroma of the wonderfully expensive cigars.

"Ahhh!" Boxer sighed. "A cigar is a cigar, but a Fidel is a smoke." The others laughed comfortably, enjoying their own Fidels enormously. "Professor," the Marine asked after several more moments, "what do you know about tank warfare?"

"Ah! Yes! Ahem. Well," Benjamin began, his nervousness gone—he was in his element. "As you know," he continued, assuming his classroom manner, "the last major tank battle in history was fought in 2052 at Lake Mistassini, in Canada, on Old Earth, and involved the 1st and 7th Armored Divisions of the United States Army against the lightly armored forces of the Chibougamou League. The Americans fielded the M1D7 Abrams main battle tank and the Canadians destroyed almost all of them. It was the worst defeat of an armored force since the battle of Kursk, in Russia, in World War Two, where—"

"The Canadians used the Straight Arrow antitank rocket, didn't they, Professor?" Secretary Berentus interrupted.

"Oh, yes. Indeed, sir. The Straight Arrow. The introduction of that weapon at Lake Mistassini virtually ended the use of tanks on the battlefield." Benjamin leaned back in his chair and smiled confidently at the others. "Uh, why do you ask?"

"Professor," General Boxer said, ignoring the question, "I understand you have a complete set of the technical manuals for the Straight Arrow."

"Yessir," Benjamin answered proudly. "They're all original twenty-first-century editions. I also have the U.S. Army field manuals and training manuals for the entire weapons system, the launcher, the projectile, everything. Why, I even have ballistic tables—"

"Could you fire one of those things?" the Marine asked.

"Oh, yes, I believe I could!" Benjamin answered. The other three men looked at one another. "Uh, why do you ask?" Benjamin asked, repeating the question.

The Secretary of War looked at Boxer, who leaned forward in his chair. "Professor, after Mistassini, we kept the Straight Arrow in our inventory for over a hundred years, just in case somebody decided to use heavy armor somewhere again. Eventually the council"—he made an apologetic gesture toward Secretary Berentus—"decided their maintenance was too expensive, considering the unlikely event we'd really need them again, so they were all destroyed two hundred years ago. Now we are planning to build as many of them as quickly as we can. We suddenly need a lot of them. We managed to locate eleven in museums, and our weapons technicians are fabricating exact replicas right now. Your technical manuals would be invaluable to us. We could just ask for a loan and I'm sure you'd give them to us. But nobody alive knows how to fire the damned things properly or how to use them tactically against heavy— *really* heavy—armor. Except you. We hope."

"Jere," President Fike said, "they were very impressed with your book, *The Employment of Armor in Land Warfare in the Twentieth and Twenty-first Centuries.* Secretary Berentus has requested the loan of your services for a while. I have agreed. There will be some travel involved. Can you hand over your department to Dr. Toppings?"

"Trish? Yes, yes, I believe she can handle things. How long would you need me?" He looked at Secretary Berentus, who nodded at the assistant commandant.

"Oh, two, three months, maybe," Boxer said. "We'll need you to help train our men in their use and then oversee the weapons' deployment in the, uh, active theater. We plan to gather on Arsenault a select group of officers and NCOs from the strike teams that'll be making the initial assault landing. Arsenault's the Confederation Armed Forces' training world. You and a task force of technicians will train them there in the use of the Straight Arrow, and you, Professor, will teach them what you know about armored warfare tactics."

"Somebody's using tanks?" Benjamin asked, as if the thought had only just struck him. It had. "Who? Where? It's unbelievable!"

"Somebody is, Professor, but I can't tell you who or where just now," Boxer replied. "We need you to help train our men. And, Professor? Every word of this conversation is classified top secret. I'm sure you understand."

Benjamin looked bewildered. "But why me, gentlemen? I'm not the only expert in this field. Why, Dr. Post over at the University of Nammuoi is fully as qualified as me to—"

"Because, Professor, you are available, and the fewer people involved in this operation the better," Boxer growled. "Besides," he added, "we've all read your books."

"Professor," Secretary Berentus said, leaning forward and touching Benjamin lightly on his right knee, "if you can't oblige us, we will understand, but let me assure you, your help is vital and we are begging for it. Hundreds, thousands, of our Marines and soldiers will die if we don't do this right. We do not have the time to go to Dr. Post and convince him to help us. We need your decision right now."

Professor Benjamin stared silently at the others. Then he sighed. "Very well, gentlemen. You can count on me. When do I leave?"

Secretary Berentus rose from his chair and pumped Benjamin's hand vigorously. "This afternoon, Professor," he replied.

Benjamin stood, slightly bemused, absentmindedly shaking the Secretary's hand. Then he turned to General Boxer. "Sir, I have studied war all my life, but I have never even held a weapon in my hands. Will I see these weapons used in real combat?"

The Marine shifted nervously in his chair before answering. "Yes, Professor, there's, uh, a good chance you might. But," he added quickly, "there'd never be any danger to you personally, I can assure you of that."

Yes, Professor Benjamin thought, his pulse quickening, I bet: no more danger than Henry's archers faced at Agincourt.

The flight to Arsenault on the CNSS *Sergeant Frank Crean* took thirty days, standard. During that time Professor Benjamin was accorded flag-rank treatment.

"Your mission," Assistant Commandant Boxer explained before he left, "is to train Marine officers and NCOs in the use of the Straight Arrow and in antiarmor tactics. They, in turn, will spread out to the units scheduled to make the assault and train the men who will go up against St. Cyr's forces. You may be required to accompany a follow-on assault element, just to be on hand if the task force commander needs any advice after the initial landing. For sure, we want you to be on the Fleet Admiral's flagship during the preliminary invasion, in case your expertise is needed. You'll go as a civilian adviser to the Fleet commander."

While on board the *Crean*, Benjamin received a full intelligence briefing on the Diamundian situation, especially concerning what was known about the armored force St. Cyr had managed to assemble. Unfortunately, St. Cyr had closed down all communication and commerce with the outside world once he seized power on Diamunde, so not many details were known about conditions there. Analysts believed he was consolidating his power and would soon ask for formal recognition from the Confederation. The Council of Worlds had concluded, after a heated debate, not to deal with the usurper, but to invade and oust him with military force. This was done over the strenuous objections of many Council members, particularly those afraid their financial interests on Diamunde would be threatened if the Confederation invaded.

"He'll be ready for us," the briefing officer had said, "but what he doesn't know is that we'll be ready for him." Professor Benjamin said nothing, but he hoped the briefer's optimism was justified. But as a historian who had studied many military campaigns in past wars, he was fully aware that in battle nothing ever went as expected.

He spent most of his time on the *Crean* studying his manuals, reviewing how the Straight Arrow worked, and rereading Guderian's *Panzer Leader*, a book he'd been told Marston St. Cyr had studied thoroughly. Life on board a military naval vessel fascinated him, and when he had free time he wandered about the ship, talking to the crew. Just before he boarded the Essay to land on Arsenault, he'd been issued several sets of garrison utilities and told he would be required to wear them while training the Marines. Standing in his stateroom, gazing into the mirror at himself in Marine uniform, he felt a surge of pride. He actually looked tough in the utilities. My God, he thought, have I missed my calling in this life? He also wondered if he'd be able to keep them after the mission was over.

On Arsenault, Benjamin was introduced to the officers and staff NCOs he would train. He was surprised at how warmly they greeted him. Many said they had read his books, which surprised him even more. And they really had, which flattered him very much. After teaching generations of reluctant scholars subjects they took only to get credit for graduation, he knew when someone had read a text. In time he was astonished at how closely these professionals had studied his books, as they sat around in the evenings, discussing how the Germans should have deployed their tanks at Kursk and the failure rate of the Straight Arrows at the Battle of Lake Mistassini.

But his first lecture was the best of his career.

Professor Benjamin took the podium. "Gentlemen," he began, and coughed. "Excuse me, but your incomparable mess sergeant served us frogs' legs for breakfast this morning and I must have a couple still stuck in my throat." Several men laughed.

"Gentlemen," he tried again, "this is an M1D7 Super Abrams from circa 2049." The huge vidscreen behind him came to life as the three-dimensional image of an armored behemoth roared down a dusty road. "The M1D7 was the direct descendant of the M1A1 developed by the automotive genius, Dr. Phill Lett, during the late twentieth century." The charging tank froze on the screen and began to revolve. "We do not know the precise capabilities of the tanks St. Cyr has developed, but from surveillance and eyewitness accounts, we are pretty sure his main battle tank is going to be very much like the M1D7, with updated weapons and propulsion systems, of course. He has an inventory of lighter armored vehicles and they are a potent threat, but it's the M1D7 we will concentrate on during the coming days. We do know that he calls them TP1s, which stands for Teufelpanzer, Model One. That's German for 'devil tank.' Marston St. Cyr is a student of the German Army armor tactics employed during World War Two."

The assembled Marines were relaxed but paying close attention.

"The M1D7 you see up there weighed 360,000 kilograms and had armor thick enough and strong enough to defeat any antitank weapon of its day. It stood four meters high, was twelve meters long, and six wide. Its 120mm main gun fired, among many others, an armor-piercing, fin-stabilized, sabot-discarding round made of depleted uranium. It could carry sixty of those rounds and had a crew of four. The tank had a top speed of one hundred kph and burned fuel—gasoline—at the rate of eight liters per minute. We do not know the consumption rate for the TP1 or anything about its propulsion system.

"A concentration of bolts from heavy plasma weapons could eventually melt through the hull of one of these things, providing you could get one to stand still long enough, or not fire back until you'd finished slagging its armor plate. Likewise, your artillery would be effective, providing a gunner could get a direct hit on the relatively thin dorsal armor plates. You could take a track off with a lucky hit or a mine, but the tank would still be a dangerous stationary gun platform until someone came along to finish the job. In a fluid battlefield situation that might not happen soon enough. In actuality, the infantryman has nothing in his arsenal that can stop a monster like this—today.

"So why did these tanks disappear from the battlefield?" Benjamin touched a control and the M1D7 was replaced by the image of a long black cylindrical object that looked like a huge writing stylus. "That, gentlemen, is why: the 75mm Straight Arrow light antitank weapon.

"The Straight Arrow combined the features of several older man-portable antitank weapons with some ingenious modifications that completely changed mobile warfare. Those older weapons were the Soviet RPD-series 40mm antitank free-flight missile and the American 66mm light antitank weapon. Where the Straight Arrow improved on these weapons was its self-contained guidance system, longer range, and devastating destructiveness. The Straight Arrow had an effective range of one thousand meters, and at that range could penetrate over four hundred millimeters of rolled homogenous armored plate.

"That baby," his enthusiasm was building now, "could be fired over open sights as a direct-fire weapon, or its self-contained guidance system could be activated to launch a heat-seeking missile for indirect fire. It was muzzle-loaded and percussion-fired, but a short distance from the muzzle the rocket motor cut in, boosting the missile to a velocity of a thousand meters per second. The rocket was fin-stabilized. The penetrator rod was made of depleted uranium, two times denser than tungsten steel. When this hit the armor of a tank, its entire kinetic energy was concentrated in a spot about the size of your thumb. The penetrator turned white hot and punched through the plate, shedding its 'skin' as it passed through. But the skin followed the penetrator through the hole and dispersed inside the tank into white-hot granules twice as dense as steel, instantly igniting everything they touched. So even if the main round itself didn't set off the fuel and ammo, the thousands of granules would. I don't need to tell you what they did to the crew."

He paused. The room was completely silent now, each man's eyes focused on the Straight Arrow, which dissolved suddenly into a tank rushing at great speed across a snowy ridge line. A bright finger of light flashed out of the left side of the screen and touched the turret of the tank. There was a brilliant bloom of white light as the round penetrated, and then the turret leaped into the air on a gout of flame. The mortally wounded tank ground erratically to a halt, burning intensely. The camera shifted then, looking down into the burned-out hulk through the hole where the turret had been. What had once been a man sat melted into the driver's seat.

The trid screen went blank. "Those films were shot by the Canadians at the Battle of Lake Mistassini in 2052. Gentlemen," Professor Jere Benjamin concluded, forgetting momentarily who he was, "let's go get 'em!"

CHAPTER
FOUR

Staff Sergeant Charlie Bass stretched luxuriously beneath the warm goose-down comforter that lay across Katrina's oversize bed. During the night the sheets had become tangled and askew and pillows had fallen onto the floor, but the comforter was huge and warm and more than adequately covered their naked bodies. Beside him, Katrina shifted her position slightly and sighed in her sleep. Her thigh came to rest against his, and its warmth seeped into Charlie and aroused him again.

Outside, the winds whistled shrilly about the buildings of New Oslo, driving tiny tendrils of snow across the rooftops; gusts whipped powdery snow ghosts into the air from the banks piled along the streets. Winter had only started in New Oslo, and already a meter of snow blanketed the capital of Thorsfinni's World. The newly risen sun glowed dimly through the icy haze enfolding the awakening city as well-bundled citizens, cheeks bright from the subzero cold, hurried about their early morning tasks. But inside Katrina's snug apartment, Charlie Bass was warm, satisfied, and happily looking forward to the coming days. Katrina had promised him that they'd take a trip into the nearby foothills of the Thorvald Mountains, where she would teach him how to ski. But he didn't give a damn if he spent the rest of the week right there in that bed.

Great Buddha's golden balls, he thought, smiling and settling farther down into the luxuriously soft mattress beneath him, this woman has taken twenty years off my age! The tantalizing odor of fresh-brewing coffee wafted to him from the kitchenette. His stomach growled. In a few moments he'd awaken Katrina and, swaddled in comfortable robes, they'd enjoy the hearty breakfast the servo had prepared for them. Then, a leisurely bath as hot as they could stand it. Then . . . Charlie Bass smiled broadly. Good, clean fun.

Best of all, almost, the prodigious quantities of beer he'd consumed the night before had not left him with a single trace of hangover that morning.

The communicator strapped to his wrist shrilled. He bolted upright; the Confederation Marine Corps knew where he was and wanted him again. Beside him Katrina's eyes opened slightly. *"Vas?"* she asked, a strand of silver-blonde hair bisecting her face as she rose up on one elbow. Her breasts drooped ponderously as she rose to a sitting position and smiled sleepily at Bass.

Bass leaned back and crossed his wrist across his chest. "Staff Sergeant Bass here, sir," he said resignedly.

"Captain Meadows, military attaché at the Confederation Embassy, Staff Sergeant. Very sorry to interrupt you like this." The captain's voice sounded loud and clear in the small apartment. An unfamiliar anger at the Corps gripped Bass momentarily but he suppressed it at once.

"Bad news, Staff Sergeant. You are to gather at once the men who came in with you and report to the embassy for return transportation to Camp Ellis."

"Do you know why, sir?"

"No, Staff Sergeant. All I know is that 34th FIST is going on deployment."

"Aye aye, sir." The communicator went silent.

"Vat is it?" Katrina asked anxiously.

Bass didn't answer immediately. "Aw, we've got to return to Bronnoysund," he said at last. A look of real disappointment crossed Katrina's face. "We're going somewhere," he added.

Katrina knew enough about the Marines' mission on her world that she did not ask where. "Oh, Charlie, honey, ve hat plans . . ."

"I know, Katie, I know," Bass said. He kissed her lightly. "When we get back, I'll have the skipper restore our R and R, and by Buddha's big balls, you and me, we'll do a month together! Okay?"

Bass swung his legs over the side of the bed and put his feet on the floor. It was ice cold. The entire ambience of Katrina's tiny apartment had been destroyed by that call. Already his mind was racing forward, how long would it take him to get dressed, how much time would it take to find Lance Corporal Schultz and the others? It would take them six hours' flight time to get back to the 34th FIST's garrison at Camp Pete Ellis. Sergeant Hyakowa and the other NCOs would already be getting the rest of the platoon ready back there even now. Where were they mounting out to this time? A desert world, a jungle world? His heart began to race. Charlie Bass was a professional Marine. Deployments, training, the myriad details required to administer and lead an infantry platoon, that's what he did, and he was good at it and he loved it.

"You muss leaf right now?" Katrina asked as she slid out the other side of the bed and into warm slippers.

"What?" Bass asked, his mind already light-years beyond where they were sitting. She repeated the question. Bass hunched his shoulders against the cold in the room and scratched one foot with the other. His body was laced with the scars of old wounds. The most recent, a long gash down his left arm, was still livid. The skin-grafting did not require a surgeon, so even a corpsman could have removed the scars easily and painlessly, but Bass insisted on keeping them. He ran a finger thoughtfully down the outside of his left arm, feeling the long groove a knife blade had gouged there on Elneal the year before. "Yeah," he answered. "But Katie—" He held up a finger and smiled broadly. "—not before breakfast, and a hot bath."

Every man in the 34th FIST was authorized one week rest and recuperation leave a year—R&R to most people, or I&I in unofficial Marine parlance, which stood for "intoxication and intercourse"—mission requirements permitting. Since the 34th was stationed on the very fringe of Human Space and subject to immediate deployment without prior notice, it was unit policy that no more than ten percent of the men could be on leave at any one time. Except for special reenlistment leaves, none was permitted offworld for any man assigned to the 34th.

Men were selected for R&R by rotation from a roster maintained by the FIST F-1, or personnel officer. There were three sites on Thorsfinni's World where the Marines were permitted to take this leave: Troms, a tiny resort town located near the equator, where in summer it often got warm enough to swim comfortably in the ocean and sometimes even get a tan on the narrow, rocky beaches; Bergen, a booming mining town about six thousand kilometers south and east of Bronnoysund; and New Oslo, the capital city of Thorsfinni's World, in the northern temperate region on the other side of the planet. New Oslo had a population of over a million and some of the amenities of a modern city on one of the more developed worlds of Human Space.

When the third platoon of L Company got its chance to send eligible men on R&R, Staff Sergeant Bass, and Lance Corporals Schultz, Claypoole, and Dean, were selected. They had unanimously elected to spend their leave in New Oslo, where the women were warm, the beer was cold, and there were sights to see.

"Best of all," Schultz said as they settled in for the suborbital flight to New Oslo, "we won't have to put up with this damned urban warfare crap for a week." Since the battle in New Obbia on Elneal the year before, the Fleet operations officer had directed that the men of the 34th FIST get additional training in the techniques of city fighting. For weeks now they had practiced assaults and withdrawals in clever mock-ups of city streets and buildings constructed just for training purposes. Schultz was weary of running up and down narrow stairways and pulling "dead" Marines out of hallways. "We'll never get to use any of this shit anyway," he muttered.

"Pipe down, Hammer," Bass said. "You know the Corps always prepares for the last war it fought. Relax, enjoy the scenery."

The aircraft broke through the cloud cover over New Oslo at about three thousand meters. Simultaneously, as if some god were illuminating the city below for the Marines' benefit, the sun broke through and bathed the metropolis in rays of weak winter radiance. Terraforming on Thorsfinni's World had not been allowed to get out of hand as it had on other inhospitable planets in the Confederation. Even so, the 'Finnis had left their cities and towns fully open to the elements instead of confining them within climate-control bubbles. The 'Finnis had the technology to build the bubbles, they just didn't want to. They had not only preserved the language of their distant Terran ancestors, but had also found a world whose rugged landscape and harsh winters replicated the Scandinavian climate their ancestors had come from, and they were going to keep it that way.

Inside the terminal the four Marines were directed to a small office marked FIST LIAISON, where they found several comfortable chairs, a workstation manned by a lance corporal, and a captain, both wearing class B winter uniforms. The walls of the room were decorated with holograms of the attractions of New Oslo, all of which prominently featured beautiful young women.

"My name is Captain Meadows," the officer began without preamble. "I am military attaché at the Confederation Embassy here in New Oslo. As an extra duty, I also run the R and R program for the 34th FIST. This is Lance Corporal Minh. Any problems or questions while you're here, contact him. Any of you ever been here before?"

Only Bass raised his hand. "Good, Staff Sergeant. Are these other men from your platoon?" Bass answered in the affirmative and the captain nodded. "Good." He smiled cryptically. "You show them the ropes, then. Lance Corporal . . ." He turned the proceedings over to Minh.

Lance Corporal Minh did not bother to get up from his workstation. The immaculately tailored class B winter uniform he wore had no badges or decorations. He clearly considered the men from the FIST an annoyance, an interruption to his otherwise very important work. He had been selected for attaché duty right out of Boot Camp and had never had another assignment in the Corps except there, at the New Oslo embassy. His high intelligence, high security clearances, and close association with the Confederation diplomatic corps had given him a very high opinion of himself.

"Here are some brochures about what to do and see in the

city," he said in a voice that reflected his bored, seen-it-all attitude. He spread out the brochures in front of him. He would not lower himself to passing them out to these boondock Marines. "If you must go outside the city, you are limited to a hundred kilometer radius. There are some fine winter resorts within that limit you might want to visit while you're here.

"We have rooms booked for you in the FIST R and R hotel downtown. They are first-class accommodations. You may stay there or anywhere else that suits you while you're here." He made a deprecating gesture at one of the holograms portraying a buxom young woman on skis. "In these envelopes is supplemental pay, in kroner, that you may find useful while you're here. The uniform after dark is dress scarlets; otherwise, wear whatever in your seabag suits the occasion. You can buy or rent cold-weather gear if you need it. Somehow, I don't think you will," he added with a sneer. "Transportation to your hotel leaves in thirty minutes. Please be back here at oh-five hours next Freytag, that is, five days from today.

"I want to do a quick download from your personnel records bracelets before you leave here, and I need to know your communicator call signs. If you need me, my call sign is R and R2. Please, don't mumble that in your sleep." Minh nodded at the captain that he was finished.

"Well, welcome to New Oslo, Marines," the captain said. "The people here are not as rough around the edges as they are back at Bronny, but they love their beer and a good time and they like Marines. While you're here, though, remember the old commandment for men in port: 'Lend and spend and not offend, till eight bells calls you out.' "

"Men," Bass said to the others as they checked into the lobby of their hotel, "I know a place here where we can get started tonight. It's eleven hours local now. Meet me down here at sixteen hours, in your reds. After tonight you're on your own."

In their room—the three had been assigned to one large suite—Claypoole bounced his seabag on the bed and began to undress.

"You guys ever been on R and R before?" Schultz asked.

"I haven't," Dean responded.

"Bullshit," Schultz sneered, "both you dukshits were on R and R the whole time we were deployed on Wanderjahr! What do you mean, you ain't never been on R and R before?" They all laughed.

"Yep," Claypoole said, "while the real men like you, Hammer, were out in the boonies back there, ol' Dean-o and me, we stayed back in Brosigville and just shot the shit out of everything that moved." Schultz clapped Claypoole on the back and laughed with him at the joke. Despite being on detached duty at the FIST headquarters the whole time, both Marines had been promoted in lieu of a decoration for heroism during the training mission on Wanderjahr.

"Well, with Charlie Bass along, we should have a good introduction to things in this town tonight," Dean said.

"Yeah," Schultz grunted, "intoxication and intercourse nonstop." Although Schultz feigned world-weary cynicism most of the time and maintained that he never felt comfortable unarmed no matter where he was, all three men were delighted their platoon sergeant had been picked to go on leave with them. "If he could lead us out of the Martac Waste," Schultz conceded, "he can get us laid in New Oslo."

"The place we're headed for is called Bjorn's," Bass told them as they waited for a cab. They huddled inside their greatcoats, turning their backs to the bitter wind that ruled Kaiser Street outside their hotel. After three hundred years, the Confederation Marine Corps still hadn't developed adequate foulweather clothing to go with the dress uniform.

The cold did not seem to affect the people crowding the streets, many of whom nodded in a friendly fashion at the four Marines. The city's citizens walked along purposefully, backs straight and heads held high, as if all of them were on the most interesting and important business. Evidently they took themselves seriously in New Olso. Evidently, also, they were prosperous, because everyone was dressed nicely despite the cold. Back in Bronnoysund, the natives dressed in practical work clothes and spit in the streets, and if they wanted to stop and gab in the streets, they did that too.

"Bjorn's has all the ingredients you need for a fine R and R," Bass said. "Beer, women, and music. Oh, and food, *lots* of food!"

Despite the fact that the place was crowded, the four Marines were shown to a table on the edge of the spacious dance floor. The raised platform for the band was empty but well-lighted, promising live entertainment later in the evening.

Midway through their second reindeer steak, they were interrupted by a loud cry. "Charlieeeeee!" A beautiful, silver-haired blonde woman threw her arms around Staff Sergeant Bass's neck and kissed him wetly on his cheek.

"Katie!" Bass exclaimed. "Gentlemen—you too, Claypoole—meet Katrina." They stood and shook hands with her. Her grip was cool and firm. "I met Katie the last time I was up here, on embassy courier duty," Bass added lamely.

Katie slapped Bass playfully on the top of his head. "Vy you didn't tell me you vas coming back again!"

Bass made an embarrassed face. "I was going to, honey, but we just got here."

Katie looked at the others. "You boys are alone?" she asked, and frowned when they admitted they were. She stood up, put two fingers in her mouth and whistled loudly three times.

"Local custom," Bass said. In a few moments three other young women joined them. Waiters brought extra chairs, and they all crowded around the small table. The food scraps were removed and replaced with huge pitchers of cold beer. Then Bass broke out cigars, and everyone lighted up.

A slight, dark-haired beauty named Jena took Claypoole's hand and sat next to him. "You must excuse I don't speak English so good," she murmured, a Scandanavian lilt making her words musical.

"Oh, your English is fine!" Claypoole protested.

"Thank you, kind sir," she responded, and smiled. Claypoole was reminded of a young woman he'd met on Wanderjahr, and he felt a sudden stab of sorrow; a sniper had killed her with a bullet that might have been meant for him. His unexpected change of mood was reflected on his face, and Jena asked if he was okay.

"Uh, oh, yeah yeah. Just gas." Claypoole smiled and burped loudly. Everyone laughed.

"Thanks for not putting it out the *other* end!" Schultz shouted, and everyone laughed even harder.

Claypoole had changed since Wanderjahr. The old wiseacre Claypoole was still around, but he showed up only occasionally now. The unhappy memory passed quickly, and Claypoole smiled at Jena, took her hand in his own and with his free arm drew her closer to him.

"Ah!" one of the women exclaimed. "Music!"

Three men had emerged from the wings carrying stringed instruments. They bowed to the audience and sat down. Each adjusted his instrument and conferred briefly with his companions. When all nodded that they were ready, the leader stamped his foot three times and, without introduction, they began to play.

In Bronnoysund sailors off the oceangoing ships and fishing trawlers often played for their own amusement in the local beer halls, sawing away or plucking enthusiastically on a variety of stringed instruments. The music was fine for drinking and for dancing across sawdust-covered floors at places like Big Barb's, the beer hall, bordello, and ship's chandler that served as third platoon's drinking headquarters when they were in town. But these players were different.

At the first notes of their playing, a cold shiver went down Joe Dean's spine, and his companions began keeping time with their fingers and toes. The music was "kinetic," it made you want to move, and soon that's just what the other patrons began to do. Men and women poured onto the wooden dance floor, stomped and shouted and whirled around while diners and drinkers shouted and clapped their hands. The music they played that night—rollicking fiddle tunes improvised long ago by hard men to enliven the rigors of life on rocky seacoasts in a time long before men could fly, imported by the first settlers from Old Earth, adapted to the harsh environment of a new world over several centuries—stayed with the Marines long after the other events of that night were only a dim memory.

* * *

Many people visited at the Marines' table over the next few exhilarating hours. The fiddlers played and the patrons stomped until musicians and dancers both were soaked with perspiration. During breaks in the music, everyone drank heartily. The beer flowed in prodigious quantities but nobody went mean.

At one point the Marines were joined by a red-faced young man who said he was a naval rating stationed at the embassy on special communications duty.

"SRA Third Hummfree," he introduced himself. Schultz rolled his eyes; Claypoole and Dean exchanged pained glances. Navy enlisted ranks didn't make any sense to the Marines.

"I was on the *Denver*, fellows," Hummfree told them, "when you were training the field police on Wanderjahr. I'm the one who figured out where the rebels had their headquarters," he added proudly.

"That's right!" Claypoole exclaimed. "Hey, that's right! So you're the guy! I remember the briefing at the brigadier's headquarters when it was explained how you did that." He clapped the young man on the back and poured him a beer from his pitcher. "He said you were too good for the navy, that the Marines should try to get you away from them."

"That was me," Hummfree said a little tipsily. It was obvious he wanted to talk about it. "Surface Radar Analyst Third Class Hummfree." He tapped his arm where chevrons would be if he were in uniform.

"Watcha say yer doin' here?" Schultz interrupted.

"Uh, I'm in the communications cell, at the embassy."

"Yeah, but whatcha *do*? You snoop around on the 'Finnis too?"

"Naw," he answered, "I work on Project Golem." Instantly his hand half flew to his mouth and an expression came across the analyst's face as if he'd just spoken an abominably filthy word. To the others in the noisy, smoke-filled room it sounded like "Project Go Get 'Em."

"That's deep-space communications and shit like that," he added quickly. "Well," the sailor said, "gotta go now. See you around, huh?"

After the man had departed, Schultz turned to Bass and said,

"Tell me the anchor clankers aren't a bunch of pussy farts," and laughed.

In the early morning hours of the following day, Schultz, gamely assisted by a laughing Miss Helga Halvorson, staggered up the stairs and into the foyer of her small apartment.

"Hold it!" Schultz commanded once they were inside. "I feel—I feel, a—*communication* coming through!" He swayed drunkenly as he brought his right wrist up to eye level. "R and R Two," he said, speaking Lance Corporal Minh's call sign into his communicator.

"Lance Corporal Minh here, sir," a tiny, sleepy voice came through the speaker.

"Commandant of the Confederation Marine Corps here, Lance Corporal!" Schultz bellowed, trying to keep his voice even and grave. "I have an important message for you and all the other rear-echelon pogues and pussy farts in this town!" Doubled over with drunken laughter, tears streaming down his face, he put his wrist between his buttocks and farted.

Two days later they were on their way to war.

CHAPTER
FIVE

The staff and major subordinate unit commanders of the 34th Fleet Initial Strike Team sprang to attention as Brigadier Sturgeon entered the briefing room. The FIST commander strode to the lectern standing to the side of the large vidscreen at the back of the small briefing stage. Normally he would put the officers at ease while he walked through their ranks, but this time he left them standing at attention while he went to the lectern, then stood at it looking at them for a moment before saying, "At ease, gentlemen." He gave them another moment to resume their seats and exchange questioning glances. The more they wondered what was going on, the sharper their attention would be when he told them. Not all of the staff and subordinate commanders of 34th FIST had ever been on an operation such as the one they were about to embark on. Then he gave them another, longer moment, long enough for some among them to begin to fidget.

"Gentlemen," Sturgeon finally began, "we are going to war." Some of the less experienced officers looked at each other quizzically. He could almost hear them thinking, *Going to war?* Thirty-fourth FIST was always going on operations, what could be different here? "Not all of you have been to war," he continued after a few seconds. "On operations and campaigns, certainly. Expeditions, too many to count. There's not a man jack in this room who doesn't have four or five campaign medals and a few campaign stars on his Marine Expeditionary Medal. Those kinds of operations are the bread and butter of the Confederation Marine Corps, it's how we earn our keep day in and day out. But we don't often go to war. Those of you who have, you know the difference. The rest of you are about to find out."

Sturgeon touched a button on the keyboard in the lectern's top. The vidscreen to his side went from gray to interstellar black studded with the patterns of unfamiliar constellations. The patterns shifted, grew, widened toward the sides of the screens. The view focused on one point of light and closed in on it until it was visible as the burning disk of a star seen close, and only it and eight planets circling it were in the view.

"This is Drummond's system," Sturgeon said as he paused the changing view. "Most likely, few of you have heard of it. But you've all heard of this place." The view on the screen began to change again, the focus shifting to the fourth planet out from the star. "This is Diamunde." The silence in the room became almost palpable when Sturgeon gave the planet's name. When the planet's orb almost filled the screen, he stopped the screen again and looked at the officers. "You all know the Confederation has fought three major wars on Diamunde. Some of you fought in the most recent of them. You know what this means. I fought in two of them myself, so I can say without hesitation or fear of contradiction that the most recent was worse than the previous one. What I've read in histories tells me the second was worse than the first. Do you see the pattern here?

"Another war has broken out for control of the gems and minerals Diamunde is so rich in. It's a war the Confederation has to put down. The 34th FIST, along with the 13th, 19th, 21st, 36th, and 225th FISTs, reinforced with Marine heavy artillery—" He let his gaze sweep over the officers again, few of whom had ever been on operations or expeditions that included heavy artillery. "—have as their initial assignment the securing of a planethead for follow-on forces from the Confederation Army." He paused to let that sink in. Six of the Confederation Marine Corps' thirty-six FISTs operating in concert to secure a single planethead was a mission of a magnitude almost unimaginable to most of the assembled officers. Those few who had experience with an operation of that size turned grim.

"Gentlemen, we are not going up against tribal warriors riding horses and firing projectile rifles. We are not going up against guerrillas accustomed to fighting a comic-opera police force. We are taking on a million-man army equipped with modern weapons, using tactics very similar to those used by the Confederation forces, and commanded by generals with experience in major wars. What's going to make this operation doubly difficult for us is, this million man army has—" He hesitated. "—tanks. Main battle tanks." He pushed another button on his keyboard and the image on the screen changed from the rotating planet to a sixty-thousand-kilogram armored vehicle rumbling at high speed across the landscape, firing a 120 millimeter gun as it went, and hitting targets four kilometers away.

Excited murmurs broke out. One officer exclaimed loudly, "Tanks? I thought they didn't exist anymore!"

"They do exist, and we're being sent to kill enough of them to make room for the army to come in behind us," Sturgeon replied sharply. He glared at the officers and they quickly became quiet. "As you well know, Marines haven't fought tanks in several centuries. We haven't even trained in antitank tactics for generations. Most of our plasma weapons are completely ineffective against heavy armor. Fortunately, the Corps is in the process of acquiring weapons that can defeat heavy armor—the same weapons that sent tanks into retirement in the first place." He shook his head ruefully. During his forty years in the Corps, he'd always fought with the most modern of weapons; now he'd have to fight his FIST with weapons so archaic he'd never seen one outside a museum. Weapons neither he nor his Marines knew how to use. Weapons with which they would have to become proficient by the time they mounted out in less than a month. Weapons they didn't have.

"Gentlemen, I'm now going to turn you over to the good auspices of Commander Campinisi, who will give you some details of what we are about to do." The staff and subordinate commanders sprang to attention as Sturgeon stepped off the stage and marched out of the briefing room.

Once he was out of sight, Commander Campinisi, the FIST operations officer, began his briefing.

"This is Marston St. Cyr. He's the vice president for Marketing and Research of Tubalcain Enterprises—or at least he was until he appointed himself a major general in something called the Diamundean Armed Forces and came up with enough main battle tanks to form several armored divisions . . ."

"You heard me," Commander Van Winkle snarled. "Main battle tanks." Thirty-fourth FIST's infantry battalion commander wanted to glare at his assembled staff officers and company commanders, but was too shocked at the news himself to pull it off. "Right now the only weapons organic to the FIST that can kill an MBT are the squadron's Raptors and the guns of our artillery battery. This battalion certainly doesn't have anything else that can do more than annoy one of those monsters—unless one sits around long enough for our massed plasma weapons to burn through it. And I can't imagine anyone, even a tanker, dumb enough to do that. When we reach Diamunde, we will be reinforced by additional Marine artillery. Each of the six FISTs in the operation—yes, I said *six FISTs*—will be supported by a general support battalion of 175mm and 200mm towed howitzers. Unfortunately, we aren't going to be able to do any training with them before the assault." Protestations interrupted him, but Van Winkle held up his hand. "We'll still be able to train with the FIST air and artillery. As a matter of fact, that's exactly what I want you to be doing between now and the time our antiarmor weapons arrive."

He held up his hand again to stop the questions that were coming at him. "No, I don't know when the antiarmor weapons will arrive. All I know is they're in transit and they have experts with them to teach us how to use the weapons.

"Here are your assignments. Company commanders, effective as soon as you return to your barracks, begin training your men in calling in air and artillery. We won't be able to kill every tank we see, but I don't want even one to survive because somebody didn't know how to call in air or artillery to kill it.

"One," Van Winkle said, referring to the battalion's S-1, or personnel officer, "fine-comb your records. I want every man in this battalion to have the rank he's supposed to have and all the decorations and commendations he rates before we mount out. Two"—the S-2, intelligence officer—"dig up everything you can find on armor and antiarmor tactics for dissemination. You can get specifics on the Diamunde armor from the F-2," the FIST intelligence officer. "Three"—the operations officer—"coordinate with the squadron and the battery for field training. We'll begin in the classroom, then head into the field. I want every man in the battalion to have both theory and hands-on for calling in air and artillery. Four," logistics, "not much for you to do until our tank killers arrive. Make sure everything is packed or ready to pack for our mount out."

Van Winkle paused to look at his officers. They all looked serious. That was good. They also all looked like they were ready to begin, which was even better. "Let's do these things." He abruptly stepped out and left the briefing room by the side door that led directly to his office. He heard his company commanders and staff scrambling to do their jobs before his office door was completely closed behind him.

"So what if they've got armor?" PFC Clarke objected. An assistant gunner in Company L's third platoon, Clarke thought he understood his weapon's capabilities. "If our guns can slag rock, they can melt armor."

As the more than ninety enlisted men of the company moved about, chairs rattled, conversations buzzed, and the noise level in the company classroom overpowered what Clarke's gun team leader, Corporal Lonsdorf, had replied, so Lonsdorf reached out and smacked the back of Clarke's head.

"I said, clean the wax out of your ears," Lonsdorf snarled.

Clarke flinched, then glared at Lonsdorf while rubbing the sting from the back of his head.

"I said," Lonsdorf repeated, leaning closer so Clarke could hear him without him having to shout, "rocks stand still and let us slag them. Armor moves. We can't concentrate enough fire on a moving target to melt armor." He looked to the front of the classroom, where Gunny Thatcher, the company gunnery sergeant, had just arrived with three other Marines, two NCOs, and a warrant officer whom he didn't recognize. "Dumb guy," he muttered at Clarke.

The two NCOs, a sergeant and a corporal, looked almost like recruiting posters in their garrison utility uniforms. The warrant officer wasn't wearing spectacles, but his somewhat bewildered expression made him look like he should be. Otherwise, he looked uncomfortable, like someone had dressed him up for a costume party.

Claypoole and Dean glanced at each other. "Spears," Dean mouthed. Claypoole nodded. The warrant officer did indeed resemble the Confederation ambassador to Wanderjahr, whom they'd met during their last deployment.

Gunnery Sergeant Thatcher looked over the assembled Marines for a moment before glancing toward the back of the room where Captain Conorado, the company commander, stood with the company's other officers and first sergeant in the passageway just outside. At a nod from Conorado, Thatcher called out, *"Attention on deck!"* and everybody immediately stood at attention.

"At ease," Conorado said as he strode briskly from the back to the front of the classroom. The first sergeant, Top Myer, followed closely on his heels, glowering to the sides. Myer's glowers didn't mean anything in particular; it was his normal expression. The other officers arrayed themselves at the rear of the room, near where the platoon sergeants had already stationed themselves.

Captain Conorado didn't glower when he reached the front of the classroom and turned to face his men, but there was instant stillness when the Marines saw his expression. The company commander looked more serious than he usually did when he briefed his men on a mount out.

"I know the scuttlebutt's gotten around," Conorado started. "You know we're going up against main battle tanks. Right now the biggest problem we have is that none of you understands what a main battle tank is, what it can do, or how to kill one. Sure, you've all seen MBTs on historical vids—and I'll bet none of you believe what you've seen in those vids. You're right in not believing a lot of what you've seen; there's a lot of exaggeration in vids. But there are things about MBTs that those vids just don't tell you. That's what you're going to begin to learn today. Behind me, with Gunny Thatcher, are three Marines who will spend the next two weeks teaching you everything they can about what MBTs can do, what they can't do, and how to kill them. You had best pay attention to them when they tell you something. If you don't, you're going to get yourself killed. And you'll probably kill a lot of good Marines at the same time."

Conorado turned to look at Thatcher. "Gunny, take over."

Thatcher snapped to attention. "Aye aye, sir." He waited until Conorado turned back toward the men, then bellowed, *"Attention on deck!"* He remained at attention until Conorado left the classroom. The first sergeant left with the company commander. The other officers stayed behind; they had things to learn as well.

"As you were," Gunny Thatcher said as soon as the captain and first sergeant were gone. He gave the Marines a moment to resume their seats before continuing. "We've got a lot to learn and a short time to learn it in. Sergeant Bojanowski"—he indicated one of the three Marines standing with him—"is a forward air observer from the composite squadron. He's going to teach us how to call in air support. Corporal Henry,"—he identified another of the strangers—"is a spotter from the artillery battery. He's going to teach us how to call in the big guns. Some of you already know how to call in air or artillery, but nobody in this company has called in either in quite a while—calls for hopper medevac or guiding hoppers in to drop off supplies don't count. So even if you already know how, think of this as a refresher course—or use your knowledge to help train the Marines who don't know how to do it.

"We'll start with artillery. Corporal Henry, the floor is yours." Thatcher and the other two Marines stepped aside and took seats in the front row. Everybody noticed that Thatcher hadn't introduced the warrant officer, and nearly all of them wondered why not.

"This," Corporal Henry began, flicking on the trid he stood next to, "is the mainstay of Marine artillery, the towed 175mm M-147 howitzer." In the trid's field, an artillery piece rotated. A Marine stood next to the big gun for scale. Its main wheels came up to his shoulders. The muzzle of the gun, elevated about fifteen degrees, was nearly twice his height above the ground. Other than its size, it would have been immediately recognizable as an artillery piece to a late sixteenth century French cannoneer. "The M-147 is called a 'direct support' weapon, but that's because it directly supports one unit, not because it fires directly at its target. It has a range of fifty kilometers with a target-error radius at maximum range of fifteen meters. The primary ammunition used by the M-147 is explosive projectiles." He paused for a moment while a gun crew appeared in the trid. It took the crew twenty seconds to load, aim, and fire the big gun. The image shifted to a masonry house, which erupted when the artillery round hit it. "The M-147 can be reconfigured for short-range, direct plasma fire by the simple expedient of replacing the breech and relining the bore." The howitzer was again visible in the trid. A two-armed rigger approached it. One arm removed the bulky back end of the piece, then the other installed something that, except for its size, resembled the breech of a blaster. Another rigger approached the muzzle and slid a tube into the barrel. The change took two and a half minutes. The crew came back to the gun, lowered its elevation to horizontal, manhandled a man-size power pack into the breech, and fired at a patch of forest two kilometers away. The Marines in the classroom imagined they could hear a whoosh as the one-hundred-meter-wide swath of woods went up, though the trid didn't have sound.

"That's what an M-147 looks like and a couple basics of what it can do. Now that you're impressed, I'll tell you how it's used." Corporal Henry spent the next two hours reciting more details about artillery uses and procedures for the Marines of Company L than most of them wanted to know.

"Be back here in ten minutes," Gunny Thatcher said when the corporal finished his introduction to artillery. The classroom

emptied faster than a gun crew could load, aim, and fire a projectile round.

Ten minutes later the gunny was standing front and center,
looking at his watch. On the dot of ten minutes he looked up
and saw the last man scrambling back into his seat. "I said ten
minutes, MacIlargie," he snarled, "not ten minutes and two
seconds."

Third platoon's PFC MacIlargie gave the gunny his best
"Who, me?" look. Thatcher returned the favor with a "You're
on my list" look. MacIlargie wished he was in his chameleons
so the company gunny couldn't see him.

"Now," Thatcher addressed the company, secretly pleased
that everybody was back so promptly, "Sergeant Bojanowski is
going to introduce you to Marine Air."

"Most of you have seen Marine Raptors in action," Bojanowski began as he flicked on the trid. He wondered why so
many of them flinched at that. He didn't know that most of third
platoon had been on the wrong end of a two-Raptor strafing run
a year earlier during a peacekeeping mission on Elneal. The trid
projection showed a flight of two Raptors flying arabesques
around each other far above ground.

"The A-8E Raptor is the Marine Corps' vertical/short
takeoff/landing aircraft," Bojanowski continued. "It has an effective combat radius of one thousand kilometers. That means
it can fly a thousand kilometers, deliver support to the Marines
on the ground, fight off an enemy air attack, and have enough
power left to fly a thousand kilometers back to base. The
Raptor's top speed is classified, but it's well in excess of Mach.
Its armament consists of four plasma guns similar to those in
the gun squad of an infantry platoon."

In the trid projection, the two Raptors sailed low over the
ground with their guns flaming a company-size formation of
man-size targets. When the aircraft completed the strafing run
along the long axis of the formation, hardly any of the targets
were left uncharred.

"The Raptor also has plasma cannons." This time the Raptors flew almost straight down from a great height. At two
thousand meters they sprayed bursts from their cannons. The

aircraft shuddered visibly as vernier jets cut in and bounced them back heavenward.

"In case you're wondering," Bojanowski said dryly, "the Raptors are subject to fifteen g's in that maneuver. The pilots wear special flight suits and are hooked into life-support systems that keep them from being injured or blacking out." The plasma bolts from the cannons looked huge, and the men compared them to the bolts fired by the blasters they used. When the bolts hit the ground, they burst into fireballs more than twenty meters wide. When the fireballs dissipated, ten-meter craters could be seen in rocky ground. A wooden structure that had been struck by two bolts was turned to ash before it could burst into visible flame.

"I only wish we had a tank on hand to show you what one of those babies can do to armor," Bojanowski said. "Now, all the attack aircraft in the world won't do the infantryman a damn bit of good unless he can tell the pilots where he is and what he wants killed. I'm going to begin to teach you how to do that now . . ."

Sergeant Bojanowski talked for two hours, complete with trid demonstrations. In the back of the classroom, Staff Sergeant Charlie Bass, third platoon's sergeant, nodded to himself. He'd wondered why Gunny Thatcher had the artillery corporal talk first, and now he understood. The trid projections of the Raptors in action were more exciting to watch than the artillery presentation. It kept the men's attention better when they were beginning to tire.

When the initial air lecture was over, Gunny Thatcher took the floor again. "It's seventeen hours," he announced. "Time for mess call. Be back here at eighteen hours." He gave the men a few seconds to express surprise and disappointment, then told them, "If any of you were expecting liberty call, you're badly mistaken. We've got six months worth of schooling to cram into two weeks, first here in the classroom, then in the field. You're going to be working, studying, and learning around the clock for the duration. You'll think you're fortunate when you manage more than four hours sleep in twenty-four. Dismissed for chow. See you back here in one hour. MacIlargie, that doesn't mean one hour and two seconds."

One hour later Sergeant Bojanowski flicked the trid back on and said, "Here's what armed hoppers can do . . ."

CHAPTER
SIX

Joe Dean looked aghast at the landscape. "I thought there was too much snow in New Oslo," he moaned. He shivered in his mottled-white winter gear. Even growing up in New Rochester on Old Earth with its severe winters, and visiting nearby Buffalo and Watertown, he'd never seen so much snow so early in the season.

Hammer Schultz hawked into a snowdrift tw' e his height. "Ain't seen nothing yet," he said. "Wait'll full winter gets here."

Dean turned to Schultz, a horrified expression on his face. Two meters of snow was understandable in the dead of winter, but so early? The wind swept the snow cover smooth and melted its surface into such a brittle crust a man could walk on it, but if he stepped too hard on a thin spot of crust, he'd sink into soft snow to his chest or deeper.

"Hammer's right," Corporal Leach said. "Last winter we had to save four men from the platoon from drowning in the deep snow. One man from second squad, he rotated out before you got here, had a leg, an arm, and several ribs broken when a snowslide from the barracks roof hit him."

"No." Dean gave his fire team leader a terrified look.

Schultz hawked again. "Yep," he said. "Wasn't even a bad winter."

Leach nodded. "Only one serious casualty and four near drownings. Not bad at all; didn't have to bury anybody."

"Don't let them spook you, Dean," Sergeant Hyakowa said as he walked up. "We hardly ever have broken bones from falling snow, and the biggest danger of dying is from exposure." He eyed Dean's cold weather gear to make sure it was sealed properly. "You do have to be careful about falling in over your head, though. Smothering is a real possibility." He dropped the infra screen on his helmet and slowly pivoted to see where the rest of the squad was. They weren't wearing chameleons, but to the naked eye the mottled white of their winter gear had the same effect. Because the winter field uniform kept body heat in, heat signatures were lessened as well. But everybody was standing in the open, and he spotted his squad members easily enough.

"First squad, on me," he called out.

In a moment the ten men of first squad, third platoon, Company L, 34th FIST, were gathered together in a tight clump, symbolically if not actually sharing body warmth. Even though none of them faced outward, all of the more experienced members of the squad spent more time looking past whoever they faced than they did looking at each other. Constant awareness of one's surroundings is a vital skill for an infantryman, so the experienced men watched for any sign of enemy, even though the only enemy they faced on Thorsfinni's World was the weather—and some defenseless targets set up for the artillery spotting practice they were about to conduct.

"Cheer up, Deano," Leach said, poking his junior man on the shoulder. "We might be in snow as deep as we are tall, but at least we're out of the damn classroom, right?"

Dean smiled weakly. "Yeah. No more trying to look awake when we're asleep." He began to brighten. They would begin practicing the things Corporal Henry had been lecturing about.

"Dean"—Hyakowa drew his name out—"you're still too boot to know how to look awake when you're asleep. That's why I'm going to make sure you get tested on something you slept through."

Dean's brightening mood crashed back into darkness and despair.

"Lima Three-five, Lima Three-five," Dean said nervously into his helmet comm unit. "This is One-one-three." The simple call signs identified Staff Sergeant Charlie Bass, the third platoon sergeant, as the recipient, and Dean, third man in the first fire team of first squad, as the caller. "I have targets. Request patch-through to Gun Control. Over."

"One-one-three, this is Lima Three-five. Roger your request for patch-through. Wait one." For this first exercise, the radio call signs and procedure were kept simple and formal. Both men knew they wouldn't be talking that way on the radio under fire.

In a moment a new voice came over the radio to Dean, relayed through the platoon's main communications net. "Lima Three-one-one-three, this is Gun Control. Over."

"Gun Control, this is Lima, uh, Three-one-one-three." Dean had to think about his call sign—he'd never used one so long and involved. Then he forgot what he was supposed to say next.

"What is your position, One-one-three? Over." The artillery radioman obviously understood Dean's confusion.

Dean looked at the unfamiliar geo-position-locator. It was unfamiliar to him because the GPL was normally a squad leader's equipment. The GPL was tied into a planet-girdling satellite system that gave his position within five meters. "I am at . . ." He read off the alphanumeric string that gave his map coordinates. Then he remembered what he was supposed to say next. "Target, earthwork structure." He looked at the sod-covered earthworks that was his target through the range-finder shield on his helmet. "Azimuth, three-two-four. Range, one-one-zero-zero. Over."

"One-one-three," Gun Control immediately read back the information. "Confirm. Over."

"Confirmed, Gun Control," Dean said after he checked the numbers. He was concentrating on the mechanics of calling in artillery, and his radio procedure was slipping.

"Lima Three-one-one-three, one spotter round on its way. Advise. Over." Over the radio, Dean heard the blast of a howitzer firing.

Dean peered intently at the target and began counting the seconds. He knew how far away the artillery was and how long it should take for a round to travel that distance. Still, he flinched in surprise when he heard the sharp crack of the supersonic round as it passed overhead, and almost simultaneously saw the flash of light and eruption of snow thrown up by the explosion. He quickly analyzed what he saw and compared it to vids he'd seen of artillery rounds hitting different surfaces. The way the snow flew up in a broad cone told him the round had been fused for explosion on contact and had gone all the way to the frozen dirt surface before it went off.

"Gun Control, adjust," he said excitedly. "Right one hundred. On my azimuth, up seventy-five." His helmet's range finder told him the round hit a hundred meters to the left of his aiming point and seventy-five meters short. "Fire one spotter."

"Right one hundred, up seventy-five," the Gun Control radioman repeated. "One spotter on its way."

This time the sonic crack and simultaneous explosion didn't make Dean flinch, though he was surprised that they occurred exactly when he expected. This round struck well within the kill radius of his aiming point.

"Gun Control, you're on target. Fire for effect. Over."

"Lima Three-one-one-three. This is Gun Control. We are on target. Fire for effect. Advise when target is destroyed. Over."

"Gun Control, Lima Three-one-one-three will advise when target is destroyed."

One round came downrange and hit within meters of the last. For this exercise, one round was all that would be fired to simulate a barrage. Dean stood, grinning proudly. The first time he'd ever called in artillery he'd hit his target with the second round.

"Not too bad," Corporal Miller said a few meters to Dean's left rear. "Of course, if that was a moving target, you would have missed it completely." Miller was more pleased than he let on, though. He knew that the artillerymen deliberately missed with their first round; Dean's instructions had been precise enough that the first shot would have been metal on target if they'd been firing for real.

On a different range a hundred kilometers to the south, Claypoole studied the drone that was his target. It was big and it was gray and it was scooting along the surface of the snow at a speed his range finder translated as more than one hundred kilometers per hour. He remembered what he'd been taught in the classroom, and knew that if the drone was traveling in a straight line, he could call anything down on it. But the drone was zigging and zagging, and once in a while threw itself violently into reverse. But it didn't have any passengers, and its driver was safely operating it from a steady seat at a console inside a shelter a hundred meters to Claypoole's rear.

"Go to it, Lance Corporal," Sergeant Bojanowski called from his observer position. "You've got to kill that baby before it kills you."

"Right," Claypoole muttered. He didn't know how he was going to manage. Well, here goes, he thought. "Fireball One," he said into his radio. "This is Spotter Ten." They were using a different communications protocol for air. "I have a target. Over."

"Spotter Ten, Fireball One. Go." No airman, not even a hopper pilot, was going to use formal radio procedure—it wasn't dashing enough.

"My position . . ." Claypoole didn't have the same nervousness about giving instructions that had bothered Dean, his worry was different. He rattled off his coordinates. "Target, MBT. Azimuth, one-seven-three. Range, six-five-seven-zero. Vector, zero-eight-six. Speed, one-zero-two. Maneuvering. Over." He didn't know where the hopper was. He couldn't hear it, and suspected that even if he stood up and looked around, he wouldn't see it. He had to give his and the drone's relative positions so the pilot would know where to look for the target.

The hopper pilot repeated the numbers, then said, "Orienting. Splash color."

Claypoole planted the laser pointer on his shoulder and sighted on the drone. Bingo, he nailed it on the first try! He tracked the movement of the drone and kept the beam of light on it.

"Ten, One. I have red light. You." The pilot didn't actually see the color, he was firing from behind a hill and read the data transmitted to his instruments from satellites.

"Hopper One, that's it. Fire."

There was a second's hesitation, then the pilot said, "Ten, what are you doing? I lost the light."

Claypoole swore at himself. The drone had made a sudden turn, almost ninety degrees, and lost the color Claypoole's laser beam was painting it with. Quickly, he found his target again and hit it with the red laser light.

"I have red," the hopper pilot said.

"You have the target."

"One Hellspawn out."

Claypoole instinctively gripped the laser pointer tighter—and lost his target when the drone took another sharp turn.

"Find it, find it, find it!" the pilot shrieked. He could slow the missle slightly, but if it lost the target for more than a second or two, it probably wouldn't have time to lock back on again.

Frantically, Claypoole found the drone and resighted.

"Got it!" the pilot shouted. "Keep it painted."

The drone sped in a straight line to the west, and Claypoole managed to track it, keeping the beam of light on the target. Suddenly, the drone stopped and went into reverse, causing Claypoole's aim to slide off. Appalled, through the sight he saw the Hellspawn pass through the space the drone would have been in if it hadn't stopped.

"You're dead," Sergeant Bojanowski called out. "Next victim." He turned to Ensign vanden Hoyt and said quietly, "You know, if that drone had a real driver instead of a controller who could see what your lance corporal was doing, that would have been a clean kill."

After two weeks of classroom and field training, with very little more sleep than Gunny Thatcher had said they'd have, the exhausted Marines of Company L reassembled in the company classroom for a briefing from their trainers.

"None of you are a danger to take over my job," Sergeant Bojanowski said. "But every one of you has the experience of painting a moving target so well that a hopper can hit it with a Hellspawn. Every one of you can talk to a flight of Raptors and rain fire on a target. You've all got the experience, and that experience will likely save some of your lives where you're going." He paused for a moment and let his gaze wash over the tired men he was addressing. "Something nobody told you before now is my last duty assignment was on Arsenault—as an instructor at air controller school. You've learned more and performed better during the last two weeks than any of the classes I taught there. You did it on less sleep than those students had, and you had to divide your attention between what I was teaching you and what Corporal Henry was teaching you."

Bojanowski stood erect. "Marines, well done! I hope you get a liberty call before you mount out. You've earned one hell of a drunken night in town." He stepped aside and Thatcher nodded to the artilleryman.

Corporal Henry took front and center. He seemed lost in thought for a moment, then said, "The only thing Sergeant Bojanowski said that I can't is that he's served as an instructor at artillery school. You did an outstanding job. If I was on a gun crew, I wouldn't be worried about following aiming instructions from anyone in Company L. And when I get back to the battery, I'm going to pass the word that you know your shit."

Gunny Thatcher stepped forward. He looked at the two trainers for a long moment before addressing them. "Gentlemen, if anybody had told me two weeks ago that every man jack in this company would be as proficient today at calling in air and artillery as they are, I wouldn't have believed them. I am personally going to see to it that your commanders know what an outstanding job you did." He cracked a brief smile. "The Marines of Company L appreciate a job well done."

"Three cheers!" someone called from the back of the classroom.

The Marines jumped to their feet and shouted in unison, "Aarugh! *Aarugh! Aarugh!*" They burst into laughter while the last "aarugh" was still echoing off the walls, and hurtled catcalls at their instructors.

"Thank you," Thatcher said as the cries of his Marines died down. "I know you have to get back to your units for your own preparations for this mount-out." He watched as the two walked down the center aisle of the classroom, shaking outstretched hands and exchanging compliments with the Marines of Company L. As soon as they were gone, he called for the company's attention.

"You look pleased with yourselves, and you should be. You did extremely well in your training. You also look like you need about twenty-four hours sleep. But you aren't going to get it, not now. Now you have to find out just what we're going to be facing." He noted with satisfaction how serious everyone became. "You're probably all wondering who the gunner is," he said, and indicated the warrant officer, who had done nothing more than observe during the previous two weeks, and who still hadn't been introduced. "This is Gunner Moeller. He's a historian from Headquarters Marine Corps. His job is to teach us all about armor, antiarmor tactics, and about the other weapons we'll use to kill tanks."

There were a few sounds of disbelief. "What's a historian got to do with it?" someone asked.

Thatcher cocked an eyebrow. "Nobody uses armor anymore. It's too vulnerable to man-portable antiarmor weapons, and too expensive to replace. The Fleet no longer has any experience or expertise in armor or the tactics to defeat it. We need a historian because they're the only people who know enough about the subject to teach us what we need to know to face armor and live to tell about it." He turned to the slender, slightly stooped warrant officer and nodded. "Gunner."

Warrant Officer Moeller looked distracted as he walked toward the trid controls. Almost absently, he reached out a hand to turn it on. "This is an M1D7 Super Abrams from circa 2050." The three-dimensional image of a monstrous vehicle appeared and began revolving. "It stood four meters high, was twelve meters long, and six meters wide. The M1D7 Super Abrams weighed more than sixty tons, and had armor strong enough to enable it to ignore any weapon short of a tactical nuke. It carried a crew of four, and sixty rounds for its 120mm main gun. The Super Abrams had a top speed of one hundred kph. It burned diesel fuel at the rate of eight liters per kilometer. Its weight was so great it could only maneuver on paved roads or stony ground with solid understrata, and could safely cross only a small portion of the bridges on the face of the Earth. It was too heavy for nearly any airlift available at the time. The logistical train it required was such that an armored battalion could only field sixty tanks." Gunner Moeller spoke in a drone and didn't seem to notice the drooping eyelids and nodding heads in his audience. "Still, despite its limitations, the Super Abrams was so awesomely powerful that it was the strongest and most desired land-war fighting weapon on Earth." The tank's image was replaced by that of a foot soldier aiming an ornate tubelike object that rested on his shoulder. "Until the infantry came up with this . . ." Moeller reached to the trid's controls and twisted the volume dial to full just as the soldier in the image fired his weapon. The loud blast shocked most of the men back to attention. The louder blast when the image switched to an M1D7 being hit and killed by the rocket made all of them jump.

Moeller chuckled. "Got you!" He continued in a livelier voice, "Now that I've got your attention, that was an M-72 Straight Arrow. It was man-portable, relatively cheap, and could kill an M1D7 Super Abrams, the tank that could withstand anything short of a tactical nuke. The Straight Arrow was the reason the M1D7 Super Abrams was the last main battle tank anybody developed and fielded. Lance corporals and below, who can tell me why?"

The right arms of almost all the junior men in the company shot up. All of them shouted out answers. Some of the answers were right.

CHAPTER
SEVEN

The gist of Warrant Officer Moeller's lecture on the history of tank warfare was that the first armored vehicles that could be called "main battle tanks" were fielded in the early part of the twentieth century during what was then called the "Great War." The first ones were basically mobile pillboxes. They mounted a couple of machine guns and had thick enough armor to stop bullets, hand grenades, and smaller artillery fragments. In short order some of them began carrying small-caliber cannons. To the infantrymen who couldn't stop them with their rifles and machine guns, they were rolling hell. So the infantry developed tank traps that reduced their mobility, and explosive charges that could knock them out of a fight even if they couldn't kill them. The reaction of the tankers was to develop bigger, tougher, faster, more maneuverable tanks. By the time the Great War ended, the tanks being fielded by all the participants were true monsters compared to those in the earliest stages of the war.

But tank development didn't stop there. Over the next twenty years the major powers of Earth continued to develop bigger, stronger, tougher, faster, more maneuverable tanks, so by the time the Second World War began, the most militarily underdeveloped of the major powers had tanks that could easily defeat the strongest tanks from the previous war. Infantrymen *really* hated that. When you're armed with a rifle and maybe a rifle grenade, there's simply no way you can expect to survive against a twenty-five-ton chunk of armor carrying a 75mm cannon and a couple of machine guns. So the infantry came up with a gizmo called a bazooka—or other names, depending on which of the great powers did the naming. One rocket from a bazooka could kill any tank in the world. Tankers *hated* that. So they made bigger, stronger, etcetera tanks to defend against the bazooka.

Tank development continued after World War II. It got to the point where nearly every national leader wanted an army of tanks to call his own, whether his country had any real use for them or not. At most, there were only a half-dozen nation-states with the development and manufacturing capability to come up with newer and better tanks, and each vied with the others in the international arms market to convince those countries that didn't have that capability that theirs were the very biggest, strongest, toughest, fastest, and most maneuverable tanks available, and that the lesser countries—of course, they didn't call them that, "developing countries" became the polite catch phrase—should buy tanks from them. And buy they did.

In the latter part of the century the leader of an insignificant desert nation, highly impressed with his tanks, decided to conquer his neighbors. What's the point of having all those tanks if you're not going to use them, right? So this desert war chieftain invaded the smallest and weakest of his neighbors, convinced that the rest of the world would see the size of his tank army and quail at the very thought of intervention.

He was very wrong. The small, weak neighbor he invaded was a major source of the world's supply of petroleum. The world at that time ran on petrochemicals, and nobody wanted this particular war lord to control a significant portion of the supply. So most of the developed world went to war against him. The war lord's opponents didn't bring as many tanks to the fray as he had, but as it turned out, that was quite all right. He'd believed the sales hype of the wrong major power, and his tanks simply couldn't stand against the tanks made by the other major powers. The war was over four days after the allied forces crossed the border.

At that point Gunner Moeller inserted a side note, partly bragging, partly a comment on how infantry kept getting ahead of tanks. The immediate lineal ancestor of the Confederation Marine Corps was the United States Marine Corps. Those Marines, like Confederation Marines, were primarily infantry, with strong organic air support, moderate artillery, and very little armor to call their own. The U.S. Marines sent two divisions and one air wing into the war. In three days' fighting, the Marines, mostly infantry, defeated ten infantry and five armored divisions and cleared enemy forces out of a third of the small country.

Moeller then returned to the major history lecture.

Infantry antitank weaponry and tactics also continued to develop. By the end of the century, a U.S. Marine infantry battalion had the weapons and tactics to defeat an armor battalion from almost any army in the world. The best tank in the world then was the M1A Abrams. It was the only tank that a well-equipped infantryman couldn't go *mano a mano* with and have a reasonable expectation of victory. But the infantry kept working on the problem, and in response the tankers with the M1A Abrams had to come up with a better tank in order to survive a fight against foot soldiers.

The result, a couple of generations later, was the M1D7 Super Abrams. That tank cost more than two fighter-attack aircraft; it took more than two hundred men to service, supply, maintain, and operate a four-tank platoon. It cost more to keep one M1D7 in the field than it did an entire company of infantry, and it was so heavy it could operate on less than twenty percent of the world's land surface. But it was proof against any weapon short of a tactical nuke, so it was widely loved and coveted.

The infantry, which had spent almost a century and a half developing ways of defeating armor, wasn't going to stand for that. They came up with the M-72 Straight Arrow.

The Straight Arrow had a reloadable launcher that fired rockets weighing ten kilograms each. Those rockets could punch their way through the side or rear armor of an M1D7 Super Abrams and explode inside, killing the crew and setting off any ammunition it was carrying. Tankers were totally baffled. The only way they could defend against the Straight Arrow was to build their tanks with even more armor plating on the sides and rear. But that made them bigger, heavier, slower, and more costly to build and maintain. Moreover, it reduced their usability to a mere ten percent of the Earth's land surface. Some earlier developments in armor design didn't necessarily increase the weight of tanks, but had changed configurations to prevent anti-tank weapons from penetrating. The tankers tried that route, but it didn't work. The only thing they were able to come up with that kept a Straight Arrow from punching through the armor and exploding inside the tank was to honeycomb the armor so much that the warhead met insufficient resistance to set it off. Which made the tanks vulnerable to other weapons. Besides, if a Straight Arrow hit that honeycombed armor, it would go in one side and out the other, probably hitting and killing a crewman on its way, and generally spewing enough molten metal from its passage inside the tank that it injured or killed the crew, fried a goodly part of its electronics, and maybe set off its ammunition supply. Whatever, the tank was killed or disabled even if the warhead didn't explode inside it.

The tankers had to throw in the hat; the battlefield belonged to the infantry again.

At this point Moeller paused and looked at the rapt Marines for a long moment before continuing. "The real problem with using the Straight Arrow for anything other than an M1D7 Super Abrams is that, to be triggered, the arming mechanism in the warhead requires a high level of resistance. When our engineers tried to engineer it down to more easily explode, it wouldn't work correctly. Munitions experts found that they weren't even effective against buildings; they simply go in one side and out the other and wreak havoc on anything they encounter along the way—but they don't explode. So, the M-72 Straight Arrow, the relatively inexpensive weapon that sounded the death knell of armor, cannot, at present, be used against anything other than the one weapon it was designed to defeat.

"The Straight Arrow is back in production, but I think you're only going to get a relative few of them for this mission," Moeller explained. "The intelligence reports we've received indicate that there are very few tanks on Diamunde with heavy enough armor to justify their use . . ." He paused because he didn't like what he was about to say. "Instead, you're mostly going to be using other antitank weapons, weapons that aren't as powerful as the Straight Arrows. When I left Headquarters Marine Corps on Earth to come here, the civilian contractors maufacturing the M-72s were getting orders to build other anti-armor weapons as well. A small supply should arrive in a few days and you'll begin training with them."

He checked the time. "Starting in an hour or so, right after evening chow, I'll begin teaching you about the other types of armor you might run into on Diamunde. Then, beginning tomorrow morning, you'll start training in the virtual reality simulator that a team from HQMC has been developing over the past couple of weeks." He shook his head. "That's when you'll find out that no matter how vulnerable to infantry weapons tanks are, they are still tough and dangerous opponents."

Actually, when Gunner Moeller left Earth for Thorsfinni's World, nobody had any idea of what kind of tanks the Marines would face on Diamunde, or what kinds of weapons they'd be given to kill them with.

"Wake up, wake up, wake up," Corporal Keto shouted into his helmet radio.

Lance Corporal "Rat" Linsman smacked the back of Claypoole's helmet. "You need your beauty rest, Sleeping Beauty?" He didn't bother with the radio, he shouted directly into Claypoole's ear.

Claypoole jumped, then peered around. "What?" He sounded groggy. After only four hours' sleep, the company had been given a three-hour orientation on the kinds of weapons they would be using in the VR simulator, then second squad had to wait outside two hours before its turn in the simulator. After two weeks of too little sleep, that wait was taking its toll on the Marines.

"You've got a target, sweetheart," Linsman snarled.

"Azimuth, zero-two-seven," Keto said calmly, now that he knew his shooter was awake. "Range, two-seven-five-zero. Target, low-rider, sitting. Mark?"

Claypoole shifted the launcher tube on his shoulder and squinted through its eyepiece at the battle-blasted landscape. Red-fringed clouds, reflecting the burning of vehicles and buildings on the ground, drifted low overhead. He noted the compass reading on the left side of the image and scuttled around to point himself in the right direction. Then he checked the range indicator on the right side of the image and looked straight ahead. Something was out there beyond the splintered trees in his field of vision, but he couldn't quite make it out. He groped for the image magnification tab on the left side of the launcher's receiver, just forward of his face. Magnification jumped from one-to-one to six-to-one and he saw the target. The low-rider tank was hardly higher than a standing man. It was long, low, and wide, and had sides that sloped shallowly. In outline, it somewhat resembled an upturned serving platter. Its low profile was supposed to make it a more difficult target for direct-fire weapons. The shallow slopes of its sides were supposed to make rockets ricochet off rather than penetrate. Neither of those design factors should protect it from the M-83 Falcon, a fire-and-forget rocket. The shooter locked on a spot on the target, then fired. The rocket would maintain a course to that spot no matter how violently the target maneuvered. Five hundred meters from the target it would jump up 250 meters and dive down at an acute angle to hit the armor flush.

"Mark," Claypoole said. The tank's angle to Claypoole was slightly closer to full front than broadside. He picked a point on the front of the tank and depressed the lock-on-target button.

"Fire when ready," Keto said.

Claypoole's right eye flicked to the sides of his aiming image to verify the azimuth and range, looked back at his marking spot on the tank, and then he pulled the trigger. Next to his ear the launcher boomed, then it bucked on his shoulder. He watched the rocket as it sped downrange. After two seconds its motor cut off and all he could see of it was a dark blur centered in his magnified sight. He estimated the rocket was halfway to its target when the low-rider turned and began speeding toward them. The rocket immediately began flashing with quick jet pulses as it adjusted its course to maintain its lock on the target. Abruptly, there was a brilliant flash and the rocket shot upward briefly before another brilliant flash sent it plunging downward.

Claypoole wouldn't have believed he could hear the spang of

a ricochet at a distance of more than two kilometers. The rocket bounced harmlessly away to the front of the low-rider. He closed his eyes and groaned.

Keto sighed loudly into his radio.

Claypoole flinched in anticipation of a slap on the back of his helmet from Linsman.

The slap didn't come. Instead Linsman said, "I always thought you didn't like me, rock head. I just never thought you didn't like me that much."

"What do you mean?"

"You just killed me."

"Huh?"

Before Linsman could reply, there was a dazzling flash of light, a *boom!* crashed over them, and the floor of the VR chamber shook violently.

"Third fire team, second squad, you're dead," Gunner Moeller's amplified voice said. "Move off the firing line and return to the briefing room."

Sheepishly, Claypoole stood up. He left the launch simulator in place for the next fire team. He blinked as the landscape he stood in vanished and his eyes adjusted to the bare walls of a room less than ten meters on a side.

Linsman glared at him. Keto had nothing to say—but Claypoole knew he'd have a lot to say later on, when the two of them were alone. The two lance corporals followed their fire team leader out of the simulation chamber, through the door next to the observation window, behind which Gunner Moeller had watched along with Captain Conorado, Gunny Thatcher, Ensign vanden Hoyt, and Staff Sergeant Bass. Claypoole felt terrible; he'd messed up badly but didn't know what he'd done wrong.

A moment later they were in the briefing room, and the five senior Marines from the observation room joined them.

"Do you know what you did wrong?" Gunner Moeller asked as Bass closed the door behind him.

"No sir." Claypoole swallowed.

"Either of you know?" Moeller asked the other two. They shook their heads. "You picked the wrong part of the target to shoot at. It looked like the right part, but it was the wrong part. You see, when I told you how the Falcons defeat low-riders and how the low-rider configuration was no defense against the Falcon, I didn't tell you the defensive tactic low-riders use to defeat the Falcon." He looked at Keto and Linsman. "Don't blame him, you probably would have made the same mistake."

Linsman glanced at Keto, but the corporal nodded at the gunner; he was beginning to get it.

Moeller turned his attention back to Claypoole. "I firmly believe that mistakes are an important part of learning. And I'd rather have you make them in a VR simulator, where the worst that will happen is you'll feel dumb, than in combat, where you'll probably get yourself and your teammates killed.

"I very deliberately had the low-rider situated so you had a clearer shot at its front armor than its side, and you took the bait. The only defense a low-rider has against a Falcon is to charge in the direction it's coming from. If the Falcon doesn't make its course adjustments quickly enough, as it didn't this time, it will be coming down at the low-rider from behind when it hits. If its aiming point is on front of the glacis, it'll ricochet off. If you'd aimed at the side, the chances are better than even that it would have hit at an acute enough angle to do its job. Maybe even before the low-rider got into range to fire its own gun." He looked at Linsman. "As you saw, it didn't take the low-rider long to close the gap to where it could hit you on its first shot." He looked at Keto. "When you fire at range like that, you have to move immediately. Most tanks have targeting computers that can locate where a threat is coming from before the threat reaches the tank, identify what kind of threat, and immediately begin calculating what its best defense is and where it has to get to in order to effectively respond to the threat.

"Incidentally, some of the other teams that shot before you didn't even manage to get the ricochet. You're the sixth team from this platoon to shoot so far. Only one of the others got a kill. You didn't do badly."

So it went for three more days. Every time a fire team entered the VR chamber, they used a different kind of tank-killer weapon. Each time they faced a different type of tank design. They were never told in advance what kind of tank they'd face, or the defensive tactics it used against the weapon they were using. There was a lot of trial and error. Mostly error. The one lesson they all learned in a hurry was to relocate as soon as they fired.

"We know what kind of tanks St. Cyr used when he attacked the Confederation embassy and took New Kimberly, but we don't know everything he has," Gunner Moeller said, explaining why they were training against so many different armor configurations. "When I left Earth, we'd gotten some reports of other tank types being used elsewhere on Diamunde. And I've got you training on every type of antiarmor weapon we've got in storage because nobody had decided what kind—or kinds—would be ready for this operation. You need to be ready to use any weapon available to kill any kind of tank you might run into."

After four days in the VR chamber with everyone continuing to make mistakes, Captain Conorado stood the company down for twenty-four hours to get some sleep.

"When do we get the real ones?" Schultz grumbled. After ten solid hours of sleep he looked like a bear coming out of hibernation. He acted like one too.

"As long as we get the real ones before we go up against real tanks, I don't care," Dean said. He'd been awake for half an hour but still hadn't stirred from his rack. The feeling of getting enough sleep was so luxurious that he didn't want to move if he didn't have to.

Corporal Leach, their fire team leader, was already up and dressing. He paused in pulling on his boots to listen. He knew the importance of using the real weapons, and wanted to hear how Schultz would explain it to Dean.

Schultz sat on his rack with his forearms resting on his thighs and his head lolling. He rolled his eyes toward Dean and cast him a "you're too dumb to live" look. His voice rumbled out from somewhere deep inside his mass. "You just spent four days in a VR chamber firing mock weapons at computer-generated images. You think that felt real?"

"Yeah, that felt real." Dean raised himself up on an elbow and faced Schultz. "It was the best computer simulation I've ever seen."

"Did you feel the wind on your face?"

"There was air movement in there, I felt it."

Schultz made a face. "That was fans. Fans don't feel like wind. Did you feel the blast when you fired the rocket?"

"I sure did feel it buck on my shoulder."

Schultz gave his head an ursine shake. "You felt it buck. What about the blast?"

Dean looked at him blankly.

"Rockets have a backblast. It's hot and violent. If you're in its way, it'll kill you. Did you feel that?"

Dean's eyes went unfocused and his brow beetled. He shook his head, uncertain about what to say, other than to admit he didn't remember that rockets had backblasts, which he wasn't about to admit.

Schultz wasn't a talker; he'd already said more than he usually did. He felt it was time to wrap up the conversation. "Until you fire the *real* weapon at a *real* target, you don't *really* know what it's like. No matter how good a VR is, it's only a simulation, and there's always a part of your mind that knows it isn't *real*." He stood, scratching himself through the underwear he'd slept in, and headed for the shower. "Morning chow, fifteen minutes?"

"Hurry it up, Hammer," Leach said, grinning. "I'm already hungry enough to eat a bear." He resumed dressing.

Schultz grunted. He shed his underwear as he went into the head. A moment later they heard the sound of splashing water.

"You gonna shower and join us or are you waiting for a prince?" Leach asked Dean.

Dean's eyes popped. He wasn't waiting for any damn prince, he liked women too much. He stripped and hit the shower much faster than Schultz had.

* * *

Corporal Dornhofer scanned the landscape through the magnifying shield of his helmet. The surface was irregular, probably crossed by more drainage ditches like the one behind him and his men. *That* ditch wasn't wide enough to hide an MBT, he thought, so maybe there weren't any larger ditches out there. He couldn't make out anything moving in the murky vista, which was shadowed by clouds, obscured by drifting battle smoke, and tinted red by burning vehicles, buildings, and flora. He slid his infra screen into place and looked for moving hot spots. There were plenty of hot spots, but none of them were moving. They couldn't all be fires, and he knew at least one of them had to be a tank. Unless the tank was in defilade. If it was, they'd just have to wait until it exposed itself. He didn't think they'd have to wait long—this was second fire team, first squad's tenth time in the VR chamber. On the other occasions, they'd never had to wait much more than five minutes before a tank showed itself. But they'd been waiting and watching for more than ten minutes. Maybe he was missing something.

He focused on one of the hot spots visible through his infras and flapped that screen up. He saw a fire in visible light. He dropped the infras back into place and focused on a different hot spot, then flipped the infras up again. Another fire. He methodically repeated the process, identifying a hot spot, then verifying it in visible light. After three minutes of searching, he found a hot spot that wasn't there in visible light. Was it a glitch in the VR programming that the tank didn't show in the visible? The Confederation Marine Corps didn't have chameleon paint that could turn its vehicles as effectively transparent as the chameleon uniforms made the infantrymen. If the Marines didn't have it, most likely nobody did. He wished his magnifying screen was stronger than four power. He checked the azimuth scale that ran across the top of his infra screen.

"Wolfman, give me the launcher, I want to look at something."

PFC "Wolfman" MacIlargie looked at him curiously, but didn't say anything as he passed over the antitank rocket launcher. They were taking turns with the rocket launchers and it was his turn, so he was pretty sure Dornhofer would give it back unfired.

Dornhofer raised his screens and settled the launcher onto his shoulder. He peered through its sights, found his azimuth, and ratcheted the magnification to eight-to-one. He spent a long moment studying what he saw.

It looked like a pile of rubble, but it had shown red through his infras. Could it be the remnant of an earlier fire, the flames gone but the rubble still warm enough to show as a hot spot? No, if it was still that hot, there should at least be some sort of visible glow emanating from it. He double-checked the range. Four thousand meters. Even if he couldn't see a glow through his helmet magnifier, it should be visible at eight power. There was an operating power source in that rubble, that was the only explanation.

Dornhofer pulled away from the sights and glanced to his sides. Both of his men, MacIlargie and Lance Corporal Van Impe, were scanning the landscape through their magnifiers. He went back to his launcher's view and swore. In a real war, he'd have let the rocket test the rubble, but his fire team would have only one opportunity to fire in the VR chamber.

He wasn't positive, but he thought the rubble had moved while he was checking his men. It was in the same place, but some of its elements seemed to have shifted. What's that? he wondered, and looked at the lower part of the pile. It seemed somehow too regular, like a series of nearly identical blocks. One of the uniform blocks fluttered. Like a skirt panel on an idling air-cushioned vehicle.

What kind of tank could move on an air cushion? Tanks were too heavy. Even the Marine Corps' amphibious Dragons, which were classed as light armored vehicles, operated near the outer envelope of weight that could be supported by an air cushion. Wait a minute. Yesterday, Dornhofer recalled, during Van Impe's turn with a launcher, they didn't have an MBT as their target. That one was a scout car that went so fast it needed spoilers to keep it from lifting off the ground. Maybe this was a simulation of a different kind of scout car. It was a weird-looking scout car, though. He squinted, hoping to bring the pile of rubble into closer focus. There, on what could be the front end, a short tube stuck out. That might be a gun. He examined the pile bit by bit and saw more details that could be something. This sheet of something could be a hatch. That hole could be a vision port. The other nub could be a machine-gun muzzle. The more Dornhofer examined it, the more he became convinced it was an enemy vehicle. His fingers flexed over the trigger and his thumb caressed the safety.

No, it was MacIlargie's turn. He'd have another chance later. This go-through, his job was spotter. He glanced at the range finder and azimuth and fixed the numbers in his mind.

"Wolfman," he said, handing the launcher back. "Target. One-four-two. Range, four-zero-five-zero. Pile of rubble. See it?"

MacIlargie took the launcher and settled it on his shoulder. He looked blasé about it, showed none of the anxiety he felt when he'd seen Dornhofer's hand on the trigger and thought his fire team leader was going to take the shot. He looked through the sights and found the aiming point. "Pile of rubble, check." He waited for instructions for where to look from there.

"Kill it."

Kill it? Kill the pile of rubble? He glanced at Dornhofer, half expecting the corporal to grin at him. But Dornhofer wasn't grinning, and he was looking toward the rubble. MacIlargie looked through the sight again and studied the pile of rubble. Maybe Dornhofer was right, maybe there was something wrong with the pile of rubble. Yeah, maybe it did have too regular a shape. There weren't any objects sticking out of it at odd angles, except the one cylinder that looked suspiciously like a gun tube. He pushed the lock-on tab and squeezed the trigger.

"Move!" Dornhofer shouted as soon as the rocket cleared the launcher. The three Marines dropped into the drainage ditch and ran. They stopped when they heard the explosion.

The shattered landscape winked out and was replaced by the plain white walls of the VR chamber.

"Very good," Gunner Moeller's voice said over the intercom. "That was a Mark 27 stealth light tank. It came in several configurations. That one was called 'urban destruction.' The job of the Mark 27 was to sit in place and pick off targets of opportunity, like a sniper. You should have found it faster, but since you didn't have any idea such a vehicle existed, I have to say you found it pretty damn fast."

CHAPTER
EIGHT

During their eight days of training in the virtual reality chamber, every enlisted man in the 34th FIST infantry battalion below the rank of platoon sergeant had a daily shot with an anti-tank weapon. They fired four different launchers, and had a different type of target on each shot. Not nearly enough to become proficient, but they were familiarized with the antitank weapons they might use and gained experience at identifying different types of targets. All officers and enlisted men in the FIST's other units, including FIST and battalion headquarters companies, the composite squadron, the artillery battery, and the transportation company, had one orientation shot with each of the launchers, at four different types of targets. That left them much further from proficient than the infantrymen, but at least they knew which end of the tubes the rockets came out of and could fight if they had to.

On the ninth day they began training with real antitank weapons, which had arrived the day before.

"I hate snow!" Dean said. Unsatisfied with the universe's lack of response, he shouted the sentiment, *"I hate snow!"* The words reverberated in the crisp air over the snowy training area designated as the tank-killing range.

"Enjoy the snow while you can," Corporal Dornhofer said. "Pretty soon you'll wish it wasn't so hot."

Dean turned in his bulky cold weather gear, his mouth open to reply. He closed it with an audible snap when he realized what Dornhofer meant. He went pensive for a moment, then said, "Snow, beautiful snow. I could bury myself in it and stay here for a long time."

"Bury yourself in it and you're likely to stay here a lot longer than you want to," Schultz said quietly. He didn't like the snow either, but he liked even less the prospect of facing tanks in combat. Particularly if they were anything like the tanks he'd practiced against in the VR chamber. Men should fight like men, he thought, not wrap themselves in armor like turtles.

Dean grumbled to himself. He wasn't getting any of the sympathy he wanted. Snow now, combat soon. The Diamunde operation was already promising to be worse than Wanderjahr. It might be as bad as Elneal.

"Do you think this will be as rough as crossing the Martac was?" he asked.

Schultz spat. He'd been point man for the crossing of the Martac Waste.

Dornhofer looked at Dean. He'd never faced armor, but he knew something more about it than they'd been taught over the past three and a half weeks. "You'll wish we were back on the Martac Waste," he said softly. He'd been the second in command during that patrol. "We all lived through that. If we'd been up against even one light tank, maybe none of us would have made it out of there."

Dean didn't want to think of a fight worse than the one they'd had against the Siad tribesmen; he always thought it was a miracle they survived Elneal. "Then we had best become as good as we can at killing tanks," he finally said.

Dornhofer clapped him on the shoulder. "You get first shot," he said.

They used specially prepared drones for the live-fire exercise. Quarter-ton, remotely piloted vehicles wore shells that mimicked the size and configuration of MBTs. Many of the shells had arrived from Earth along with the shipment of antitank weapons. The variety of shells was smaller than the number of simulations they'd faced in the VR chamber. Partly that was to make construction easier and faster. Mostly, it was because by the time the weapons were ready to be shipped, more was known about the situation on Diamunde—and how St. Cyr's forces were equipped. The drones were faster and more agile than the tanks they mimicked, which would make them harder to lock onto. The brass thought that would make better training.

The three Marines positioned themselves on the reverse slope of a hard-packed drift. Dornhofer was on the left, Schultz on the right, and Dean in the middle with an M-83 Falcon on his shoulder. Dean's body lay at a forty-five-degree angle from the launcher.

"Target," Schultz said. "Dead on. Three thousand."

Dean looked through the eyepiece of the launcher. Schultz was right, a low-rider was straight ahead, churning directly toward them, a corona of thrown-up snow glistening around it. Painted in a mottled gray, red, and black pattern, it stood out clearly against the snow. Even if he aimed for the front glacis, Dean knew this would be an easy kill. "Got it," he said. He rested his fingers on the trigger and his thumb hovered over the lock-on tab as he waited for Dornhofer's commands.

"Ready to lock?" Dornhofer asked.

"Ready to lock," Dean replied.

"Lock on."

Dean pressed the lock-on tab. "Locked on."

"Wait until it passes two thousand," Dornhofer said. At the drone's speed, it would only take it a few more seconds to close within two thousand meters.

Dean's eye kept flicking back and forth between his lock-on point and the range finder. Twenty-two hundred meters. Twenty-one fifty. Twenty-one hundred. Twenty fifty. His fingers closed on the trigger.

Suddenly, the drone veered to its left. Dean twisted his shoulders and upper body to the right to keep it in his sights. The drone passed the two thousand meter mark in a straight line, crossing the Marines' front. At the same time Dean squeezed the trigger he heard both Dornhofer and Schultz shout, *"No!"* There was more shouting, but he couldn't make it out.

He screamed at the sudden pain that flashed over the backs of his legs. Before the scream was completely out of his mouth he felt himself being pummeled and rolled about, pressed deep into the snow. The backs of his legs felt like they were on fire. He tried to draw in a deep breath to scream again but only filled his mouth and throat with snow. He gagged and choked, but couldn't breathe. He struggled, but there was too much weight on him, too much pounding and wet on the backs of his legs. He couldn't roll over, couldn't sit up, couldn't get rid of the snow in his mouth and throat. All he could see was black. The black began to rim with red and he knew he was about to pass out.

Suddenly, he was yanked up and flopped over. A rough hand scooped snow away from his face, a finger forced itself into his mouth and pulled out snow. Hands grabbed his shoulders and yanked him to a sitting position. Something thumped his back hard, then something else shoved into his stomach and up. The little air that was still in his lungs was expelled violently and forced the snow out of his throat. He gasped for breath and choked as some snow began to clog his tubes again. Again something thudded into his back, and he coughed until he could cough no more. Then he shook all over, but he was able to breathe.

"Slowly," a voice next to him ordered. "Breathe slow and deep. Slowly. Do it with me. In." He took in a breath. "Out." He let it out. "In . . . out," at a steady, slow pace. Dean breathed with the voice. After a moment his trembling stopped and he looked toward the voice. It was Doc Gordon, one of the medical corpsmen.

"Are you okay now? Can you breathe all right?" Gordon asked.

Dean gulped in more air and nodded.

"Say it. Let me hear your voice."

"I'm okay. I can breathe." His voice sounded foggy, but he thought it was clear enough.

"What were you trying to do, kill him?" Gordon snapped at Dornhofer and Schultz.

"We were trying to put out the damn fire," Dornhofer snapped back. He was angry—at Dean for making the mistake he had, at the corpsman for snapping at him, and at himself, for not making sure Dean knew not to do what he did.

Schultz didn't say anything, he just spat to the side.

"By burying his head in the snow and pounding on the backs of his legs? You should have laid him on his back and pressed his legs into the snow, that would have done it." Gordon turned back to Dean. "Lay down and roll over, I want to check you out."

"Do I have to?" Lying on his stomach was how he'd gotten in trouble in the first place. He didn't want to do it again.

"Lay your head on your arms, that'll keep your face out of the snow." Sometimes corpsmen seemed to be mind readers.

Reluctantly, Dean lay on his stomach. He flinched when he saw how close his nose and mouth were to the snow, but relaxed when he realized his folded arms really were holding his head up and he could still breathe.

Gordon's exam only took a second. "We've got to get this man into a warm-tent." Then to Dean, "You aren't badly hurt, but the back of your trousers are burnt off. You'll get frostbite if we don't get you into a warm-tent and get your clothes changed. Think you can walk?"

"Yeah." He needed help standing up. He saw but didn't really notice Moeller, vanden Hoyt, and Bass standing nearby.

The three watched them walk away. Gunner Moeller said, "I don't think anybody will need any more instruction on keeping themselves out of the backblast of the launchers."

The day before mount out, Brigadier Sturgeon held a final briefing for his staff and subordinate commanders.

"Gentlemen, the first thing for us to remember is that all of our information on the Diamundean situation is at least six months out of date."

The only way anything, including information, could travel between planets at a speed faster than light was by starship. Radio and laser wouldn't do the job of interstellar communications because it would take more than four centuries for a broadcast from the farthest reaches of Human Space to reach Earth. Even the shortest interstellar transmissions would take ten years. Starships, on the other hand, traveled at a speed of slightly more than six and a quarter light-years per day. Information from the most remote part of Human Space could travel the distance in little more than two months on a starship. Diamunde was situated about seventy-five light-years from Earth. A fast courier could deliver news from one to the other in less than two weeks. On Earth, the politicians and other policy makers would badger the intelligence people to rush through their analysis of the information and make projections and predictions in less time than a conscientious person would want to spend on it. Then the politicians and bureaucrats would chew on it for a while, massage it awhile longer, spin it around to see how it looked from different angles. Finally, they'd take what they considered the relevant parts of the information, package them with their decisions and directives, and ship them off to the people who needed to take action.

The wonder of it all was that 34th FIST on Thorsfinni's World was able to get any military intelligence about the situation on Diamunde in as little time as just over six months. But the situation on Diamunde was a major economic issue for the Confederation of Human Worlds, and huge fortunes and a great deal of power were at stake—not to mention the lives and livelihoods of billions—so decisions were made and directives issued at, for politicians, breakneck speed.

In a swift and bloody coup, Marston St. Cyr had conducted a hostile takeover of Tubalcain Enterprises. In days he had consolidated his power in New Kimberly, the capital city. In less than one week he had wrested control of the rest of the planet's industrial and mining companies—hence, its wealth. He then demanded that the Confederation of Human Worlds formally recognize him as head-of-state. Further, as CEO and major shareholder of all of Diamunde's mining concessions, he required that all commercial dealings with Diamunde be conducted with his office.

To back him up, St. Cyr had the largest armored land army mankind had seen in centuries. Agents on the ground had positively identified two different kinds of tanks in his army, and had physically counted five thousand of them. There were probably more, a good deal more.

St. Cyr also had a spacegoing navy, but it consisted of little more than several dozen armed freighters incapable of travel beyond Drummond's system, and wasn't thought to be much of a danger. The Confederation Navy expected to make short work of it.

The Confederation government "refuses to deal with someone with so much blood on his hands and violence in his heart," the communiqué said. "The people and proper government of Diamunde must be restored. To that end, the Confederation Marines will assemble a six-FIST force to make a landing and secure a planethead for follow-on forces of the Confederation Army to land and restore order."

"And that's what we are going to do," Sturgeon concluded. "Does anybody have any questions about that? Are there any other issues we should deal with before we mount out? Then get your people saddled up. Dismissed."

The officers and sergeants major stood and began filing out. Sturgeon watched them for a few seconds, then headed for his office. Commander Van Winkle and Sergeant Major Parant of the infantry battalion intercepted him.

"Sir," Van Winkle said, "I have—" He felt Parant's elbow nudge him. "We have one other issue, sir, but it's not something I felt appropriate to bring up at the meeting. Especially not when everybody has so much to do."

Sturgeon lifted an eyebrow at him, then dipped his head toward his office. "Come on in and tell me about it."

After closing the door, Sturgeon invited the other two Marines to sit, which they did, gingerly. He didn't offer them anything to drink.

"Commander," the brigadier said when he took his own seat and leaned forward to cross his arms on his desk. Van Winkle looked uncomfortable, Parant seemed stern.

"Sir," Van Winkle said, "it's about Charlie Bass."

"Oh, no. Don't tell me he's gotten himself in trouble again."

"Nossir! Absolutely not, sir."

Sturgeon sighed with relief. "Then what about Charlie Bass?"

"We're going on a very tough assignment. We're liable to lose a lot of Marines in this war. Charlie Bass has tempted the gods of war too many times for me to feel absolutely confident he'll survive. Sir, I don't want to risk having Charlie Bass die as a staff sergeant. I—" He glanced at Parant. "We want to promote him back to gunnery sergeant. But I don't have an empty gunnery sergeant billet to put him into—and I don't want to give him up to some other command either."

Sturgeon leaned back and gave the two infantrymen a speculative look. "You want to promote him to a company level rank and leave him as a platoon sergeant, is that what I hear you saying?"

"Yessir."

Sergeant Major Parant nodded vigorously.

Sturgeon rolled his eyes toward the ceiling as if thinking, though his mind was already made up. He abruptly leaned forward. "It'll take us a couple days to settle in on the ship. Then we'll have the best ship-board promotion ceremony we can."

"Thank you, sir!"

Parant stood and stepped to Sturgeon's desk. He reached a hand across it. "Thank you, sir. Outstanding. This will do no end of good for the enlisted men's morale."

Startled, Sturgeon reached out and shook Parant's hand. He remained on his feet as the two left his office. Alone, he shook his head. The Confederation Marine Corps had revived an ancient tradition that had been discontinued sometime in the mid–twentieth century, the "graveyard promotion." Certain senior men were promoted on retirement, and their retirement ranks were then higher than any rank they had actually served at. This could turn into a literal "graveyard" promotion for Charlie Bass. How could that possibly be good for the men's morale?

On the appointed date and time, 34th FIST assembled with all its men and equipment at the appointed place. The Confederation Navy had Essays, surface-to-orbit shuttles, waiting for them. The twenty-four Dragons of the FIST, already loaded with the Marines of the three infantry companies, immediately drove into the eight Essays navy personnel directed them to. The ground crews secured the Essays for launch, then retired to their bunkers. The Essays launched at ten-second intervals, the roars of their rocket-assist engines sweeping over the navy spaceport. As soon as the rockets had the vehicles clear of the ground, they cut off and the Essays' main engines took over and they flew upward in relative silence. At fifteen thousand meters they circled until cleared to climb to orbit altitude, then shot upward in formation, heading toward the parking orbit of the CNSS *Tripoli*. The *Tripoli*'s position in its orbit required the Essays to approach it from below to catch up with it. When they were near, jets would propel them into matching altitude a kilometer to the starship's rear, then pulses from their rear jets would accelerate them to close the distance; pulses from their top jets would keep them from climbing to a higher orbit. The *Tripoli*, a Crowe-class amphibious assault battle cruiser, opened the hatches of one of its four docking bays to admit the eight Essays.

All the Marines had been through at least several launches. Even MacIlargie and Godenov, the newest men in third platoon, had been through five launches since enlisting in the Marines. The first was the civilian shuttle that ferried them to the troop transport that shipped them to Boot Camp on the Confederation military training world, Arsenault. During Boot Camp they'd gone through the complete launch-and-landing cycle during the phase of training that took place on Arsenault's moon. The third time was when they lifted off Arsenault for transshipment to Thorsfinni's World and their first duty assignment with the 34th FIST; then again at the beginning of the FIST's deployment to Wanderjahr, and finally the return only a couple of months ago. Older, saltier Marines, such as Claypoole and Dean, who had been with the 34th six months longer, had seven launch-and-land cycles as Marines—the extras having occurred during the deployment to and return from Elneal. Soon-to-be Gunnery Sergeant Charlie Bass had been through so many launch-landing cycles that he had lost count.

After the first few crushing seconds of blast from the rocket engines that lifted the Essays off the surface, the trip to orbit was a picnic. They all relaxed. They could afford to—everyone knew the landing would be an entirely different matter, and not only because of resistance they might meet on the surface.

The Essays' only view ports were in the coxswain's compartment. That didn't matter to the Marines, who were in Dragons that only had vision slits, up front, for the crew. The Dragon commanders had no reason to open their command hatches inside the Essays. Even if there had been anything to see, there wasn't enough headroom to raise the hatches.

In sum, none of the Marines could see anywhere anyhow. All they could do was go along for the ride. The passage of time and the Essays' subtle shifts in attitude and changes in the direction and force of what they experienced as gravity were all the indications the Marines had as to where they were on their journey to the starship. When they began floating against the webbing that held them into their seats, they knew they were in orbit and chasing the *Tripoli*. They felt the thrusts of the control jets as they matched altitude and velocity with the starship more as resistance from the webbing than as weight. The pinging and clanking of the magnetic clamps that secured the Essays to their berths in the docking bay were all they needed to tell them they were aboard the starship. They waited a few more minutes while spacesuited sailors snaked flexible tunnels to the exit hatches of the Essays and secured airtight locks. Only then did sailors undog the hatches of the Essays. Three pairs of sailors, a petty officer and a rating in each pair, pulled their way into each shuttle. The ratings carried spools of cable.

"You know the routine, Marines," the petty officer in each pair said. He began unreeling the cable as the Marines unhooked themselves from their webbing. The petty officer handed a clamp that was on the lead end of the cable to the Marine on the port side of the Dragon's hatch. The Marine hooked the clamp onto his belt. The petty officer reeled out more of the cable, exposing more clamps at two meter intervals. Each Marine in turn took a clamp and attached himself to the cable. When all the Marines and the Dragon crew were attached, the petty officer led them out of the Dragon and the cables from the three Dragons in the Essay were linked together. Then he led the linked Marines out of the Essay into the bay and through a hatch into the interior of the starship. The ship was in null-g, and would remain so until it left orbit.

Eight strings of Marines followed sailors up, down, and sideways along tunnels, some of which would be passageways, others ladderways once the ship was underway.

On the surface, the rest of the Marines of 34th FIST were boarding other Dragons. Some of the Dragons belonged to the port, but most of them were ship's complement off the *Tripoli*. As soon as the Marines were aboard the Dragons, they drove onto more Essays—half of which were from the *Tripoli*. The second flight launched a half hour after the first. This flight would have to gain a higher altitude than the starship's and wait for it to gain on them before they could maneuver to its docking holds.

A third flight of ten Essays from the *Tripoli* landed at the air station of Camp Major Pete Ellis. The FIST's ten Raptor assault aircraft and ten hopper troop-carrier aircraft boarded them, two per Essay, and launched for orbit.

Two hours after the first flight of Essays launched, the entire FIST was aboard the CNSS *Tripoli*.

CHAPTER
NINE

The CNSS *Tripoli* was a Crowe-class amphibious assault battlecruiser. It was designed to carry two full combat-armed FISTs. The 13th FIST, which was always glad to leave its home base on New Serengeti, where the Marines never felt welcome, was already on board when the Crowe swung into orbit around Thorsfinni's World.

The *Tripoli*'s troop accommodations were luxurious compared to most other navy vessels the Marines had mounted out on. Each major troop hold was designed for one company and was subdivided into squad-size compartments. In each squad compartment the racks were stacked only three high, which gave the men room to roll over without bumping the man sleeping above. Each squad compartment had its own head. The company commander and executive officer shared what amounted to a small stateroom; the company's four other officers shared an only slightly larger stateroom. The six senior noncommissioned officers—the first sergeant, gunnery sergeant, and four platoon sergeants—had an even larger stateroom. The squad leaders had it the best—the ten from each company shared two compartments the size of squad compartments.

The "keel up" design of the "amphibious assault" part of the Crowe class allowed for sufficient VR chambers for Marines headed to an operation to maintain or increase their proficiency in weapons and tactics—including squad-level movements. Included in the design were sufficient gymnasiums for all the Marines of both FISTs, should the starship be loaded to capacity, to keep in top physical trim. The gyms and some of the VR chambers could also be used as briefing rooms or classrooms.

As a battlecruiser, the Crowe could outfight any known space-ship or starship from any of the independent human worlds, and virtually any ship short of a dreadnought from the Confederation Navy. One Crowe-class amphibious assault battlecruiser, with an escort of a few destroyers, could defeat any of the lesser worlds in Human Space. The five Crowe-class starships of the Confederation Navy together with a strong enough amphibious task force of the Confederation Army behind them, could defeat any but the strongest worlds in the Confederation.

Diamunde wasn't one of the strongest worlds, but it was far from being one of the lesser ones. But the mighty warships weren't going to engage in battle against the planet, only against its ships. Diamunde was too valuable for the Confederation to risk doing serious damage to the planetary infrastructure and surface. The Crowe-class ships were being used only because they were the most efficient means of transporting six full Marine FISTs while allowing the Marines to continue training with the still-unfamiliar antiarmor weapons. When the three Crowe-class amphibious battlecruisers and their destroyer escorts converged on Diamunde, they would meet the largest interstellar amphibious invasion fleet ever assembled. The Confederation Army was committing five hundred thousand combat troops to the fight.

The gymnasium compartment HL/q/v/14-3 was assigned to the exclusive use of Company L, 34th FIST. Every day, when they weren't in the VR chamber or the mess line, the Marines of Company L were in HL/q/v/14-3 working out individually or in organized calisthenics or athletics. Captain Conorado was determined that two months aboard ship weren't going to cost any of his men muscle strength or endurance.

During the *Tripoli*'s first hop, the compartment was used for another purpose. On the fourth day all of the gymnasium equipment was stowed away and a small platform was raised at one end. The men of Company L assembled in parade-ground formation. The uniform of the day would have been dress scarlets, had they brought their dress uniforms. There was a susurration of voices in the ranks as the Marines asked each other what the formation was about, and speculation when nobody knew. The noise level grew louder when the officers and senior noncommissioned officers of the other companies in the battalion crowded in behind them, then were followed by all the officers and senior NCOs from the rest of the FIST's units, including the FIST and battalion headquarters. Everyone was present except the FIST and battalion commanders and sergeants major.

Of the more than two hundred Marines in the compartment, only Captain Conorado and First Sergeant Myer, both on the raised platform, knew what was going on. Conorado stood at ease, calmly looking over the assembled Marines. Myer, also at ease, less calmly eyeballed the side entrance to the compartment.

At a signal from someone in the passageway who only he could see, Myer snapped to attention, faced front, and bellowed, "COMP-ney, A-ten-HUT!" The heels of the Marines standing in formation slammed together with a thunderous clap.

Brigadier Sturgeon strode in with Commander Van Winkle immediately behind him. Sergeants Major Shiro and Parant followed them. FIST Sergeant Major Shiro had a rolled sheet of parchment in his hand. The four senior Marines were in their dress scarlets; they had room in their kits to carry them. They mounted the platform and stood facing Conorado and Myer.

"Sir, Company L and attachments all present and accounted for," Conorado said sharply. He didn't salute his commanders; the gymnasium compartment wasn't an area where the Marines wore their hats, and they didn't salute "uncovered."

"Thank you, Captain," Sturgeon replied. The six men then formed a single line along the back of the platform.

Sturgeon spun in a sharp about-face to look at the assemblage. "We are Marines," the FIST commander began without preamble. "We take care of our own. We honor our own. There are some of you, and some who aren't with us in this compartment, who a month ago were serving in positions above the rank you held then. You were promoted in recognition of this before we left Camp Ellis. There are some of you who a month ago had decorations or letters of commendation coming to you that you hadn't yet received. You have received them. We are assembled here today to give recognition to another outstanding

Marine. I'm sure everyone will agree that this recognition is richly deserved. Many, perhaps most, of you will think a higher recognition is deserved." A wry smile twisted his lips. "We honor our own, but sometimes the honor we wish to give is beyond limits we cannot pass. We are Marines. We do our best. Our best is always enough." He turned his head to Van Winkle. "Commander."

"Sergeant Major," Van Winkle said in a voice loud enough for everyone to hear, "call Staff Sergeant Bass."

"Staff Sergeant Bass, front and center," Parant called out in a voice that made Top Myer's sound soft.

Bass suffered an instant of startlement, then stepped forward and marched to the platform.

"Sir, Staff Sergeant Bass reporting as ordered." He flicked his eyes questioningly at Parant, who studiously ignored him.

"FIST commanders sometimes have levels of authority unknown to brigade commanders in the past," Sturgeon said to the assembly. "The commander of a FIST on a remote outpost such as Camp Ellis has levels of authority that other FIST commanders don't. The commander of a FIST on a combat operation has further levels of authority. That means I have certain extraordinary powers. I'm going to exercise one of them now." He held out his hand and Shiro slapped the rolled parchment into it. Sturgeon unrolled the parchment, looked at it, then let it roll itself back up. "Commander," he said, handing the parchment to Van Winkle, "would you like to do the honors?"

"I certainly would, sir. Thank you very much." The infantry commander unrolled the sheet of parchment and began in a loud, clear voice, "To all who shall see these presents, greeting: Know ye that reposing special trust and confidence in the fidelity and abilities of Charles Bass . . ."

When Van Winkle finished reading through the Marine promotion warrant, a document that hadn't changed its wording in centuries, he glanced at Sturgeon, who nodded. Van Winkle said, "Sergeant Majors."

The two sergeants major stepped up to Bass. Each withdrew something from a pocket.

"Charlie," Shiro said, "this was pinned on me by my com-

pany first sergeant the first time—the only time, I might add—
that I was promoted to gunnery sergeant." A pointed reference
to the fact that Charlie Bass had already been a gunnery sergeant
twice before and was busted both times. He pinned gunnery
sergeant's chevrons on one collar.

"This was pinned on me," Parant said, "by the"—he quickly
glanced at Van Winkle—"the second best battalion commander
I ever served under." He pinned chevrons on Bass's other collar.

The two sergeants major shook Bass's hand, then returned to
their positions.

"Gunnery Sergeant Bass, my hearty congratulations," Sturgeon said, shaking his hand. Lower, he added, "I'm sure you
understand why we had to wait until we were en route before
your promotion."

Van Winkle shook his hand and said, "Richly deserved,
Charlie. Though I'd rather it was a bar." But Charlie Bass always refused a commission; he thought he was of more value as
a noncommissioned officer.

Conorado added his congratulations.

"I'll see you after formation, Charlie," Myer said softly,
smiling.

"You'll have to ambush me, Top," Bass said and smiled back.
Myer chuckled.

"Gunnery Sergeant Thatcher," Sturgeon said as soon as the
congratulations were completed, "you are still Company L's
gunny. All other gunnery sergeants rest easy. Gunnery Sergeant
Bass is still third platoon's platoon sergeant. Nothing changes
except the number of rockers Gunny Bass wears on his rank insignia. That and the size of his paycheck." He chuckled briefly,
then said, "That is all." He looked at the other officers and senior NCOs on the platform, pivoted, and marched out of the
compartment with Van Winkle, Parant, and Shiro following.

When the commanders were gone, Conorado nodded to
Bass, who marched back to his position.

"Today we honored one man," Conorado said when Bass
was back in position. "But I like to think that one man could not
have been honored if the entire company wasn't as good as it is.
I also believe the company couldn't be as good as it is if that one

man wasn't the outstanding Marine he is. Gunnery Sergeant Bass, you have been honored. In return, you honor all of us by being the Marine you are. First Sergeant, dismiss the company." He strode off the platform and out of the compartment.

Myer waited until the company commander was gone, then faced the Marines. "COMP-ny, dis-MISSED!"

Working out and VR weapons training weren't the only things the Marines had to do during the voyage; the navy wasn't that dumb—no way they'd want to inspire a mutiny from two thousand overworked and bored Marines. The *Tripoli* also had a library well-stocked with books—archaic hardcopy as well as digital—educational programs, and games. There were also several vid theaters, two-dee and trid, with enough variety that a Marine could attend one every night without having to see a repeat of anything.

Which is not to say the *Tripoli* had all the comforts of home. The stock in the ship's store had a limited variety, and access to it was equally limited. The vid and trid theaters were cramped, and during long features it became very easy to tell if the Marine alongside you was showering after the gym. Short features, especially military comedies like *General Clinton's War*, became very popular. Nothing could be taken from the library—of course, some Marines found out how to defeat the ship's security system. Marines always figure out how to do what they aren't supposed to. Neither alcohol nor tobacco was allowed in any of the troop areas—and the Marines weren't allowed in those parts of the ship where alcohol could be drunk or tobacco smoked. Naturally enough, several Marines found ways around that restriction as well, and there was more than one drunken party in a smoke-filled squad compartment. And, of course, there were no women. Well, there were women in the *Tripoli*'s crew, but the Marines couldn't get close to them even though from time to time a navy woman's duties would bring her to a place where the Marines could see her. It wasn't only navy policy that kept the Marines and the women apart. The navy women didn't want to get close to those dirty Marines with their hungry reputations.

There was sound logic and good reason for the restrictions and minor discomforts inflicted on the Marines. Marines are cargo. Cargo is something ships pick up in one place and drop off at another. When Marines are taken from one place to another by the navy, they're frequently dropped off at someplace nasty. The navy doesn't want to make the Marines so comfortable they want to stay on board ship when they get to where they are supposed to be dropped off. Nossir!

Twenty-fifth-century space flight used the Beam Drive for hyperspace transit between star systems. The Beam Drive used the Beam Constant, which allows travel at a light-years-per-day speed, which is calculated as an irregular number that begins with 6.273804 and continues on from there. What with the irregularity of the Beam Constant, the movement of the celestial spheres, and the space-time curvature, interstellar navigation is something less than an exact science. No starship navigator, no matter how good, knows with any real precision where his ship will pop back into Space-3. This means that interstellar navigators have to plan a margin of error when they plot their courses. The plotted arrival point is always at greater distance from the outbound jump points than the radius of the circle of error, as it's called. It really wouldn't do to have an inbound ship suddenly return to Space-3 in the same spot from which an outbound ship is attempting to make a jump. When two or more ships are traveling together, they also have to consider each other's plotted arrival points, to avoid coming out within each other's circle of error. Just in case. Since the margin of error increases with distance traveled, ships in convoy go in short jumps and reassemble in formation each time they return to Space-3. Otherwise, after a single long jump, they would be scattered over a horrendously large sphere on arrival. Which won't do at all for warships boldly sailing into a hostile environment.

The *Tripoli* was traveling with an escort of destroyers, so it made the transit in jumps. Top-of-the-line warships have the best navigators, so the *Tripoli* Amphibious Battlegroup made the entire journey in just four hops, and never had to take more than one standard day to "regroup" at the conclusion of a hop.

That was exceptionally good for a voyage of about 240 light-years. The final hop took them out of hyperspace nine days out of Drummond's system.

The battlegroup reassembled in formation and began its ponderous journey through Space-3 into the system and the planet to which it was to send in the Marines. Three days out it was met by a courier boat from the blockade force that had been gathering over the past month. The courier boat transported the Commander Amphibious Battlegroup and the two FIST commanders to Fleet Admiral Wimbush's flagship, the CNSS *Lance Corporal Samuel Ogie*, for the final planning session for the amphibious assault landing. The meeting was almost a waste of time for the commander of the 34th FIST. Even if the overall mission to Diamunde hadn't been a Confederation Army operation, a Marine brigadier ranked too low to be allowed to speak.

CHAPTER
TEN

Sitting quietly and virtually unnoticed in a remote corner of the briefing room on board the CNSS *Lance Corporal Samuel Ogie*, Fleet Admiral Wimbush's flagship, Professor Jere Benjamin thought, Good luck, fellas, but if you believe this plan'll work . . .

Since he had done such a good job with the Marine trainers in the use of the Straight Arrow and antiarmor tactics, Professor Benjamin had been attached to Admiral Wimbush's staff as a "civilian adviser," and as such was permitted to sit in on high-level planning conferences.

Benjamin had studied enough military history to know that the more complicated a plan was, the less chance it had to work properly. The plan for the invasion of Diamunde, he thought, relied too much on two very unpredictable factors: the army's ability to reinforce the Marine beachhead on time, and Fleet intelligence estimates of the enemy's strength at the two proposed landing sites. It was the landing site that was under discussion just then.

Lieutenant General Hank "Box Kicker" Han, commander of the army forces assigned to the Fleet, was addressing Admiral Wimbush. "Sir," he said, "Oppalia is the ideal spot for a landing. It has all the facilities we need to establish a base of operations: a spaceport, a seaport, communications facilities, transportation systems, everything. Surveillance has not revealed any significant enemy forces there, and if any show up before we reinforce the Marines, they can fortify themselves until we get in. It's an ideal target for an operation like this."

Admiral Wilber "Wimpy"—but never to his face—Wimbush

sat back in his chair and stroked his chin. Wimbush was a cautious, thoughtful commander who never committed himself without considering every possible ramification, especially any that would get him in trouble. "Andy?" He turned to the Marine task force commander, General Anders Aguinaldo.

"Well, sir, we Marines weren't made to fight from behind fortifications." This elicited polite laughter all around. "And I agree with Hank that Oppalia should be our primary objective after we've secured a planethead. But I don't want to get bottled up in a built-up area if we do meet resistance. City fighting is a bitch. We can't use our heavy stuff in street fighting, so it's man-to-man, house-to-house, and it'll take time and it'll cost us lives. And if we have to fight in the city that'll only make follow-on landings more difficult." He punched a button on his console and a detailed map of the coast thirty kilometers north of Oppalia sprang into focus. "I favor the landing here, on the outskirts of the Debeers Drift. We can secure the beachhead in twenty-four hours, the army comes in and we all push overland to Oppalia.

"Besides, because there's a significant civilian population in the city, not to mention an important industrial infrastructure, we can't use preparatory fires to soften up any resistance that might be there before we go down. We'll be going into a potentially hot landing zone without any prep. If we come in over the beach, we can slag the goddamned dunes and then push south to the town. If there is any significant enemy force there, it's them who'll be besieged and not us."

"There aren't any enemy forces there," Rear Admiral David "Davey Jones" Johannes stated emphatically. Admiral Johannes was in charge of Fleet Intelligence.

"That you know of," General Aguinaldo pointed out. "With our reliance exclusively on string-of-pearls satellite and drone surveillance, they could have a division of tanks hidden down there, and how would we know?"

"Andy, surveillance hasn't revealed any signatures that would match those of armored vehicles," General Han interjected.

"Jesus Christ, Hank, they've got mining operations going on down there. The place is covered with clouds and fog most of the year! Has anybody considered there may be no way to distinguish the infra signature of a tank from that of an earth mover? And how the hell do you tell? Nobody's surveilled tanks in more than 250 years! And besides, we've only had surveillance since the Fleet arrived and deployed its string-of-pearls, five days ago." The cordiality between the senior officers, which had been forced all along anyway, was beginning to weaken.

Admiral Johannes cleared his throat preparatory to making a pithy remark, but he was interrupted by Admiral Wimbush, who wanted to head off a confrontation. "Andy, if you go in up there in the north, isn't that favorable terrain for motorized warfare? Won't we run the risk of being attacked in force by St. Cyr's First Armored Division? Intel reports them only a hundred kilometers from the drift, at Hefestus's Tourmaline mining complex."

"Sir, that's only an hour and a half from Oppalia for St. Cyr's main battle tanks, and besides, Fleet Air, in addition to the FIST's organic air, will give us the cover we need if they attack us before the army follows on."

"That's right, sir," Rear Admiral Benton "Benny" Havens, commander of the Fleet air arm, said. "We'll have St. Cyr's air assets knocked out by midnight on D minus one. We'll have effective control of the skies over the entire hemisphere before the Marines land."

"Admiral, it's still exposed territory, and it has none of the logistical facilities we need to support the multicorps-size force the army's going to have to put in there," General Han interjected. Admiral Wimbush was an experienced logistician, as was General Han, whose last ground combat command had been an infantry platoon many years before. They both lacked experience handling operations of the size they were soon to launch. "Besides, we lose the element of surprise. The drift is an ideal landing zone; St. Cyr is bound to have his eye on it."

" 'Surprise' my—" General Aguinaldo paused and looked for another word. "St. Cyr knows we're coming and he's smart enough to figure it'll be one of several likely places, an ideal spot for a landing, so that's why I say we go in there. He'll expect us to go in elsewhere, where the landing is more difficult, to maintain the element of surprise, but I bet this guy understands us better than we think, and I bet he's counting on our landing at Oppalia because it has all the logistical facilities we need to support an invasion. The SOB's a genius, we're told. Do the obvious and apparently stupid thing and it may throw him off." He did not want to add that if St. Cyr knew anything about Admiral Wimbush and his staff, he'd know for sure they were planning on landing at Oppalia. It was too safe an option, with little apparent risk. But he also knew he was losing the argument.

"One other point, Admiral," Aguinaldo continued. "I'm very concerned about the rules of engagement."

"What about them?" Wimbush asked, surprised. "I thought they were very clear."

"They are, Admiral. Especially on one point. They are very clear that there is to be, if at all possible, no damage done to infrastructure. With all due respect, sir, we're going to be fighting against tanks. It won't be possible to avoid severe damage to infrastructure."

Wimbush smiled condescendingly and shook his head. "General, you shouldn't be concerned at all on that point. You won't be fighting anyplace where there is civilian infrastructure to damage."

"Oppalia, sir. We'll be fighting there."

"General"—there was an edge of annoyance in Wimbush's voice—"you heard the intelligence report. There won't be any fighting in Oppalia. Let's drop this unproductive line of discussion."

Aguinaldo settled back in his seat and gave Wimbush a level look that made the admiral very uncomfortable.

In the back of the room Benjamin gently nudged Rear Admiral Gary B. Clark, the Fleet surgeon. Clark sat with his feet up and his blouse unbuttoned, the picture of nonchalance. He considered himself a doctor first and a flag officer second, or maybe third, since he also liked rock climbing and shooting white-water rapids in his leisure time. The two had become friends over cigars in the admirals' mess.

"Arnhem," Benjamin whispered into Clark's ear. Clark raised an eyebrow. "I'll explain later," Benjamin said.

Back at the conference table, the admiral had made his decision: "Gentlemen, I appreciate Andy's concerns, but all things considered, we go in at Oppalia." General Han sighed and smiled and the other members of the staff relaxed visibly. General Aguinaldo nodded his assent. The decision was made. He was thinking of how best to carry it out, his personal reservations about the admiral's decision now past discussion. He wanted to get back to his own staff and start planning for the landing.

Wimbush shook off his annoyance at Aguinaldo's impertinence. "One more item, gentlemen, and then you can all go back and start drafting your operations orders. Hank, the army has got to come through on time. How are your boys set?"

"No problem, sir. We'll have the Third Corps in there no later than D plus three and the Ninth Corps by D plus five. That'll be 120,000 men. We have two more Corps in reserve that we can have in by no later than D plus ten if we need 'em. Gentlemen, that's the equivalent of two ground armies, nearly 500,000 men, and we'll have the firepower of the entire Fleet in orbit to boot. Neither this St. Cyr nor anybody else in Human Space can stand up to figures like that. Intel tells us St. Cyr can't field more than 250,000 men, tops, four divisions of armor, eight thousand tanks of all kinds, maybe only four thousand of those TP1 Main Battle Tanks. The Marines will only have to hold out, er, I mean secure the facilities for two days, max. It'll be a walkover for Andy's boys, Admiral, a walkover." He nodded to General Aguinaldo. "Tell your boys they can bring their golf clubs to this one, Andy." General Aguinaldo permitted the right side of his face to twitch slightly in response while the rest of the staff laughed politely.

"Hank, I have precisely 350 Straight Arrow antitank rockets in the hands of my men. We're going to need a hell of a lot more than those when we break out of Oppalia."

"No sweat, Andy, no problem," General Han answered, making placating motions with his hands. "We have a thousand more en route, and we'll have 'em on the ground not later than D plus five. Thousands more are in production and scheduled for delivery to the Fleet by D plus ten at the very latest. The

Council has given production of these weapons absolute top priority. Your men will have 'em when they need 'em."

Admiral Wimbush conferred briefly with an aide and then said, "Okay, Hank, you've got the green light. Your readiness reports convince me your boys are combat-loaded and ready for this operation. Pass on to your commanders my personal congratulations for keeping their units in such tip-top shape."

"You'd better get ready for some casualties, Gary," Professor Benjamin said to Admiral Clark as they walked down the companionway outside the briefing room.

"The Intel boys guess wrong on this one?"

"I don't know about that, but military intelligence has always been an iffy game. Anyway, I've been talking to some of the army's battalion staff, you know, over beers, and if the admiral believes those readiness reports General Han's been filing, he's on thin ice. Hell, Gary, commanders have flushed out their readiness reports ever since the first Roman legionnaire lied to his Centurion when he told him he had his basic load of spear points. Commanders never report bad news to headquarters! I'm not accusing General Han of falsifying reports, but how often does any four-star general get down to company level and inspect rifle bores and Dragon engines himself?"

Admiral Clark nodded. He'd experienced a similar problem in the medical field. "What's this 'Arnhem' thing you mentioned?"

"Ah, place in Holland, back on Old Earth, where the Allies dropped some parachutists during a World War Two operation, September 1944, I think. Would've worked perfectly, except there was 'unexpectedly heavy' German resistance when the guys jumped in. They wound up in a shooting gallery, thousands killed and captured. If this St. Cyr guy is so smart . . . Jesus, Gary, am I ever glad I'm not going in with the Marines."

They paused outside the Fleet Medical Staff bay. "Well, Jere," Clark said, "I'm not a proctologist, but if you're right, looks like we might need one—to get those golf clubs out of old Box Kicker's rear end after the Marines are through with him."

* * *

General Aguinaldo sat facing his commanders. "We're going in at Oppalia," he announced. Nobody said a word but each man realized this was bad news from an infantryman's viewpoint. They fidgeted in their seats. But the decision had been made and now they would carry it out. No sense protesting.

"I know this is a night operation, but gentlemen, the harder the task, the more we like it, so I know you will carry this off to perfection. Intel says no sign of enemy presence there."

"That's Fishface Johannes's evaluation, sir?" a stocky major general named Jack Daly asked. He would command the division that would compose the assault element.

"Yeah, Jack. Don't take that to the bank, though. Gentlemen, I want you to prepare for stiff resistance, maybe even armor. I've never downplayed the risk of a combat operation to my staff. I have a bad feeling about this. I hope I'm wrong, but I want you to prepare as if I'm right."

"Sir, I notice the operations plan calls for the army to reinforce us on D plus three. Will they?" the brigadier commanding the 22nd FIST asked. "If you'll recall, on the Auberge landing nine years ago, the army failed to reinforce. I'm sure you all recall the disastrous results of that operation very clearly."

General Aguinaldo hesitated before replying. "Yes. Hank Han may be a box kicker, but he knows how to get the beans and the bullets to the right place at the right time. That goes for the thousand Straight Arrows as well. Okay, who's up to snuff on urban warfare?"

"The 34th FIST," Daly answered at once. He nodded at Brigadier Sturgeon sitting at the far end of the table.

"Ted, you lead the way in," Aguinaldo said. "Gentlemen, D-Day is in seventy-two hours. H-Hour will be three hours local time. This will be a night landing. You have the basic op plan, with the Fleet intelligence estimates and logistical annexes. Have your op orders for the assault to me tomorrow at this time." He stood up, signaling that the meeting was over.

"Jack," Brigadier Sturgeon said, accosting General Daly before he could leave the conference room. "We have the Straight Arrow, my men are trained in its use, but we don't have nearly enough if we run into a big armored force down there. We've got to be assured we'll have air and artillery support if we do."

"Ted, you have 'em, you have 'em," Daly replied, clapping Sturgeon reassuringly on the shoulder.

"Goddamn, Jack, we're going into a built-up area, at night, lousy weather—"

"Ted, look on the bright side. At the most, you'll only have to be there two days. And you're not going in alone, the rest of us'll be there right behind you, and then you'll have 120,000 dogfaces to reinforce you. And you've known Andy for years, he always looks on the dark side—that's good, that's good— but this'll come out all right, Ted. Think of what we'll be up against once we move out of Oppalia." He clapped Sturgeon on the shoulder again and walked off.

Brigadier Sturgeon stood by himself for a moment. He shook his head. He just couldn't think ahead to the breakout. What waits for us down there? he asked himself. Shaking his head again, he walked off to the debarkation port to catch the shuttle back to his own transport.

CHAPTER
ELEVEN

"Attention on deck!" First Sergeant Myer bellowed.

The assembled men of Company L sprang to their feet.

Captain Conorado marched briskly into gymnasium compartment HL/q/v/14-3 and down the aisle in the middle of the rows of benches that had replaced the exercise equipment that normally filled the space.

"Seat the men, Top Sergeant," Conorado said as he stepped onto the small stage that faced the ranked benches. The company's other officers followed him into the gym and took places at the rear of the room.

"Aye aye, sir," Myer replied. He glared out at the men. *"Sit!"* he bellowed. The momentary clanking, thumping, and bumping of the men resuming their seats almost drowned out the rest of what the first sergeant said. "If there's any ruckus or grab-assing, you'll sit at attention."

There wasn't any ruckus or grab-assing as the 120 enlisted men of the company looked intently at their skipper and waited to hear what he was going to say.

Conorado spent a few seconds looking out at the faces staring back at him. He wondered how many of them would die in the next seventy-two hours.

"In two days," he began, "at nine hours ship-time, we will board orbit-to-surface craft to conduct an amphibious assault. One hour later, at three-thirty local time, we will go over the beach at the city of Oppalia. Oppalia is a major industrial city. It has a fully developed seaport and spaceport, and it's a transportation hub. Our job is to secure both ports for the ingress of follow-on army forces." He paused for a few seconds to allow his Marines to hoot and cry out a few disparaging words about the army. The hoots and cries cut off immediately when he resumed speaking.

"It is the belief of Fleet Admiral Wimbush, who is in overall command of this operation, that the bad guys have no significant defenses at Oppalia. This belief is based on extensive intelligence gathered by the string-of-pearls and by reconnaissance drones. The nearest known enemy force is the First Armored Division, located at a mining complex a hundred kilometers away. We should have at least two or three hours, maybe longer, to secure Oppalia and set up our defenses before the First Armored can mount up and get to us. By then we should have four entire FISTs on the ground and in position around the city, and another FIST either already moving in with us or on its way.

"As you know, the First Armored Division comprises fully half of the enemy's known armored forces. I assure you, if twelve hundred tanks attempt to attack four thousand Marines armed with Straight Arrows, those tanks will die in very short order.

"The army command believes, and the Fleet Admiral concurs, that this will be an essentially unopposed landing. We will secure the ports, the army will make planetfall behind us and go out to do battle against the tanks, and we can pull some liberty. That's the plan," he said very dryly.

"There's one other thing you have to be aware of. Since we will make planetfall in a major city that is vital to the economy and postwar redevelopment of Diamunde, there is a restrictive rule of engagement in effect. We are to avoid, to the greatest extent possible, damaging the infrastructure. That means we can't knock down or burn up buildings, we are to leave civilians and their housing alone, and we are not to tamper with the public utility systems." Conorado paused a moment to let the implications sink in. "That's right," he said when he saw appalled expressions wash over a few faces, "under no circumstances are we allowed to invoke the Negev Protocol."

More than twenty years earlier, Marines on a peacekeeping

mission in the Negev district of Alhambra repeatedly came under fire from villages that were supposed to have only civilians in them. One squad on patrol came under particularly heavy fire and could see a large number of armed men preparing to assault them. The corporal leading the squad called in artillery to bombard the would-be attackers, and destroyed the village in the process. The brigadier commanding the mission backed up the corporal, so did the entire Marine chain of command. Ever since, the "Negev Protocol" was invoked when massive destruction of lives and property was the only thing that stood between Marines and death. They were being forbidden to use Negev in this war.

Conorado did his best to keep his face neutral. "I say again, Fleet Admiral Wimbush and his intelligence staff are positive that there are no enemy forces in or near Oppalia. Therefore, destruction of infrastructure shouldn't be an issue regardless of this rule of engagement." He left unsaid that the prohibition against invoking Negev was also why the artillery wouldn't be landed until after Oppalia was secured.

"Your platoon commanders and platoon sergeants will give you more detailed briefings between now and the time we board the assault vehicles. Those briefings will include maps and VR chamber exercises. Are there any questions?"

It was normally a rhetorical question. What it means in Marine is, "Did I say anything you didn't understand?" It is not an invitation to question whys and wherefores. But PFC MacIlargie was too new to realize that, so he asked the question so many others had but wouldn't ask—and it wasn't about Negev.

"Sir, if the landing's going to be unopposed, why are we making it at night?" MacIlargie may not have known this wasn't the kind of question he was supposed to ask, but he did know that night amphibious landings were uncommon—when Marines put on a display of strength, they want to be seen doing it.

"MacIlargie, your platoon sergeant and I will have a talk with you afterward," Top Myer boomed. MacIlargie shrank back to the bench.

Conorado turned his head so few of the men could see his face and murmured, "No you won't." Then he turned back to the company. "That's a very good question, PFC MacIlargie. Unfortunately, nobody told me. Maybe it's so we can move through the city and get into position without civilian traffic getting in our way." He shrugged. "Ours not to reason why, ours but to do. Any other questions?"

This time there were the expected none.

"All right, then, I'll leave you to the first sergeant, who I'm sure has a few words of wisdom for you."

"Attention on deck!" Myer bellowed, and the men sprang to attention as Conorado marched out of the compartment.

Top Myer waited until Conorado and the other officers were gone, then nodded at the senior NCOs, who secured the hatches to prevent anyone's leaving—or entering unannounced. He clasped his hands behind his back and paced from side to side on the stage, glaring out at the men. Maybe it was only MacIlargie's imagination, but it seemed to the young Marine that the first sergeant glared at him more than anyone else.

"Were you listening to that briefing?" Top Myer suddenly barked out. "Did you hear what the skipper said?

"We are making a nighttime assault landing. The skipper said the port is 'supposedly' poorly defended. The 'nearest known' enemy force. It is the 'belief' of Wimpy Wimbush. Intelligence gathered by string-of-pearls and drones. We 'should have' two or three hours. There 'should be' four FISTs. The 'army command believes.' The last time I heard an army command believe something, it was that an asshole and an elbow *might* not be the same thing." He glared so fiercely that none of the Marines dared laugh.

"You've all heard the old maxim, 'No plan, no matter how good, ever survives first contact with the enemy.' Well, I heard so many 'ifs' in the skipper's briefing, I don't think this is a good plan to begin with. I'm going to forget every part of it after 'we are making an amphibious assault into a major city with a major seaport and spaceport and we're doing it at night.' I'm going in expecting major resistance. Any man in this landing who doesn't go in expecting major resistance isn't likely to live long enough to get his feet dry.

"Let me tell you something about who we're going up against. Diamunde doesn't have a government, not what any of us know as a government anyway. A government ultimately has to answer to the people it rules. A democratically elected government can be voted out of office if it doesn't perform up to the people's expectations. A kingdom has to keep its people happy or face a coup or a war of succession. If a tyranny is too repressive, it will be overthrown.

"Diamunde doesn't have a government. The whole damn world's a company town. Today's Diamunde is a wholly owned subsidiary of Tubalcain Enterprises—an interstellar conglomerate. The people of Diamunde aren't citizens or even subjects. They're employees. Anyone who doesn't like the way the place is run either keeps it to himself or gets fired. That's a one-way ticket on the next outbound starship with no job, no home, and no friends waiting at the other end of the ticket. It was a little bit different before the recent hostile takeover by this Marston St. Cyr character." He looked like he wanted to spit, but didn't have a place to do it. "Until then, if you got fired by Tubalcain you could go to work for the Hefestus Conglomerate, or one of the few remaining smaller corporations.

"So who does a corporation have to answer to, you may ask? It's stockholders, that's who. They're the people who want to make money from the corporation without having to do any work for it. The stockholders aren't on Diamunde, they're spread throughout all of Human Space. They don't know what's going on here. If they do, they probably don't care. What they care about is their dividend payments. They take a look at their credit statements once in a while, and if the amount they get from their holdings in Tubalcain is big enough, they're happy.

"What's the worst that can happen to St. Cyr and his corporate cronies? Well, some stockholders might decide to get a new board of directors. But boards have staggered elections. That means it can take years to change the majority view in a board of directors. But it won't happen. Look at what St. Cyr did to the old board when it didn't want to do what he wanted. The son of a bitch killed them. So what alternative do the stockholders who don't like what's going on have? They can sell their stock to people who don't care, that's what. And St. Cyr stays in power. How many more people will he kill?" He shook his head sadly. "I don't even want to think about it.

"Some of you may be wondering how come we're conducting our landing at a major city. Nobody told me this, but here's what I think is the reason. The high commanders think St. Cyr won't want to fight in Oppalia because he won't want to risk damaging such an important part of the planet's infrastructure. Just like we can't invoke Negev." He shook his head at that folly. "If I was in his position, I'd be willing to have it completely destroyed rather than let an invader have it. That's why I think we're going to face strong opposition.

"There's something else here that's bothering me. Tubalcain is very rich—richer since this takeover. When you look back through history, you can see that there's a pretty direct correlation between wealth and political power. The richest people, those who control industry, manufacturing, mining, banking, and all other forms of production, have the greatest access to and influence over the people who run government. There wasn't any attempt at negotiation with St. Cyr, just a quick decision to go to war. And we have been ordered to avoid damage to infrastructure. I have to wonder if someone's being influenced here, and who's doing the influencing."

Top Myer stopped abruptly and a look of consternation flashed across his face. "I don't want anyone to repeat what I just said," he growled.

There were nods and murmurs from the Marines. They understood that the Top had just said something that could be taken the wrong way by the wrong people. Even if he did glare, growl, and bark at them too much, nobody wanted the first sergeant to get in trouble.

"That is all, people. Platoon sergeants, take over." First Sergeant Myer headed for the nearest exit.

"First platoon, company area, on the double!"

"Second platoon, stay in place!"
"Third platoon, VR chamber!"
The final briefing and training was about to commence.

CHAPTER
TWELVE

Klaxons blared throughout the amphibious battlecruiser *Tripoli*. The carefully modulated female voice that came over the ship's speakers intoning the ancient words, "Commander Landing Force, prepare the landing force for landing," galvanized the Marines of 34th FIST into action.

"First squad, fall in," Sergeant Hyakowa called from where he stood in the passageway just outside the squad compartments. Throughout 34th FIST's areas, other squad leaders were also calling their men to the ready.

"Second squad, on me," Sergeant Eagle's Cry, a few meters away from Hyakowa, commanded. Thirty-fourth FIST's areas reverberated with the thudding of feet on metal.

"Guns up," Sergeant Kelly shouted. The commands of other squad leaders echoed along the passageways.

Before the squad leaders finished calling for their men, the Marines of third platoon were scrambling through the hatches to line up in front of their squad leaders.

Gunnery Sergeant Bass, virtually invisible in his chameleon field uniform, stood watching at one end of the passageway. Ensign vanden Hoyt, like Bass, visible only as a face hovering in midair, stood observing at the other end. Between them, the squad leaders were readily detectable only by the Straight Arrow tubes slung over their shoulders—their hovering faces mere blurs behind their helmets' infra screens. The men of the platoon also had their infra screens down, so they could see more of each other than just the Straight Arrow tubes every third Marine carried at sling arms. The rushed manufacture of the antitank weapons hadn't allowed for any chameleon effect on the weapons. Instead, they were a drab, light-absorbing green.

As the Marines lined up before their squad leaders they flipped up their infras, fully exposing their faces. As soon as they were in formation, the squad leaders flipped up their own.

Hyakowa stepped sharply to his first fire team leader, Corporal Leach, to give him a final inspection. The inspection was perfunctory and mostly manual—he couldn't see Leach's gear and had to touch it to make sure it was present and secured. He moved on to Schultz and gave him an even more perfunctory inspection—he knew Schultz would be the most ready man in the platoon, maybe in the entire FIST. His inspection of Dean was more detailed. Even though Dean had acquitted himself well during the two operations he'd been on, neither had involved an amphibious combat assault. He looked into Dean's eyes. Leach's eyes had been tensely ready. Schultz's eyes were relaxed, almost sleepy. Both of them had made combat assaults before and survived them, they knew what to expect. Uncertainty and nervousness showed in Dean's eyes.

"We're Marines, Dean," Hyakowa said crisply. "We're gonna get some!"

"Kick ass, take the names of the survivors," Dean replied.

Hyakowa clapped him on his invisible shoulder and moved on to Sergeant Ratliff.

The squad leaders completed their inspections and reported their men ready in less than five minutes.

"Marines," vanden Hoyt said in a voice that wasn't a shout, but carried clearly to each man in the platoon, "we are about to go into the unknown. Thirty-fourth FIST is the first wave. Companies L and M will cross the beach in Dragons, Company K will be directly behind us and cross in hoppers. We will have air cover from our Raptors. Thirteenth FIST," the other FIST on the *Tripoli*, "will follow in two waves at half hour intervals. We will cross the beach in the small hours of the morning. Intelligence says the landing should meet little or no resistance. That's nice to hear. But we're Marines. Marines are always ready for the unexpected. Even though the bad guys aren't supposed to be waiting for us to show up then and there, be ready to breathe fire as soon as you step off the Dragons. Let me hear it."

The men of third platoon roared out, "OOH-RAH!" Vanden Hoyt's eyes flicked to his left in surprise—Lance Corporal Dupont, the platoon's communications man, was "oohrahing" along with everyone else.

"Sta— Gunnery Sergeant Bass!" vanden Hoyt said.

"Aye aye, sir," Bass called back. He didn't need to be given any more orders, he knew this routine too well. "Platoon, right face!" he commanded, then paused for a beat while the Marines of third platoon turned to face him. He took off his helmet to allow the men to see him in visual. "Follow me. *Route* step, *march!*" He led the way through the maze of passage- and ladderways to the number-one well deck, where 34th FIST's Dragons waited in the seven Essays that would carry the two lead companies to the surface of the planet. Ten more Essays held the hoppers and Raptors of 34th FIST. The final three Essays in the cavernous hold stood ready to carry the FIST's command and combat support elements to Diamunde's surface. M Company simultaneously entered the well deck from a different direction. Shortly, Company K would enter the well deck and board the hoppers waiting on five of the other Essays.

The Marines had drilled on boarding the vehicles several times over the past few days—the boarding was eerily quiet, few sergeants or corporals had to speak up to redirect Marines going the wrong way.

Bass stopped at the open hatch of the Essay third platoon would ride down to Diamunde's sea and waved Hyakowa past. The first squad leader headed directly to the Dragon two-thirds of the members of the platoon would ride in and stopped by its ramp to wave his men through. He entered the Dragon behind MacIlargie and walked the length of the vehicle's interior, making sure his men were properly strapped into their acceleration webbing before taking his own place next to the ramp and locking down. The ramp was wide enough that Eagle's Cry was able to board and inspect his men without having to wait for first squad to finish.

Four minutes after Bass entered the well deck, all of third platoon was secured for launch. Vanden Hoyt had brought up the rear from the troop compartments and was the last to strap in.

The Dragons' computers registered that each acceleration position was occupied and all locks properly secured, then simultaneously notified the Dragon commander and the Essay's computer.

"Dragon One, secured and ready," the first Dragon commander redundantly reported to the Essay's coxswain.

"Dragon Two, secured and ready," the second Dragon's commander reported.

The third Dragon commander echoed them.

"Essay Alfa zero-four, ready to drop," the Essay's coxswain reported to the well-deck officer, though the Essay's computer had already made the report. The redundancy of voice and computer reporting was to protect against failure of the sensor system and to provide assurance that not only were the troops properly secured for launch, but the vehicle commanders and coxswains were alert and aware of their individual situations.

As soon as all Essays reported themselves ready, the well-deck officer said, "Well deck, stand by for zero atmosphere." Even through the walls of the Dragon and the Essay outside it, the Marines could hear the whisper as the well deck's air was sucked out.

"Open drop hatch," the well-deck officer ordered.

Inside the Dragons the Marines felt rather than heard the opening of the bay hatches beneath the Essay.

"Stand by for null-g," the ship's female voice intoned.

The Marines braced themselves for a sudden loss of weight.

"Null-g," intoned the ship's voice. "Three, two, one, mark."

The ship's gravity generators shut off. Everywhere in the ship and on its surface, people and objects slowly drifted upward from whatever direction had been "down" for them. In the Dragons, there was a slight shifting of webbing as weight went away from the overhead support straps and the newly floating masses were pulled into equilibrium by the deck straps.

The klaxons blared once again throughout the ship and within the Dragons. The computer's female voice said soothingly, "Land the landing force."

The magnetic clamps that had held the Essays to the overhead of the well deck suddenly reversed polarity and the Essays were ejected straight down from the ship.

The Marines all shouted, screamed, or bellowed to "equalize the sudden pressure" of the launch.

One second and three hundred meters from the already closing bay doors, the Essays' engines fired up and added three g's of forward momentum to the four vertical. The roar of the Essays' engines, soundless in the space outside it, was loud enough inside to drown out the screams of the passengers it carried in the Dragons. Small rockets on the bottom of the Essays blasted to cancel the downward motion of the entry vehicle; the aft retros fired more strongly than the forward ones to angle them so the main rockets gave the entry vehicles a slight downward thrust. Little more than ten seconds after launch, the Essays were already past the two-kilometer-long battlecruiser; only the downward thrust from their main engines kept them from being flung into a higher orbit. Finer adjustments brought the seven Essays together in formation.

"Essay Alfa zero-four clear of the ship," the Essay's coxswain reported. "Position in formation visually verified." The other Essay coxswains made the same report.

"Wave one, properly formed," reported the chief petty officer in command of the formation. "Request permission to commence atmospheric entry."

"Permission granted. On my mark, commence atmospheric entry. Four, three, two, one, mark."

The coxswains were all listening in on the command circuit. At "mark" they punched the buttons that controlled the topside attitude jets of their Essays. The Essays' computers received confirmation from the ship's launch control computer then executed the command. Small vernier rockets above the Essays' noses pulsed to angle the reentry vehicles sharply downward and convert their orbital velocity into downward speed. Five seconds later the main engines shut off and the Essays went into an unpowered plunge at a glide angle calculated to take them fifty thousand meters above the surface in five minutes. There, wings would deploy and forward thrusters would fire to drop speed to something that could be controlled by powered flight.

"Sound off," Hyakowa ordered into his helmet comm unit as soon as the decible level in the Dragon was low enough to be heard.

"Three-one-one-one, okay," Leach immediately reported.

"Three-one-one-two, ready," Schultz replied.

"Three-one-one-three, here," Dean said.

"Three-one-two-one . . ." Ratliff said, and on through the rest of the squad until every man had reported. On the other side of the Dragon, Eagle's Cry had his squad report, as did every squad leader on every Dragon in the Essay formation. Squad leaders reported to platoon leaders, who reported to company commanders, who reported to the battalion commander, who reported to the FIST commander who was riding to the surface with the first wave—the executive officer would follow with K Company and the air element. Seconds after Commander Van Winkle's report of all Marines ready reached Brigadier Sturgeon, the formation of Essays reached atmosphere and the shuttle craft deployed their wings and hit their retro rockets. The Essays shuddered violently and the men in the Dragons were bounced and rattled about in their acceleration webbing.

"High speed on a bad road," was how Marines described the fall from the top of the atmosphere to the beginning of powered flight fifty kilometers above the surface. It was an apt description. The fall through the middle thermosphere felt like the Dragon was driving at top speed on a coarsely graveled road, the gravel getting coarser the farther down they went. The lower thermosphere was an eroded roadway with potholes and bumps. In the mesosphere, some of the potholes seemed deep enough to swallow the Dragon whole, and some of the bumps should have flipped it over.

The Essay formation spread out during its drop to the top of the atmosphere, so by the time the breaking rockets and deploying wings cut their speed and the angle of the shuttles' dives, the Essays were two kilometers away from each other. That gave the coxswains the space they needed to rein in the reentry vehicles without risking collision. Once the Essays' wings were fully extended, huge flaps extended from them to further decrease the Essays' speed. When the wings finally bit into the thickening air hard enough for controlled flight, the coxswains turned off the braking rockets, fired up the atmosphere jets, and maneuvered the craft back into formation and into a velocity-eating spiral that slowed their descent as well as the shuttles' forward speed. At one thousand meters altitude the coxswains pulled out of the spiral and popped drogue chutes. At two hundred they angled the jets' vernier nozzles downward. Seconds later the shuttles rested on the surface of an ocean, a hundred kilometers off the shore of Oppalia.

"Ready landing craft to hit the beach," the shuttles' coxswains ordered.

"Landing Craft One, ready to hit the beach," said the first Dragon's commander.

"Landing Craft Two, ready to hit the beach," said the second Dragon's commander, and so on throughout the formation.

The Dragon commanders revved up their engines; the vehicles' curtains fluttered and they rose from the force of the air cushions that lifted the Dragons off the deck. On command from the chief petty officer commanding the formation, the coxswains opened their aft hatches and lowered ramps, and the Dragons drove out to splash onto the surface of the water. In seconds twenty Dragons were in a column, zipping at top speed across the wave tops toward the distant shore. At their top water speed of more than 140 kilometers per hour, the Dragons would cross the beach in about forty minutes. During that time the commanders and leaders, from Brigadier Sturgeon on down to the newest fire team leader, reviewed with their subordinates what they were going to do if things worked as planned. And they reviewed their options if intelligence was wrong.

Twenty minutes after the wave of Dragons flowed off their Essays, five more Essays opened their hatches and tilted forward at seven thousand meters altitude. Ten troop-laden hoppers slid out of them. The hoppers' engines revved up immediately and they were in controlled flight by the time they free-fell a thousand meters. The hoppers gathered in formation and headed after the Dragons. Fifteen minutes after the hoppers slid out of their Essays, ten Raptors slid out of five more Essays at twenty thousand meters. It took two thousand meters of free-fall for the Raptors' engines to kick in and take control. The Raptors gathered together and made one wide orbit before they streaked toward Oppalia. Both flights were synchronized to cross the beach at the same time the Dragons did.

Since the highest rank attainable in Marston St. Cyr's army was Major General, the rank he had selected for himself, brigadiers commanded corps, colonels divisions, and lieutenant colonels brigades.

While Lieutenant Colonel Naseby Namur did not understand the reasoning behind St. Cyr's army reorganization, he did know how to follow orders. For two months now he had sat with his command, the First Tank Brigade of the First Armored Division, at Oppalia, watching the miners go to work every day. Of the 410 Main Battle Tanks assigned to his brigade, 405 of them were ready for action, although during the time he had been at Oppalia, he was under strict orders to perform no maneuvers with the behemoths.

During that time, his men had practiced tank gunnery in virtual reality chambers, attended to the endless maintenance tasks to keep their tanks and vehicles ready for combat, endured forced marches across the desert to keep themselves in top physical conditioning, and practiced maneuvers on sand tables. And the weather during that time of year in Oppalia had been terrible—cold, windy, wet; clouds and fog hid the sun for days on end. All that work and military routine was necessary not only to keep the brigade in fighting trim but to keep the men occupied, otherwise they'd all go nuts. The miners had their families and friends to return to at night; his men lived in drafty warehouses temporarily converted into troop barracks. Still, morale was high.

Lieutenant Colonel Namur had spent the day in the motor park with his tank commanders, inspecting engines and weapon systems. It had been tedious work. He had just put his feet up and was about to pour himself a glass of wine when his communicator bleeped.

"Lieutenant Day, sir." It was the brigade staff duty officer. Irritated, Namur asked what it was. "General St. Cyr, sir. He wants all commanders to sit in on a secure videoconference in five minutes."

Namur swung his feet heavily to the floor and walked slowly to his command post, where his staff had already assembled. They stood when he entered. "Seats," he commanded. They had just returned to their chairs when St. Cyr's image appeared on the huge vidscreen set up at one end of the storage room that had been converted into the brigade command post. Everyone jumped to attention.

"At ease, gentlemen." St. Cyr's voice boomed over the audio system. He was sitting at a desk, wearing an ordinary soldier's battle dress uniform. His only badge of rank were two silver stars on a bracelet he wore around his right wrist. "A Confederation Navy amphibious assault fleet has arrived in orbit around Diamunde," he announced. "We are already under attack here in New Kimberly. Our intelligence service estimates a force of at least 120,000 troops will be landed somewhere on Diamunde within the next seventy-two hours." The men in the command post looked at one another nervously.

"I am addressing all my commanders at once on this net because we are not sure just where the invasion force will land. As of right now you will put all your commands on one-hundred-percent combat alert. Stay in constant touch with my headquarters. Hold the invading forces if you can, delay them if you can't. You will be reinforced. That is all." The screen went blank.

For several seconds nobody stirred. Then Namur was on his feet. "Battalion commanders! Issue live ammunition to every man. I want fifty percent of our tanks manned, engines running at all times; two shifts, twelve hours each. S-4, get down to the spaceport, I want command-detonated mines everywhere down there. Sergeant Major, get me the mine operator on the horn right now—we're closing the goddamned thing down."

Awakened from a deep sleep by the insistent shrilling of the communications console beside his bed, Gregory Gurselfanks, operator of the Oppalia mining complex, answered sleepily.

"Namur here, sir. The Noncombatant Evacuation Order is now in effect. Get your people to safety at once. Enemy attack is imminent." The connection went dead; Namur had said all that needed to be said. Weeks before his staff had worked out an evacuation plan with Gurselfanks. Food supplies had been prepositioned deep within the mines, enough for the 3,000 miners and their families to survive for two weeks. Overland evacuation routes and transportation had been arranged for those civilians who might want to flee to New Kimberly or some other refuge.

Gurselfanks, wide awake by that time, bounded out of bed. Within minutes he had assembled his staff and his people were gathering their few personal belongings. One thousand of them opted to flee Oppalia for a small village in Rourke's Hills. Weeks later their remains were found inside their burned-out vehicles halfway there. Flying 2,000 meters above the desert at a speed in excess of Mach 3, Admiral Wimbush's Raptors had mistaken them for a fleeing enemy column.

The next few hours were controlled pandemonium. Finally Namur was able to find a moment to sit down. He asked a sergeant to bring him a cup of coffee. He glanced at his watch: already past three hours, and dark as pitch outside. He hoped in a few minutes he might be able to get some sleep, although it would have to be right here, in his command post. He was just putting the coffee cup to his lips when his wrist communicator bleeped. It was St. Cyr himself, broadcasting in the clear.

"Colonel Namur. The invasion force will land in your area!"

A tremendous explosion shook the building, and Namur spilled the hot coffee on his legs. He never noticed. "General," he shouted, "they're already here!" and was out the door.

CHAPTER
THIRTEEN

"Shore's in sight," Corporal Duguid, the Dragon crew chief, said into the squad leader circuit in his comm unit. "Everybody get ready. We're going feet dry in three minutes."

"Roger," Hyakowa and Eagle's Cry said simultaneously.

"Look alive," Hyakowa said into his all-hands circuit. "Less than three minutes."

The Marines ran through the checklist for hitting the beach. They checked their webbing, no longer in the horizontal acceleration attitude but in the vertical surface-transit mode. Each man made sure his weapon was on safe and had a battery in the well. They checked the rest of their gear, then flipped down the infra screens on their helmets. Instantly the view inside the Dragon changed. The dim red lights that were the only illumination in the vehicle had shown twenty barely seen faces hovering at intervals along the two sides of the troop compartment. Through the infras, twenty ill-formed, bulky bodies glowed red.

The Dragons maneuvered to change their formation from one line twenty abreast to two lines ten abreast. They couldn't go ashore in the harbor proper, it was too heavily built up with wharves, piers, and seawalls, so there was no place low enough for the Dragons to climb over. To the north and south of the bay were points of land. The point to the south was smooth, gently sloping beach, ideal for coming ashore. The Dragons headed toward the north point, which was boulder-strewn and sloped upward at nearly thirty degrees. General Aguinaldo and his staff had chosen that as the landing spot because they thought—hoped—it wouldn't be as well-defended as the southern point.

"Stand by for rough road," Corporal Duguid said, but not all the Dragon crew chiefs alerted their Marines. The Dragons cut their speed from full to one-quarter so suddenly that the Marines were thrown toward the front of their vehicles. Only the webbing kept them from being dashed against the front wall of the troop compartments. The Dragons lurched and yawed violently as they abruptly transitioned from level travel on smooth sea to climbing over the rocks. The undercarriages screamed and clanged from striking boulders as the uneven surface ripped tufts of air cushion from underneath. The Dragons rocked and rolled their way up the slope, clattering so loudly no one inside them could hear the hoppers that whooshed by overhead or the Raptors that screamed in above the hoppers.

Fifty meters beyond the water line, the top of the slope abruptly turned level. The Dragon drivers increased vertical air pressure to maximum as they topped the slope. Still, as the Dragons shot up over the lip of the slope they lost enough cushion that the front ends of the vehicles slammed against the ground, rattling everyone aboard. But the cushions puffed back up almost immediately, and the drivers prodded the Dragons back up to over one hundred kpm.

The sudden increase in speed was the only thing that saved them.

In response to Lieutenant Colonel Namur's abrupt command, Company C of the 552nd Battalion, First Tank Brigade—forty-five TP1s strong—raced to its shore defensive positions at the north point overlooking the harbor entrance. The tanks were taking their places among the half-dozen ferrocrete bunkers, which should have been enough to successfully defend that rocky slope, when the first wave of ten Dragons roared over the slope's edge and picked up speed.

The gunners in the bunkers knew the Marines were coming, they'd watched through their infra scopes as the amphibians reformed into two ranks and turned north. Namur's men knew the Dragons would have to drop speed to negotiate the slope. They thought they'd have time to take careful aim as the Dragons topped the slope, and be able to blow their targets away before they were level again. They hadn't counted on the speed of the Marine vehicles. Only four of the six bunker guns got shots off before the Dragons were too close for them to shift their aim. Only one of the four hit a Dragon with a high explosive round.

Overhead, the hopper flight carrying Company K continued toward its landing zone. Above the hoppers five of the ten attack craft in the flight of Raptors continued with them. The other five peeled out of formation and flew an aiming run over the defenses before circling around to come back with their cannons belching fire.

The nine surviving Dragons opened fire with their guns, firing as much to confuse the enemy as to hit targets. In seconds they were passing through the still moving TP1s. The tanks slewed about, tried to bring guns to bear on the rapidly moving targets. But the Marines were too mixed up with the tanks and bunkers; none of the tankers could find a target where a miss wouldn't hit one of their own. The tanks slewed more, attempting to find open targets. Drivers responding to their tank commanders' excited orders yanked and twisted steering yokes and stomped on accelerators in attempts to ram the Dragons. But the Dragons were faster and more agile and managed to avoid the tanks as they sped through them and headed for the safety of the twisting roads through the nearby industrial area.

By then, guns blazing, the second wave of Dragons had topped the slope and was roaring toward the defenders. The Marines weren't concerned about hitting friendly targets—they were using plasma weapons; the Dragons had their shields up, they wouldn't be hurt by a shot from one of their own. Of course, the plasma guns wouldn't do a lot of damage to the tanks either, but they could blind the tanks, burn off their antennas and sensors, fracture their periscope glass and camera lenses. And the plasma could get inside the bunkers. The second wave killed two of the bunkers, then was among them and the tanks, following the first wave inland. The second wave of Dragons barely missed the Marines who piled out of the one Dragon that was hit. And two of the tanks, trying to ram Dragons, collided with a thunderclap.

* * *

The shaped-charge round that had hit the Dragon was designed to take out medium tanks. It blew through the relatively light armor of the left front of the Dragon, burst through the thin panel separating the crew cab from the troop compartment, cut a diagonal across the right forward corner of the troop compartment, and detonated when it impacted the starboard wall of the vehicle. Most of its explosive blast and the molten metal it spewed forth went beyond the Dragon to spend itself harmlessly in the open. But the shell didn't pass through harmlessly. A flying chunk of shrapnel ripped a chunk out of the base of the driver's neck, and another piece gouged a deep furrow in Corporal Duguid's arm. More shrapnel tore into the control panel and disabled the vehicle. Four infantrymen in the troop compartment were injured, and Corporal John Keto was killed outright when the round plunged through his chest on its way to the starboard wall.

"Find a target and kill it," Duguid snapped at the unharmed gunner as he slapped a field bandage onto his wounded arm. He then turned to try to save the life of his driver.

"Everybody out!" Hyakowa knew the Dragon was dead as soon as he felt the way it swerved when it was hit. He pounded the heel of his hand against the panic button at the side of the closed exit ramp to open it and was out before the ramp hit the ground. The uninjured Marines and one of the wounded were right behind him.

"Spread out!" Hyakowa shouted. As soon as he saw they were following his orders, he looked beyond the downed Dragon to the line of defenders and swallowed. The second line of Dragons was speeding through the bunkers and tanks, the first wave disappearing down the streets and around the corners of the nearby industrial section of the city. A quick glance told him that two of the bunkers were dead. But he saw far too many tanks, none of which looked any worse than inconvenienced by the damage inflicted by the Marine light armor. As he watched, the Dragon he'd come ashore in killed a third bunker. "Oh, hell," he muttered. He knew that was going to bring fire. "Over the edge," he commanded on his comm unit. Glances to his sides showed man-sized splotches of red flowing toward the top of the slope and the cover it offered. He dashed back to the Dragon to check for wounded and get any survivors out.

PFC MacIlargie, though wounded himself, was half carrying Lance Corporal Van Impe out. "Keto's dead," MacIlargie gasped. "Everybody else is out. I patched Van Impe up."

"What about the crew?"

MacIlargie shook his head.

Hyakowa looked into the Dragon. "Get him to cover," he ordered. He ran forward.

"We're fighting," Duguid snarled at him. He didn't think his driver was going to make it. "Get out of here, mud-Marine."

Hyakowa backed off and headed for his men.

Behind him another shaped-charge round slammed into the Dragon. Its gun stopped firing.

Then the five Raptors swooped back down, cannons flaring.

Five bolts from one cannon, so close together that they looked like a stream of fire, struck the top of the engine compartment of one tank. The force of the impact knocked the turret loose and tipped it forward like a jauntily worn cap. Then their heat enveloped the ammunition compartment and set off the sixty-odd rounds in it. The heavy vehicle burst apart, chunks of armor flung about like papier-mâché. The multiton turret tumbled into the air and crashed down on top of another tank, bending its cannon out of shape.

The second Raptor melted a hole through the side of a tank. The acrid smell of molten metal was joined by the stench of burnt flesh from the crewmen who didn't live long enough to realize they were being burned to death. Three more tanks died in flames before the Raptors began to orbit for another run.

Five tanks were dead, a sixth helpless with the loss of its cannon barrel, and two others were damaged from their collision. The company commander knew that his mission had failed, the Dragons had gotten through. He also knew that if his tanks stayed in the open, another run from the Raptors would kill more of his tanks—and his tank commanders couldn't take the chance of standing out of their turrets to use their antiaircraft weapons. He ordered a retreat with all speed. The tanks were back among the industrial buildings before the Raptors could hit them again. The Raptor commander called off the second firing run before all of his birds had fired at the bunkers. The Raptors had another mission: defend the Dragons. They flew off to complete that mission.

Hyakowa listened to the departing Raptors, then cautiously raised his head to look above the lip of the slope. Four of the bunkers were obviously dead. The other two were just as obviously still alive. He slid back down before any of the remaining defenders could spot him through their infra scopes. Quickly, he took stock. He had nineteen Marines including himself. Three were wounded, one too badly to fight, maybe too badly injured to move. The rest of the company had moved inland. The next wave of Marines was half an hour off, if it even came ashore at this point. The two remaining bunkers were too strong for his Marines to assault—unless he wanted to kill them with Straight Arrows. But the two squads only had six of the rockets, and firing them would surely bring unwanted company—and he needed to preserve the six antitank weapons for use against tanks, not against bunkers that could be bypassed. He had no choice—no matter how badly Van Impe was injured, they had to move, they had to rejoin the company on their own.

He turned on his squad leader's situation HUD and flicked on the map overview. The map showed the streets of New Kimberly to scale and ground elevations in schematic. His position was marked with a blue circle, the company's destination was a blue X. A few red dots marked enemy disposition. He ignored the red dots; he wasn't going to depend on the HUD to tell him where the enemy was. He'd checked the map display before the wave of Dragons reached the shore. It hadn't shown enough red dots in the entire city to make up an armored company, let alone a company waiting to meet them at the shore. He scanned the map seeking a route that might give them a chance of reaching the rest of the company without losing more men. He saw several routes that weren't too roundabout. The most difficult part would be getting off the rocky slope without being spotted by the defenders in the two bunkers—or by any tanks that might still be around.

He turned off the HUD and looked around inside. Even though the infra didn't show details, he could tell that every man, except the unconscious Van Impe, was looking at him as the senior man to tell them what to do, where to go.

He heard a voice call from the Dragon.

"Nobody stopped to check for survivors?" Captain Conorado asked when his communications man, Corporal Escarpo, gave him the platoon commanders' reports: First and second platoons and the assault platoon made it through all right. One Dragon, with third platoon's two blaster squads, was stopped and presumed killed at the beach.

Escarpo's shrug went unseen in the predawn dark. How was he supposed to know?

Conorado was silently swearing at himself. He should have known at the time that one of the Dragons was hit. He should have given the order himself to check for survivors. This was a failure on his part; Marines were never supposed to leave their own behind. No time for self-recriminations now, Companies L and M had to reinforce Company K and secure the spaceport. Company K was already engaged with enemy armor. Thunder rolled toward the Marines of Company L—the roar of Straight Arrows firing, the blast of main battle tank guns, the ear-splitting shriek of Raptors swooping low to fire their cannons, the stuttering of Dragon and hopper cannons, the louder blasts of tanks exploding. Less than a kilometer ahead the night strobed brilliantly with the flashes of plasma bolts and the explosion of tank rounds, sometimes punctuated by bigger blooms of light as killed tanks erupted.

"Sir," Escarpo said. "F Three wants the actual."

Conorado accepted the offered handset with one hand and flipped up his infra with the other so he could snug the earpiece under his helmet. "Lima Actual here, go Foxtrot Three," he said crisply.

"Lima Actual," came back the voice of the FIST operations officer. Conorado could hear explosions behind the voice, explosions that reached him through the air a split second later. The FIST headquarters was closer to the fighting than he was. "Another company of bad guys is approaching rapidly from the southeast. Move your company to intercept and stop them. Details follow. Do you copy? Over."

Conorado toggled on his HUD. Colored lines and dots appeared etched in the air in front of his eyes, put there by his small belt computer, which received the data transmission from HQ and recorded it. He focused on the circled blue dots that represented his company and the circled red dots that indicated the approaching enemy. "Roger, Foxtrot Three, I see them. Over." Part of his mind was already calculating the route the company would take to intercept the tanks.

"Kill them, Captain."

"Roger, Three. Do they have infantry support? Over."

"Not that we know. Foxtrot Three out."

Conorado gave the handset back to Escarpo. "Not that we know," the operations officer had said. That told Conorado there was a serious intelligence breakdown. The intelligence officer should know details like that and pass them on to operations. Conorado didn't have time to worry about foul-ups higher up. He flicked on his commanders' circuit and spoke to his platoon commanders and sergeants. "We're moving out this way." He traced three lines on the map display on his belt computer. The computer immediately transmitted the data to the HUD displays of his senior men. "First platoon, your route." He made the center line blink. "Second platoon, yours." The line on the right blinked. "Assault platoon and headquarters group." The leftmost line blinked. "Third platoon, accompany first. Move now." He started out himself. Around him the other Marines of the company HQ group also began heading toward their interception point. Through his infra he saw the men of the assault platoon advancing ahead of him. "Everybody see the red dots? Armor. We don't know what kind. It may or may not have infantry support. We're going to kill them before they can join the main fight."

Conorado's HUD showed the blue dots of his company split into three groups that followed the three lines. He turned it off.

One hundred men with small arms, antipersonnel guns, and twenty-four Straight Arrow antitank weapons were on their way to intercept and kill forty-five tanks. He repressed a shiver.

CHAPTER FOURTEEN

"We went six blocks," Schultz reported. "Didn't see or hear anything." He stood in a recessed doorway half a kilometer from the landing beach, facing Sergeant Hyakowa. Dean huddled next to him.

"You're sure nobody's coming that way?" Hyakowa asked the men he'd sent ahead to scout their route.

Schultz didn't say anything. He thought the predawn light was bright enough for Hyakowa to see his "That's a dumb question" expression. He had no way of knowing whether someone out of his hearing or sight might be moving to cut across the route he'd taken. But he and Dean—Hyakowa had insisted that Schultz not go alone—had gone out by one street and come back by another. They hadn't found anything to indicate enemy presence in the immediate vicinity or moving their way.

Hyakowa looked at Dean, who nodded, agreeing with Schultz. The senior squad leader cocked his head and listened to the distant sounds of battles, fights they'd been hearing since before they got off the landing slope. One, the first one they heard start, sounded like it was at the spaceport—at least it was in that direction and could be the right distance. "Lead the way," Hyakowa said, then flicked on his squad and squad leaders circuits. His squad leader's radio had three groups of frequencies: one was selective and allowed him to talk to his own squad, either all of them at once or a few of them selectively; on another he could talk directly to the other squad leaders in the platoon; the third went up to the platoon and company command. He hadn't been able to raise anyone on the platoon or company frequencies.

Between interference caused by the buildings around them and electronic interference, he wasn't able to transmit or receive much more than a hundred meters. He flicked on both the squad all-hands and the squad leaders circuits. "Let's move it out, people," he said. "The rest of the company needs us." He dropped his infra back into place to watch the two squads begin their movement.

Schultz moved close to the buildings on one side of the narrow, winding access road they were following through a light industrial area. Dean and Corporal Leach, their fire team leader, paralleled him on the other side of the road. Then came the second fire team, Ratliff, Chan, and Godenov. Dornhofer brought up the squad's rear with MacIlargie, whose wound wasn't severe enough to prevent him from walking and using his weapon. Second squad followed them, carrying Van Impe and Duguid on two litters. They had hidden the bodies of Corporal Keto and the two dead Dragon crewmen in a building— Hyakowa thought that none of the people who normally worked in this area would come to work today, not with all the fighting going on in the city. He was willing to leave the dead hidden to be taken care of later, but there was no way he would leave a wounded Marine behind. Sergeant Eagle's Cry and PFC Clement, the other walking wounded Marine, formed the rear point.

Satisfied that the two squads were moving out in as good order as possible under the circumstances, Hyakowa fell in behind Ratliff.

Company L barely got into position before the van of the oncoming armored company reached them. The vehicles, fifteen TP1s, thirty medium tanks, and an armored staff car, came barreling in two columns down the middle of the broad boulevard leading from the city proper to the spaceport. Any infantry that might be accompanying the tanks couldn't keep up with them. Second platoon, on Company L's right flank, didn't wait for orders from Captain Conorado.

"First squad," the second platoon commander coolly ordered

over his platoon command circuit, "fire one Sierra Alfa, kill the nearside lead tank. Second squad, fire one Sierra Alfa, kill the tank behind the leader. Platoon, pull back as soon as Sierra Alfas are fired."

Second platoon was spread out in a colonnade of monuments and ornamental trees that shielded travelers on the boulevard from the ugly sight of the industrial area between it and the port. The trees afforded little protection from the guns of the tanks, but the monuments were heavy and close enough together to prevent the tanks from mounting an orderly charge. The industrial area began less than fifty meters behind the colonnade, a warren of small and medium three- and four-story buildings plunked down wherever was convenient or where there was space. Streets wended mazelike through them. If the tanks could be enticed to follow the Marines into the warren, they could be isolated and picked off one at a time. Maybe.

Two Straight Arrows fired almost simultaneously. The first squarely hit the TP1 leading the near column. The huge tank bucked violently and skittered out of control toward the far side of the boulevard, slamming into and knocking over a medium tank in the far column before skidding to a stop with its sides bulging, seams burst, turret canted. The medium tank that was second in the near column lifted several inches off the pavement then crashed back down, broken and dead. A second later it erupted as its ammunition cooked off. The closest following tanks were moving too fast to stop before they piled into the dead tanks ahead of them. The drivers twisted their steering yokes and stomped their drive petals to maneuver between and around the wrecks. One medium tank spun almost a complete 360 degrees before it skidded off the roadway and slammed into a monument. The impact shattered the ferrocrete base and toppled the bronze statue on top of it onto the tank's engine cowling, where it hit with a thud that shook the vehicle. A second medium slid sideways into the back of the medium killed by the Straight Arrow. A TP1, whose driver wasn't able to see the knocked-over medium tank in time, slammed into the damaged tank and began climbing over it. The medium shrieked and partly collapsed beneath the monstrous weight. The TP1's treads came fully off the pavement and it stalled. The remaining tanks managed to avoid the growing pileup.

The Marines of second platoon were on their feet, sprinting for the buildings to their rear before the missiles hit the tanks. They made it to temporary safety as tanks farther back in the double column, which had more time to slow their speed and avoid collisions, fired wildly into the colonnade.

Seventy-five meters to the left, the first platoon commander assessed the situation through his infras as soon as the tanks came into view and realized what second platoon was probably going to do—it was what he would do in the same position. "Platoon sergeant," he ordered, "take first and second squads and put them in the buildings to our rear. Assault squad, wait for my orders." He looked around to check the disposition of his assault squad, saw too many red splotches, then remembered the rump of third platoon was attached to his platoon. He switched to the circuit that allowed him to talk to the other platoon commanders. "Three-six, go with the rest of my platoon," he said. Having that extra assault squad with its two Straight Arrows could come in very handy very soon. He was senior to vanden Hoyt, so there was no question of who was in command in the platoon.

"Let's move back, Three," vanden Hoyt murmured into his all-hands circuit. Third platoon's assault squad went with him, back into the industrial warren.

First platoon's commander and assault squad watched as the two tanks were killed and the nearest survivors reacted with wild maneuvering. They felt like cheering as they watched another TP1 and two medium tanks crash into obstacles. Their elation didn't last, as other tanks began speeding through the gaps.

"Team one," the first platoon commander ordered, "kill the Tango Papa on the left. Team two, kill the medium on the right." He waited for the double explosion that told him the two missiles were fired, then commanded, "Pull back, on the double," and began sprinting toward the industrial warren. Halfway there he paused to look back and was rewarded by the sight of his infra screen flaring a red that nearly blotted out his entire vision, caused by another exploding medium tank that he hoped would block the boulevard. But when his screen cleared enough, he saw a splotch of moving red that told him the TP1 his first team had shot at was unharmed. He flipped his infra screen up for a better view and groaned. The Straight Arrow that should have taken out the TP1 had been wasted on the armored staff car. When he got the chance, he was going to have to chew someone a new asshole for that.

Lieutenant Colonel Namur, momentarily shocked by the sudden destruction of a half dozen of his tanks, had just taken the vehicle commander's position in the driver's module of his command car when a Straight Arrow passed straight through the passenger compartment, killing both the brigade S-3 and S-2 before exiting through the opposite side and detonating inside a nearby building, where it started a raging fire.

The vehicle's hull armor, vaporized by the Straight Arrow warhead as it bored its way through, skittered around inside the passenger compartment in the form of white-hot globules of molten metal, igniting everything combustible, including the men's clothing. The bodies of the two officers, cleanly decapitated by the round, slumped blazing at their consoles, but the two sergeants who accompanied them were pounding frantically at the release buttons of their safety harnesses.

Namur and his driver were largely protected from the initial blast by the armor plate that separated the driver's module from the compartment behind it, but within seconds everything around them was in flames too. The driver threw himself out of the vehicle through his escape hatch and rolled desperately on the ground, the lower half of his body wrapped in flames. Namur exited through the commander's hatch and, ignoring his own painful burns, raced around the vehicle, now entirely engulfed in flames, and dragged his struggling driver to safety behind a partly demolished wall. There they crouched, their clothing smoldering, listening to the screams of the sergeants still trapped inside.

Namur's mind whirred, blocking out the screams of the men frying inside the vehicle: He would not be able to replace the two officers who'd just been killed. He'd have to deal with brigade intelligence and operations himself now. His driver only then realizing how badly he'd been burned still thought they were lucky to be alive.

"What do we have?" Hyakowa asked. He'd sent Schultz and Dean to recon the engine noise that had been growing louder as the Marines slipped through the past several blocks.

"A tank company on that side street." Schultz pointed in the direction he and Dean had gone.

"I think it's the same company that hit us on the beach," Dean added.

"Why do you think that?"

"We counted thirty-four of 'em. One had a bent cannon, and I saw one on the beach get its cannon bent. Three others looked like they were in a crash."

"How could you see that?"

"They set up lights to work under."

"Hammer?"

"He's right."

"There's only thirty-four?" Hyakowa remembered there were supposed to be forty-five tanks in a company. Five were killed on the beach, there should be forty.

Schultz shrugged. "Could have been more."

Dean agreed.

"What else were they doing?"

"Nothing," Schultz said. "Just working on the damaged tanks."

"They looked like they were trying to get them back in operation," Dean added. "One of them had its treads off. I don't think they'll be able to straighten out the bent cannon, they'll have to replace it."

"What kind of security did they have out?"

Schultz lifted his infra screen high enough to spit.

"We didn't see any," Dean answered. "They probably think all the Marines are ahead of them, at the spaceport."

Hyakowa thought for a moment, considering his options. He had to get his two squads back to the company, which was still a couple of kilometers away. The company needed the men and the tank killers they carried. They could easily bypass the tanks if the tanks stayed where they were. But then there'd be a company of tanks behind the Marines, and that wouldn't do.

"What are the streets like?" the sergeant asked while he studied his HUD map. If the street layout was accurate . . . "Can we bottle them up?" He made two marks on the map and transmitted it to Schultz and Dean.

"East mark," Schultz said after looking at the map. "Move it right a notch, up two."

"Like this?" Hyakowa made the adjustment and retransmitted.

"Like that."

Two shots and they could stop or at least slow down an entire tank company—and still have four Straight Arrows when they rejoined Lima. Hyakowa made his decision.

"Chief, Rabbit, to me." In a moment the first and second fire team leaders joined him. He transmitted the map to them. "Here's the situation." In a few words he told them what he wanted. Schultz and Leach would wend their way through side streets, through buildings if they could, to the far, easternmost, end of the tank column. Dean would lead Ratliff to a position covering the rear of the tank company. Each pair would take one S.A. When Schultz and Leach got into position, they'd take out the lead tank. When Ratliff and Dean heard their shot, they'd take out the rear tank. Then everybody would reassemble at another spot he marked on his map—he'd lead the rest of the unit there while the four were getting into position.

"Questions? Then do it."

Leach and Schultz raced to the north side of a building directly east of their position. Dean led Ratliff south and they climbed through a window in a long building that ran east-west. As soon as the red splotches that showed the two Marines dropped out of his infra vision, Hyakowa signaled on his all-hands circuit and moved out with the rest of the Marines to the assembly point.

Vanden Hoyt and Bass saw how first platoon's platoon sergeant was deploying his men inside buildings facing the boulevard.

"That way?" vanden Hoyt asked, nodding toward a darker shadow between the dark shadows that were buildings under the star-lit sky. It looked like the mouth of a narrow alleyway that led deeper into the industrial complex.

"That way," Bass agreed. "I'll take point." He sprinted toward the doorway of a one-story, framework building flanking the alley's entrance.

Vanden Hoyt signaled the assault squad to follow Bass and brought up the rear of the truncated platoon.

Bass paused next to the door and flipped down his night vision screen. Using night vision and infra together slightly reduced the effectiveness of each, but neither one by itself might provide enough guidance inside a darkened building at night. He yanked the door open violently and dove through the doorway, tumbling halfway across the night-black room inside. As he tumbled he looked around with an infantryman's eyes, the muzzle of his blaster always pointing where his eyes looked. Before he came out of the tumble and bounced to his feet, he knew no one was in the room with him. Clarke, the first man in the assault squad, dashed into the room, spun to the side and came to a stop with his back against the wall next to the door. He quickly looked about, aiming his blaster where he looked. The only red he saw on his infra screen was Bass. Lonsdorf and Stevenson were right behind him. In seconds all of them were in the room. The room seemed to be a reception area of some sort. It held a smallish secretarial desk and chair, a settee, a couple of chairs, a low table, a coffee maker, and some computer data storers. The room was crowded with the nine Marines.

Vanden Hoyt didn't know what, but he could tell Bass had something in mind. He said curtly, "Lead on, Charlie."

Behind the room was a corridor that ran the length of the building. Bass led the way to the corridor's end. At each door along the hall he stopped long enough to kick the door open, or look in if the door had a window or was already open. The building was unoccupied except for the Marines. There was a door at the corridor's end. Bass opened it onto a narrow passageway. Directly across was the door to another building. This building was of sturdier construction than the office building, masonry and metal sheathing.

Bass turned back and raised his right arm to let his sleeve slide down and show his arm. He made a few hand signals. Lonsdorf and Clarke joined him in the passageway, against the wall on either side of the door. The others flattened themselves against the sides of the corridor. When everyone was where he wanted them, Bass looked at the door. It had a push plate and opened in. Arm still bare and visible, he gave Lonsdorf and Clarke some signs. They nodded. He put his hand against the push plate, shoved, and stepped aside.

The door swiveled slowly open on its gimbals. No light or sound came through the widening gap. As soon as the door was open far enough, Lonsdorf pushed himself away from the wall and dashed inside. Clarke was immediately behind him. Their paths crossed as they rushed at sharp angles away from the door. Bass ran inside on Clarke's heels. He zigged and zagged a few paces, then went prone behind a blocky something he barely saw in the darkness. The three Marines swept the interior of the building with their eyes but saw nothing threatening. The first building had windows that admitted enough light for their vision screens. This building was windowless; the only light came from the open door, and the vision screens were almost worthless. The darkness didn't affect the infra screens, though. Those screens showed no people but the Marines, and no operating machinery.

Bass stood. "All clear," he murmured into his all-hands circuit. Behind him vanden Hoyt led the other Marines in. He moved on, around and past the looming shadows of hardly seen light-manufacturing equipment, some freestanding, others table mounted. The platoon followed him. Ten minutes later he and vanden Hoyt were putting everyone into position in an area where the streets were barely wide enough for a TP1 to navigate, and many led to cul-de-sacs.

Vanden Hoyt nodded approval. "This is a good place to be when they come in after us."

"And if they don't come in after us," Bass said, "we'll convince them that they should."

Half a kilometer away they heard sporadic cannon fire from the tanks as the monsters hunted Marines. Twice they heard Straight Arrow rockets firing, followed closely by the explosions of killed tanks.

The long walls of the assembly building Dean and Ratliff entered were lined with windows that began not far above street level and continued almost to the ceiling. As long as they stayed close to the side walls, the dim splashlight afforded by the stars was enough to keep them from bumping into things. Deeper, they'd have to use their night vision screens, which neither wanted to do. Ratliff would have been more comfortable with Chan, or even MacIlargie—even though he and Dean were in the same squad, Dean wasn't in his fire team and he didn't know him as well as he did his own men. "Where are we going?" he asked as soon as they were in the building. Dean told him and he took the point.

When they left the building at its far end, they had to run across a wide street. They ducked inside another building, two-story this time, climbed to the second floor and went its length. They found themselves in a room that overlooked a short street leading into a lit up rail-switching area filled with tanks and the low din of shouting men working on the heavy beasts. One TP1 was clearly silhouetted just beyond the short street, barely inside the switching area.

"Are you sure two hits will block that area?" Ratliff asked. "There are only two ways out?"

Dean nodded. "Hammer and I got a lot closer than this. We looked at it from several spots. We only saw two ways in. That's all the map shows too."

Ratliff grunted. He didn't trust the maps, and even though he knew Dean was a good Marine, he didn't know in his guts that he could absolutely trust his scouting reports. But he trusted Schultz implicitly. If the Hammer said there were only two ways, there were only two ways.

"Gimme," he said, and held out a hand.

"What?"

"The Straight Arrow."

"It's mine. I'm a good shot with it."

"I'm a better shot. Gimme." Ratliff didn't know for a fact that he was a better shot with the S.A. than Dean was. But he did know how good a shot he was, and didn't know how good a shot Dean was. All hell was going to break out when they fired at the tanks. He wanted to make sure the way to them was blocked, that all they'd have to worry about was getting away from these windows before any tank fired at them, not worry about tanks rumbling after them. If one shot was all they were going to get, he was going to take it.

Hesitantly, almost resentfully, Dean handed the rocket over. "Where are we going to shoot from?" he asked.

"Right here."

Dean's eyes went wide. "We're inside a room. We should shoot it outside."

Ratliff settled the tube on his shoulder and put his eye to the sight. "I've got as pretty a sight picture as you can get right here. No need to go outside and try to find another spot. Probably won't find a cleaner shot anywhere else."

"B-But the backblast . . ." Dean sputtered. His legs twitched as he remembered the burns he'd gotten when the backblast from an S.A. washed over them during training.

"That's why we left the door open." Careful not to alter the position of the rocket, he turned his head and looked back. "Most of the backblast will go out the door. There won't be enough left to bounce off the walls and hurt us."

"But—"

"We do it from here."

From a few hundred meters away they heard the muffled,

echoing *whoosh* of a rocket being fired. Then a closer explosion, and the switching yard flared with the explosion of a tank. Ratliff took quick, careful aim and fired the Straight Arrow.

CHAPTER
FIFTEEN

Vanden Hoyt and Bass quickly took stock. There were only nine of them. They only had two tank-killing Straight Arrows. Worse, something had gone wrong with their communications, they couldn't talk to anyone except the seven members of their assault squad. They had to rely totally on what they could hear to know what was going on with the battle that raged around them.

It was obvious from the sounds that the tanks had come through the colonnade and gone after the rest of the company. The wide dispersal of the explosions—mostly tank guns—made it evident that the Marines were spreading throughout the industrial area. None of them seemed to be coming this way at the moment.

"We need to set up a barricade just beyond there," vanden Hoyt said, pointing to a turn about fifty meters away. They were leaning out a first-story window overlooking the narrow road along which they'd emplaced their few Marines. The road snaked its way through two rows of buildings with no passages wide enough to admit a tank intersecting it. At this place the road went straight for three hundred meters before taking a left turn.

Bass nodded, examining the area. "Right. If we lure them in here and block the road behind them we can get a lot of tanks trapped. I'll check it out." Before vanden Hoyt could object, Bass slipped out the window and darted to the corner.

The road beyond was just as narrow as before the corner. A TP1 could drive along the road, but it had no maneuvering room. Set up a roadblock, and the tank wouldn't be able to turn around, it could only back up. If the other end was blocked as well, however many tanks they managed to lure in would be blocked. But what could they use to make a barrier? He looked at the buildings lining the road. They were two- and three-story masonry structures, some with a lot of windows, some windowless. If they could bring down a few walls, that might do it. But there was that rule of engagement that forbade any unavoidable damage to the infrastructure. Knocking down walls would certainly damage the infrastructure. He shrugged mentally. They didn't have any explosives to knock down the walls anyway.

He tried a person-size door of a nearby windowless building. It was unlocked and swung open to a touch. Inside, when his infra showed no people or operating machinery, he slid the infra screen up and his night vision screen down. It was a warehouse stacked with crates. Most of them seemed to be on skids. He went to the nearest crate and found it was sealed shut. He looked around but didn't see anything at hand to unseal it with. Muttering to himself that a crate wasn't infrastructure, he stepped back, set his blaster to low power, then fired a grazing shot along a top edge of the crate. The plasteel bubbled and split where the fireball ran along it. Careful not to touch the hot surface with his hands, Bass pried a split open a little farther with his combat knife, then prodded inside. He gave a satisfied grunt. Whatever was inside the crate was hard, heavy, and gave out a metallic ring when the knife blade hit it.

Now, how could he get this crate and several others into the road?

Deeper in the building he saw a squat machine with a lip on uprights. He looked closer and saw wheels under the machine. It was a freight mover, exactly what he needed. He ran to the mover. "So what if I've never driven one of them," he said to himself. "I learn fast."

The assembly of buttons on the operator's lap console were totally unfamiliar to him, nothing like the controls in any vehicle he'd ever driven, and none of them were labeled with words—not that he'd be able to read them via the night vision screen. But he could make out icons on some of the buttons.

The one with the up arrow and the one with the down arrow seemed pretty obvious, but he couldn't be sure of any of the others. He felt along the edges of the console and found grips on its sides. Probably driving controls. But how did he start it? Maybe that button that didn't seem to have an icon and looked vaguely red. He pressed the unmarked button and was rewarded by the whirring of a motor. Experimentally, he pressed first the up then the down arrows. The verticals squealed and clanked and lifted and lowered the lip, just as he'd suspected. He twisted and tilted the hand grips one at a time to see what they did. One moved him forward, left, and right. The other controlled speed and moved him backward.

Confident that he knew basically what he was doing, he rumbled forward to a crate and maneuvered to slide the lifting lip under its skid. It took more maneuvering than he'd thought it would. Lip under the skid, he pressed the up button. The lifter groaned as it hoisted the crate, then began to tip forward as it kept lifting after the crate was cleared of the warehouse floor. Quickly, Bass hit the down arrow and lowered the crate. He peered at the console again. One of those buttons had to tell the lifter to stop lifting. Maybe the one with the two horizontal lines on it. He hit the up button again and then the horizontal lines as soon as the crate was clear of the floor. The lifting stopped. All right! Now, how to get the crate out of the building and onto the road? It was too wide to get through the door he'd come in by. He got off the mover and walked to the wall. There, where he couldn't see it from where he'd been, was a double door that looked wide and high enough. It was locked. It was also wood. Telling himself a door wasn't *serious* infrastructure, he went back to the mover.

Again, it took more maneuvering than he'd expected to align the front of the mover with the door, but after several attempts he was aimed straight at it. He told himself it took so much maneuvering because he couldn't see through the crate he was hauling. Then he accelerated as fast as the mover would go and rammed through the door. The wood was thick and hard, it resisted. But it couldn't resist long, and with a rending crack, it splintered all around its locking mechanism and slammed outward, to crash against the sides of the building. Still accelerating, the mover jumped across the road and slammed into the building across the way. Bass barely threw it into reverse in time to keep it from going through.

That was when somebody took a shot at him.

The bolt passed through the operator's compartment behind him, close enough that he felt the heat of its passage—he could smell the acrid aroma of burnt hair. Bass dove out of the mover and hit the ground prone. He belly-crawled away from the mover, keeping it between him and the direction the shot had come from. Wait a minute, the shot came from the direction the Marines were in. He twisted around to face back, but remained flat on the street.

"Cease fire!" he bellowed. "Who do you think you're shooting at?"

"Charlie, is that you?" came vanden Hoyt's voice.

"No shit it's me. Who do you think?"

"What are you doing, Charlie?" He could hardly get the question out he was laughing so hard.

Bass rose to his feet and began stomping toward his platoon commander. "Why are you shooting at me?" he demanded when he'd cut the distance in half.

By now the officer had himself under control. "We heard the crash. I thought a tank was coming through the building at us."

"No, it was me. Had to get through a locked door." Bass stopped and looked at the wall he'd nearly driven through. Tanks were bigger and stronger than movers. If a mover could burst through one of these walls so easily, a blockage wouldn't work.

Vanden Hoyt saw where he was looking and guessed what he was thinking. "I've seen the vids too, Charlie. A tank can go through one of those walls. But they can't go sideways. There isn't room in this road for a tank to turn. That's why we picked this place, they don't have maneuvering room. If we block the ends so they can't get through, they'll be stuck."

Bass grunted; the ensign was right. He hoped. "If nothing else, they'll be slowed down."

"Any more movers in there? The job'll go faster if more than one man's doing it."

There were two more movers in the warehouse. And another two in the next warehouse. Vanden Hoyt and Bass made their plans while other Marines built the barricade. In fifteen minutes they had a barrier of heavy crates six meters high and even wider across the width of the road, and more crates stacked against the inside wall of the warehouse. They would have done more but a platoon of tanks entered the area they were in.

Dawn was breaking.

Dean turned to run out of the room as soon as Ratliff fired at the tank, and was knocked back by the blast of superheated air that bounced off the wall next to the door. He barely heard Ratliff say, "Got it!" The blow of hot air wasn't enough to daze him, but all of his attention was taken by the fire that suddenly licked all around the frame of the door—the door that was their only way out of the room.

Ratliff turned and swore when he saw the fire. "Don't stand there, let's go!" he shouted. Putting action to words, he ran through the growing flames, shielding his face with an upflung arm. Dean followed, and they both got out with no more than a light singeing. Dean began to slap at the smoke wafting from one sleeve as he ran behind Ratliff. Then they were staggered by the concussion from a tank round that hit the ceiling of the room they'd just vacated. A few pieces of shrapnel zinged through the air past them and they were peppered by bits of debris.

"You okay?" Ratliff asked.

"I'm okay."

"Then we better get out of here right now."

Another round hit in the room behind them. The flames grew, sending flickering light ahead of them. The sound of another cannon shot was almost drowned out by the roar of many tank engines starting up.

"Positions, everyone," vanden Hoyt ordered into his all-hands circuit. None of the five Marines operating movers took the time to turn off the motors; they didn't have time to waste. Besides, the low whirring of the motors would be inaudible under the roar of the tank engines.

Bass sprinted to the building from which he and vanden Hoyt had examined the narrow road, and dove through a doorway just before the first tank rumbled into view. Clarke, who had been operating one of the movers, raced with him. They made it into a stairwell before that tank passed a window in their line of sight. Corporal Lonsdorf and Lance Corporal Stevenson were waiting for them on the second floor. Lonsdorf had found a position where he could see out while still being shielded from any infra devices the tanks might have. He had the team's Straight Arrow. Stevenson stood by with the assault gun.

"How many?" Bass asked when he reached Lonsdorf. Until the fighting started, they were avoiding radio communications in case the tankers were able to monitor their frequencies.

"Six so far," the assault gun team leader replied. "They've got real good spacing, twenty-five meters between tanks. If it was us, not all of us would get caught." If Marines moving in a column ran into an obstacle, they wouldn't bunch up behind their point, they'd maintain interval. If the Diamundean Armed Forces were well enough disciplined to maintain their interval, fewer than a dozen tanks would fit into the four-hundred-meter length of the narrow road between its entrance and the roadblock.

"Let's hope they aren't as good as we are. Any sign of infantry?"

"Negative." Lonsdorf shook his head and grinned. His training had taught him that properly trained and equipped foot soldiers could defeat armor unless the tanks had infantry to protect them.

"Here's hoping they aren't as good as us. Let's get into position." Crouching low enough that their heat signatures couldn't be seen by the tankers, the Marines headed for the back stairs. Lonsdorf led; he'd scouted the route while Bass and the others were preparing the roadblock. When they reached the door that gave egress to the street the tanks had come down before turning onto the narrow road, Bass took the lead again.

He stood next to the closed door and listened. He didn't hear any tanks still coming, all the noise was in the direction the tanks were headed in. Cautiously, he cracked the door open and peered out. Nothing was visible coming toward him. He eased the door open farther and stuck his head out. The last tank, a TP1, was fifty meters away, making the turn. Halfway into the turn it suddenly stopped.

Bass ducked back in. "Damn! Its turret is reversed."

"They saw you?"

"No, I don't think so. The tank commander was standing up, but he was looking ahead instead of to the rear." Marines called the tail end of a column the "rear point," which always watched to the rear so no one could come up behind them unobserved. This tank was supposed to be guarding the rear, but the commander wasn't looking that way.

"Can I get a shot?" Lonsdorf asked, hefting the S.A.

"Maybe. You'll have to." If Lonsdorf couldn't get a shot and kill that tank, the trap would fail and they'd all get killed. Bass moved out of the way.

Lonsdorf opened the door the rest of the way, got onto his belly, eased his upper body through the doorway, and laid the S.A. tube across his shoulder. The rumbling of the TP1's engine increased. Lonsdorf fired, but a brief burst from the TP1's plasma gun hit near him before it was cut off by the explosion when the S.A. struck the tank. The combination of plasma bolt and blast overwhelmed Lonsdorf's shield and the assault gun team leader went up in a flash.

Bass swore. Clarke gagged. Stevenson gripped his assault gun tightly and said, "Let's get some."

"In a minute," Bass said. He took a quick look outside to make sure the tank was dead and blocking the road, then flicked on his command circuit and called vanden Hoyt. "Six, this is Five. We blocked the entrance. They're trying to push the tank we killed out of the way." The dead tank was already rocking back and forth as the tank ahead of it worried at it. But the dead tank was at an angle at the corner and the tank ahead of it couldn't push it in a straight line.

"Five," vanden Hoyt said back, "we were right—they can't

swivel their turrets, all their guns are pointed forward. Put the plan into effect."

"Roger, Six."

"Everybody all right?"

"Negative, Six. Three-two-one is down."

"Bad?"

"The worst."

There was a pause before vanden Hoyt said, "Roger, Five. Carry on. Six out."

Bass flicked off the transmitter and used voice to speak to his remaining men. "They can't bring their guns to bear. Let's get behind them and take out anyone brave enough to stand up in the turret."

Stevenson was the first one out. He tried to climb onto the dead tank to make himself level with the turrets of the line of tanks in front of him, but Bass ordered him away from it.

"That thing's too hot, it's ammo could cook off. Let's stick with the plan."

Stevenson kicked at the dead monster, then entered the building across from the one they just vacated. A second-story window overlooked the three-hundred-meter road. Bass could see thirteen tanks, five TP1s and eight mediums edging back and forth, but mostly back. Close at hand a medium tank kept rocking backward, bumping the dead TP1 in hopes of moving it out of the way. Near the far end of the column a tank commander stood tall in his turret, talking into a radio.

Stevenson sighted in on him as soon as he and Clarke had the assault gun, a heavier, rapid-fire version of the standard infantry blaster, set up.

"Not yet." Bass put a restraining hand on the gunner's shoulder. He scanned the row of tanks, looking for other open turrets. He saw one. "Fifth tank up, the TP1. Think you can put a burst into it?"

"You know I can."

"Six," Bass said into his command circuit, "can somebody take out the dumb guy? We can get number five from my end."

"Affirmative, Five. Wait until the dumb guy's down."

"Roger." Then to Stevenson, "Somebody else'll get him. Soon as he goes down, pour some fire into that open turret.

"Got it."

"That's probably the platoon commander," Bass said softly of the standing man, the one he'd called "the dumb guy" when he talked to vanden Hoyt.

"Yeah," Stevenson said. "I'd like to get me an officer."

"You'll probably get another chance. But if you fire at him first, that hatch might close before you can—"

Thirty meters away to their right front, two blasters fired. Both of them hit the standing officer. Before the man completely collapsed, Stevenson was pouring fire into the open turret of the closer tank. He thought he heard abruptly cut-off screams as the bolts hit around the bottom of the forward lip of the hatch opening and spattered plasma inside the tank.

The tank lurched when the dead driver fell onto his controls, then rolled forward and slammed into the rear of the medium tank in front of it. Tortured metal shrieked and gears ground loudly as the medium being pushed tried to reverse, but the TP1 was too heavy and powerful, and the medium lacked the power to stop the heavy tank that was slowly shoving it toward the next one in line.

Other tanks started swiveling on their treads, trying maniacally to turn in the narrow space so they could shoot back, but the space was too narrow for them to turn or to get any momentum to bull through the walls that hemmed them in.

"Want me to try for the command tank?" Stevenson asked. The hatch the dumb guy had stood in was still open.

"Think you can get into it?"

"I can try." At nearly three hundred meters, it would be very difficult to strike the lip of the open hatch at an angle that would ricochet plasma into the tank crew compartment.

"Do it."

Stevenson carefully took aim and pressed the firing lever. A stream of plasma bolts so close together that they looked like a stream of fire shot out of the muzzle of the assault gun and splattered on the turret.

Almost immediately, the other assault gun added its stream

of plasma at the command tank. Between them, they managed to get enough fire on the open hatch to overheat and ignite the oxygen inside it. The tank swerved wildly, stuttered, then sat still, looking almost deflated.

"Cease fire," Bass ordered. "I think you killed it." He clapped Stevenson on the back.

One TP1 was dead. Two more had their crews killed, and maybe enough of their controls and electronics were fried to keep them from being used again without major repairs. A medium tank was slowly being mangled between two TP1s. It was beginning to look like the assault squad was winning its battle against the tank platoon. Then the farthest visible tank fired its gun at the wall in front of it and crashed through the weakened structure. Inside the building it found space to turn around, and came back out with its gun pointed toward the Marines.

"Time to get out of here," Bass said. They ran. Over the command circuit Bass heard vanden Hoyt ordering the rest of the Marines away from their positions. They headed for the rendezvous point. It wouldn't take the remaining tanks long to escape the trap now, and the Marines only had one rocket left.

"Are they bottled up?" Hyakowa asked when the two killer teams rejoined the unit.

"We killed ours," Leach reported. "They aren't getting out that way in a hurry."

"Same here," Ratliff said.

Hyakowa looked at them in the dawn light. He could see them in part because he knew how to look at a man in chameleons. He could also see Ratliff and Dean because where the fire had singed their uniforms, the chameleon effect wasn't working anymore.

"You look like you were in more of a firefight than you bargained for."

Ratliff shrugged. "That's the hazards of firing a rocket inside a structure."

Amazed at the calm understatement, Dean looked at him. If they'd been a little slower getting out of that room, or if the angle of the shot had been a little different, they might have been burned to death.

"Now, again, are they trapped?"

Schultz spat to the side. No fighter worth the name is ever trapped for long.

The two men looked at each other, wondering if the tanks really were trapped. "For a little while," Leach finally said. Ratliff nodded agreement.

Hyakowa's mouth twitched. "I hope for long enough. I managed to get contact with a flight of Raptors, long enough to give them the coordinates. They said they'll check it out on their way back from their strike at the spaceport. If they've got any ordnance left, they'll use it on those tanks."

Schultz spat again. From the sounds of the battle in the direction of the spaceport, he didn't think the Raptors would have anything left.

"We can't dwell on it," Hyakowa said. "We still have to get back to the company. Here's where we're going." He transmitted the HUD map with the overlay he'd made showing their route. "Let's move it out."

CHAPTER
SIXTEEN

The advance of the 493rd Battalion of the First Tank Brigade against the Oppalia spaceport ground to a halt by mid-morning. The first wave of six hundred Marines of the 34th FIST had been quickly reinforced by the FIST's remaining four hundred Marines. Not long after came the 13th FIST and its thousand Marines. The thousand infantrymen, supported by twenty Raptors that were able to fly unimpeded by the badly mauled Diamundean air forces, had killed or damaged fifty-one of the battalion's 133 tanks. Afraid to launch a direct assault against the Marine positions, the survivors hunkered down under cover and turned their engines off so the Marine infras couldn't spot them.

If the tankers had known that the infantrymen of the two FISTs were down to twenty-seven Straight Arrows and had no other tank-killers, that sixteen of the Marine Raptors were sitting idle at an expeditionary airfield waiting for resupply of ordnance, and the four Raptors still in the air only had enough power left in their cannons to take out three tanks, they might have been bolder. The Marines of 34th FIST had lost a hundred men killed, another thirty or more wounded. Thirteenth FIST's casualties were a little lighter. Plasma weapons tend to kill, and most of the Marine casualties were the result of fire from plasma weapons.

It's a fact: a properly trained and equipped infantryman can go *mano a mano* with a tank and have a reasonable chance of coming out on top; a thousand infantrymen without tank killers are just so much mincemeat for eighty-two tanks.

But Major Kleidsdale didn't know the Marines were improperly equipped to take on an armored battalion, much less a full brigade, so he ordered his tankers to take cover. And he gave his tankers orders to make full use of all passive vision devices and to concentrate their fire on Marines carrying rockets. He hoped the Marines would get bored and come looking for his battalion. While his staff wracked their brains trying to come up with a better plan, Kleidsdale listened in on the brigade's tactical net.

The 19th and 225th FISTs were in full control of the seaport after mangling the 552nd Battalion. Lieutenant Colonel Namur was holding the 687th Battalion in reserve, waiting for one of the other battalions to make a breakthrough that the reserve battalion could exploit. Lots of luck, Kleidsdale thought. The 552nd had faced all four FISTs as they came over the beach and was in even worse shape than the 493rd. Kleidsdale switched to the command net to see what he could learn of the situation on the rest of Diamunde and wished he'd done that earlier.

The rest of the First Armored Division, the Fifth and Eighth Tank Brigades, had mounted up and were on their way to Oppalia! In another hour, two at the most, relief and reinforcements would arrive. The division, Major Kleidsdale was sure, could defeat the Marines. He turned off the radio and assembled his staff. Had he continued listening for a few more minutes, his staff meeting might have proceeded a bit differently.

"Hellcat Flight, this is Hellcat Lead," said Lieutenant Commander Ragrun, commanding officer of VFA 112, "check in."

"Hellcat One," came the voice of Lieutenant Cehawk, the Hellcats second in command.

"Hellcat Two," chimed in Lieutenant Brush.

One by one, in order, the sixteen pilots of VFA 112 reported in. Using all of their vision-enhancing and emission-detecting devices to aid in their search, the Hellcats' Raptors were flying in combat formation at angels thirty, looking for Diamundean aircraft to engage and destroy. During the four hours they'd been flying they saw sign of many bogies, but none were flying. Every Diamundean aircraft they spotted was on the ground, crashed and shattered by them over the past couple of days. They thought the Marines on the ground in Oppalia should be having an easy time of it with nothing more than a few tanks to worry about.

"Hellcat Flight," Ragrun said, a chuckle bouncing under his words, "we've been given a change of orders. Higher-higher thinks we bounced all the baddies and are wasting our time up here." He paused a couple of beats to give his pilots a chance to laugh at his wit, then continued, "The First Armored Division has been observed moving out of its base. Higher-higher thinks the spam-cans are on their way to bother our mudpuppy brothers on the ground in Oppalia." He paused again, pleased with his choice of words. "We are to intercept and convince them they don't have invitations to that particular party."

"Turkey shoot!" exclaimed Lieutenant (jg) Dule.

"Bunny hop!" from Ensign Prowel.

"Stand by for tacmap." Ragrun tapped a series of buttons on his tactical control panel and transmitted the overlay map to his squadron, showing them where they were and where they were going. The pilots acknowledged receipt of the map data.

"Close on me," Ragrun said, more businesslike. "Prepare to board the express elevator to the ground floor."

The pilots laughed and cheered. After four hours of looking for bogies that had already been shot down, going after spam-cans that couldn't shoot back sounded exciting.

Captain Hormujh stood tall in his commander's position, hips level with the turret hatch of his Teufelpanzer One. His Company B, 261st Tank Battalion, Eighth Tank Brigade, First Armored Division, was given the honor of leading the division to the rescue of the besieged First Tank Brigade in Oppalia. Impatient, he positioned himself behind his company's lead squad instead of between the lead and middle platoons, as was usual in a tank company column. He wanted more direct control of the point than a company commander normally had. He was in a hurry to get to Oppalia and begin the counterattack. In his opinion, the First Tank Brigade had always been overrated. He thought the Eighth was the best in the whole Diamundean Army. Had the Eighth been in Oppalia when the Confederation Marines came ashore, he believed, no rescue would need to be mounted. And, of course, he thought Company B of the 261st was the best tank company in the entire army. He'd stake his life on it. In his haste to get to Oppalia to demonstrate that superiority, he had already increased the interval between his company and Company A from two hundred meters to a kilometer and a half.

The pass through Rourke's Hills was less than two kilometers ahead. Rourke's Hills was an ancient mountain range, eroded down to ridges and hills that rose mere hundreds of meters at its greatest heights. Most of the littoral plain between the hills and the sea was buildup from that erosion. In a straight line, the pass through Rourke's Hills was fifteen kilometers long. The way the road twisted around the remnant mountains, the passage was closer to thirty kilometers. Aside from his impatience to get to Oppalia to begin the counterattack, Hormujh wanted to get through the pass as fast as possible. The Confederation Navy had full control of the air, and it flew the same kind of aircraft the Confederation Marines did. Intelligence reported Marine Raptors attacking and destroying ground targets, some of which might have been tanks—the intelligence reports were fuzzy on that point. If the Marine Raptors could attack and destroy tanks, the navy Raptors probably could as well, though he suspected the navy pilots weren't as good at attacking ground targets as the Marines were. Regardless, if Raptors came, he didn't want to be in the pass when they arrived.

"Baker Two-one, this is Baker Papa," he said into his communicator. "Speed it up, we don't have all day here."

A few hundred meters ahead the lead tank sent up swirls of dust as it accelerated to ninety kilometers per hour. The interval between Company B and the rest of the First Armored Division increased more rapidly. Captain Hormujh decided to disable the battalion circuit on his communicator before the battalion reassembled. That way he could claim he never got the order to slow down that was coming at him now from the battalion command.

The Hellcats had plummeted to angels two and were cruising in a tight, bomber formation north over Rourke's Hills. There were several passes through the ancient mountains, but one pass was on an almost direct line from the First Armored Division's base and the port city of Oppalia. The string-of-pearls had detected the division headed toward that pass. The Hellcats were to fly directly to the pass, then make a starboard turn and head inland until they intercepted the division's van, then blow the hell out of it.

"Stand by to hang right in two mikes. Mark," Lieutenant Commander Ragrun said into his squadron circuit. "Confirm."

"Hang right in one fifty-five," Lieutenant Cehawk said.

"Starboard flip in one fifty," said Lieutenant Brush.

"Go right in one-four-five," came from Lieutenant (jg) Dule.

Prowel confirmed. At five second intervals the pilots confirmed receipt of the order. The Hellcats were forty-five seconds from their next maneuver when Ensign Hagg, the most junior and last member of the squadron to reply, gave his acknowledgment. The squadron flew on at four hundred knots.

"On my mark, peel right," Ragrun said half a minute later. He began counting down to the turn. ". . . three, two, one. Mark!"

The Raptors of VFA 112 peeled off to the right onto an eastern heading.

"Tally ho!" Lieutenant (jg) Blackhead suddenly cried.

"Fish in a barrel," Ensign Cannion shouted simultaneously.

Below them, traveling at a high speed through the pass, were forty or fifty tanks.

"Angels four, turn about," Ragrun ordered, no humor in his voice. The pass was narrow here and had frequent turns. If the Hellcats were going to strike the tank column below them, they'd have to be very careful not to wipeout themselves. "Orbit," he ordered as soon as the squadrons had reversed their direction of flight and gained altitude.

"Flight one, recon," Ragrun ordered. He tipped his wings and dropped out of the orbiting formation with Lieutenant Brush on his wing. "Throttle back," he told Brush. Both pilots reduced speed to two hundred knots. Ragrun dropped into the pass and cut his airspeed even further. He glanced up and grimaced when he saw rock slopes extending a couple of hundred meters above him, then he lowered his eyes and kept his attention riveted on the channel he was following. Here, not much more than a hundred meters above the roadway, the pass was barely seventy meters wide. He had almost no maneuvering room. Brush flew a few meters to his left rear, his eyes locked on the near point of Ragrun's left wing; he'd follow that wing tip as precisely as he could.

There they were! Ragrun spotted the company of speeding tanks as he made the next turn. All the tank commanders were standing in their turrets. He wished the pass went straight long enough for him to dare breaking Mach; the sonic boom would rattle the cages of those tank commanders. Probably wreak havoc in the interiors of the tanks as well.

Ragrun and Brush flew on past the column of tanks. Part of Ragrun's mind wondered where the rest of the First Armored Division was. Maybe the First Armored had changed its direction since the report he'd gotten, maybe this one company was all that was using this pass. But most of his mind was examining the pass itself, learning its twists and turns and analyzing how to attack the tanks in it. If his planes came in low for strafing runs, they'd have to fly very slowly in order to give themselves maneuvering room to avoid hitting the walls. The only other choice was the attack they called the "screaming meemie," which was hard on both the planes and the pilots. But the damn jarheads used the screaming meemie. On one of the few occasions during the voyage to Diamunde that Marine Raptor drivers were allowed in the Hellcats' wardroom, some of those damn jarheads had laughed about how much fun the screaming meemie was!

Well, Ragrun resolved, no pilot worth his salt was going to let any jarheads claim they enjoyed doing something navy pilots wouldn't do. At least with the screaming meemie they wouldn't have to worry about hitting the walls. But where were the rest of the tanks?

Captain Hormujh didn't duck when the Raptor flight zoomed overhead. He merely glared up at them until they disappeared around the next bend. If they came after his tanks again, they were in for a big surprise. If the Raptors were going to attack in

this section of the pass, they'd have to fly very slowly. He spoke
a few words into his communicator, then looked to his rear and
had the satisfaction of seeing five of his tank commanders
lifting assault guns from the interiors of their tanks and mounting them on top of their turrets. He faced front again and saw
two more tank commanders already had their assault guns
mounted. He was very pleased with his foresight. He suspected
he was the only company commander in the entire division,
perhaps the entire army, who realized the value of top-mounted,
free-swiveling guns for antiair defense. Other tank commanders of all levels, from company to division and maybe higher,
probably believed the propaganda that said the planes would fly
too fast for the guns to hit them without extensive radar and
computer guidance systems, and that the tanks' armor was
strong enough to defeat the weapons carried by the Raptors
anyway. Here, certainly, any man who knew how to press a
firing lever could hit an aircraft. And Hormujh didn't believe
the Confederation pilots would bother attacking a target they
couldn't damage.

Yes, those navy pilots would be in for a surprise if they dared
come back at Company B of the 261st.

Where was the rest of the division? The question wouldn't
leave Ragrun alone during the short flight back to the orbiting
squadron. It almost interfered with his ability to mark his
tacmap. But "almost" didn't count, and the tacmap was ready
when he and Brush resumed their positions in the formation.
All business now, he briefed his squadron.

"Hellcat Two, take Division Four west and find the rest of
those tanks. We only have one company down there, our orders
are to go after the division."

"Roger, Hellcat Lead," Lieutenant Cehawk said. "Division
Four, on me. Let's go get 'em." Four Raptors peeled out of orbit
and flew east, gaining altitude and speed as they went.

Ragrun didn't say anything to Cehawk, he continued issuing
orders to the rest of his squadron. "Divisions One, Two, and
Three, stand by to receive tacmap." He pressed the button that
transmitted the tacmap. He continued without waiting for re-

ceipt acknowledgments. "You can see where we are and where they are. It's narrow in there. I don't want to risk losing anybody because his speed was just a little too high or he was aiming too carefully and wound up running a wall. We're doing screaming meemies, by flight in division waves."

He was interrupted by a few groans. "I hate screaming meemies," Ensign Franks moaned.

"Belay that, people. It's the only reasonable way. First Division will be the first wave. Flight One will hit the head of the column while Flight Two hits the rear. Then Division Two. Flight Three will hit just behind the head of the column while Flight Four hits the center on a ten-second delay. Division Three will do the same for the back end of the column. Fifteen seconds between divisions. With any luck, we can kill that entire column in three passes. On my mark, break orbit, angels ten. Three, two, one. Mark!"

The twelve remaining Raptors angled away from each other out of the orbiting formation, then powered up for a steep climb. When they reached angels ten, they were almost directly above the tanks in the pass.

"Remember," Ragrun gave his final orders, "fifteen seconds between divisions. Division One, tally ho!"

The four Raptors of Division One heeled over and screamed almost straight down toward the tanks in the bottom of the pass.

At angels four Brush swiveled away from his flight leader and twisted in a 180-degree turn so they flew head-to-head.

At angels two, Ragrun locked his sights on the lead tank and pressed his cannon trigger. The cannon spat out seven plasma bolts before the dive pullout took over and cut the main engine and fired the vernier jets in the Raptor's nose. The jets stopped the aircraft's nose-groundward plunge and allowed momentum to carry the tail down. When the Raptor was pointed up almost vertical, the main engines flashed back on and it shot upward. To the untrained eye it looked like the Raptor hit an unseen wall not far above the heights above the pass and bounced. Twenty-five meters away Brush went through the same fire-and-bounce maneuver.

Nearly a kilometer away Flight Two used the same maneuver to hit the column's rear tank. Fifteen seconds later Flight Three struck the second tank and bounced upward. Seconds after that Flight Four hit a tank in the middle of the column. Then Division Four came down and hit two more tanks.

When the lead tank was hit by the cannon fire, Captain Hormujh was too shocked to react for an instant, but only for an instant. Then anger took over. Intelligence had failed to give warning of this tactic. Someone would pay for that failure. If he couldn't force the issue officially, he'd deal personally with whichever intelligence officer was responsible—and he didn't care how much rank that officer had. He looked up and saw four specks that rapidly grew in size, obviously four more Raptors coming down for another strike. Before he could speak into his communicator to warn his tankers, the sonic shock wave from the first Raptors hit and staggered him. In the front and end of the column, tanks swerved out of control as the shock wave slammed inside the tanks and shocked the drivers. The force of the blow put out the fires licking from the two damaged tanks.

Before Hormujh could recover, the shock wave from the second flight hit, and hit him even harder. This time tanks in the middle of the column went out of control. The column was in total disarray after the Third Division struck. Despite the rumbling of engines and clanking of treads, the pass sounded eerily silent after the third shock wave passed.

Hormujh recovered and looked up. High above he saw tiny dots as the Confederation Navy Raptors orbited to regroup for another strike.

"Report," he snapped into his communicator. In seconds he knew the worst. Four tanks were destroyed. Two others were severely damaged, most members of their crews killed.

"Assault gunners, aim up. We'll try to discourage them when they come down again." He didn't know at what altitude the Raptors opened fire, he hadn't even seen how low they got before they stopped their plummet. He suspected it was beyond the effective range of the assault guns. Still, seeing fire coming at them might make the pilots lose concentration on their aiming and cause them to miss. One might even lose control and crash.

He saw the Raptors break orbit.

"There, that didn't hurt, did it?" Lieutenant Commander Ragrun asked when all of his Raptors were orbiting. "Any educated guesses as to how many we killed?"

"I think we got them all," Ensign Prowel said.

"I don't know. They're awful tough," Ensign Franks said. "They'll probably be ready next time and flame some of us."

Ragrun gritted his teeth. He really should relieve that Franks, he thought. But a man deserved every possible chance. So far he hadn't allowed any bad guys to get away. Ragrun was about to give the order to make another strike when Lieutenant Cehawk's voice broke into the circuit.

"Hellcat Leader, this is Hellcat Two. We found the main body. They're approaching the east entrance to the pass."

Ragrun thought for all of a second. Their orders were to hit the division's van. Well, they'd done that. One damaged company wasn't going to be much threat to the Marines at Oppalia. They could hurt the enemy more by striking the main body. If the main body was close enough to the entrance of the pass, they might be able to destroy enough of the front tanks to block the entrance, and that would do the most good.

"Hellcats," Ragrun ordered, "break orbit and form on me east. We're going after the main body."

CHAPTER
SEVENTEEN

The admirals and generals assembled at fourteen hours for an updated situation report.

"Benny," Admiral Wimbush said to Rear Admiral Benton Havens, the Fleet Air Arm commander, "your Raptors went in first, so you begin. What have your attack planes done, what are they doing now?" Wimbush carefully avoided looking at the Marine generals; he didn't want to face the glares they were giving him.

"Thank you, sir," Benton said. He stood and walked to the map display. "As you can see"—he pressed buttons on the display's console, and a map appeared showing the 420,000-square-kilometer theater of conflict—"we effectively destroyed the Diamundean air forces during the two-day air campaign prior to the amphibious landing." A chart appeared on the right side of the display. It showed an hour-by-hour tally of contacts between navy Raptors and Diamundean aircraft and the results of those contacts. The numbers were impressive. In two days of conflict, Fleet Air claimed 230 contacts that resulted in 539 Diamundean aircraft shot down against the loss of only six navy Raptors. Equally telling was the frequency and spacing of contacts—they were most frequent during the middle of the first day, then declined until there weren't any at all during the last ten hours before the Marines landed. Havens pressed more buttons, and symbols appeared on the map. Yellow dots indicated contacts that resulted in no kills; red and yellow flames showed enemy aircraft shot down; red X's showed navy Raptors that were knocked out of the air. There were almost as few yellow dots as there were red X's.

"Well, Benny, it certainly looks like your people have done their job."

The grinding of General Aguinaldo's teeth was quite audible in the briefing room.

"What are they doing now?" Wimbush continued, as though he hadn't heard Aguinaldo's teeth.

"Sir, I have eight squadrons on combat air patrols looking for any Diamundean aircraft foolish enough to take to the air." He pressed more buttons. The contact symbols disappeared and eight curving lines representing the combat air patrols took their place. "The CAPs aren't having any luck, so they're being diverted to attack Diamundean armored columns whenever one is spotted moving toward Oppalia." He pressed another button and seven red and yellow flames appeared. "That's where we made interceptions."

"How many tanks have your Raptors killed?" Wimbush asked eagerly.

Havens paused before replying. Should he give the possibly inflated numbers his squadron commanders reported, or should he give the probably more realistic numbers his intelligence chief developed? He decided to look good. "Sir, my squadron commanders report 157 tanks killed, mostly TP1s." He paused again, this time for dramatic effect. "Gentlemen, that's an entire battalion of armor destroyed from the air before it could get into position to engage our Marines."

"And they're still hitting the tanks?"

"When I left my command center to come to this meeting, three of my squadrons were engaging enemy armor. I did not include those engagements or their results in the report I just gave."

Admiral Wimbush nodded. "Impressive numbers, Admiral. Thank you." He sighed with relief. At least Air was doing its job. He turned to Rear Admiral David Johannes, the Fleet intelligence officer.

"Admiral Johannes, can you give us an update, please."

Davey Jones Johannes cleared his throat and touched a finger to his collar as though he meant to loosen it, but changed his mind at the last instant. He stood up facing Wimbush, but didn't step to the front of the room to operate the map display console or look at the admirals and generals while he give his report.

"Sir, the First Armored Division at the Tourmaline mining complex has come out as we suspected it might. But either it is weaker than we thought or it didn't sally in full force. It seems to have only two brigades instead of the three we expected." He flinched when Major General Daly, the Marine assault commander, snorted, but went on. "The Second Armored Division has not moved from its defensive positions around New Kimberly. Another unit, which we have tentatively identified as the Fourth Armored Division—" Professor Benjamin barked a laugh. Johannes flicked his eyes in his direction but didn't turn his head far enough to see him. "—has moved from its concealed positions in abandoned mines in the Crankshaft sector and is moving toward Oppalia. It is currently stalled 250 kilometers south of the landing beaches, where two of Admiral Havens's squadrons are engaging it. What we think is the Ninth Armored Division is rounding the north end of Rourke's Hills and is about six hours from Oppalia. I believe Admiral Havens has a squadron on its way to intercept that division." He looked at the air commander, who nodded. "The 15th Heavy Division, which is comprised of tanks and self-propelled artillery units, is moving into position to intercept any forces that land at Debeers Drift." He stopped talking and waited uncomfortably for a question.

"Thank you, Admiral," Wimbush said somberly. He still refused to look at the Marine commanders. "General Han, how are your landing preparations proceeding?" Admiral Johannes sat greatly relieved at not being asked about the origin of those four additional divisions.

The army commander rose to his feet and stepped to the front of the room. The intelligence screw-ups weren't his fault, he didn't need to be afraid to face the Marines. "Sir, I have every expectation that at dawn on the day after tomorrow, Third Corps will have its first elements on the ground. By the end of the day, Third Corps will be driving the four—" He looked at Johannes. "It's four now, isn't that right? Third Corps will be pushing the four divisions now closing on Oppalia back into the hinterlands. Or I should say the remnants of those four divisions. Between Benny's squadrons and my soldiers, four divisions will have a very short life expectancy. Two days later, Ninth Corps will be on the ground. If Third Corps hasn't had the opportunity to do it by then, Ninth Corps will destroy the Second Armored Division and occupy New Kimberly. I believe that should end this war."

"So nothing has changed in your plans or preparations?" Wimbush asked hopefully.

"Nothing, sir. Everything is proceeding as expected."

"Thank you, General." General Han resumed his seat.

Admiral Wimbush could no longer avoid looking at the Marines. "General Aguinaldo, the seaport and spaceport have been secured, is that correct?"

General Aguinaldo stood and marched to the front of the room; Major General Daly marched with him. The Marines assumed positions of parade rest, feet spread, hands clasped behind their backs. Aguinaldo fixed the assembled admirals and generals with the kind of look that general officers normally only use on incompetent subordinates who they are about to relieve of command.

"Sir," Aguinaldo began, "the 13th and 34th FISTs have occupied the spaceport. The 19th and 225th FISTs have the seaport."

"Thank you, General—" Admiral Wimbush began, but Aguinaldo spoke over him and continued.

"Admiral Johannes, get your people on the stick!" he snapped. The intelligence commander jerked as though struck, and his face turned a deep red. "The First Armored Division is neither weaker than previously believed nor did it leave part of its strength in the Tourmaline mining complex. The First Tank Brigade of the First Armored Division is in Oppalia. It greeted the first wave of my landing force. The four FISTs on the ground are fully engaged with a superior force of enemy armor."

He looked at General Han. "My Marines haven't had a chance to break out their golf clubs yet." Han had the grace to blush.

"Ge-General, we—" Admiral Wimbush tried to interrupt. Aguinaldo shot him a look that shut up the top commander. Wimbush looked thoroughly flustered.

"My Marines have been planetside for ten and a half hours. They have suffered nearly fifteen percent casualties." He looked at Admiral Clark; nobody could tell if he was looking for confirmation or defying the Fleet surgeon to dispute his figure.

"That's right," Clark said.

Aguinaldo nodded at him. "At this point, the Diamundean forces have suffered worse casualties, but that's only to be expected when anyone goes up against Marines. Our best intelligence, not my FIST commanders' initial reports"—he looked pointedly at Admiral Havens, who flinched—"indicate we have destroyed 103 of the First Tank Brigade's tanks. However, that leaves about three hundred more that my Marines are facing. The problem we have is, the assault waves went ashore with only 240 Straight Arrows. The four FISTs planetside only have ninety-seven S.A.'s remaining—not quite enough to kill one-third of the remaining tanks they're sharing the city with.

"If Major General Daly commits his remaining two FISTs, and I commit my Straight Arrow reserve, that will give the Marines planetside enough power to kill all but about thirty-five or forty of the remaining tanks—provided every shot scores a kill. Which leaves the landing force with nothing other than antipersonnel weapons with which to face the Diamundean armor that gets past Admiral Havens's eight squadrons.

"Gentlemen . . ." The way he said the word clearly indicated he thought they were anything but. "There is no way eight squadrons can stop three armored divisions—let alone however many more there may be that we don't know about." He glared at Johannes.

"Now, at this moment, the Diamundean forces have broken off. We suspect they don't realize how lightly armed my Marines are. But if they do sally forth, the infantry and Raptors of the four FISTs can probably defeat them, albeit with heavy losses. If they remain in hiding, I don't have enough strength to dig them out, so the FISTs must remain in position waiting for the enemy to move. While they are waiting, the enemy gets reinforced. Those reinforcements will be powerful enough before D plus three for them to mount an attack, even if they think every Marine on the ground is carrying a tank-killing rocket. If that happens, I dare say Third Corps will be unable to make its landing.

"We," he dipped his head toward Daly, "are open to suggestions as to how to proceed."

None of the admirals or generals had any suggestions other than for the Marines to hang in there for another two days. But before the meeting was over, Rear Admiral Havens agreed to commit twelve of his sixteen squadrons to slowing down the advance of the three known divisions. General Han, believing they wouldn't be needed later, offered to strip five hundred Straight Arrows from the IX Corps and give them to the Marines. "In a straight-up trade for golf clubs," he added in what sounded entirely too much like gallows humor. Those promises secured, the Marines marched out without waiting for Admiral Wimbush to dismiss them.

At sixteen hours the resupply of Straight Arrows reached 34th FIST. It took less than half an hour for the new rockets to be distributed to the infantry units. By then, third platoon was whole again, and Sergeant Hyakowa and the two squads with him had rejoined the company an hour earlier.

Ensign vanden Hoyt shook his head after he took delivery of sixteen tank killers. "Typical. They don't give us enough to do the job until after we need them the most."

"And even then they don't give us enough to finish the job," Gunnery Sergeant Bass grumbled. Still, he was pleased by the delivery. Third platoon had only used four of its initial issue of twelve rockets. The platoon was down to twenty-eight men, including the two of them, after losing Corporal Lonsdorf and Lance Corporal Van Impe. Bass took one Straight Arrow for himself. The command element should be too busy with running the platoon to actively engage enemy tanks, he decided. Still, it was always possible they'd find themselves in a situation where they wouldn't have a choice in the matter. "How do you want to distribute them?"

Vanden Hoyt didn't comment on the S.A. that Bass appropriated for himself. "The gun squad has the most to carry with its own weapons," he said. "And it's short a man. They still have one, right?"

Bass nodded.

"Give guns to two of them. That way every man except the squad leader and the gunners will have one. Split the others between the blaster squads."

"Leaves us an extra."

"Who's the best shot with them?"

Bass thought for a moment. "Probably Dean and Claypoole."

"They're in different squads. Give it to Eagle's Cry, he hasn't lost any men, right?"

Bass nodded and spoke into the squad leaders' circuit. "Squad leaders up. Hyakowa and Eagle's Cry, bring a pack animal."

In a few moments the three squad leaders joined them. Hyakowa's and Eagle's Cry's eyes lit up when they saw the stack of new rockets.

"Now we get them!" Eagle's Cry exclaimed. "Life would've been a lot easier earlier today if we had them to begin with." He was both relieved and glad of the resupply.

"Yeah," Sergeant Kelly said dully. The death of Corporal Lonsdorf was weighing on him, even though he knew that having more Straight Arrows earlier probably wouldn't have saved his life.

Hyakowa was fully business. "How many do we each get?" He noticed that Bass had laid one at his side.

"First squad, take six. Second squad gets seven," vanden Hoyt told them. "Guns gets two."

"Guns is the platoon's heavy weapons," Kelly snapped, suddenly angry. "How come we only get two? That gives me only three rockets for six men."

"Because you've got the guns," Bass said calmly. "You're already carrying extra firepower and weight."

"I've got four men who aren't carrying the guns." Kelly quickly scanned the stack of rockets and saw the odd number. "The guns are only good against tanks if they're unbuttoned. There's an extra. Let me have it."

Vanden Hoyt and Bass looked at each other. Bass gave an almost imperceptible nod.

"You've got it," vanden Hoyt said.

Kelly's anger dissipated as quickly as it had overcome him. "Thanks," he said.

"That gives me eight rockets for my nine men," Hyakowa said. "Who doesn't get one?"

Bass fixed an eye on him. "If you don't know your men well enough to decide that yourself, maybe I should make Leach the squad leader."

Hyakowa returned the look. "I know my men well enough," he said. "Just wanted to make sure you hadn't made up my mind for me."

Bass laughed.

Eagle's Cry turned to Godenov, the man he'd brought with him. "Now you know why I needed a faithful gun bearer," he told the PFC. "Pick up a load and let's get back to the squad."

Godenov's face twisted in a sour expression. Six Straight Arrows weighed more than fifty kilos. It wasn't fair of Eagle's Cry to expect him to carry all of that. But when he got to the pile of rockets and started to pick them up, Eagle's Cry hefted three to carry himself. Godenov's sour expression went away; his squad leader was an all-right guy.

Twenty minutes later vanden Hoyt was on the all-hands circuit giving the platoon the orders he'd just received. Thirty-fourth

FIST was moving out. Now that they had enough tank killers to do the job, they were going to find where the 552nd Tank Battalion was hiding and kill it.

CHAPTER
EIGHTEEN

Company B, 261st Tank Battalion, sped across the plain west of Rourke's Hills, avoiding the highways and roads Captain Hormujh believed the Confederation Navy Raptors were searching. The forty operable tanks that remained in the company after the air attack in the pass would reach Oppalia in three-quarters of an hour. Every tank that had the capability—only seven of them—was searching the sky for aircraft, paying special attention to the swatch of sky directly overhead. Hormujh grew furious at the memory of that unexpected attack. Who would have suspected that anyone could strike that way? He wondered how many times a Raptor could survive the stresses of that maneuver before it began to fall apart. Enough, he decided—enough times to destroy his company.

His tank's communications man and that of his executive officer scanned the frequencies, searching for messages that would tell him what was going on elsewhere. He was particularly interested in the movement of the rest of the First Armored Division as it made its way through Rourke's Hills. That movement was not orderly. He learned that the squadron that hit his company had moved off to attack the main body, and that squadron was relieved by two more squadrons. Many tanks—security concerns kept anyone from giving out numbers over the air—were killed by the attacking aircraft. Progress was piecemeal. Individual small units—battered companies, even platoons—made it into the pass and continued west, but the bulk of the two brigades was scattered east of the mountains, doing their best to evade fire from the attacking Raptors. A battalion or two had made it back to the base at Tourmaline and taken cover in the mines. Elsewhere, the Fourth and Ninth armored divisions were also having problems with Confederation Raptors. Only the Third Armored Division, slipping carefully along the west face of Rourke's Hills, was moving unmolested. Somehow, Third Armor hadn't yet been detected. Hormujh wondered how long that would last.

He wondered why there was so little activity in Oppalia. Yes, the First Tank Brigade had suffered heavy losses, but the invasion force had landed with only a few thousand men. Surely those few thousand had suffered heavy losses as well. The brigade should be fighting, but the communications he was able to intercept indicated otherwise.

He checked the time. In half an hour or a little more, his company would join the fight against the invaders at Oppalia. Then they'll see how real tankers fight infantry, he thought.

General Aguinaldo glared at the situation map in the air command center as though by sheer force of will he could make it change what it was showing.

This map, unlike the one in Admiral Wimbush's briefing room, was a real-time projection from the string-of-pearls. The computer that ran the map held a trid view of all the land in the theater of operations. Any part or all of the landscape could be shown in an overhead view or from nearly any angle. The computer overlaid tank icons onto the map. The icons were modified according to the best estimate of the condition of the tanks represented. Other flickering icons showed the Raptors that were attacking the tanks. On a small scale map that showed a large area, the icons were oversized. On a larger scale map, where a smaller area was shown, the icons could be to scale.

The current map showed Raptors attacking the Fourth Armored Division south of Oppalia. More than fifty tank icons smoldered red, indicating they'd been killed. The rest of the tank icons, more than eleven hundred, were scattered over an area larger than the two thousand square kilometers shown on the map—and all the icons were moving north. Aguinaldo glanced at the inset in the lower right corner of the map that showed where the main view was within the theater of operations. He estimated the tanks would reach Oppalia in four hours. He looked back at the main map in time to see two more icons turn red.

"Admiral Havens," he said with cold calmness to the air commander, "your boys seem to be doing well."

"Thank you, General," Havens replied grimly. He didn't want the Marine in his command center. Even though a full general of Marines was a lower rank than an army general, a Marine general outranked a rear admiral. Still, Havens could have banished the Marine from the center, but he didn't want to face the embarrassment of the general disobeying him. And Aguinaldo had already demonstrated his ability to cow Admiral Wimbush, who outranked him, so he couldn't expect any support from that direction if he tried to exclude Aguinaldo and failed.

"There are about twelve hundred tanks in a Diamundean division, isn't that right?" Aguinaldo asked.

Havens nodded.

"And you have three squadrons attacking the Fourth Division?"

Havens nodded again, reluctantly. He had an idea where this was going, and he didn't like it.

"It's been some time since I studied mathematics," Aguinaldo said almost conversationally, "but I think that works out to a ratio of twenty-five tanks to one Raptor. Am I right?"

"Your ability to do ratios doesn't seem to have suffered," Havens said tightly.

"How long do you think it would take one Raptor to kill twenty-five tanks?"

The muscles in Havens's jaw bunched. He could read the activity on the sitmap as well as Aguinaldo. There were too many tanks and not enough Raptors to stop them. It was evident that many of the Raptor attacks were missing their targets. He didn't answer.

As the two flag officers watched the map, a Raptor icon turned red and disappeared.

"What are your losses?"

Havens closed his eyes for a moment. "Seven," he said, so softly the Marine almost missed the word.

"Against the Fourth Division?" Aguinaldo asked, a hint of sympathy in his voice.

"Yes," Havens said softly.

"Similar against the others?"

Havens could only nod.

Sympathy came clear in Aguinaldo's voice now; he knew too well what it was like to lose men. "Air power alone has never won a war. Never will. All it can do is soften up the enemy so the infantry doesn't suffer as much when it goes in to make the final kill. Admiral, soften up those tanks so my Marines have a chance against them." He almost added, "please." He turned and left the command center. The weight of many Marines' lives pressed on his shoulders but failed to bow them.

Oppalia was both a major transportation hub and a mining and industrial center. Its million inhabitants worked hard, and then they played just as hard to work off the stresses and exhaustion of work. At that hour, well after the whistle signaled the end of the workday for most of the city's people, the streets in the entertainment and dining district through which Company L maneuvered should have been teeming with throngs of diners and revelers. Instead, the streets were empty and an eerie quiet ruled. Sidewalk tables in front of bistros sat vacant and unattended. Nightclubs, through whose open doors the sound of music and gaiety should have blared, squatted shuttered and dark. Theaters that normally had lines of people at their box offices stood abandoned. Stores and boutiques filled with the most fashionable goods imported from scores of planets should have been awash with shoppers; instead they stared, seemingly despondent, onto the empty streets. The half light of dusk, filtered through the atmospheric effluvia of mining and industry, gave the place a surreal appearance.

"Where are they?" Claypoole asked nervously when he joined Lance Corporal Linsman in a recessed doorway. Linsman had become his acting fire team leader, with Corporal Keto's death.

Linsman shook his head. He had no idea where the people who lived here were; he hadn't seen any more sign of them than Dean had. The city being so thoroughly abandoned made him shiver.

"What are *we* doing here?"

Again, Linsman shook his head. Nobody had told him what they were looking for or why anybody would think the Marines should search through a dining and entertainment district for tanks. "Maybe this is where their infantry is hiding." Like most of the Marines, he found it very difficult to believe that anybody would make an army without infantry.

"How sure are you they've got any infantry?" he asked.

Linsman shrugged; he wasn't sure of anything.

"Third fire team . . ." Eagle's Cry's voice came over their helmet radios. "Second fire team reports there's an alley twenty meters ahead of you, your side of the street. They see what looks like an open door in the alley. Check it out."

"Roger," Linsman replied. Second fire team was on the other side of the street. First fire team was fifty meters ahead and hadn't seen an open door when they went by. "Let's go," he said to Claypoole.

They slipped out of the recessed entryway and crept forward, almost touching the front of the building. Even though their chameleons made them effectively invisible to the naked eye, neither wanted to take the chance there wasn't anybody out there with infras who could spot their heat signatures. The fronts of the buildings were still warm from the sun that had shined on them recently; maybe they were warm enough to mask the Marines' heat signatures. A sign announced the building across the alley was the Barzoom Theater, "Presenting a One Minute Play Festival." Linsman peered into the alley when they reached it. Thirty meters down it he saw a wedge of shadow, probably a half-open door at the side of the theater. The alley was about two meters wide, too narrow for most vehicular traffic. The door must have been for cast and crew, rather than deliveries. Maybe it was an exit from the auditorium. With a light touch, he summoned Claypoole to follow him. Linsman slipped along the wall opposite the door, Claypoole following five meters behind him along the wall with the door. That way they could both fire at the door with minimum risk of Claypoole hitting Linsman.

Halfway to the door Linsman whispered, "Hold it." He thought he heard voices. He listened carefully. There seemed to be something just on the verge of audibility, but he wasn't positive. It sounded like it was coming through the doorway—if he was actually hearing anything at all. He took a couple of steps back, closer to Claypoole.

Speaking as quietly as he could, knowing Claypoole's helmet radio would amplify his words so the other Marine could hear him, he said, "Move to three meters from the door. I'm going to move forward and see if I can spot anything inside. If I haven't seen anything by the time I get past the door, I'll tell you what to do next."

"What if you do see something?"

"I'll tell you. Now move."

Stepping lightly, Claypoole eased forward. When he was three meters from the half-open door, he stopped and looked across the way. His infras showed him a red, man-size splotch four meters beyond the door. He smelled urine and glanced down. A fading red glow showed him where someone had emptied his bladder. Why didn't he go inside? Claypoole wondered. Surely there are facilities inside the theater. Then he stopped worrying about it. He looked back at Linsman and saw his red splotch shrink downward as Linsman dropped into a crouch, then moved closer as he came back. He saw an arm come out of the red and reach across to touch him. He followed Linsman back to the mouth of the alley.

"Birdie," Linsman said into his radio when they reached the street. "There's four tanks in there."

"How'd they do that?" Eagle's Cry sounded incredulous.

"Damfino. Looks like they drove over the seating and crushed it, though."

"What do they have, Rat?"

"Two TP1s, definitely. I think the other two are mediums. I only saw a few people. I think maybe most of the crews are in the tanks."

"Any other doors on the side of the theater?"

"Negative. Maybe around back."

"Wait one."

They waited until the squad leader made a report to the platoon commander.

In a couple of moments Eagle's Cry's voice came back. "Second squad, we got some bad guys in the Barzoom Theater. Okay, listen up. I reported. The boss wants us to see if we can get clean shots at them. First fire team, go around back, see what's there. I'll check the front doors."

It was a small block. First fire team was back in little more than five minutes. "There's a vehicle entrance in the back," Corporal Bladon reported. "Looks big enough for a TP1. There's also a personnel hatch. Both are closed. I didn't want to alert anybody, so I didn't try the doors to see if they're locked."

"That's okay, we probably can't go in that way anyhow," Eagle's Cry said. "Wait one."

They waited while he reported the new findings. The next voice they heard was Bass's.

"Second squad, listen up. Birdie, send a fire team to cover the back and kill any tank that comes out. Have a fire team cover the side door with blasters in case any crewmen try to get out that way. Bring the rest of the squad, we're going in the front door."

"You heard the man, people," Eagle's Cry said. "First fire team, did you see a position where you can cover the back door and have enough room to fire your Straight Arrows?"

"Affirmative," Bladon replied.

"Go. Let me know when you're in position. Third fire team, cover the side exit. Second fire team. On me."

Linsman signaled Claypoole with a light touch, and the two took positions at the mouth of the alleyway, Linsman on the left and Claypoole on the right. They lay prone, their blasters pointing at the door. Claypoole made a disgusted face; he had to put his blaster to his left shoulder, and he was a right-handed shot. Then he put his discomfort aside. The corner of the building gave him cover from fire from the alleyway.

A moment later Corporal Bladon reported that first fire team was in position behind the theater.

"First fire team, Third fire team," Eagle's Cry said, "maintain positions. Second fire team, let's go inside."

Claypoole wondered where Gunny Bass was, why he wasn't giving the orders. He thought, from the directions Bass gave a few minutes earlier, that the platoon sergeant had joined them. Shouldn't he be giving the orders now? He gave a mental shrug. Maybe Bass was letting Eagle's Cry run the squad; maybe Bass was doing something different. He stopped thinking about it and concentrated on the side door. After a few moments he began concentrating on staying alert. What was it now, sixteen, seventeen hours since the Essays 34th FIST rode down from orbit were launched from the *Tripoli*? He suddenly realized he'd been awake for twenty hours or longer, and most of that time was under stress: first was the final preparations for landing, then the launch and hitting the beach and the fight on the beach; then finding the rest of the company—and evading the enemy when they could. During the afternoon lull, when they still expected to be counterattacked at any moment, he'd eaten a meal. As near as he could recall, that was all he'd eaten since morning chow back on the *Tripoli*. He blinked a few times, gave a jaw-stretching yawn. He rolled his shoulders, bunched and relaxed muscle groups all up and down his body in the exercises he'd been taught to maintain alertness. He looked back into the street in both directions to make sure nobody was coming up behind him and Linsman. Then he settled back to blast anyone who came out the side door. His consciousness faded and drifted.

The sudden crackle and sizzle of blasters from inside the theater snapped him back to full awareness. Abruptly, Claypoole's earphones, which had been silent since Eagle's Cry gave the order for the second fire team to follow him into the theater, were filled with the shouts of men in deadly battle.

"Did you get him?" Corporal Saleski called.

"I'm pretty sure," Lance Corporal Watson called back. Blaster fire drowned out any follow-up Saleski might have asked.

"Over there, get him before he gets away," Eagle's Cry shouted.

"They're going for the tanks, stop them!" Bass said, his voice booming. The blaster fire intensified.

"Look alive, Third team," Eagle's Cry shrieked.

Someone burst out of the side door.

The sudden firefight that he could hear but not see inside the theater tightened Claypoole's nerves so taut he didn't need the warning. His hand closed on the firing lever before his conscious mind knew he had a target. His plasma ball hit the Diamundean tanker a split second before Linsman's did, and the man flashed briefly into flame from the double hit. His charred corpse crumpled to the pavement. A second tanker tripped on the body and almost fell, sending Claypoole's second shot over him. The tanker looked wide-eyed at the mouth of the alleyway, his mouth gaping open in terror. Even in the dimness, Claypoole could see the whites of the man's eyes. He didn't hesitate, he lowered his aim and shot again. But the man was back up and trying to run away, the bolt blasting through his thigh. He shrieked and pitched forward, clutching at the limb. Claypoole hadn't seen a weapon. He didn't bother to shoot the man again, instead looked back to the door for someone else to come through it.

"Good shooting," he heard from Linsman. "If he lives long enough, maybe he can tell us where some of the others are hiding."

"First fire team, get ready!" Eagle's Cry shouted, and Claypoole became aware of the engine noise that had begun while he and Linsman were shooting at the two tankers who came out of the door they were guarding.

"Take cover!" Bass called.

Over the rumbling of the tank, Claypoole heard the staccato crackling and whoosh of a plasma gun firing a long burst. None of the Marines in the building had an assault gun. Claypoole knew someone had to be firing a plasma gun on a tank. The engine noise changed pitch and the sound of gears grinding and treads turning echoed from the theater. The rising pitch of the engine became a roar, followed by a crash as the tank drove through the doors at the back of the building. That crash was followed almost immediately by the blast of an antitank rocket and an explosion when the Straight Arrow hit the tank. That was followed a second later by an even louder explosion when the tank's ammunition was set off. Debris clattered loudly, then the ground shook when the tank's turret thudded to the ground. More debris rained down in the back street. Then there was a moment's silence.

"Eagle's Cry, report," Bass said, breaking the silence.

"Second squad, report by fire teams," Eagle's Cry ordered.

"First team, we're all okay," Bladon reported.

"Second fire team, everybody's all right," Saleski said, relief clear in his voice.

"Third is fine," Linsman said. "We've got a prisoner, if he's still alive."

"Get him," Bass said. Then added, "All right, people, we've got a fire starting in here. I think we should move to a safer position. Anybody know how to drive a tank?"

As the squad assembled in front of the theater, Bass reported to vanden Hoyt. He used the circuit that allowed all the members of the squad to listen in.

"Three Actual," Bass reported, "Three-five. I've got some good news and some bad news."

"Give it to me, Five," vanden Hoyt said. His voice sounded dull; Claypoole suspected he thought the bad news was heavy casualties in second squad.

"First bit of good news is, we captured three tanks."

"WHAT?"

"Yeah. They're inside a building. We killed their crews, we own the tanks."

"What's the bad news?"

"First bit of bad news is, there were four tanks. We killed one of them when it tried to get out and it's blocking the exit for the other three so we can't get them out."

"Give me the rest of the bad news, how many casualties?"

Bass glanced at the tanker whose leg was barely hanging on. "Nineteen dead, one wounded. But he looks like he's going into shock, we need a corpsman if we're going to keep him alive."

"Nineteen dead? But there were only ten of you!"

"Hmm?" Bass's face shields were up; the Marines could clearly see his grin. He was deliberately holding back the fact that they were all right. "Yeah, that's right. But any day ten Marines can't swab the deck with twenty dismounted tankers is the day those ten Marines should be retired."

"Charlie," vanden Hoyt said with more than an edge of anger, "are you telling me we don't have anybody down?"

"I'm not telling you that, I thought you knew it." Bass's eyes twinkled.

Vanden Hoyt's sudden, breathy release of tension was clearly audible over the radio. "Stop jerking my chain, Charlie. Anything else to report?"

"There's a fire started inside the building. We don't have a lot of time to do it, but I'd really like to get those tanks out of there. We could sure use them."

Another voice broke into the transmission; it was Captain Conorado. "Lima Three-five, this is Lima Six Actual. Is there another way out of the building? Over."

"Six Actual, Three-five. Only through a wall. Over." Bass switched from casual talk to almost formal radio procedure.

"The building's on fire, is that right, Three-five? Over."

"Affirmative, Six Actual."

"Then the building's coming down anyway. If you've got anybody who can drive a tank, drive them through the damn walls, Three-five. Do you copy?"

Bass grinned wider than before. "Roger that, Six Actual. Over."

"Lima Six Actual, out."

"You heard the man, Charlie," vanden Hoyt said. " 'Drive through the damn walls.' Doc Gordon's on his way to patch up your prisoner. Lima Three Actual, out."

Bass was still grinning. "I say again, anybody have any idea how to drive a tank?" He was sure it was only a matter of time now before the 552nd Tank Brigade was totally defeated. If he knew about the other armored units battling their way toward Oppalia, though, he probably wouldn't have felt so good.

CHAPTER
NINETEEN

The new day found the Fourth Armored Division stalled south of Oppalia. The tankers were under what cover they could find, which was precious little in the open land. Severely battered Navy Air halted its operations against the Fourth shortly after nightfall, but not before it had killed some three hundred tanks. To the north, the Ninth Armored Division took cover in a densely wooded area, its drivers ordered to kill their engines in hope of dissipating their infrared signatures before the Raptors killed the division. The Third Armored Division, still undiscovered, was perched at the foot of Rourke's Hills, less than an hour away, hesitant to launch an assault against Oppalia. The navy attack against the Fifteenth Heavy Division succeeded in making it withdraw, but it withdrew in order and could still make a strike toward the Marine ground force. Only the First Armored Division was in full disarray. Some of its elements had made it back to the safety of the Tourmaline mining complex. Others were playing dead on the plain between Tourmaline and Rourke's Hills. Only scattered small units of the First Armored Division, little more than a battalion's worth, had made it through the pass and across the littoral plain to the eastern fringe of Oppalia. Captain Hormujh, commander of Company B, 261st Tank Battalion, found himself the senior officer among those small units, which made him their battalion commander.

Captain Hormujh had chafed the evening before when Lieutenant Colonel Namur ordered him to take a defensive position. Now that the sun was up and the tanks of a full battalion were under his command, he was even more impatient to engage the invaders. The scouts he'd sent out on foot overnight reported back that the Marine expeditionary airfield was only three kilometers away from his makeshift battalion, and the navy airfield a couple of kilometers beyond it. He was sure that if he was given the go ahead to attack, he would quickly eliminate a big part of the major danger to the tanks. He waited with growing impatience for Lieutenant Colonel Namur's reply to his latest report.

In orbit on the *Ogie*, the Confederation command had a serious problem to deal with.

Rear Admiral Havens's face was drawn; he looked like he'd had several sleepless nights instead of only one. He also looked like he'd rather be someplace else.

"Gentlemen," he said, standing in front of the map display that showed the positions of the two stalled divisions and the two that had withdrawn, but not the unknown Third Armored, "my pilots have accomplished their primary mission." His voice was tired and he didn't sound like he fully believed what he was saying. "They have halted the advance of two divisions on Oppalia, and driven two others back with heavy losses." He touched the console and several hundred red icons appeared on the map. "Our best intelligence estimate"—he nodded to General Aguinaldo—"aided by low-flying reconnaissance drones, is that we killed nearly nine hundred of St. Cyr's tanks, and possibly fifty mobile artillery pieces." He paused and seemed to be searching for what to say next.

"There's been a price," General Aguinaldo said into the silence.

Havens nodded. "We've lost fifty-two of the 190 Raptors we committed to the fight." He shook his head with disbelief. "Their ground forces have proved better at fighting my Raptors than their air forces were." He cleared his throat and gave a shake of his head before continuing. "I can replace nearly all of my losses with the four squadrons that haven't yet been committed, but that would leave Navy Air without reserves. In short, if we resume our attack today, we don't have enough aircraft to destroy the four divisions that we know about."

Admiral Wimbush listened to Havens's report with growing consternation. If the Diamundeans resumed their attack toward Oppalia, there was no question they could defeat the Marines and wipe out the planethead. Such a defeat could prevent the army from landing and cost the invasion force the entire campaign. That would prematurely end the careers of every one of the admirals and generals in the room, most notably his own.

"What do you propose to do, Admiral?" Wimbush asked, not sure he was going to like any answer his air commander would give.

Havens managed not to flinch when Wimbush called him "Admiral" instead of by name. "Sir, I think we should hold back any attack until somebody moves. If one of the divisions resumes its advance, I will commit all of my squadrons to stopping it."

"What if more than one resumes its advance?" General Han asked. He was also well aware of the risk to the planethead.

"We stop one, then move on to the next," Havens said weakly.

Han shook his head. His best option seemed to be to move the landing of III Corps up a day. He'd have to check with Lieutenant General Bosworth, the Corps commander, and see how far along his preparations were.

Wimbush turned to the senior Marine, "General, how long can your Marines hold out?"

"Against a multidivision armored attack, with just a few hundred Straight Arrows, our organic air, and no artillery?" Aguinaldo didn't think that question deserved an answer. "I'm going to commit one of my two reserve FISTs. That way my Marines will have a better chance of knocking out the First Armored Brigade in a hurry. That might discourage the other divisions from resuming their advance." He looked at Havens with a mix of sympathy for his losses and anger for the losses his own Marines faced.

Then Wimbush broached the subject that bothered him even more than the loss of aircraft.

"Admiral Johannes, why are we not getting string-of-pearls surveillance over Oppalia?"

The intelligence chief looked to be in even greater distress than the air commander.

General Aguinaldo went bolt upright—nobody had told him they'd lost string-of-pearls surveillance. His people on the ground didn't know that; he had to get the word to them.

Sergeant Eagle's Cry blinked against the harshness of the rising sun. He squinted to shield his eyes, but all he saw moving was the detritus of unswept streets lifting as the sun turned on the local atmospheric engine and set eddies of air into motion. He looked to the other east-facing window in the living room of the third-floor apartment his squad used as an observation post in its overnight position. He saw Lance Corporal Justice Goudanis's face hovering a meter and a half inside the window. Goudanis was keeping watch seated at a small table, far enough from the window to be unobservable from outside, close enough to have a wide field of view. His blaster lay across the table, pointing out, his hand rested on the weapon. A Straight Arrow tube stood propped against the side of the table. Goudanis shielded his eyes by tipping his head down so the lip of his helmet shaded them.

"You can't see all the way to the horizon that way," Eagle's Cry said.

Goudanis shrugged. "Don't need to," he replied, his voice thick from lack of sleep. "They won't be coming from that far away." Goudanis turned away from the window to look toward his squad leader. "They're probably less than a hundred meters from us. That's all the farther I have to see." He turned back to the window. "Someone told me that last night."

Eagle's Cry smiled lightly. He was the one who'd told Goudanis the Diamundean forces were probably no more than a hundred meters away. Eagle's Cry glanced out the window again to make sure nothing had changed since he looked away, then said, "I'm going below to get everybody up. I'll send someone to relieve you in a few minutes."

Goudanis grunted in reply.

Eagle's Cry had to go out onto the street to reach the rest of his squad. Most of them were in the shop that occupied the first floor of the building. Bladon and Nolet were inside, looking out the display window.

"See anything?" the squad leader asked.

"Nothing," Bladon said. Nolet shook his head.

"Better chow down now, we might be moving out soon."

"You know something you haven't told us?" Bladon asked.

"You know nobody ever tells squad leaders anything until they have to do it." He went through the shop to the room in back. Idly, he wondered where the people were who lived and worked in the entertainment and dining district. The Marines hadn't seen any civilians during their advance the previous afternoon, and no one was at home when they occupied the upper story apartments to use as overnight observation posts. He dismissed the thought.

Five Marines were asleep in the back room—Linsman and Claypoole, and Corporal Barber's assault gun team. Barber opened his eyes as Eagle's Cry entered the room.

"Sun's up," Eagle's Cry said in an ordinary voice. "Reveille, reveille."

Barber sat up and stretched. The others rolled over and groaned. They'd all taken turns on watch; nobody had enough sleep the night before.

"Can't be, it's too early," Claypoole mumbled.

"Gimme another ten minutes," Neru murmured. Barber reached a leg out and kicked his gunner's boot. Neru yelped, then sat up stretching and yawning.

"Rat, you and Claypoole go upstairs and relieve Juice. Take chow with you and eat."

"Sure." Linsman sat up and loudly cleared the night phlegm from his throat. Rubbing his eyes, he stood. "Let's go, Rock. No amount of beauty sleep's going to do you any good."

Claypoole groaned, then arched his back and jumped to his feet.

Eagle's Cry continued to the back of the shop. As he went through the rear exit he heard Linsman say, "Stop your complaining, it's your own damn fault. Nobody made you enlist in the Marines, it was your decision. You're just getting what you deserve for doing something so dumb."

The street in back of the building was just wide enough for a medium tank, and one was sitting there. Brigadier Sturgeon had been delighted by the capture of the three tanks. He wanted to take them and use all three for the defense of the expeditionary airfield, but the entire infantry chain of command from Eagle's Cry all the way to Commander Van Winkle objected. They'd found them, they wanted to keep them. Sturgeon relented and let them keep one medium. Even though everybody from the battalion commander on down wanted the tank, possession went back down that chain to the squad that captured it. So Sergeant Eagle's Cry found himself the proud owner of a medium tank. It would have been a wonderful addition to his squad—if he had any idea of how to use a tank. But he didn't, so he parked it out of harm's way overnight. Corporal Bladon's fire team occupied it during the night. One man was supposed to be on watch at all times while the other two slept. Bladon was standing in the commander's hatch when Eagle's Cry stepped into the street.

"Did you learn anything?" Eagle's Cry asked his senior fire team leader as he clambered onto the tank.

"Sure did," Bladon replied. He shook his head. "These Diamundeans must think their tankers are a bunch of dummies. Everything's marked with symbols. Even an illiterate could figure out how to do it from the markings. And the ones who can read, well, there's a manual at every station." His eyes were red-rimmed.

"You get much sleep last night?"

Bladon shook his head. "We were too busy learning about this tank. It was after twenty-four hours before I made anybody stop and go to sleep." It was just past six hours now, which meant none of them had gotten any more than six hours' sleep.

"Well, get them up and chow them down. Then you can tell me what you think you can do with this tank."

A few minutes later Ensign vanden Hoyt and Gunnery Sergeant Bass showed up, eager to learn what they could about the tank and how they could use it.

* * *

Captain Hormujh was finally given the permission he wanted to attack the airfields. He didn't bother to hold any sort of staff planning sessions or devise an elaborate plan. He felt there was neither time nor need for them. He knew the city, and so did most of the company and platoon commanders under him. This would be a quick and dirty raid where so many things could happen it didn't make sense to plan for any of them. The instructions he gave his subordinate commanders were simple. He told each of them which streets to follow west to the Marine airfield and where to stop—he hoped it was out of hearing of the airfield. His next order would be to assault. The biggest problem he saw with these orders was that the part of the city his tanks were going through was residential—it wouldn't provide them with much in the way of cover from either visual or infrared detection. But all of his commanders had shot down Raptors on their fight to the city, and the reports he'd heard from the other divisions told him they'd also had success against the Confederation Air. His only question was, if the Confederation forces saw his battalion approaching, would they be willing to attack inside residential neighborhoods?

He needn't have worried. The Marine and navy group commanders at the expeditionary airfields didn't know that the satellite views they had of Oppalia and environs hadn't been updated for several hours, and consequently they had no idea that they needed to provide their own aerial security. The Navy Air groups were sending out flights of Raptors to observe the stalled divisions, and remind the Fourth and Ninth Armored that they were still there and able to resume their attacks. The Marine group commander had one squadron, ten Raptors, flying in the front of the infantry positions, while the other four squadrons on the ground sat fueled and armed, with their pilots standing by in a ready room. None of the air units knew a battalion of tanks was approaching them.

Captain Hormujh stood in his commander's position with a stillness that belied the impatience with which he waited for the last of his company commanders to report that they were in position. He forced himself to maintain communications silence, with only the tersest acknowledgments of each company's arrival at its jump-off point. When the last commander reported in, he gave a two word command: "Attack now."

One hundred eight tanks, half of them TP1s, rolled forward at top speed.

The first hint the pilots of Marine Attack Group 33 had that the morning was about to change from quiet was when the box in the ready room squawked, "*Scramble, scramble, scramble. Bogies on the ground, in sight and approaching fast!*"

"Is this a joke?" Captain Hans "Pappy" Foss yelled back at the box. He was out of the door by the time his words finished leaving his mouth. Whether he thought "bogies on the ground" was a joke or not, he reacted automatically to the *"scramble"* command. He'd covered better than half of the sixty meters to his Raptor when the oncoming tanks finally registered on his mind—they were half a klick away and closing fast. "My God," he murmured, and threw his sprint into overdrive.

Foss's crew chief was climbing out of the cockpit when he reached it. "All revved and ready to go, Pappy," the corporal shouted over the roaring of the Raptor's engines.

Foss nodded at his crew chief as he jammed himself into the cockpit and rammed on his flight helmet. He raced through the shortest preflight checkup he'd ever made: He checked that the ground and air brakes were both off, the engine was powered up far enough to get him off the ground, and glanced around to make sure his ground crew had cleared off. Then he twisted the collective to aim the exhausts down for vertical takeoff and shoved the accelerator to max. The Raptor shot up. A round from a TP1 sailed through the air below his rapidly rising aircraft; a second's delay on his takeoff and the round would have killed him and his Raptor.

"Black Sheep Four, Sheep Three. Are you airborne?"

"That's an affirmative, Black Sheep Three," came the laconic voice of Ensign Geiger, Foss's wingman. "You want to do this in orderly fashion, or ethnic fire drill?"

"Let's start off orderly. Angels one." Then he had to twist the collective to horizontal flight because his altitude was already passing through angels one. A quick glance to his left rear showed Geiger in the wingman's position meters away from his wing tip.

Foss rolled his Raptor onto its right side so he could get a clear look at the ground and whistled. More than a hundred tanks were overrunning the airfield. A dozen billows of thick smoke laced with flame showed where several Raptors hadn't made it off the ground. He leveled off and looked around for other Raptors. He saw some, but not as many as he expected to see. Then he looked around the edges of the airfield and saw rising smoke in three more places, places where Raptors started to take off but didn't make it all the way up. As he looked, he saw another Raptor that was limping along a couple hundred meters below him explode.

"Jesus Muhammad," he murmured, then into his radio: "Who's in command up here?" Silence answered his call. The radio was set to the Black Sheep's frequency, maybe another squadron commander was airborne, but it seemed like he was the senior pilot in his squadron. "Black Sheep, Black Sheep, this is Black Sheep Three. Form on me, at angels two." He twisted the collective and shot up. At angels two he looked around and saw four Raptors forming on him and Geiger.

"That's it, just six of us?" he asked.

"I saw Yamata's plane get hit on the ground," came the voice of Ensign Mann.

"The skipper got hit as he was lifting off," someone else said. Two other pilots reported they'd seen someone's Raptor killed on the ground. Six was all that were left.

Foss gave another quick look around. The survivors of the other three squadrons didn't seem to be as well-organized. It looked like it was up to him to start the party.

"Black Sheep, Black Sheep. Angels eight, screaming meemies. Acknowledge."

Crisply and in order, the five pilots confirmed angels eight, screaming meemies. Foss led his understrength squadron to altitude at a sharp angle, then swung around so they were almost directly above the airfield.

"By flights, pick a target and go for it," he ordered. "I expect to see everybody back up here in about four-five." He rolled to his right and nosed down. He blinked. Where did they all go? Of all the tanks he'd seen on the ground just a minute or two earlier, only a half dozen were still in sight. He locked his laser sight onto one and asked, "Got it, Roy?"

"Got it," Geiger replied.

"Let's get it." He powered his dive.

Geiger peeled off Foss's wing to hit the target from a slightly different angle.

At angels three Foss hit the trigger and saw the stream of plasma bolts plunging toward the rapidly growing tank. At angels two he threw in the forward jets and boinged back up. He was able to focus his eyes again and draw breath without pain when he was back at angels four. He looked to his side and saw Geiger in place, bare meters from his left wing tip. At angels eight he orbited and looked down. Four tanks and a lot of Raptors were burning. "Where did the rest of those tanks go?" he asked no one in particular.

Those tanks were halfway to the navy airfield. Thanks to the Marines getting hit first, the navy pilots had an extra minute's warning before the provisional tank battalion hit them. Unfortunately for the navy pilots, they had more aircraft, and many of them had to run farther to reach their Raptors. Then again, none of them really expected whoever was attacking the Marines to simply swarm through and keep going. Captain Hormujh caught more than half the navy Raptors still on the ground. His tankers had a ball, especially enjoyable after the hell the navy Raptors had put them through the previous day.

Admiral Wimbush looked at Admiral Havens with profound disbelief. "I think I need to see a doctor about my hearing," Wimbush said. "Would you kindly repeat what you just said?" His voice cracked on the last syllables.

Rear Admiral Havens looked even worse than he had that morning. Still, he managed to dredge up a strong voice. "Sir, twenty minutes ago Diamundean armor launched a surprise attack on the expeditionary airfields at Oppalia. They destroyed sixty-three of the Raptors at the navy airfield."

"Sixty-three?" Wimbush repeated weakly.

Havens could only nod.

"Out of how many?" Wimbush didn't really need to ask; he knew there were only 138 navy Raptors planetside. He asked the question simply to give himself time to think. General Aguinaldo didn't give him that time.

"Before those tanks hit the navy airfield, they hit the Marine airfield," the Marine commander said stonily. "They knocked out twenty-one of the forty Raptors I had on the ground. Including the ten I had in the air, I only have twenty-nine left planetside. Thirty-nine including the ten still in orbit. Admiral, I'm afraid we have an intelligence problem that was serious and is rapidly getting worse."

Wimbush looked at Rear Admiral Johannes. "When will the string-of-pearls be fully operational again?" he whispered.

"Sir, we are using shuttle craft to reposition satellites. Hopefully, we'll have Oppalia covered again in several hours."

"Several hours?"

Johannes nodded numbly. No matter what happened from here on out, he was sure his career was over.

CHAPTER
TWENTY

Company L was still in its overnight positions. The word that filtered down was both battalion and FIST reconnaissance units were up ahead looking for enemy hiding places. Nobody in the company complained about having to sit around and wait. D-Day had begun too early and gone too late. Facing tanks with too few antitank weapons had been the most frightening thing most of the members of the company had ever done. The company lost five men dead and seven others evacuated with wounds or other injuries—heavier casualties than all but the most experienced of them had ever seen. It didn't matter to most of the Marines that they gave far worse than they got, D-Day had been hard, damn hard. They were able and willing to keep going, to search out more enemy tanks and kill them. But everybody—well, nearly everybody—in the company was glad for the respite.

Lance Corporal Dave "Hammer" Schultz stood glaring out a third-story window. Without looking to see if anybody was below, he spat.

Corporal Leach laughed.

Lance Corporal Joe Dean, who was looking out the other window, glanced at Leach and wondered what was so funny.

"Hammer, who'd you just spit on?" Leach asked.

"Don't matter," Schultz said with a grunt.

" 'Don't matter'? What if Commander Van Winkle was passing by and you spat on him?"

"Deserves it."

Leach's eyes bugged. "Why does our battalion commander deserve to be spat on?" This should be fun, he thought.

"We're sitting."

"So what?"

Schultz finally turned from looking for enemy to look at his fire team leader. "Marines ain't supposed to sit. We're supposed to kill." He resumed looking for someone to kill.

"Yeah." Leach nodded slowly. "But where are the people we're supposed to kill?"

"There." Schultz waved a hand in a way that indicated just about everyplace to the front.

"That's why we're sitting, Hammer. They're out there someplace, but nobody knows where. We can waste a lot of time and energy trying to find them, and maybe expose ourselves and take more casualties. Maybe use up rockets we can't afford on targets that aren't real. Both Battalion and FIST have recon out there, so when we go, we go where the bad guys are and don't waste effort or resources trying to find them. When we know where they're at, we'll go get them."

Schultz spat out the window again. This time he looked, but not until after he spat.

Dean shook his head and returned his attention to the front.

Overhead, the Raptors that had been flying to the FIST's front all morning turned and headed in the direction of the airfield.

The wait wasn't as long as Schultz made it seem. At ten hours, Company L got orders to move out. Their objective was a sports arena a kilometer and a half away. Recon reported there was a company of tanks hiding in it—and tankers on foot were providing outlying security; recon had fixes on a dozen four-man observation posts at ranges of up to five hundred meters from the arena. Third platoon led the way. Its first objective was to silently take out all the OPs between them and the arena. Naturally, *most* of the observation posts were between them and the arena, little of the security was on the other sides.

"Recon found them, why didn't recon take them out?" Claypoole grumbled as second squad prepared to move out from the storefront of the building they occupied overnight.

Linsman gave him a you-dumb-guy look. "That's not recon's job," he said. "Recon's supposed to find them, we're supposed to fuck them."

"All right," Claypoole conceded with full lack of graciousness, "then why doesn't FIST send Raptors in to hit them?"

Linsman couldn't resist anymore—he lashed out and slapped the back of Claypoole's helmet. "They want it done quietly. There's nothing quiet about a Raptor strike." He shook his head, and added almost to himself, "Dumb guy."

Claypoole glared at him, and for a moment he thought Linsman had called him "new guy," the hated sobriquet he'd gotten rid of two campaigns earlier.

"Gather around, people," Sergeant Eagle's Cry called. "Listen up carefully," he said when all of his squad members were close enough to hear his normal voice. He made marks on a civilian street map of Oppalia. The map indicated individual buildings as well as streets. "This is where we are." He made an X. "This is the arena." He drew a circle around a symbol on the map. "There are listening posts in buildings here, here, and here." He made three more X's, each on a different block; the building indicated by the middle mark faced a two- or three-square city block park. "We're going to approach them from this direction." He traced a line along streets that took them out of the way and allowed them to come at the building farthest to the right from its side. "We can go this far riding on the tank." He made another mark about halfway to the first observation post. "Second fire team will enter the building through the side door." He continued to make marks as he talked. "The OP is on the third floor. Third fire team, when second reports they've made their kill, you leapfrog to this building. It'll be tricky; recon didn't find any side door, and the rear door is jammed and can't be opened quietly. The OP is on the first floor." He shook his head. "Recon didn't say why it's on the first floor. Then third team leapfrog and get the third OP. It's on the second floor. Remember to do it as quietly as possible—we don't want to alert anyone we're coming." He looked at his men solemnly. "If you see anyone talking on any sort of communicator, hold off until they get off it. Questions?"

"What about first fire team?" Bladon asked.

"You've got the tank, you provide support if we need it. Stay two blocks behind the rest of the squad. I'll let you know if we need your help."

Corporal Bladon glowered. He didn't like being left out of the action this way. "Third fire team's shorthanded, let them have the tank and we'll take out an OP or two."

Eagle's Cry shook his head. "You're the ones who spent the night in the tank. You know how to use it, they don't. Besides, it takes at least three men to operate one of those tanks, and third fire team only has two men. Any other questions?"

"What do we do after we take out the OPs?" Goudanis asked.

"Don't be so anxious. I'll let you know when I find out. Ready? Let's do this thing."

They all headed for the tank.

"Listen, Birdie," Bladon said, walking next to his squad leader, "put Linsman and Rock in the tank with me. They both know how to drive. We can show them what they need to know about driving the tank, and show them how to operate the gun."

Eagle's Cry shook his head. "Still takes three men."

"Put Clement with them, or Nolet. Let one of the other fire teams be short."

Eagle's Cry stopped and faced Bladon. "Tam, you're my senior fire team leader, my most experienced. I need my most experienced man commanding that tank."

Bladon shook his head sharply. "I'm most experienced on foot, I don't have any more experience with tanks than anyone else in the whole FIST."

"You've got more time *sitting* in a tank than anyone else, you *studied* them more than anybody else. That makes you more experienced. You found the tank, you wanted to keep it, it's yours." He sighed. "Tam, you're probably going to have more than your share of the shit before this day is over. Now let's get going."

Reluctantly, Bladon dropped the subject.

In a couple more minutes second squad was all in or on the

tank and rolling to the point where the second and third fire teams would drop off and move ahead to kill the observation posts.

"What are they doing?" Claypoole asked nervously. "Do you think they got spotted and taken out?" He and Linsman were crouched with Eagle's Cry, waiting at the side of the building second fire team had entered five minutes earlier, the building with the first observation post to be killed.

"Snooping and pooping," Eagle's Cry replied softly. He was almost successful at keeping the concern out of his own voice. "It takes time to get to the third floor and into position without being spotted. Even with chameleons. Maybe the OP's reporting in and they have to wait." He shrugged.

"But what if—" Claypoole's question was cut short by the *crack!-sizzle* of a blaster.

Eagle's Cry held up a hand to forestall any questions. He listened carefully to his helmet comm. After a few seconds Corporal Saleski reported, "We got 'em."

Eagle's Cry let out his breath in a *whoosh*. "Let's go." He rose to his feet and trotted around the front of the building. Hugging the fronts of the buildings, the three Marines hurried to the next corner. A moment later, second fire team exited the building and followed. Two blocks farther back, Goudanis rolled the medium tank forward.

They were in a mixed residential area—mostly single houses and small apartment blocks, with a scattering of convenience stores and restaurants at ground level. Most of the buildings abutted each other; the few that didn't open directly onto the sidewalk seemed to be eating or drinking establishments that used the space between their front walls and the sidewalk for outdoor seating.

"Your turn," Eagle's Cry said to Linsman and Claypoole when the three of them ducked into a recessed bistro frontage short of the next corner. "Unless they've got some kind of infra or motion detector spy-eyes out there that recon didn't spot, they can't see you coming until you get there. Ready? Go."

Claypoole padded rapidly to the corner behind Linsman. They ran with a shuffling, gliding motion that made almost no noise. After several long seconds they reached the corner, crossed the street, and dropped to a knee next to the shop front recon had reported held a three-man observation post. Claypoole looked across the way at the park. Straight-boled trees grew in it, the foliage of the trees beginning three or four meters above the ground and continuing upward another twenty meters or so. That was why the OP was on the ground floor—the men in it could see under the trees; in an upper story, their view would be blocked by the trees.

Linsman put his head close to Claypoole's and whispered, "I'm going to take a look." A moment later he whispered, "Back."

The two Marines eased back toward the corner.

"Here's the situation," Linsman said in a low voice when they were at a safe distance. "It's a butcher shop. The door's open. One man is inside the window on the far side of the door. He doesn't seem to be paying a lot of attention. One is lying on a counter on the right side, maybe sleeping. I didn't see the third man. Damn, I wish we could go in the back way." He shook that thought off; wishing wouldn't change anything. "Here's what we do. I'll go in first and get the one on the left. You come in on my heels and go for Sleeping Beauty. We'll use our knives. Then we have to find the third one. Use our knives if we can, blast him if we can't."

"They'll see our knives," Claypoole said—the Marines' combat knives weren't chameleoned.

"We'll be too fast. And like I said, the one man watching isn't paying much attention. He probably won't see the knife until it's too late for him to react. The other one's sleeping, he won't see anything at all."

"Okay." Claypoole took a deep breath and tried to calm himself. Not knowing where the third man was bothered him.

"Put your hand on my back. Stay with me. I'm going to run. Let's go." Linsman stood and waited until he felt Claypoole's hand. "Go."

The two ran. Claypoole did his best to keep in step with Linsman, but he couldn't see the other Marine's feet to avoid stepping on his heels. The *tock-tock* of their footfalls were swallowed up by the park and didn't echo. In seconds they reached the butcher shop and Linsman pivoted right, through the door, then left to the watcher. Claypoole lost his pacing and his toe clipped the side of Linsman's heel when Linsman turned left. Claypoole staggered a step or two, then regained his balance and headed toward the man lying on the counter. Behind him, he heard the clatter of the watcher falling. He was still a couple of steps from the man on the counter when a door in the rear of the shop flew open and a blaster bolt flashed through the room. The bolt sizzled just past Claypoole, hit the front window and melted a wide hole in the glass. Claypoole glanced toward the rear door and saw a man in a gray uniform standing in the doorway, pointing a blaster. The man had a screen suspended from the front rim of his helmet and seemed to be looking straight at him. The muzzle of the blaster swung toward him.

"He's got infras!" Claypoole shouted as he dove under the counter his man was on. A blast shot through where he would have been if he hadn't dropped. He heard the man on the counter scrambling to his feet. Then he heard a scream and a gurgle and the blasterman thudded to the floor.

So did the man on the counter. He bumped into Claypoole and his eyes popped because he was touching someone he couldn't see. Even so, he reached out with both arms, groped at his invisible opponent, and locked his arms around him in a bear hug that squeezed the air from Claypoole's lungs. Claypoole was on his right side, his knife hand trapped under his body. The tanker tightened the bear hug while Claypoole struggled to suck in a breath as he twisted his knife arm free then shoved the blade into his opponent's kidney. The tanker gasped and arched his back, reaching a hand around for the knife, but Claypoole pulled it out and sliced the man's exposed throat. The tanker spasmed and thudded his heels on the floor while Claypoole skittered away from him.

The fight was over. They'd been in the butcher shop for ten seconds.

Claypoole rose to his feet and shuddered. It had been close, closer than it should have been. He looked at the man in the back of the shop and saw Linsman's knife being pulled out of his throat.

"He saw you, didn't see me," Linsman said as he wiped the blood off his knife on the man's gray shirt. "I threw my knife. He was sure surprised. So was I. That trick hardly ever works, even in the gym."

Claypoole shook his head, smiled.

Then Linsman got on the comm unit to report their kill.

Third platoon successfully killed all seven of the observation posts assigned to it. Killed: all twenty-seven of the Diamundean tankers were dead, no prisoners. The infantrymen of 34th FIST assembled in platoons a block beyond the arena's surrounding open areas, and platoon sergeants checked their platoons' loads of antitank weapons. Company L was the main assault force and would approach from the south. If they needed help, K Company was to the west and would come to their aid. Mike Company was stationed east of the arena to kill any tanks that broke out and tried to escape. The Marines heard tank engines rumbling from the direction of the arena.

There was no time now. They didn't know how often the OPs were supposed to report in, or where they were in the reporting cycle. As soon as the platoons were all assembled, Company L moved out at a trot, straight down the streets toward the arena. Each platoon carried a dozen Straight Arrows. Not enough to kill an entire company, but Commander Van Winkle didn't think the Diamundeans would stand and fight to the last tank. Either they'd surrender or they'd try to run. If they ran, there were two more companies of tank-killing Marines waiting to stop them.

But the tanks of Company F, 687th Tank Battalion weren't going to simply wait in the arena for someone to show up. Before Company L was in position, tanks began pouring from the arena.

"Take cover!" vanden Hoyt ordered on his all-hands circuit. He dropped next to a wall and stared forward in horror and disbelief. The tanks were rolling out of the arena. A whole platoon, maybe more, was already in the open space between his platoon and the building they were supposed to assault. A squad of the tanks were already entering the street in front of his lead men.

"First squad, kill the point tank," vanden Hoyt said urgently.

Sergeant Hyakowa, directly behind Corporal Leach and the first fire team, said, "Chief, kill the point." He used his infras to see where the first fire team's rocket carriers were, then rolled into the middle of the street to get out of the way of the Straight Arrow's backblast.

Schultz was already up on one knee, his rocket tube resting on his shoulder. "Mine," he said.

"Get him," Leach agreed.

Dean dove away from Schultz. He'd already been scorched by an S.A.'s backblast, he wasn't going to let it happen again.

The tank was almost too close to safely fire the rocket, but Schultz ignored the behemoth and took careful aim at the seam where the gun mount met the front glacis. He fired. The rocket struck the front of the tank. The depleted uranium casing of the warhead punched straight through the 300mm-thick armor and spewed globules of molten metal into the interior. The driver was densely speckled by the fiery liquid all up and down one side. His death was agonizing but quick. The gunner got the full force of the round when it bored through his belly, so he never knew he was dying. The tank commander, standing up in the hatch, was hit repeatedly in the front of his legs. He screamed and tried to lift himself out of the turret, but was flamed by a shot from Hyakowa's blaster. Hyakowa leaped to his feet and raced away from the still moving tank. The tank's other two crewmen lived a tiny fraction of a second longer before the exploding ammunition box tore them apart. The tank bounced up from the force of the explosion. Its turret was jarred loose when it hit the ground and it canted but didn't come off.

On the other side of the street Eagle's Cry shouted, "Let's go," as soon as he saw the turret wasn't going to land on anyone running by it. He broke past his second fire team and led the way. "Here!" he ordered, and stopped in the middle of the street directly in front of the dead tank. The five men of his squad who were on foot joined him. Directly in front of them the second tank in the column, a TP1, was trying to back up but was blocked by the tanks behind it.

"Oh, shit," Corporal Saleski exclaimed. Bladon had a tank, he wanted one too. "Second fire team, let's take that tank."

"NO!" Eagle's Cry shouted, but Saleski ignored him.

Watson and Clement ran with their fire team leader. None of the three believed that even if the tankers had infras and could see them that they'd be able to bring their guns to bear and shoot them before they were on the tank.

The tankers didn't bother with infras or aiming, they just started firing their plasma guns. A burst from the commander's gun turned Saleski and Clement into ash. The turret gun swept the back of the dead tank and around its right side. It flamed Eagle's Cry and sent Linsman and Claypoole, who were just rounding the left corner of the tank, staggering back. Leach was leading his fire team along the side of the tank when the gun fired and he took the full force of the plasma spray.

Claypoole, who had been behind Linsman, recovered first. He quickly glanced to his rear to make sure no one was in his backblast area, then fired his rocket. The second tank belched loudly, then burst at its seams. Watson barely jumped off it in time. The concussion from the explosion slammed him down and rolled him violently into the gutter, where he lay still.

Behind the rest of the platoon, Bladon stood tall in the hatch of his tank. Coolly, he directed Goudanis to fire the main gun and gave him aiming adjustments as the medium's main gun drilled rounds into the tanks trying to exit the arena.

Six more men from third platoon managed to reach spots where they could fire their Straight Arrows. They killed five more tanks. First and second platoons didn't have tanks coming up their streets. They reached open ground without resistance and fired all their rockets.

The fourteen tanks of Company F, 687th Tank Battalion, that

weren't killed by the Marines in the first three minutes of the uneven battle tried to run. They ran right into Mike Company. None of the tanks or their crews survived the encounter.

CHAPTER
TWENTY-ONE

"Admiral," General Aguinaldo said late in the afternoon of D plus one. The Marine commander had bulled his way past the phalanx of officers and enlisted men who were supposed to keep people—most particularly, angry Marine generals—out of Admiral Wimbush's office. "I have committed all of my infantry and aircraft to the fight in Oppalia. All I have remaining to commit is my artillery, which the rules of engagement forbid me to use. So far my Marines have killed close to half of the armored brigade that was holding the city. But the cost has been severe." He planted his fists on Wimbush's desk and leaned dominantly over the senior officer.

Wimbush leaned back in his chair and did his best not to look cowed. He wished his chair wasn't bolted to the deck so he could move it back a few inches.

"One of my platoons has lost six men dead and two others so badly wounded they're out for the duration," Aguinaldo went on. "That's eight men out of the thirty who were in that platoon when it went planetside." He didn't mention that no other platoon had suffered as severely as third platoon, Company L, 34th FIST, nor did he mention that this one platoon had killed at least fourteen tanks and captured three others. "My remaining Marines can kill the rest of that brigade, but there are three armored divisions within easy striking distance of the city. The navy doesn't have enough aircraft left to stop them if they move. I need help down there, and I need it now. If the Diamundean divisions move on the city, they will overrun the landing force. Then we will have no planethead and this operation will fail.

"Have I made myself perfectly clear, Admiral?"

"General—" Wimbush began. His voice squeaked and he cleared his throat for another try. "General, Third Corps can begin feeding its divisions to the surface tomorrow. Can you hold out that long?" He did his best to look like the man in command—which he didn't feel he was—rather than a supplicant.

"If those three Diamundean divisions don't move, yes. But if they do, there is no way my Marines can hold. And those tanks can move at any time, even before the army lands its first soldier tomorrow."

"I understand this, General. I'll have General Han get cracking on it right away." Wimbush cleared his throat again to cover the swallow he took to ease the dryness.

Aguinaldo stood up. "Tomorrow," he said flatly. "At the earliest. I'm losing Marines even as we speak, Admiral. We might not have a planethead for those soldiers to land on tomorrow. I request permission to land my artillery." Wimbush opened his mouth to tell the Marine he couldn't do that, but Aquinaldo kept talking and wouldn't let him speak. "Thank you, Admiral. I will have my artillery commence landing immediately. We can save the situation yet. Sir, when you need me, you will find me planetside, directing my forces. I will accompany the artillery down." Without waiting for a reply, he made an about-face and marched from Admiral Wimbush's office.

Wimbush sat for several long seconds, the fear and uncertainty he felt quivering his body. This Diamundean situation was totally out of hand. St. Cyr was far better equipped than anybody had any idea. The operation was about to become a disaster, if it wasn't already. At best, the court of inquiry he was going to face would demand his retirement. At worst, they would recommend a court-martial. He cleared his throat again and spoke a couple of soft words to himself to make sure his voice worked, then called out, "Yeoman, get General Han for me. On the double."

"Aye aye, sir," barked the petty officer first class who ran the admiral's errands.

Ensign vanden Hoyt wanted to withdraw third platoon so it could lick its wounds and they could hold a memorial service for the six Marines it had lost. Four men dead in a matter of seconds. He shuddered. And he'd already lost two men killed and two others severely wounded. That casualty rate simply didn't happen to a Marine platoon. The Confederation armed forces itself was almost the only power in Human Space that had weaponry capable of inflicting that level of casualties on shielded Marines. In the twelve years he'd been in the Corps, he'd never seen a platoon lose eight men on an entire campaign, much less four in one firefight. Vanden Hoyt dropped his helmet, then plopped down under a tree near the secured arena and hugged his knees to his chest. The veteran Marine found himself on the verge of tears. Six men dead in his platoon, and they'd been planetside for less than a day and a half. What kind of leader was he that he could lose that many men? He was the platoon commander, and his men and their lives were his responsibility. He had failed his men, he must have been somehow derelict in his duty. He should see Captain Conorado and get himself relieved of command.

A short distance away, Gunnery Sergeant Bass said, "Take over the platoon, Wang. Deploy them for defense."

Sergeant Hyakowa followed Bass's gaze, saw the platoon commander's half-hidden head, and nodded. "Sure thing, boss." Then into his comm unit: "Squad leaders up." He swore at himself. Second squad didn't have a squad leader anymore. "Bladon up," he added, calling the senior fire team leader from second squad.

Bass took off his helmet and sat next to vanden Hoyt. For a long moment neither man spoke. Bass waited for the younger man to become aware of his presence, and to give him time to compose himself.

"They were good Marines," Bass finally said. "Good men too."

Vanden Hoyt's nod was almost hidden from view.

"Every man in this platoon lost friends today. Most of us have lost friends before." He paused, wondering whether he should say the next thing on his mind, decided he should. "We'll all lose friends again. We're Marines. Marines fight. When men fight, men die. That's the way it goes."

"It's my fault," vanden Hoyt said, so softly that Bass almost had to ask him to repeat himself.

"It's not your fault. Eagle's Cry got overconfident. So did Saleski. That's why they died. For a moment, just a moment, they thought their chameleons gave them invulnerability instead of lending them invisibility. They exposed themselves to weapons that could overwhelm their shields."

"Right. And if I'd done a better job, they wouldn't have made that slip. It's my fault."

Bass nearly snapped. He felt the loss of the six as deeply as vanden Hoyt did, probably more deeply—he'd known those Marines longer, been on more operations with them, pulled liberty and leave with them. They weren't just men he led, they were friends as well, Marines he knew and respected.

"Mr. vanden Hoyt," he said sharply, "neither of us was in a position to see what second squad was doing. Even if one of us had, it happened so fast we couldn't have done anything to keep those Marines from dying. It's not your fault, it's not my fault, it's nobody's fault. Men get killed in combat, Marines get killed. That's all there is to it."

"It's the leader's responsibility. That makes it my fault."

"The leader on the scene, the only leader with the immediate capability of controlling the situation, was Eagle's Cry. Following your logic, that means it was his fault." Bass hated saying that. "But that's false logic."

Vanden Hoyt turned red-rimmed eyes toward Bass. "In less than a day and a half this platoon has lost six men dead. I've never seen such heavy casualties. It doesn't happen."

This time Bass did snap. He twisted to face the ensign, grabbed the front of his shirt and shook him. "Mr. vanden Hoyt, straighten yourself out. It does happen. A couple of years ago I was with a reinforced platoon that was nearly wiped out in one firefight that didn't last much longer than the fight we just had. Nobody got blamed for that one. Shit happens, Ensign. And when it does, we wipe it off and keep going."

Vanden Hoyt looked at him, shocked. He didn't know whether he was more shocked by being grabbed and shaken or by what Bass said about a reinforced platoon being nearly wiped out. He opened his mouth. Closed it. Opened it again. He didn't know what to say. He shook himself, then sat erect, took hold of Bass's hand and removed it from his shirt.

"Gunnery Sergeant, is the platoon properly deployed?" he finally asked.

"Properly deployed for defense, sir." Relief was audible in Bass's voice.

"Then carry on. We have a job to finish." He picked up his helmet and stood.

"Aye aye, sir." Bass also stood. He put his helmet on as he stood up, nodded at vanden Hoyt, then looked around for Hyakowa.

Vanden Hoyt watched Bass walk away. The platoon sergeant was right, he realized, they had a job to finish, and this was no time to quit. But the lives of his Marines were his responsibility. He still felt he had been derelict in fulfilling his duties. When the war was over, he thought that he might tender his resignation. He'd have to give that very serious consideration.

His thoughts were interrupted by a call from company headquarters for the platoon commanders and platoon sergeants to assemble.

"Artillery's joining us," Captain Conorado said as soon as his senior men were assembled. "The first batteries have already landed and are taking positions behind their respective FIST lines. Company L has been assigned security for the general support battery." The general support battery had bigger guns than the direct support batteries that were part of the FISTs. By changing barrels and breech inserts, they could fire 75mm, 145mm, or 200mm high explosive or penetrating rounds. They could also mount assemblies to fire plasma bolts that were the largest science and engineering could make work under battlefield conditions. The general support batteries were the most destructive weapons in the Marine arsenal. The platoon commanders and platoon sergeants looked at each other with wonder. General support batteries were rarely committed to combat. "You will meet the Golf Sierra battery when it lands and escort it to its position. Here's a map of where Golf Sierra is going to set up and your assigned positions around it." Conorado transmitted the HUD map. "Save it and pass it along to your squad leaders. We will be resupplied with Straight Arrows at the spaceport. Any questions?"

"How soon will the Dragons get here?" the first platoon commander asked.

Conorado cocked his head, listening to a growing drone. "Sounds like they're arriving now. You better get back to your platoons."

They went.

Captain Hormujh was exultant following the destruction his makeshift battalion wreaked on the two expeditionary airfields. He wanted to continue wreaking havoc on the invaders. Despite his impatience to keep bringing the battle to the Confederation Marines, he took his battalion to ground at Lieutenant Colonel Namur's order. The brigade commander promised him that his battalions would shortly launch a counterattack. Hormujh's battalion, Namur said, would best serve by attacking the enemy's rear once it was engaged from the front. Hormujh had to agree with Namur on that. But it was the brigade commander's plan of action, rather than his superior rank, that compelled Hormujh to quell his impatience and take his battalion into hiding.

Finally, the order for the counterattack was given. Hormujh fought to slow his breathing, suddenly rapid from the adrenaline surge that met the order. He looked at his watch and tried to make the time move faster by force of his will. The minutes ticked by slowly until the fifteen minutes he was to wait passed and he could finally give the order to move out. His first objective was the spaceport, where there had been much activity for the past three-quarters of an hour. If the Confederation forces were feeding in reinforcements, their landing had to be disrupted as quickly as possible, and the reinforcements already on the ground had to be mangled before they got organized. If supplies were being landed, he would destroy them before they could be distributed.

One hundred ten tanks, mostly Teufelpanzer Ones, rolled toward the spaceport where the Marine artillery was landing.

* * *

"Captain Pelham? I'm Conorado. My company is to escort your battery to your position and provide security for you." The spaceport stank with exhaust fumes from the Essays. The ground trembled with their launches and landings. Wind gusts thrown by the Essays buffeted them. Even with helmet communications, Captain Conorado had to shout to make himself heard over the roar of the Essays that were bringing the big guns planetside.

The artillery commander stuck out a hand. "Glad to meet you, Coronado."

"Conorado," the infantryman corrected as he shook hands.

"What? Sorry." Pelham waved a hand, indicating the Essays. "So much noise, I can't make out what you're saying. Where are we going?"

"Are your guns ready to move?"

Pelham looked to the side of the spaceport where his six twenty-ton, towed artillery pieces were hitched to heavy equipment movers, and a train of twenty Dragons carrying his gun crews and loaded with ammunition and spare barrels and batteries were waiting. "Ready whenever you are, Captain."

Conorado pointed toward the Dragons holding his company. "Mount up and follow us." His company already had its resupply of tank killers, enough so nearly every man in the company had one.

"Roger." Pelham turned and trotted to his command Dragon.

A moment later, back in his own Dragon, Conorado gave the order to move out. A moment after that he gave the order for the Dragons to spread out and take cover and for his infantrymen to dismount and deploy—more than a hundred tanks suddenly were roaring into the spaceport field with their guns blazing.

An Essay, just launching after off-loading its artillery cargo, was hit by an armor-piercing, high-explosive round. The round exploded in the Essay's cargo bay and tore gaping rents through its body. It dropped back to the field and skittered into another shuttle. Fire engulfed the two shuttlecraft.

Another AP-HE round slammed through the open cargo hatch of an Essay that was off-loading artillery ammunition and set off an explosion that shattered three nearby Essays and rocked every vehicle in the spaceport. When the smoke cleared, there was a crater twenty meters deep and eighty meters across where the Essay had been.

In less than half a minute's time every Essay that wasn't able to get off the ground was hit, fifteen orbital shuttlecraft killed or severely damaged.

By then the Marines of Company L were dismounted and deployed. Their first Straight Arrows were already aimed.

Schultz was the first to fire. He aimed broadside at a TP1 in the middle of the spaceport. "That one's for Chief, you bastard," he muttered as the rocket penetrated the tank's armor and split its seams. He looked to his side and grabbed Dean's S.A. off his shoulder. "You ain't going to fire it, I will," he shouted at Dean's astonished face. He fired and hit an oncoming TP1 just under its turret. The tank staggered and slewed to a stop. "That's for Eagle's Cry! You aren't killing my buddies and getting away from it, you sons of bitches!"

Dean looked at him, astonished, and backed away. As deadly as Schultz was, Dean had never seen him angry before. He suddenly thought that anywhere near Schultz was a dangerous place to be.

Schultz looked around for another unfired S.A.; he had more Marines to avenge. He didn't see anyone with a tank killer he hadn't fired. He looked back at the field, saw what he wanted to see, and waited with his blaster in his hands.

"You ready?" he snarled at Dean when another tank came close. "Let's get it." He bounded to his feet and ran at a tank as it sped by. He leaped at the tank and clambered onto its side.

Dean, thinking Schultz's action was suicidal but not knowing what else to do, followed. Somehow, he managed to get onto the rear deck of the tank. Almost immediately he knew he didn't want to be there—it was burning-hot from the engine's cooling fins.

Schultz was on top of the tank now, trying to wrest the commander's hatch open. It wouldn't budge, it was dogged and secured from inside. Drastic measures were required. He remembered in training that the gunner, Moeller, had said a blaster could burn through a tank's armor if the tank stood still long enough. Well, this tank wasn't going anywhere, not without taking Hammer Schultz along for the ride. He stood up, braced his legs against the side of the turret, and began shooting at one spot on the commander's hatch.

"Keep them off me," he yelled at Dean.

Dean goggled through his infras at Schultz, convinced more than ever that the man was crazy. He climbed to the other side of the turret so he was off the cooling fins and looked around for any tanks that seemed to be paying attention to them. His infra vision was totally blotted out by the large, red splotches of burning Essays and tanks. What seemed like a lifetime ago, on Elneal, he'd witnessed a scene that looked like a Bosch painting of hell. When he raised his visor so he could see, what met his eyes made that remembered scene look more like purgatory. The spaceport field was covered with burning vehicles, the dead tanks outnumbering the destroyed Essays. Debris was scattered everywhere, much of it glistening red with fresh blood. Unidentifiable chunks may have been, some certainly were, bits and pieces of people. Shadows that were tanks moved rapidly through the flames and smoke. Almost instantly Dean realized that even with infras, tankers wouldn't be able to see him and Schultz on top of this tank. And just as quickly, he realized other Marines wouldn't be able to see them either.

"Hammer, we've got to get off this tank," he shouted, and grabbed Schultz's arm.

Schultz shrugged Dean's hand off. "If you don't care about Clement or Keto, you go." He returned his attention to burning a hole through the commander's hatch.

Dean looked at the hatch. It was growing concentric rings of red, white, and red around the spot where Schultz was shooting. He wasn't going to leave Schultz alone, no matter how crazy and suicidal he thought this was. He shuffled around to the front of the turret and straddled the main gun, then added his own fire to the hole Schultz was burning, and ignored the heat that washed over him from the hole they were trying to burn through the armor.

A sudden clank behind and below him made him twist around.

The driver's hatch was open and a soldier was beginning to emerge with a hand weapon. Dean pointed his blaster and pressed the firing lever. The bolt burned the tanker's head half off. He started to turn back to the commander's hatch before it clicked on him that the interior of the tank was now open to him. He dropped down, managed to stick his blaster's muzzle through the open hatch and fire just as someone inside pulled the dead body out of the hatch. Over the roar of the tank's engine he heard a scream from inside. Encouraged, he fired at a different angle, then another and another and another. The tank lurched into a different direction. Dean, on his knees, shifted to another position and fired several more bolts into the tank. When there were no answering shots or screams, he ducked low and looked inside. Nothing moved in his view. He lowered himself and poked his head inside. He saw five charred corpses and a slow dribble of molten metal from the commander's hatch.

"Hammer," he shouted, standing up, "we did it! We killed them."

Schultz paused in his firing to look at Dean. "You sure?"

Dean pointed at the open hatch. "Take a look, you don't believe me."

Schultz looked out at the burning field. "Let's get off this tank," he said, "before our guys shoot us by accident."

CHAPTER
TWENTY-TWO

General Han, army forces commander, stared intently at Brigadier General Harry Sommers, his chief of staff. The one-star general nervously fidgeted before his commander's desk. The news he had just delivered was disastrous, and as the messenger, he feared he'd be the one shot. He also had other reasons to fear retribution, one of which was that he hadn't bothered to verify the readiness reports subordinate units had submitted to General Han before their deployment orders were issued.

The Confederation Army required all combat units to submit semiannual readiness reports to their higher headquarters, and periodically inspection teams visited every unit with a check-list, to verify readiness independently. But since the army's combat commands were spread out all over Human Space, the intervals between submission of reports and actual on-site verification were usually vast. To make matters worse, individual commanders' careers often hinged upon the readiness reports, and no one was ever willing to admit his unit wasn't deployable. Most commanders fudged the reports, hoping to make them good before the next inspection team arrived. The whole system was a joke among army men, but they still played the silly game because no one had the courage to tell the truth, and, until that day, luck had been with them.

Now the chickens had come home to roost. The III Corps, already in orbit around Diamunde, was reporting that most of its heavy mobile weapons required spare parts to make them combat ready. The Corps commander deployed, fully aware of that shortcoming. He'd counted on making the necessary repairs en route, not an unusual practice. But those spare parts were on a freighter whose Beam drive had broken down, and the ship was now days behind the rest of the reinforcing fleet. Nobody knew when it would arrive. Worse, the Corps had mounted out so quickly that many units barely had the basic load of ammunition required for the infantrymen's personal weapons, much less that required to supply their heavy artillery in sustained combat.

"I'll have that bastard's ass," Han muttered, referring to Lieutenant General Bosworth, commander of III Corps. "Damn," he hissed, and pounded his desk, "rely on the navy to screw things up!" He meant the freighter whose Beam drive had broken down. The chief of staff remained silent. He knew the blame was with the army staff, not the navy. General Han knew it too, and he also knew that as overall army commander for that phase of the invasion, his head would be the first to roll. Now he bitterly regretted that offhand remark he'd made to General Aguinaldo, that the Marines should take their golf clubs down to Diamunde with them since the invasion would be a "walkover." He didn't even know if General Aguinaldo played golf. Probably not. The Marines were too straitlaced for golf.

"Goddamnit, Harry, why the hell didn't you check this crap out for me! That's what a goddamned chief of staff does!"

The portly brigadier general spread his hands helplessly. General Han knew it would do him no good to get on Sommers. He was force commander; the ax would still fall on him first and hardest.

"Well," General Han sighed, "I better go tell the admiral."

"You mean to tell me," Admiral Wimbush asked General Han after he'd explained the problems with the III Corps, "that the Marines, who've been getting slaughtered down there for two days now, can't expect reinforcement for six more goddamned days?"

"Yessir, until Ninth Corps get here. Unless the freighter gets here first, of course. Any word on her position, sir?" General Han was as calm as if he were inviting the admiral to play a few holes of golf with him in the morning.

The admiral stared in disbelief at the army general. Admiral

Wimbush controlled himself with effort. "That— That," now he lost control, "asshole corps commander of yours deployed without all his goddamned gear and you sat on your damned ass and let him do it. You bastard! You promised me . . ." Admiral Wimbush rested his head in his hands. What was this going to do to his career? he wondered. Marines were always a problem to anyone who desired order and probity in life, but dead Marines could ruin a man's chances for advancement.

"Will the Ninth Corps be ready to go ashore when it gets here?" the admiral whispered.

"As far as we know, sir."

Admiral Wimbush looked up as if he'd been shot. " 'As far as we know'? Did you just say 'As far as we know'?"

"Sir, they will be ready," General Han answered, but his voice did not carry conviction, and the admiral sensed that instantly.

"You worthless sonofabitch," Admiral Wimbush said evenly. "All you had to do was walk through the door the Marines kicked open for you. This is the biggest operation either one of us ever participated in and the most important command I've ever gotten. Probably my last, thanks to you. Okay, General, you get your worthless ass out of that chair and you drag it down to General Aguinaldo's headquarters on Diamunde and you tell him how you have left him holding the bag."

General Han blanched, not because he was afraid of General Aguinaldo's understandable wrath—Han may have been an arrogant stuffed shirt, but he was no coward—but because Admiral Wimbush was the one who should have told the Marine ground commander the bad news, not a subordinate. General Han realized in that dreadful moment that it was Wimbush who was afraid of the Marine general.

"One more thing, General. After General Aguinaldo is through with you, you are relieved. That stupid Corps commander of yours is relieved. I'm putting Third Corps under General Aguinaldo's direct command until the army sends in an officer capable of leading troops in battle. I'm the senior commander here and it's my decision to make. Let your high command scream all it wants to. Let them answer to the Marines. Now get out of here," he finished wearily, putting his head back into his hands.

General Han sat stunned for a moment before he rose. He had never in his life been talked to like this. Privately, he despised Admiral Wimbush as the quintessential naval manipulator, one who advanced his precious career upon the merits of capable subordinates. He wanted to stand up and bury a fist in the pudgy admiral's face. But he couldn't respond, he was helpless before Wimbush's onslaught, because he knew he deserved it. Slowly, he walked to the door.

"General," Admiral Wimbush said from behind him, "isn't it the custom in the army for an officer to salute a superior when being dismissed from his presence?"

General Han turned and stared back at the admiral. That was too much. "Fuck you," he said after a moment, and stepped through the door.

General Aguinaldo surveyed the spaceport from a hopper he'd commandeered for his personal use. He shook his head. The extent of the destruction was astonishing. He'd rarely seen its match in his forty-five years as a Marine. As soon as he'd landed, an hour before, he'd gone straight to Major General Daly's division headquarters for a firsthand report on the ground situation. Then he'd gone on a tour of the lines, intending to visit each of the FIST HQs and as many of their infantry and Dragon companies as possible before he headed for the expeditionary airfield to see for himself the condition the squadrons were in.

The First Tank Brigade began its counterattack while he was with Company B of the 21st FIST, the first company he visited. Even as confident as he was of the combat prowess of Marines, he was impressed by the ease with which the men of Company B killed the tank platoon that attacked them. So intent was he on watching the battle that he didn't notice the stream of plasma bolts from a medium tank commander's gun that just missed him until his sergeant major, who was wise enough to take cover, reached up and pulled him down.

"I'd appreciate it if you turned on your shield, sir," the sergeant major said.

Only then did Aguinaldo realize he hadn't turned on the shield that would protect him from plasma bolts. Another burst shot overhead.

"Thank you, Sergeant Major," he replied. "But if a burst like that hit, it would overwhelm the shield." He poked his head up to look again. "I don't see anybody firing single shots."

He didn't see anyone firing anything—Company B's fight was over. Moments later he got word of the attack on the space-port and headed to it.

Now, from the orbiting hopper, he could see the fifteen Essays that were down—a very significant portion of the fleet's orbit-to-surface capability. The landing of reinforcements—when they get around to joining the show, he thought bitterly—would be slowed by the loss of the Essays. Fortunately, most of the artillery had landed and dispersed before the attack—even though much of their ammunition and supplies had been destroyed. Scattered throughout the landing field were close to eighty dead tanks, some still smoldering. Heavy movers were already shoving the hulks off the field to clear space for Essays. Around the periphery of the field, buildings were burning. Other buildings showed damage.

At least his Marines had done their job. Damn, one infantry company against an entire tank battalion. That company was going to get a citation. He'd make sure as many of its men as possible also got individual medals for their heroism. He wondered, not for the first time, why the Diamundean Army didn't have infantry in support of its armor. Very early in the history of armored warfare, back in the beginning of the twentieth century, commanders had learned how terribly vulnerable tanks were to infantry, and that they needed infantry to defend them against the enemy's foot soldiers. That was a lesson St. Cyr seemed not to have absorbed. Well, Aguinaldo wasn't going to be the one to point out his mistake to him—not until this war was won, anyway.

The hopper suddenly turned out of its orbit and flew away

from the landing field. Before Aguinaldo could ask why, the pilot's voice came to him over his headset.

"Sorry about the unexpected maneuver, sir, but an Essay is coming down and we had to get out of its way."

Aguinaldo looked up and saw the rapidly growing silhouette of an approaching Essay making a "tactical" landing. He glanced back at the landing field and hoped the Essay's coxswain was good enough to come in somewhere the field was clear. They couldn't afford to lose any more Essays.

The Essay landed safely and a small party of men emerged. They ran from the Essay, which launched as soon as they were at a safe distance. Aguinaldo wondered who the newcomers were and why an Essay drop was wasted on five men when weapons and ammunition were so desperately needed. He saw a Marine join the newcomers, and a moment later received a call that he had important visitors. He told his pilot to land near the small group.

At first General Aguinaldo did not think he had heard General Han correctly. The Marine commander was dead tired, he'd been up since landing and nearly killed by enemy tank gunners several times as he made his way from one trouble spot to another, bolstering morale with his presence among the desperately fighting infantrymen, bucking up a bewildered commander with a hand on the shoulder and a few intense remarks and then dashing back to his headquarters to better coordinate his attacks.

"Excuse me, General? What did you say?" Aguinaldo looked as wary as he sounded. General Han closed his eyes briefly and steeled himself to repeat the disastrous news.

"Sir, Third Corps cannot deploy with its heavy weapons as planned." He swallowed. "I just learned this morning that they mounted out without the spare parts they needed to—"

Han stopped talking when he saw the expression coming over Aguinaldo's face. Anders Aguinaldo came from an old Filipino-Dutch family—wiry, swarthy, he was a Filipino with a Dutch temper, for which he was famous throughout the Fleet.

The Marine's face was now turning a remarkable shade of dark brown.

"When will I be reinforced?" Aguinaldo asked in a very small voice.

"Six days, sir, when Ninth Corps arrives." Aguinaldo said nothing, just stared at the army general silently. "Third Corps mounted out with a lot of deadlined equipment they failed to tell us about. Their commander counted on performing maintenance en route, but the freighter carrying the Corps' spare parts broke down before a jump. We don't know when it might reach us here."

"What if Ninth Corps is in the same shape?" Aguinaldo said quietly. Had Han known the Marine better, he would have realized the calm was only skin deep. He had reason to be. Han's news could mean total defeat for the invasion force.

Now it was General Han's turn to remain silent. The answer to that question was obvious, and so devastating he refused to say it aloud. "You now have direct command of the Third Corps, sir. General Bosworth and I have both been relieved, and we will be returning to army headquarters on the first available shuttle."

"You goddamned fool!" Aguinaldo shouted. "You army bastards have never come through when the Marines were holding the line! Never! Now you and whatsisname leave us holding the bag again and scoot off home. I ought to leave you two here and take my Marines home."

Han jumped to his feet. He was about the same height as Aguinaldo but stockier, like his Korean forebears. "I've had enough of this crap from you and your goddamned admiral!" he shouted. One of General Aguinaldo's aides, standing just outside the room, quietly closed the door, but the shouting now got so loud everyone in the command post operations room could hear the generals inside. The enlisted men grinned at each other, despite the fatigue that gripped everyone in the landing force. Nothing is so sweet as to witness officers falling out; the higher their rank the sweeter the sound, especially since it was the army getting chewed out.

Aguinaldo stood up and leaned across his desk. "You get

your ass back to army headquarters, General," Aguinaldo shouted, "and you explain why my men died in this damned place! Because you fucked up! Better still, you tin soldier," Aguinaldo's voice dripped with sarcasm at the insult, "you tell their families why their men died here!"

Han's face drained white. He had once been a platoon leader and he'd seen combat. He knew he was responsible for the debacle, but to hear it put into words by another military man, his superior officer now but more than that, a renowned fighter like Aguinaldo, brought the terrible load of his failure home. He sat down hard, utterly deflated. Aguinaldo remained standing for a moment and then he sat down too.

"I—I . . . Yes, I am responsible for this, General," he said quietly. Aguinaldo was surprised to see tears in the man's eyes as he spoke. "Give me a blaster and a set of chameleons and put me into a rifle company," Han said, his voice hoarse with emotion. "I—I—I can't go home like this." He gestured helplessly. "Forty years a soldier, and now . . ." His voice trailed off.

Aguinaldo had calmed down now. "Well . . ." he began.

"Sir." Han straightened his back. "My staff, General Bosworth's staff, they stand ready for your orders. They are good men, General. They will serve you well. Don't take any of this out on them."

"Well, ah, General, I can't use any sixty-year-old riflemen, but I appreciate the offer. How soon can Third Corps begin to land?"

"Immediately."

"Do they have any heavy weapons that will work?"

"Yessir, some." Han passed a microchip to the Marine. "There's a complete report on the Corps' readiness status. They will be of some help to you. Enough, I hope, to . . ." He left the sentence unfinished. From outside came the rumble of a heavy artillery barrage and Han flinched. He stood up. He had completed his mission here, it was time to leave.

General Aguinaldo stood up. "I was a bit harsh a few moments ago," he began.

"Sir, would you talk to Admiral Wimbush?" Han interjected, desperation written all over his face. "I'd like to stay with you in some capacity, help out in some way. I'll defer my rank and gladly put myself under your command."

Aguinaldo offered his hand. "No, General, that's not possible," he said firmly. "I appreciate the offer, though." He was beginning to feel a twinge of sympathy for the army officer, but he suppressed it. He had a battle to win.

"Sir? Can you hold?" Han asked as he turned to go.

Aguinaldo shrugged. "Will a kwangduk shit in your mess kit? We have no intention of 'holding,' General. We're going to break out and kick some ass. We're Marines."

CHAPTER
TWENTY-THREE

"What do you mean, the army's not coming?" Lance Corporal Joe Dean demanded.

Lance Corporal Dave Schultz, the bearer of the news, didn't look at Dean. His eyes kept scanning the street and buildings to their front, vigilant for signs of the enemy. He'd just returned from a platoon NCO meeting where the junior leaders of third platoon, Company L, had been given a briefing on the situation. He spat a long stream of saliva. "They ain't coming. Army ain't ready." He spat again and finally turned to look at Dean. His eyes were hard, his face rigid. Anger twitched the corner of his mouth. "Dean, understand this. The army don't like Marines. Never has. Army gets a chance to get some Marines fried, they take it." He looked back to the front. "They ain't ready. They ain't coming." Anger started a tick on his cheek.

Schultz's anger wasn't directed at Dean, who he thought should be in charge, nor was it directed at the army, which was guilty of leaving the Marines in an untenable position. His anger was at being appointed acting fire team leader. A fire team leader was a corporal, a noncommissioned officer. Hammer Schultz wasn't an NCO, a leader of men. He was a career lance corporal. He'd argued that Dean should take over as acting fire team leader even though Dean was junior to him. But Bass and Hyakowa had taken him aside and explained to him, as only sergeants can explain, that as the more experienced man he had to be in charge. He'd fought in cities before, Dean hadn't. He'd fought against regular armies before, Dean hadn't. His chances of survival were better if Dean followed his lead than the other

228

way around. Besides, he'd have to answer to them if he refused. Schultz had cursed and threatened, but a sergeant and a gunnery sergeant had just too much power and he finally acquiesced. With absolutely no grace.

"What are we going to do?" Dean asked. Uncertainty made his voice small; he knew there were hundreds, maybe thousands, more tanks facing them, and the Marines were running very low on Straight Arrows again.

Schultz rippled his shoulders in a half shrug. "Take as many of 'em with us as we can." He settled his blaster into a more ready position. Even if he no longer had a weapon that could kill a tank, maybe a tank commander or a driver would have his head sticking out of his hatch. Them he could kill.

Schultz suddenly cocked his head and put a hand to the side of his helmet to listen to an incoming call. He acknowledged the call, then turned to Dean. A death's head grin split his face.

"Remember that Corporal Henry back at Camp Ellis? Taught us artillery spotting?"

Dean nodded, wondering why Schultz asked.

Schultz nodded back, in the direction of the general support artillery battery they were screening. "We're going to spot for them. Let's go." He examined the Oppalia street map he had, then flipped his chameleon screen down and disappeared like the Cheshire cat's smile.

Dean dropped both his chameleon screen and his infra. He followed the red blob in his visor that was Schultz.

Six FISTs, complete now that their artillery was planetside, had landed. Their front lines, the infantry and Dragons, should have been more than three thousand men, but casualties had reduced that number to somewhat fewer than 2,500. They had to secure a perimeter that included both the seaport and spaceport and the many square kilometers of the city that the Marines had driven the First Tank Brigade out of. Fewer than 2,500 men to secure that perimeter and advance it. Fewer than 2,500 men on foot and in light armored vehicles to take on the remaining 250 tanks and defeat them, then occupy the entire city of Oppalia and hold it against an expected counterattack from as many as four armored divisions. The Marines did not, could not, cover the entire perimeter they had, there simply weren't enough of them. The perimeter had gaps that whole tank battalions could drive through without opposition. It was into one of those gaps that Schultz led Dean.

A ten-story building, one of Oppalia's tallest, stood at one end of a broad, two-kilometer-long boulevard. Stunted elms imported from Old Earth to line the boulevard struggled to wrest nourishment from the alien soil.

"We can see from up top," Schultz said when they reached the building. He looked around for street signs, then at the name of the building.

The two Marines had to slag the locking mechanism of the main doors, which set off alarms. They entered the deserted lobby. Dean looked around apprehensively, expecting security guards to come running.

"No one's here," Schultz said. "Everybody's hiding somewhere."

Dean realized Schultz was right. "Besides," Dean added, "they can't see us. And two Marines can deal with a whole company of private security, right?"

Schultz didn't bother replying. He walked deeper into the lobby.

Dean looked around and headed for a bank of lift tubes.

Schultz saw where he was going and snapped, "This way."

"What? Where are we going?" Dean asked as he scampered after Schultz.

"Stairs."

"Stairs? It's a long way up, Hammer. Let's take the tube. That'll be a lot faster and easier."

Schultz shook his head. "What if the power fails? Be a long fall."

Dean looked wistfully toward the lift tubes. He didn't relish the idea of climbing the stairs. But he had to acknowledge that Schultz was right about the possibility of a power failure. Now that he thought about it, he was surprised the city still had power at all.

The wind, mere gusts at street level, was a steady, strong breeze on top of the building. They went to the east-facing parapet and looked out over the city. From up above, the unpopulated streets looked even emptier than they had from ground level. The eerie lack of people-noises in a city made Dean imagine he could hear his heart beating inside his chest even over the low roar of the wind. The only relief from the emptiness was a couple of kilometers to the south they saw several Dragons clustered in an open park. To the north, a patrol of three Dragons nosed along a residential street. Otherwise they saw no movement or other sign of people.

Dean shivered at the eeriness of it—a city that size should be teeming with people. Even in the midst of a battle, he expected to see movement. But other than the one patrol, there wasn't any. Neither was there any noise of fighting. All along the perimeter, the Marines had beaten off the First Tank Brigade's counterattack. Now the Diamundeans were licking their wounds and the Marines were waiting for reinforcements and resupply that they no longer expected. The entire city waited, hushed. Not even Diamunde's native avians cried their songs.

Schultz called in their location. He used street names and the building's name to tell where they were. Technical difficulties kept the satellite crew from closing the gap in the string-of-pearls so the Marines were relying on civilian street maps to give locations.

The two Marines waited and watched.

General Aguinaldo intently studied III Corps' readiness report. Major General Daly read the screen over his shoulder. When Aguinaldo had seen enough to have a general grasp, he leaned back and said to Brigadier General Sommers, General Han's one-time chief of staff, who was now working for him, "It looks like the 10th Light Infantry Division can land right now. Is that right?"

"Yessir," Sommers said, his voice mirroring his uncertainty about how to deal with the Marine general who'd so suddenly and unexpectedly become his boss. "The 10th can begin boarding Essays within a half hour of receiving orders."

Aguinaldo heard the nervousness and stared at the army brigadier general, his expression daring Sommers to add a qualifier.

"Sir, I inspected the 10th myself. They're ready."

"Except they only have one Straight Arrow per squad."

Sommers swallowed. "That's right, sir. The heavy equipment still hasn't arrived, but we have Straight Arrows."

"Third Corps has enough S.A.'s to arm every man in the 10th Light, and every one of my Marines. Isn't that right?"

"Yessir." Sommers swallowed again and thought quickly. He knew the Marine would accept nothing less than instant action. "Sir, I have palletized S.A.'s that can be boarded on Essays immediately for distribution planetside." Sommers saw Aguinaldo's face darken, and hastily continued. "Sir, another one or two S.A.'s can be issued to each squad in the 10th as they board their landing craft. This can be done without slowing them down."

"Then do it. I want the first echelon of the 10th Light Infantry Division planetside in one hour." Aguinaldo turned to Daly to give him further orders.

Sommers saw he was dismissed and rushed from the command room to issue a communiqué to the commanding general of the 10th Light. The army was going to come through for the Marines. He didn't know how, but he knew a major general who would hang if the 10th didn't begin landing on time.

Schultz and Dean watched the still city for an hour and a half, reporting in at twenty-minute intervals. None of the other combination observation post/spotter teams had any more activity to report than they did. The only elements of the six FISTs that made contact were the reconnaissance teams that prowled the city looking for the hiding places of the First Tank Brigade. Recon's job was exactly that—they found the tanks. It was someone else's job to fix them and kill them. None of the tankers had any idea they were found.

By nineteen hours enough reports had made it back to Marine headquarters for General Aguinaldo to be reasonably sure he knew where enough of the tanks were for him to kill the First

Tank Brigade. He issued orders. Marine artillery would open
fire on all known hiding places. Then the six FISTs would advance into those places and take the survivors prisoner—or kill
them if they tried to fight. The 10th Light Infantry would follow
the Marines and clean up anyone they missed—which should
be just about no one. In another hour the entire city would be in
the hands of Confederation forces.

But the best made plans never do survive the first shot. Marine artillery opened fire on schedule and was answered by
counterbattery fire, not from the First Tank Brigade, but from
the lead elements of the Third Armored Division. Because of the
continuing gap in the string-of-pearls satellites, no one saw the
Third Armor racing from the foot of Rourke's Hills to the city.

"What? I'm awake," Dean said when Schultz poked him
sharply with an elbow. He looked where Schultz pointed. "Oh-
mygawd." Through a gap between buildings a couple of kilometers to the northeast, he saw a line of tanks flitting in a
direction that would take them across the front of their position.
The only question he had was would the line of tanks intersect
the boulevard they watched over. "We've got to report this."

"Report what?"

"The tanks."

"What are you going to say, we see tanks? How many, where
are they going? We don't report until we know." Schultz slid his
magnifier screen into place and the gap suddenly looked like it
was a hundred meters away. "You look there." He pointed to the
other end of the boulevard.

Casting glances toward the gap, Dean watched the boulevard. "How many are there?" he asked when he didn't see any
more tanks.

"I counted fifty," Schultz said. He didn't add that fifty didn't
include the number that passed before he started counting.

"Where are they going?"

Schultz didn't know, so he didn't answer.

A moment later they knew. The lead tanks turned onto the
boulevard a few blocks from the far end. At that same moment,

the artillery opened fire on the known hiding places of the First Tank Brigade.

The Third Armored Division was armed with a weapon the Marines hadn't seen on tanks before—rockets. One tank in every squad of the battalion turning onto the boulevard in front of Dean and Schultz had a launcher that could send rockets straight up. Each platoon had a tank with a guidance system that could direct the rockets to their targets. Each company had one tank with a radar that could detect shells passing through the air and track them back to their origin. The one company of the battalion that was on the boulevard quickly deployed to begin counterbattery fire.

Schultz made his report as soon as the first tanks came into view in front of them: "More than fifty tanks, maybe a whole battalion. Range of lead tanks, seven hundred meters. Azimuth eighty-seven degrees. Speed sixty kph. Coming directly toward me."

"Keep them in sight, we'll get back to you," was the response.

"What are they doing?" Dean asked when the company stopped and deployed.

Schultz shook his head. He hesitated about making another report without knowing. Then he saw the radar and launch tubes rise from the tanks and, as unexpected as it was, knew what the tanks were doing.

"Lima Six, break, break," he shouted into his radio, interrupting someone else's report of new activity. "Tanks in sight are readying counterbattery fire. Over."

"Counterbattery fire?" asked Corporal MacLeash, who was manning the op radio. "Are you sure?" Only artillery was supposed to be able to conduct counterbattery fire. He'd never heard of tanks firing counterbattery at artillery.

"They've got rockets," Schultz said. "Counterbattery."

"Wait one," MacLeash said.

While they waited, the command tank's computer made its calculations and transmitted them to the guidance systems. There were nine bellows of smoke and blasts of noise, and nine rockets lifted into the air. Five hundred meters up they turned from their vertical flight and arced to the west.

"Tell artillery they've got incoming on the way," Schultz said into the radio, totally ignoring proper procedure.

Just out of sight, around the corner from the company they could see, nine more rockets shot upward.

CHAPTER
TWENTY-FOUR

Two salvos of nine rockets each crashed down on 13th FIST's artillery battery. The six guns were dispersed; a hundred meters between them and revetments gave them some protection, but not as much as they needed. In the first salvo, one rocket landed directly on the breech of a gun, destroying it and killing its entire six-man crew. A second rocket struck the top of a revetment, staggering the gun as shrapnel shredded four of its crew. Two other rockets struck between revetments and caused little damage, another shot long and missed everything, and one was a dud. One missile rocket landed next to the fire control center, killing everyone in it. But the rocket that caused the most damage landed on an ammunition carrier. The massive secondary explosion toppled one gun, bent the tube of a second and jammed it into the breech, and killed twelve of the battery's Marines. The second salvo finished the job. Thirteenth FIST's battery was left with one usable gun and just fifteen of its seventy-one men still alive and functioning.

By then 34th FIST battery had adjusted its aim and fired its first salvo at the counterbattery tanks. The 19th and 21st FIST batteries were aimed and loading.

From the top of their building, Schultz and Dean watched as the tankers readied another salvo. Then the artillery struck. The first six-round salvo was fused for contact and did limited damage except for one round that hit the tread cover of a tank, disabling it. Shrapnel from another round tore the guidance system off the top of a tank, and fragments from a third round damaged the tracking radar on the command tank. Three tankers who didn't button up quickly enough were hit by flying fragments. Then the second two salvos hit, one immediately after the other, and they were more effective, as they were fused for air bursts and destroyed or disabled the rest of the rocketry control systems mounted on the tanks. They also set off four rockets sitting in their launchers and killed those four tanks.

Then another tank company, one out of sight of the two Marines, launched a salvo. When the roar of the rockets died down, Dean and Schultz heard the rumbling of many engines as the tanks displaced—those tanks weren't going to be caught by another counterbattery barrage.

The tanks withdrew directly into the path of the infantry battalion of the 36th FIST, most of whose Marines were carrying Straight Arrows. It was a brief, bloody, and thoroughly one-sided encounter: just ten of the eighty-five tanks got away. Thirty-sixth FIST suffered seven fatalities and fourteen wounded. Farther to the north, the 225th FIST's infantry ran into another battalion of the Third Armored Division and scored an even more lopsided rout. The Marines of the 13th FIST, seeking vengeance for their artillery, advanced in the middle and pinned down a regiment from the Third, held it in position and whittled it down until massed fire from the remaining artillery zeroed in on it and reduced the tanks to rubble.

General Aguinaldo, seeing the victories the Marines were achieving over the newly arrived Diamundean division, scrapped his earlier plan and quickly devised a new one.

"All FISTs will advance on line," he told his assembled staff and his combat element commanders. "General Daly, don't let anyone get ahead of the rest. I want all available air assets with tank-killing capability flying over the infantry."

He turned to the commanding general of the 10th Light Infantry Division. "General Ott, I want you to put one reinforced battalion behind each FIST to reinforce them in the event my Marines find a weakness to exploit—or to give them a hand if they encounter heavy resistance. Your battalions will be under the command of the FIST commanders. Your remaining battalions will be in reserve."

Ott grimaced; army commanders always hate the idea of soldiers being under the command of Marines. But he himself was under the direct command of a Marine, so his subordinates were as well. "Yessir, we'll do that."

Aguinaldo noticed the grimace. "Don't worry, General. The army's distrust of Marine fighting abilities is returned in spades. My FIST commanders won't throw your soldiers' lives away— they wouldn't trust them to do it right."

Ott's face turned deep red. But he wisely held back the retort he wanted to make.

Aguinaldo turned to the Navy Air commander on the ground. "Captain Sprance, Navy Air has suffered severe losses, but you still have more aircraft than I do. You will have half of your squadrons flying outside Oppalia to stop or slow down any additional tank divisions attempting to follow the Third Division. Distribute the remainder of your squadrons to the FISTs to supplement their remaining aircraft. They'll be under the command of the FIST squadrons."

Captain Sprance looked even more pained than General Ott had. Marine Air was supposed to supplement Navy Air, not the other way around. But General Aguinaldo was in full command of the planetside operations and he had to obey. "Aye aye, sir."

"Good. Do it. We commence in thirty minutes."

The senior commanders scrambled to get back to their commands, talking on their radios as they went, issuing preliminary orders to subordinates.

Less than twenty-five minutes later, half the navy squadrons lifted off for their screening patrols. Twenty-eight minutes after the order, Marine aircraft and the remaining navy squadrons took off to cover the FISTs. On the dot of thirty minutes, the Marines began their advance with the 10th Light Infantry Division moving sharply in trace. Thirty-one minutes after the order was given, a radio call came in from a navy squadron flying to the southeast:

"There's one hell of a sandstorm coming your way. We're at angels twenty-two and we aren't above it. It seems to go all the way to the ground, and it gets thicker lower down. It's bad enough that I don't think we can make it back to Oppalia and land safely before it hits."

Lieutenant Colonel Namur gazed out the observer's port of his command vehicle. A very bad sandstorm was coming. He didn't need the weather reports to know that. All Diamundeans in this hemisphere were used to these storms. What was bothering him now was not the weather but the dispatch he'd just received from General Headquarters:

GHO/PZKFWI24C4IZ/2045L

TO MY BRAVE FIGHTING MEN AT OPPALIA:

YOU HAVE RESISTED THE INVADERS HEROICALLY. THEY MUST NOT, REPEAT, MUST NOT BE ALLOWED TO BREAK OUT OF THE CORDON YOU HAVE SO VALIANTLY ESTABLISHED. YOU MUST FIGHT TO THE LAST MAN TO ASSURE THIS DOES NOT HAPPEN. ANY MAN WHO SHOWS THE LEAST DEGREE OF RE-LUCTANCE TO FIGHT ON IS TO BE SHOT. ANY COMMANDER WHO GIVES UP EVEN ONE METER OF OUR SACRED SOIL AT OP-PALIA WILL BE EXECUTED.

/s/ St. Cyr

Official: Stauffer, Col., GS, Chief of Staff

Is St. Cyr insane? Namur asked himself. In his mind, the question was entirely rhetorical. What kind of an order is this? he wondered. Execute his men? We should have stopped him when he attacked the embassy. How could we have ever expected to win a war against the Confederation? Now he has committed us to this fight without proper support and he wants us all to die here? *For what?*

No! Namur pounded his fist onto the computer console. His driver looked up in alarm. "Everything okay, Colonel?" he asked.

Startled out of his mutinous reverie, Namur glanced guiltily at the enlisted man. "Everything is fine, Scithers." He recovered his composure and punched a code into the communications console to access a secure net to Third Armored Division headquarters and Colonel Irvin Rummel, the division commander. The image of the division chief of staff, a major whose name Namur could never remember, popped onto the vidscreen.

"The colonel's not available right now," the major informed Namur at once.

"When will he be?"

"In an hour or less, sir."

"Where is he?"

"He's discussing General St. Cyr's latest order with his staff right now, sir."

Namur nodded. Everyone in the army was probably studying that order just then. "Get him, Major."

"But sir, he's in with his staff—"

"I don't care. Get him. Now."

The major hesitated only an instant, and then the screen went blank. Outside, the wind had picked up, visibility quickly decreasing. It was going to be a major storm. Good, Namur thought. Just what we need.

While he waited for Colonel Rummel to come up on the net, Namur commanded the onboard computer to plot the most direct course from Oppalia to a coordinate in Rourke's Hills. The computer gave him two routes based on the difficulty of the terrain and weather conditions that were expected to prevail throughout the area during the next twenty-four hours. It also calculated the probability of detection based on what it knew of the brigade's available electronic countermeasures suites and the enemy's surveillance and detection capabilities.

The computer gave Namur two projections: (1) A default displayed every five minutes whenever the computer was in use. At the present rate of combat intensity at the continued fuel and ammunition consumption levels, and presuming there were no more casualties, the brigade could sustain its presence in Oppalia for two more days. (2) Using either route, the brigade could reach the designated coordinates in the hills in two to three hours with zero possibility of being discovered by reconnaissance or surveillance aircraft.

Colonel Rummel came on the screen. "Nase, what is it? Are you under attack?" The colonel looked old and tired and there was a note of alarm in his voice. The fact that he addressed Namur by his first name indicated just how quickly the artificial protocols of a peacetime army evaporated under actual combat conditions. Namur had always liked the old colonel, even though privately he thought he'd have made a better division commander than Rummel. Rummel had started life as a private in an infantry company. Like most shavetails, he'd never forgotten what it was like to be enlisted, so he always tried to take care of his troops. Namur respected him for that. But Rummel was not the kind of commander to buck GHQ on his own authority.

"General St. Cyr's order—"

"Ah, yes, Nase, we're discussing that right now—"

"Sir, I am withdrawing my unit to Rourke's Hills," Namur announced. Colonel Rummel said nothing, but he did not look surprised. "We can hold out here two more days after the storm lifts, providing the Marines don't attack," he continued. "Once in the hills, we can refit and fight on. But I am not going to sacrifice my command. I am not throwing any more lives away."

Scithers looked at his commander sharply.

"You know what that means, Colonel?" the division commander asked. "Look," he continued quickly, "we've just about agreed to do the same thing. Once my staff supports a withdrawal move, I'll get the other brigade commanders to see it that way. I think we can get Corps to go along, and then army headquarters. Hell, Nase, with *all* of us in on it, St. Cyr'll find his hands tied. He can't execute everyone!"

"Maybe, maybe not," Namur replied. "But I don't have time to wait for you to get the others on board. The storm will reach its highest intensity a little after dark. I'm moving then." He punched a button on his console. "I have just forwarded to you the coordinates of our new position in the hills. I'll see you there." With that, Namur broke the connection. He crumpled up St. Cyr's order and threw it to the floor. Ignoring the insistent beeping on the communications console, a warning that a high-priority message was coming through—no doubt Rummel trying to reestablish the connection—Namur began contacting his battalion commanders.

It grew very quiet in the command module. Outside, the wind screamed as the storm closed in on Oppalia and the command vehicle, buffeted by the violent gusts, rocked gently back and forth on its suspension.

Scithers, his face bathed in the green light from the driver's console, grinned. Boy, he knew the old man had balls, but this . . . This almost made it worthwhile, being in this goddamned army.

"Break off your patrols," General Aguinaldo ordered when Captain Sprance reported the storm. "Have them find a place to land." Then he realized he was talking to an intimidated sailor, and amplified, something he wouldn't have done with a Marine. "Someplace where there aren't enemy divisions, and have them establish security patrols."

He didn't bother telling Major General Daly to get his aircraft to safety; the Marine would already be doing it. Aguinaldo focused his attention on what to do with the ground forces. The winds and the particulates being blown about would make the artillery next to useless, so the guns had to batten down until the storm abated. On the other hand, the storm could give the Marines and the 10th Light Infantry enough cover to slip right up to the Diamundean positions without being detected—even though the soldiers were wearing urban camouflage uniforms instead of chameleons like his Marines. Get right on top of the tankers, even inside the buildings most of them were hiding in. Possibly capture most of the tanks, instead of killing all of them. It was a tempting thought, but not tempting enough. According to the meteorological reports, Diamundean sandstorms raged at wind speeds of up to 150 kilometers per hour. Gusts could double that. There wasn't only the sand in the storm, which clogged breath, to worry about—the winds were strong enough to throw about sizable objects, and even men could be carried away. No, he didn't think his Marines would function very well in the storm, it would subject them to too much hazard. And if his Marines would have trouble functioning in the storm, he damn well knew the 10th Light couldn't manage either. He turned to Daly and Ott.

"Have your men take cover from the storm." He added for Ott, "Inside sturdy buildings." After the fiasco with III Corps, he distrusted the army even more than before.

The storm raged for three days. Long enough for the infantrymen to run out of rations. Fortunately, many had holed up in private homes and fairly well depleted the larders in those homes. A few found themselves in food stores and were able to eat their fill of whatever they wanted. Those unlucky enough to have had access to only the rations they carried were famished by the time the storm abated. No one had to worry about water, though—the waterworks still ran properly.

After three days, the winds abruptly dropped to mild zephyrs. The Marines and soldiers slowly, cautiously, stepped into the clear air. Their ears felt odd, hollow and stuffed at the same time, from the lack of wind-roar. They shook their heads and popped their ears, trying to balance pressure on their eardrums. As long as they didn't look down at the ten or fifteen centimeters of dirt, dust, and sand still settling on the pavement and piled in drifts against building sides, everything looked sparkling clean. The air itself seemed to glow.

A mechanical clanking and ratcheting spun Dean and Schultz to their right. A metal monster was rolling out of a building fifty meters away.

Dean didn't hesitate; he glanced to his rear to make sure his backblast area was clear, propped his Straight Arrow on his shoulder, aimed, and killed the monster.

"Wasn't a tank," Schultz said laconically.

Dean looked at him quizzically. "Then what was . . ." He looked at the beast he'd just killed. There was no gun-spouting turret on top of it. There were no observation slits, or visible crew hatches. It had big tires, no treads. Forward of the tires were round tubes half a meter in diameter, pointing down on both the front and sides. A pliable, bubblelike canopy, shredded by fragments from the explosion, filled its upper rear quadrant. As he examined the monster he saw another one bump into its rear, back off, then again bump gently forward.

"What?" Dean asked, not expecting an answer.

"Check it out," Sergeant Hyakowa said. He had run out of the building just after Dean fired and was standing behind him and Schultz.

Schultz began sloshing through the loose, ankle-deep covering on the pavement. Dean followed. The second monster stopped bumping against the one he'd killed and sat waiting.

"And hurry," Hyakowa called after them. "We don't have all day."

Schultz paused at the side of the monster and looked down, then clambered onto it. He found many access hatches, but nothing a man would use to enter a crew compartment. He dropped back to the ground.

Dean edged through the huge doorway while Schultz was examining the monster. The interior of the garage, he guessed it was, was lit, but he didn't see any people inside. What he did see was a dozen vehicles like the one he killed, all of them rocking gently on their wheels, waiting for whatever signal would set them in motion. Other than their size, nothing about them seemed threatening.

"You killed a street cleaner," Schultz said when he finished his inspection.

"A what?"

"An automated street cleaner." Schultz pointed to the bottom side of the dead street cleaner.

Dean saw retracted, circular brushes. "The tubes, they're suction," he said softly.

Schultz didn't reply, it was obvious.

They returned to Hyakowa.

"Automated street cleaners," Dean reported.

Hyakowa shook his head as if to say, "Of all the dumb things to do . . ."

Dean flushed bright red.

"I guess if they have storms like this very often, automated street cleaners are the best way to deal with it," Hyakowa said. Then into his radio, "Let's move it out. We have to get to the tanks and kill them." If they didn't move during the storm, he added to himself. He looked through his infras to see that his squad was moving and stepped out himself.

They didn't find any tanks.

CHAPTER TWENTY-FIVE

Lieutenant Colonel Naseby Namur had not slept a wink the past seventy-two hours; he had had little sleep at all since the invasion at Oppalia. Close to physical exhaustion, he was still thinking clearly, however, and he knew the peremptory summons to Major General St. Cyr's command bunker, in the hills just outside New Kimberly, meant the end for him, one way or another.

Namur was not sure he would actually be executed. St. Cyr needed good combat commanders too desperately just then to kill them off himself. It was heartening that St. Cyr had ordered him back to New Kimberly "for an interview" instead of dispatching a goon squad to execute him on the spot. But with Major General Marston St. Cyr, one never knew. Everyone in the army was familiar with his disposal of Tubalcain's board of directors. At the time, St. Cyr's military followers had been pleased by the executions, seeing the directors as mere feckless civilians with no vision. But those same officers had reason to regret their former nonchalance at St. Cyr's harsh methods.

From an early age Naseby Namur had been destined for a military career in the Tubalcain armed forces. The company had sent him offworld to an excellent military academy, and for one semester he had actually been an exchange student at the Confederation Military Academy, where he struck up friendships with some of the men now opposing him. He still thought of them as friends. They had their jobs and he had his.

Namur turned into a good soldier and rose quickly in command of Tubalcain troops. Marston St. Cyr noted the young officer's potential and recruited him into his clandestine armored

corps. At first Namur and the other officers St. Cyr had lured
into repudiating their oath to Tubalcain Enterprises worshiped
him. St. Cyr was a commanding figure with real presence, and
he promised the young officers not only promotion, but genuine
military glory commanding troops in the armored force he was
building.

St. Cyr's easy victory over the forces of the Hefestus Conglomerate seemed to confirm that he was a military genius. But
then little things started to go wrong, details a professional like
Namur could not ignore. First was the harsh discipline St. Cyr
imposed on his men. Under his command, court-martials were
the preferred method of dealing with even small infractions of
military discipline. Initiative in disciplinary matters was taken
out of the hands of small-unit commanders, and morale among
the enlisted men plummeted as a result. St. Cyr instituted a
system of spit-and-polish, enforced by court-martial, that also
eroded morale in the ranks. Working with armored vehicles,
even in garrison, requires infinite attention to logistics and
maintenance. The work is heavy, hard, and dirty. But no one
was excused from the frequent and elaborate military reviews
conducted by St. Cyr's inspectors, and woe unto the mechanic
or gunner discovered with dirt under his fingernails!

And the promised promotions had never come. Under Tubalcain's board, Namur had been a lieutenant colonel in command
of an infantry battalion. Under St. Cyr, who decreed nobody
could outrank him as a major general, Namur commanded an
armored brigade but was still only a light colonel. It was not that
pay and emoluments meant so much to an officer like Namur;
they did not. But what irked him and his comrades in St. Cyr's
officer corps, all of whom were in similarly underrated command positions, was that in other armies he would be a brigadier general and wear the insignia of that rank. So important are
the bits of tin and cloth of military rank to the professional soldier that his morale and self-esteem suffer if he is denied these
symbols of trust and authority once he thinks he has earned them.

But worst of all was the simple fact that Major General
Marston St. Cyr, a genius of corporate strategy, had no concept
of military tactics. He blithely ignored the hard-learned lessons

of the past: armored forces are only successful if fully integrated with the other arms of infantry, artillery, and air. Tubalcain's swift and total victory over the forces of the Hefestus Conglomerate had convinced St. Cyr, over the strenuous objections of his commanders, that he could also destroy the Confederation forces using his armor alone. Thus Namur's brigade had been denied its full complement of infantry and artillery support, and St. Cyr's formidable air forces had been destroyed by the Confederation's air arm before they could be used against the Marines at Oppalia; St. Cyr's air forces had been dedicated to protecting his capital at New Kimberly.

So now Naseby Namur, who had skillfully fought the Marines at Oppalia and miraculously escaped death in the maelstrom of that fight, was possibly headed for execution by one of St. Cyr's firing squads far behind the lines. Namur's only consolation was that his men had fought and died valiantly not for Marston St. Cyr, but for Lieutenant Colonel Naseby Namur. He had told his ranking officer, his second in command by default since all the other officers were dead or wounded, that if he did not return from New Kimberly, he should surrender to the Marines what was left of the brigade at the first opportunity.

Namur had been sitting quietly for over an hour just outside the door to St. Cyr's command bunker. Harried staff officers kept coming and going throughout that time, glancing surreptitiously at the haggard brigade commander as he sat there in his filthy uniform. They couldn't help noticing the burns and lacerations on Namur's hands, folded in his lap, and the large ugly scar healing on the left side of his neck. Worst of all was his expression, bloodshot eyes, vacant and fixed as if staring at some far-off object. As they passed by the battle-scarred colonel they turned their eyes away quickly and guiltily. They should have been at the front too, but instead, in the command bunker, were safe from everything but the rising tide of vituperation that seemed by then to characterize St. Cyr's staff meetings.

From far above where he sat came the roar of plasma bolts scourging the earth's surface as Admiral Wimbush's battle cruisers probed for a weakness in St. Cyr's defenses. Suddenly there was a huge crash and the solid rock shook underneath Namur's chair. Alarms shrilled and men ran and shouted in the corridors outside the war room suite. The sharp odor of ozone and molten rock filled the room. Evidently, a stray bolt had found one of the camouflaged entrance shafts and bored its way into the complex. The staff officers coming and going blanched and swallowed nervously, but Namur's battle-scarred face only twitched in a tight smile. Close just didn't count for him anymore.

Namur started as someone laid a hand on his shoulder.

"You can go in now, Colonel," an aide said gently. Namur glanced up at the man. He wore the insignia of a full colonel, and Namur recognized him as Clouse Stauffer, the former security chief St. Cyr had elevated to chief of staff. Stauffer looked haggard and drawn himself. A good sign, Namur thought, when staff officers begin to experience the hardships of war. With an effort, Namur rose to his feet and entered St. Cyr's inner sanctum.

St. Cyr looked smaller than the colonel remembered him from only a few weeks ago. He sat quietly behind his desk and regarded the brigade commander through half-closed eyelids. Namur advanced to within six paces of St. Cyr's desk, came to rigid attention and saluted smartly. "Lieutenant Colonel Naseby Namur, commanding First Brigade, First Armored Division, reporting as directed, sir!" St. Cyr returned the salute with a perfunctory gesture, and Namur snapped his right arm back to his side. He stood there for a full minute before St. Cyr said anything.

"You were one of my best officers, Colonel," St. Cyr began. "I did not give you a divisional or Corps command, because I wanted you on the front line, facing the enemy, where you could do me the most good. Now you have disobeyed my order." St. Cyr sounded more disappointed than angry.

"Sir—"

St. Cyr waved him into silence. "It is essential that all commands hold, Colonel. I am preparing a counterstroke, but I need time to get my forces together. Only you can buy me that time, Colonel."

Namur made no reply. For the moment, he couldn't make any. He was surprised at how the interview was going.

"Colonel, you can buy me that time. Will you do it?" St. Cyr asked quietly. His expression turned almost imploring as he looked up at Namur standing rigidly in front of his desk. "I have the assurances of your division and Corps commanders that they will do their best, but that will not be good enough unless officers like you lead our men with conviction. Can you do it?"

When he turned on the charisma, Marston St. Cyr was irresistible. "Yes sir," Namur said without hesitation.

St. Cyr nodded curtly. "Very good. You are now a full colonel. Return to your unit. You are dismissed."

"Clouse," St. Cyr said to his chief of staff after Namur had departed, "can we get a hyperspace drone through to Cinque Luna?"

"We'll probably have to try several, but I think we can get one through the blockade, sir."

Cinque Luna was one of St. Cyr's staunchest allies. "It is time now for them to introduce a resolution in the Confederation Congress to sue for peace," St. Cyr said. The war was lost, he knew that. The time commanders like Namur would buy for him would not be used to mount any kind of counterattack—St. Cyr had no weapons or reserves for that—but to engineer his escape. Val Carney, Cinque Luna's representative at the Confederation Congress, could get the votes needed to stop the war. He was one of Tubalcain's most prominent stockholders, and the livelihoods of many other members of the Congress were also tied to Tubalcain's fortunes.

Since only the Congress could declare war, a resolution to sue for peace would be binding on the Council. St. Cyr was confident his allies could get the resolution passed. Those members who were not tied to Tubalcain and St. Cyr would be on the fence anyway. The Confederation's campaign against Diamunde was proving very costly in terms of treasure and lives. In any democracy there are always those who are not willing to pay the price for victory. St. Cyr was counting on their support.

From far above where they sat, came the faint roar of another barrage from the Fleet's heavy plasma weapons, still searching for a weak spot in the headquarters' defenses.

"Clouse, summon the commander of my Lifeguard Battalion," St. Cyr ordered. He had deliberately sequestered a battalion of Teufelpanzers in the mountains. Their very existence was a closely held secret. When the negotiations were concluded, he would have some work for them to do. Marston St. Cyr smiled. It's never over till it's over, he thought, and leaned back in his chair.

Slowly, Colonel Namur's driver guided his heavily armored landcar across the desert. It used an infra system to navigate, and used a fuel-cell power pack that left virtually no heat signature; the armor plate would insulate even the occupants' body signatures from sensors, further insurance that they could not be detected by sensitive infrared surveillance systems. He drove cautiously because the terrain was extremely rough. They could not use the main roads, even in the violent sandstorm raging across the waste through the night, because the Confederation Fleet subjected the road networks to intermittent interdiction fires all night long in every kind of weather. So they were forced to travel cross-country all the way.

Namur's driver, Corporal Scithers, was stoic, a quiet young man when others were around, but when alone with his commander he could rattle on endlessly about weapons and vehicles and other military matters. Scithers had been driving Namur's command car when it was hit in the opening fight of the battle at Oppalia—how many days ago was that?—and he had escaped with severe burns on his legs, which had only begun to heal and were still very painful. But in the last days he had had his fill of combat, and fatigue hung heavily about him too, so now he was uncharacteristically quiet as he paid close attention to his driving.

"The war will be over soon," Namur said, just to be saying something.

"Good," Scithers answered. He cursed as he swerved to avoid a rock outcropping and then shifted the vehicle into its lowest gear to climb a thirty-degree slope.

"We might even win," Namur added.

"Good," Scithers grunted. The car crested the slope. Through his infras Scithers saw a stretch of flat tableland expanding before him. He glanced at his map console. Sixteen kilometers to the northwest lay the brigade and reasonable if only temporary safety. Scithers relaxed a little. "Well, sir—" A plasma bolt streaked by the passenger's side of the car like a flash of supercharged lightning, followed almost instantly by a second bolt that smashed into the car's engine compartment. The vehicle slewed crazily to a full stop then burst into flames.

His clothes on fire, Namur wrenched his door open and threw himself onto the desert floor. He rolled in the sand and smothered the flames. The landcar burned furiously behind him; the corporal was still inside the burning vehicle!

"Scithers!" Namur screamed. He jumped to his feet and ran back toward the car. Scithers was still strapped into the driver's console, fruitlessly beating at the flames that engulfed him. His flesh was on fire and every time he raised an arm to beat at the flames around his head, shreds of burning skin sloughed off his hands.

"Help me! Help me!" the corporal screamed. His hair blazed brightly. He twisted his head about violently, as if looking for his commander, but the fire had already burned away his eyelids and cooked his eyeballs, and with each tortured breath he sucked flames into his lungs. *"Eeeeeee!"* the human torch shrieked.

In one part of Namur's mind the thought registered that it was a wonder the corporal was still alive in there, but Namur was not thinking now, he was acting on instinct—he staggered back several meters, drew his side arm and shot Scithers in the head. He stood there breathing heavily for a time, staring at the ground, afraid to look back at Scithers's funeral pyre, before holstering his weapon and starting off wearily in the direction of his brigade. Far above the howling wind he could clearly hear the roar of the Raptor that had attacked them, circling its kill.

How could they have spotted them in this storm and the darkness? he wondered. If the Confederation naval forces had systems that could guide pilots through this stuff ... Namur paused. He shook his head. A sudden thought struck him:

Where was St. Cyr going to get the forces to mount the counter-attack that he and his men were to buy the time for with their lives? Namur knew his army's order of battle thoroughly, had committed it to memory. All available forces were engaged. He stumbled along a few more paces and then stopped dead in his tracks. There was no reserve left. All combat forces were engaged. If St. Cyr even tried to consolidate any frontline units into a significant assault force, those goddamned Raptors would destroy it before it could strike. St. Cyr could never mount any counterattack. Then what . . . ?

"Fuck you!" Colonel Namur shouted into the sky, and he wasn't talking to the Raptor.

CHAPTER
TWENTY-SIX

By the time the storm broke over Oppalia, the First Tank Brigade and Third Armored Division were hidden in badlands a hundred kilometers southeast of Rourke's Hills. The Fourth and Ninth armored divisions had also withdrawn, the Fourth to a densely canopied forest south of the badlands, the Ninth into its mountain redoubt north of First Division's Tourmaline home. The Fifteenth Heavy Division was hunkered down in hardened positions around New Kimberly, along with the Second Armored Division.

Technical problems continued to plague the string-of-pearls so there was still no satellite surveillance over the area of operations. General Aguinaldo was going to have to rely on aircraft and the FIST's unmanned aerial vehicles for intelligence, but the UAVs wouldn't do much good until he had some idea where to send them—their range was too short and the area to be surveilled too vast for them to be sent out on effective random patrols.

The infantry moved out of the city. General Aguinaldo put the Marines to the east, the direction he suspected held the greatest threat. He divided the ten thousand men of the 10th Light into three parts: he put one regiment south of the city and a second to the north, and kept the third in reserve.

Major General Ott argued against dividing his division but couldn't refuse the direct order Aguinaldo gave him. He suspected that if he tried to refuse, the Marine would relieve him and put a Marine in command of his division. Probably a brigadier, an officer who had no experience or training in the command of a division. Even divided, the 10th Light Infantry was better off with an army general in command.

Aguinaldo champed at the delay but couldn't send six FISTs and one light infantry division after the armored divisions, not even once the Raptors located them. In order to have any chance of victory against the tanks in the hiding places they'd chosen, he'd have to send all of his strength after one division. That would leave Oppalia and its vital spaceport vulnerable to the other enemy divisions. He had to wait until the rest of III Corps came down. Then he'd have the strength to go after the Diamundeans and still defend the city.

The day after the storm broke, the 37th Division began landing. A medium infantry division, the 37th had armored personnel carriers similar to the Marine Dragons, and each battalion had an organic heavy-weapons company with weapons powerful enough to destroy medium tanks with one hit. Other infantrymen were armed with TP1-killing Straight Arrows. It took the 37th two days to fully assemble planetside. Aguinaldo briefly considered sending his Marines and the 37th after the Fourth Armored Division because he knew their combined strength could defeat the Diamundeans hiding under the forest canopy. But if the Third Armor launched a lightning strike from the badlands to aid the Fourth, the resultant casualties would likely be greater than he was willing to absorb. Besides, the 10th Light couldn't defend against anything heavier than a two-brigade attack, and Aguinaldo knew two complete tank divisions and a heavy division were within striking distance of Oppalia. Allah and the Nine Buddhas only knew how many more divisions might be out there. Besides, it had taken the 37th so long to move from orbit to surface, he doubted its combat readiness.

The 106th Heavy Infantry Division was ready to begin landing when the last of the 37th touched down. It landed faster—much faster. The ass-chewing that Aguinaldo had directed at the commanders of the 37th Infantry Division was a potent spur to speed. The never-spoken but always present threat of being relieved and replaced by Marines was an even greater spur. Moreover, there was a matter of pride for the major general commanding the 106th and the colonels commanding the division's brigades. They knew full well how army and Corps command had screwed up. They were determined to show fighting Marines that all army leadership ranks weren't filled with incompetents. The five infantry battalions, three hopper squadrons, and four artillery battalions of the 106th were all planetside less than twenty-four hours after the last of the 37th touched down.

The following day the 2nd Infantry Division, a medium division like the 37th, landed quickly and efficiently.

Finally, five days after the storm that allowed the First Tank Brigade and the Third Armored Division to escape, General Aguinaldo had enough strength on hand to take the battle to the enemy. He assigned the defense of Oppalia to the 106th and 37th divisions. He'd need their strength later for the assault against New Kimberly. And he'd think about what to do with IX Corps when, and if, it was able to land. The 19th, 36th, and 225th FISTs, and the 10th Light Infantry Division, were to go after the First Tank Brigade and Third Armored Division in the badlands. Major General Daly was in command of that task force. The 13th, 21st, and 34th FISTs, along with the 2nd Infantry Division, under the joint command of 34th FIST's Brigadier Sturgeon, were to kill the Fourth Armored Division in the forest.

Aguinaldo got arguments from both army generals.

"Sir, I must protest," Major General Ott said. "As fine a general officer as I know General Daly to be, he has no experience commanding a division."

"General," Aguinaldo replied calmly. "Allowing for the 10th's lack of air, vehicles, and organic artillery, and despite its superior numbers, your division does not match the *force* General Daly has been commanding since day one of this war. He is more experienced than you are at commanding an operation of this size."

The Marine's relaxed demeanor reminded Ott of nothing so much as a native life-form on Lechter. The Barsoomian trapper looked innocent, rather like a coating of algae on rocks, but when enough weight moved across its center, it suddenly wrapped up its sides, engulfed whatever animal was on it, injected it with a paralyzing toxin, and began to digest it. When he was a captain commanding a company on Lechter, a squad had patrolled across one. There were no survivors.

When Aguinaldo saw that his point was accepted, he said, "General, I believe your foot soldiers will be better able to move rapidly and unseen in the badlands than one of the heavier divisions. That's why I'm sending the 10th—I think you can do the job."

"Thank you, sir," was all Ott could say.

Major General Flathead, commander of the 2nd Division, wasn't discomfited by Ott's abortive confrontation. He had a stronger position.

"Sir, this is preposterous," he began. "I'm a major general. Sturgeon's a brigadier. I outrank him."

Aguinaldo looked at him levelly. "That's easily enough remedied."

Flathead opened his mouth to continue, then realized the un-spoken threat had just been spoken. He turned livid, but closed his mouth. He hoped there would be an inquiry into the lack of readiness of III Corps and that he'd be called upon to testify; it was General Han's fault he was facing the embarrassment of having not just a Marine, but a junior Marine, in command over him. He wanted to see Han humiliated. It didn't occur to him that if he and the other division commanders had their divisions better prepared in the first place, there wouldn't have been a problem with III Corps' readiness and Han wouldn't have been relieved.

It took Task Force Daly two weeks of hard, grinding, slow movement through the hills and gullies of the badlands to corner and kill the elements of the Third Armored Division that didn't immediately surrender. They didn't kill the First Tank Brigade. As soon as the brigade's battalion commanders saw the desert camouflage of the advancing 10th Light, they sent out emissaries under white flags to arrange surrender.

Task Force Sturgeon had a harder time, though what turned out to be the antiarmor phase of the operation only took one week. All elements of the Fourth Armored Division fought to the last tank. The surviving tankers then became infantrymen and melted deeper into the forest, where they had to be found and killed or captured piecemeal. That took another month. That phase of the operation was conducted primarily by the Marines, who knew how to operate in platoon-size and smaller units. To the 2nd Infantry Division, a "small-unit" action was battalion-size, and their battalions couldn't function well where the tankers had gone.

Ninth Corps' heavy equipment finally arrived and its five divisions began landing. They didn't land as quickly as the 106th and 2nd divisions had because General Aguinaldo's attention was focused on the two task forces that were hunting down the Third and Fourth armored divisions.

The 10th Heavy Infantry Division was the first to land. It arrived just in time to help defend Oppalia from an assault made by three previously undetected Diamundean divisions that came up from the south. Three days of heavy fighting broke those divisions and sent them fleeing back to the south. Aguinaldo sent the 37th and 106th divisions after them. They were gone for five weeks.

Once the south and southeast were cleared, Aguinaldo sent the massed artillery of III Corps to the Tourmaline mining complex. The big guns battered the face of the mountain until it collapsed, sealing the First Armored Division inside. At last, seven weeks after the First Tank Brigade was driven from Oppalia, it was time to deal with the forces defending New Kimberly. Six Marine FISTs and two army Corps, all battle-tested if not battle-worn, lined up to assault the three divisions defending the capital city.

That was when the cease-fire order arrived from the Confederation Council.

CHAPTER
TWENTY-SEVEN

"Madame Speaker," Perry Anolitch, the representative from New Olifants intoned, "Madame Speaker, I request the august members of this august body be polled individually and by voice to confirm that—"

He was interrupted by shouts and groans as other congressmen, supporters and opponents of Val Carney's resolution to declare a cease-fire on Diamunde, voiced their opinions.

"—to confirm that the count is correct," Anolitch finished. With the electronic poll showing 248 members against the cease-fire and 252 for the measure, the vote was, so far, a clear victory for Carney.

Just three votes were needed to swing the ballot Chang-Sturdevant's way. In the event of a tie, the speaker, a nonvoting member, was empowered to break the deadlock. The speaker was Madame Piggot Thigpen of Carhart's World, an outspoken ally of Marston St. Cyr, but she shifted her vast bulk angrily and gestured at the sergeant-at-arms to proceed with the voice vote.

Wearily, he began to poll each member of the Congress. "I ask the Honorable Gentleman from Aardheim: How do you vote, sir?" Aardheim was against the cease-fire. He took a full five minutes to respond.

The recount could take several days. Already Anolitch and his colleagues were talking frantically to unpolled delegates who had voted for the measure while Val Carney and his allies appealed to those same delegates not to change their votes.

"Look there," Madame Chang-Sturdevant said to Marcus Berentus as they sat watching the vote on closed-circuit video from the private chamber reserved for the President's use. She nodded toward the screen, which showed Carney and Thigpen engaged in a whispered conversation.

"Hmph," Berentus grunted. "And they tell us there are no sentient life-forms harmful to the human species."

"Marc!" Chang-Sturdevant laughed in spite of herself. The two politicians were grotesque by themselves but, together like that, they resembled a circus sideshow duo, Jack Sprat and his fat-eating wife, licking their political platters clean: Carney thin as a rail, his sharp nose and chin almost touching; Thigpen a grotesque mound of fat, her eyes mere slits in a face as round and red as a setting sun. She constantly swiped at the rivulets of perspiration running down her flushed cheeks, and people in her vicinity had to be careful to avoid getting hit. Carney, deeply absorbed in what he was saying, was oblivious to the droplets that splashed onto him now.

"He probably enjoys her showers," Berentus said.

"I've heard she doesn't like men very much."

"Well, the feeling is mutual."

"Marc, I certainly hope this conversation is not being recorded."

"No, ma'am, not that I'm aware of."

After a moment Madame Chang-Sturdevant, shaking her head, changed the screen and they watched a prominent delegate, one whose turn was way down the roster to vote, dozing peacefully at his desk. Beside her, Berentus remarked, "This antiquated recount procedure is one of the weakest aspects of our system."

Madame Chang-Sturdevant only shrugged. All parties used the parliamentary maneuver occasionally. She sighed. "What travels about comes about. I used it once when I was in Congress, and who knows, it may work for us this time." She paused. "But don't count on it, Marc. Our forces have had some hard fighting on Diamunde, which may have cooled the enthusiasm of some members." She shrugged again. Her nonchalance belied how she really felt—betrayed and disgusted. If St. Cyr pulled off the political coup, those who died attempting to stop his butchery would have been sacrificed in vain. From where she sat at the moment, he had pulled it off.

"And don't forget St. Cyr's money," Berentus added bitterly. "All those good men's lives wasted because of these damned money-grubbing cowards . . . excuse me, Madame President! I am no politician; you know that. But we have that bastard by the short hairs, ma'am, all we need is a little more time and he's history."

Madame Chang-Sturdevant nodded. The voting droned on and on. Eventually the President of the Confederation Council of Worlds dozed off herself.

The recount took six hours. The final tally was 250 members against a cease-fire and 250 for it. Madame Piggot Thigpen smiled, her several chins jiggling merrily. She cast her vote. The measure passed.

Perry Anolitch rested his head in his hands.

Madame Chang-Sturdevant got to her feet. "Dispatch a drone to Admiral Wimbush immediately, Marc. Order him to initiate a cease-fire upon receipt and to open negotiations with St. Cyr as soon as possible." Berentus nodded, bowing silently to the inevitable. "But Marc," Chang-Sturdevant added, "tell the admiral to be very careful. Very careful. St. Cyr cannot be trusted. He may yet do something that will permit us to nail him. Nothing's over till it's over."

Jon Beerdmens, Chief of the Confederation Diplomatic Corps, shifted his huge bulk and farted loudly. His chair had been made to his exact specifications by craftsmen on New Brooklyn; the meal he'd just eaten had been prepared in the headquarters cafeteria. Eating there always made his innards rumble embarrassingly. Others who ate the cafeteria food didn't seem to have that problem. He wondered why. Perhaps it was the shurdlu sausages dripping with fat, the boiled cabbages grown on Eatoin and the Creme of Greece soup he enjoyed so much. The chef knew which foods Beerdmens liked best, and since he was the Chief of the Corps, his favorite dishes were always on hand when he was in town.

Beerdmens raised himself slightly and fanned the air vigorously. He wondered, as he always did, why one's own farts never seemed to smell as atrociously rotten as those expressed by others. He sat back down heavily. The padded cushions under his 153 kilos hissed as they absorbed his weight and lowered him slowly back into a comfortable sitting position. Fumes lingering in the fabric under him rose, silent and deadly, into the still office air. He punched a button on the climate control console to freshen the air exchange. It labored mightily, silently, but, ultimately, ineffectively to do his bidding; in the twenty-fifth century there were still tasks so difficult that mere machinery was unequal to them.

Beerdmens belched loudly. The sound reverberated like a shot in his spacious office suite. He looked about self-consciously, hoping his secretary, sitting just outside, hadn't heard. "Excellency, you have a visitor," that very same person announced over the intercom.

"Not now, Grace!" he said petulantly. Gad, he couldn't have someone coming in here now, not with that odor.

"Excellency, it is Madame Wellington-Humphreys. She is on your calendar for—"

"Oh, very well. Uh, Grace, tell her to wait a minute, would you?"

The air exchanger was not working fast enough. With some effort Beerdmens got out of his chair and waddled, swiftly and gracefully for so large a man, to the nearest window. He pressed a control pad, and instantly cool afternoon air flowed in. He stood there, shaking out his clothing and waving his arms. Satisfied that the aroma had dissipated, he waddled back to his desk and sat down with a huge sigh. The chair quietly readjusted.

"Send in Madame Ambassador now, Grace."

Madame J. Wellington-Humphreys swept into the room. She carried with her the faint but pleasant aroma of very expensive perfume. She was, as always, ravishing.

"Excellency," she said with a small bow toward Beerdmens.

"Madame." Beerdmens leaned forward and extended his hand across his desktop. It was far easier than trying to get up again. "Forgive me, but recently I sprained my ankle, and must receive you like this," he lied with an embarrassed smile. "Please, be seated, Madame. Would you like some refreshment?"

"Very thoughtful of you, Excellency! Yes, please. Would a glass of Katzenwasser 'thirty-six be any trouble? I'd like it served with just a tiny pinch of Cerebrian garlic, if possible, and perhaps a pipe of thule on the side?"

"Ah, Madame, an excellent vintage! Thule, of course! John . . ." Beerdmens punched a pad on his communications console and gave Wellington-Humphreys's order to his steward. "And the same for me," he added.

Wellington-Humphreys wrinkled her nose slightly and looked about the room. Beerdmens sought to distract her. "Ah, Madame, you've been to Wanderjahr, haven't you?" Damn, he thought, I must get maintenance to work on that air scrubber. Back to matters at hand: The champagne and the mild narcotic thule were Wanderjahr's chief exports, and Beerdmens enjoyed both enormously.

"Yes, Excellency. I was there on a diplomatic mission when that dreadful Spears person was our ambassador. I understand Spears is retired and Kurt Arschmann in jail."

"Indeed. Good riddance to them both."

"I rather liked Arschmann," Wellington-Humphreys said. "They put some—some—nobody in charge after Kurt was arrested." John arrived and served the drinks and pipes of thule. "The military made quite a mess of things there, I understand," Wellington-Humphreys continued, sipping her champagne.

"Don't they always?" Beerdmens laughed. "For them the best solution to any political crisis is to kill as many people as possible. That brings me to the reason I asked you to come back here. Been following events on Diamunde lately?"

"Well, I've been busy on Dagondxi, as you know. Got the Samovarians and the Mercers to agree on a border treaty, and that was damned hard, let me tell you!" Beerdmens nodded sympathetically. "So not much time to follow events elsewhere. But yes, I know we had to send in the Marines to deal with this—this whatsisname. . . ."

"Marston St. Cyr. Yes, it's been a terrible mess, Madame. Again, the Marines and the army have succeeded in killing a lot of people to no discernible advantage to anyone. So the Congress voted to negotiate. That is where you come in."

Wellington-Humphreys nodded and finished her drink. She picked up the small pipe of thule and inhaled through the narrow stem as the tiny ball of narcotic glowed merrily in the bowl. "You need a negotiator," she said.

"Yes. The best. The very best. That's why I called you back."

"Thank you, Excellency. Actually, with negotiations on Dagondxi nearly complete, I can leave them in the hands of my subordinates. What is my authority?"

"You will be Ambassador Plenipotentiary."

Wellington-Humphreys started. Ambassador Plenipotentiary! She would be empowered to act with the full authority of the Confederation on Diamunde. "My relationship with the military commander out there?"

"Admiral Wimbush, Fleet commander, will be instructed to give you his full support. You are in complete charge of all diplomatic operations, and the admiral will be subordinate to you in all matters except those of a strictly military nature. The usual arrangement."

"When do I leave?"

"At once, Madame."

Wellington-Humphreys smiled. She was ready for the assignment and fully confident in her ability to bring it to a successful conclusion. A good job in Diamunde might mean . . . well, Beerdmens would die or retire someday. Modern medical science could only do so much to prolong the life of a man who treated his body so irresponsibly. And when he was gone . . .

"I must warn you, Madame," Beerdmens said, seeing the self-satisfied smile crossing Wellington-Humphreys's face, "that this St. Cyr is a very dangerous person. He is not to be trusted. I am afraid to say this, Madame, but you may, this one time, find the presence of a strong military force an excellent negotiating tool—and a safety net."

"You are saying that about 'Your Huggable Military Force,' Excellency?" Wellington-Humphreys laughed.

Beerdmens laughed too. "Your Huggable Military Force," YHMF, for short, was one of his favorite expressions, used to show his disdain for the choice of military force over that of diplomatic persuasion.

"What will my Letter of Instructions say about a military escort?" she asked. Every diplomatic mission was authorized a military escort. The size of the escort depended on the mission and the desires of the chief diplomat.

"You must have one, Madame."

"I don't need one, Excellency," Wellington-Humphreys replied, a sharp edge to her voice. "They are only an encumbrance. I have never needed one up to now. You know how I feel about Marines." Diplomatic escorts were always Marines. Wellington-Humphreys harbored a special dislike for military men, one shared by most of the Confederation Diplomatic Corps. In her opinion, Marines were only good for breaking things.

"Well, you *will* have one, Madame, that is final. But just beware of this St. Cyr, Madame. That is all I am saying."

"I can handle him," Wellington-Humphreys replied, taking another deep drag of thule.

Outside Beerdmens's office Wellington-Humphreys paused by Grace's workstation and leaned over to whisper in the older woman's ear, "Grace, the old bastard let out one of the most horrible farts on record!"

Through the closed door Beerdmens heard the women's laughter and wondered what could be so funny.

Julie Wellington-Humphreys had been a child of privilege destined never to suffer the pain of work or worry. So when at the age of twenty she announced imperiously that she intended to enter the Diplomatic Corps, her parents had been both pleased and horrified. Pleased, because diplomacy and government had been the avocation of Wellington-Humphreyses for generations; horrified, because to them it was no place for their daughter. But Julie was not to be dissuaded. Like all Wellington-Humphreyses before her, she was intelligent, boldly self-confident, determined, and used to getting her way.

A raven-haired beauty in her youth and tall for her sex, age had only improved Julie Wellington-Humphreys's looks. By the time she turned forty, a streak of gray had formed in her hair that swept back from the center of her forehead. As she aged the gray turned to white but the rest of her hair remained as black as in her youth. She cultivated an aloof expression, looking down her patrician nose at people when she spoke to them in the slow drawl affected by members of the Diplomatic Corps. But she spoke a dozen languages fluently and understood dozens more dialects, was a shrewd observer, and an excellent judge of character, priceless assets for any diplomat.

Upon the occasion of her first ambassadorial appointment, Julie Wellington-Humphreys had changed her name to "J. Wellington-Humphreys." She had never married and had no lovers. She had no time for marriage or dalliance. Besides, she had never met a man, or woman, up to her standards. But she had never met Marston St. Cyr. More to the point, she had never met the men of third platoon, Lima Company, 34th FIST.

CHAPTER
TWENTY-EIGHT

Brigadier Sturgeon's landcar glided smoothly along the rainswept streets of New Kimberly, en route to Ambassador J. Wellington-Humphreys's reception at the newly refurbished Confederation embassy.

The brigadier had been surprised when Fleet Admiral Wimbush requested his presence the day before for a personal interview onboard the *Ogie*.

"Ambassador Wellington-Humphreys arrived yesterday to begin negotiations with St. Cyr the day after tomorrow," the admiral said. "She's already been in touch with the bastard, and there's going to be a huge reception at the site of our old embassy tomorrow evening. This reception is an ice-breaker, get the parties together, press some flesh and mellow everyone out over food and wine so they can get down to work the next morning. Since you Marines provide the security for our embassies, I asked General Aguinaldo to designate one of his commanders to do the same for the Ambassador. He picked the 34th."

"Thank you, sir."

"Don't thank me, Brigadier, thank the general," Wimbush replied. He had regained much of his old confidence now that it seemed the initial debacle over the landing had resolved itself. If the negotiations proceeded well, he might still find himself a seat on the Combined Chiefs of Staff. "The reason I wanted to talk to you about this assignment, Brigadier, is because I want to impress on you that nothing, and I mean nothing, can be allowed to go wrong. Nobody trusts St. Cyr, Brigadier. I want you to pick your best men for this job and have them stick to Ambassador Wellington-Humphreys like—like—"

"I understand, sir."

"Here is the communiqué from the Confederation Council that lays out our relationship to this diplomatic mission," Wimbush said as he handed it to the brigadier.

"Whew," Sturgeon exclaimed as he read. "She's 'Ambassador Plenipotentiary.' That means—"

"That means, Brigadier, that she outranks all of us."

"Sir, I promise you I'll detail my best men to this assignment. My very best men."

The car continued through the darkened streets, rain pelting off its screens. Inside, the vehicle's instrument panel lights glowed green on Brigadier Sturgeon's face as he spoke. "Since the men of Ensign vanden Hoyt's platoon will accompany Ambassador Wellington-Humphreys during these negotiations, they'll be closer to her than white on rice, so I want them and you there with me at this reception tonight to meet her," Brigadier Sturgeon told Captain Conorado as he handed him the heavily gilded formal invitation.

It read, "Brigadier Theodosius Sturgeon, Commander, 34th Fleet Initial Strike Team and party." It was the "and party" that got Conorado's attention.

"We don't even get a mention?" he asked the brigadier, handing the invitation back to him.

The brigadier waved it off. "This is an official Diplomatic Corps reception. To those people *I'm* on a social scale just a cut above the caterers, so you know where that puts the rest of you. The reception's at nineteen hours. I'll pick you up at 1830. Uniform is full dress with medals. Make sure Charlie Bass is sober." He smiled. "Your battalion commander didn't tell me why you recommended these men, Captain. I know why you picked Bass, anybody'd guess that, but why the others for the escort?"

"Vanden Hoyt because he's clean-cut, reliable, has good judgment, can act decisively in a crisis, and he's an old-fashioned gentleman. That boy's headed for flag command someday, sir, the hard way—he's going to earn it. Dean, you know, sir. He's quick-witted and will follow orders. MacIlargie, well, he's got potential as a troublemaker, sir, but he has a very good nose for trouble. And he personally flamed three enemy tanks in the Oppalia planethead, so he's got guts. With this goddamned St. Cyr involved, the Ambassador'll need a gutsy watchdog by her side."

The brigadier nodded. "I'm so damned glad this thing is about over, Captain." He sighed. "These last weeks have been the worst fighting I've seen in years. Our casualties—" He decided not to discuss casualties with an officer whose company had suffered so severely. "Well, this is the best chance we've got to end this damned farce. Let's get on with it, then."

"Sir, just what are 'flaky croissants'?" Ensign vanden Hoyt asked from the rear of the brigadier's landcar. He was reading the menu from the by then well-thumbed copy of the invitation Brigadier Sturgeon had given to Captain Conorado earlier in the day.

Gunnery Sergeant Charlie Bass leaned over the ensign's shoulder and said, "Yessir, that 'creamy Bernaise sauce' on the 'tenderloin tidbits' sounds pretty suspicious to me."

Captain Conorado laughed. "Stand easy, Charlie, or I'll have you on field rations the rest of this mission."

Dean and MacIlargie, sitting behind Bass and the officers, smiled broadly but kept quiet.

"Hell, sir, at least I know what's in 'em. Look at this." He pointed to "Crème Brûlée with Crusty Brown Sugar Topping."

Ensign vanden Hoyt smacked his lips. "Sounds good to me, Charlie." He poked Bass in the ribs.

Bass snorted and folded his arms over his chest. "Ensign," he said, with the superior air of an experienced noncommissioned officer, "when you're as salty as I am, you'll appreciate the culinary delights of a cold beer, a greasy reindeer sausage, and a fine cigar, instead of this—this milk and cookies slop these goddamn dilettantes live off of."

"Gentlemen," the brigadier said, "that menu is being catered by Ridgewell's. Do any of you know who they are?" When there was no response he continued, nodding his head. "Ridge-well's is a four-hundred-year-old catering firm that has sub-sidiaries on every world worth mentioning in Human Space. They are the most exclusive and expensive caterers in the Confederation.

"Once, oh, fifteen years ago or so now, when I was com-manding the legation guard on Carhart's World—you remember Carhart's World, Charlie—some billionaire offworlder who was on a hunting expedition there hired Ridgewell's to cater a supper for his party. The nearest subsidiary was seventy-five light-years away. They put the goddamn meal in a hyperspace drone and shipped it all the way to Carhart's World! The damned stuff was still hot when it got there. That cost him more than all of us will earn if we spend the rest of our lives in the Corps."

"Which we will," Bass added firmly, indicating he didn't care a damn for billionaires, catered meals, or Ambassador J. Wellington-Humphreys.

"Sir," Captain Conorado said, "what kind of person is this Ambassador J. Wellington-Humphreys?"

Brigadier Sturgeon turned in his seat so he could speak di-rectly to the men behind him. "Old family, old money, educated at the best schools, long history of outstanding service in the Diplomatic Corps. Arrogant, though. Thinks she can bring this mission off on the force of her own considerable personality, without any help from us."

"Damned stuck-up farts," Bass muttered, meaning the entire Diplomatic Corps. The brigadier exchanged a quick glance with Captain Conorado. This was not the Charlie Bass they had known before Diamunde. The strain of the past few weeks was showing. Bass's platoon had been in the heaviest fighting during the Oppalia breakout operation. But they were all tired.

"Well, there are exceptions," the brigadier said. "Remember old Jay Benjamin Spears, back on Wanderjahr?"

"Yessir," Captain Conorado answered. "He was with you when you pulled off the raid on whatsisname's hideout."

"Turbat Nguyen-Multan," the brigadier answered. "Yep, they threw away the mold when they made old J.B. He stood tall when we raided that old bastard. By the way, he received the Legion of Honor that I recommended him for on that occasion." The Legion of Honor was the highest military decoration a civilian could be awarded for heroism. "But I agree with you, Charlie, most of the diplomats I've met wouldn't have made a—" He gestured helplessly with one hand, searching for the appropriate phrase.

"A pimple on a kwangduk's ass," Charlie Bass said.

"Uh, right, Charlie," the brigadier answered. He turned to address vanden Hoyt, MacIlargie, and Dean directly: "After tonight you men will be Ambassador Wellington-Humphreys's personal security escort for however long it takes her to conclude negotiations with St. Cyr and end this war, is that understood? You men will stick to her like another skin. You will be her shadow."

The three Marines replied in one voice, "Yessir."

Brigadier Sturgeon and his party moved slowly through the reception line. Ambassador J. Wellington-Humphreys stood next to C. Bowles Cabot, the newly appointed Confederation Ambassador to Diamunde, who stood next to Degs Momyer, who would be Minister of Finance in the new government the Confederation was assembling to replace the directorial boards of the conglomerates. Momyer's secretary stood just behind him and whispered the names and titles of the visitors into his ear so he could whisper into C. Bowles Cabot's ear. C. Bowles Cabot in turn whispered into J. Wellington-Humphreys's ear, "The Honorable Clancy Drummon, President of Drummon Associates, and Lady Maybelle Drummon," and so on. The arriving guests briefly shook hands with the dignitaries, murmured a few words, and passed on into the reception hall for refreshments.

"Brigadier General Theodosius Sturgeon, commanding the 34th FIST, Confederation Marine Corps, and party," the secretary whispered to Momyer, who whispered the information to Cabot, who whispered to the Ambassador, just loud enough for Brigadier Sturgeon to hear him. He winced. He was not a "brigadier general." That was an army rank. Anyone could see he was a brigadier of Marines by the silver novas glittering brightly on the gold-fringed epaulets fixed to each shoulder of his stock collar tunic. He shook hands with the minister, then Ambassador Cabot, then paused for a moment before taking Ambassador J. Wellington-Humphreys's extended hand in his own.

"Madam Ambassador." He bowed and gracefully brushed his lips over the back of her hand.

"Brigadier," she drawled, dragging the title out into three long syllables, looking down her nose at the Marine. "It seems," she drew the word out into two syllables, "I shall be spending some time in the com-pah-nee of your Marines." Her lips curled in a brief smile. Popinjay; size thirty-two waist, size five hat, she thought, and then: Still, he really looks splendid in that uniform. He did, bloodred tunic over gold trousers, his decorations splashed over his left chest; on each side of his tunic stock collar shone the bright rampant-eagle emblem of the Confederation Marine Corps. The brigadier introduced the other Marines. When he came to Bass, and he stepped forward to take J. Wellington-Humphreys's proffered hand, she wrinkled her nose as an expression of annoyance came over her face. Bass had smoked a cigar just before leaving that evening, and the fabric of his uniform was still redolent with—to him, anyway—its fragrance.

"I'm very pleased to meet you, ma'am," Bass said, his voice just a little too loud.

"You are the one," she whispered involuntarily.

"Ma'am?" Bass asked.

The Ambassador shook her head. "Nothing," she said, catching herself.

When she arrived on Diamunde she had reviewed the files of the men picked to accompany her. She'd glanced, half amused, at the files for vanden Hoyt, Dean, and MacIlargie; earnest, sincere-looking young men, inexperienced in everything important, good only for military or police details. But she lingered over Bass's file. She hardly noticed the citations for bravery, which were mostly meaningless to her. But what stuck with her was the fact that when on a peacekeeping mission on a place called Elneal, he had killed a formidable warrior chieftain in a knife fight. "Nobody fights with a knife anymore!" she had exclaimed aloud. That fact both excited and repelled her. And now that knife-fighting throwback was standing there, eagerly expecting her to give him her hand.

She glanced at the resplendent uniform tunic covering the expanse of his chest. Under that tunic was a man of considerable physical power, a man like her, used to getting, within certain limits of course, his way every time.

Bass took the Ambassador's hand awkwardly and self-consciously gave it a brief shake before letting go. His hand was warm, she noted, but callused. So this is the hand that drove the knife home, she thought as Bass passed on through the reception line.

Her greeting of the other Marines in her escort was perfunctory, and they continued on through the line feeling very much that they had been summarily dismissed from the royal woman's august presence.

The Marines passed into the huge reception room where drinks and hors d'oeuvres were being served. Waiters flitted everywhere, hoisting silver platters heaped with tidbits or stacked with drinks. Bass snatched a long-stemmed glass of some effervescent wine and gulped it down.

"Charlie, you're supposed to sip that stuff, not chug it down," Captain Conorado cautioned the platoon sergeant.

"Aw, I'm dry as the Martac Waste, Skipper," Bass explained, grabbing at another glass.

"Well, that's Katzenwasser 'thirty-six, Charlie," the captain said, slowly savoring his wine, "a vintage imported champagne."

"Imported from where?" Bass asked, making a face as he sipped it.

"Wanderjahr, Charlie."

"Jesu!" Bass exclaimed loudly, and several heads turned in his direction. "I should've known it. No wonder they're so fucked up back there. This stuff tastes like a liquid fart!"

Again Conorado and the brigadier exchanged nervous glances. Then the brigadier laughed. You tell 'em, Charlie! he thought. If he'd had his way, this war would be over now, St. Cyr dead or in prison, his forces smashed, no need for all the diplomatic playacting, all this bowing and scraping and "madam-may-I-

introduce" crap. But the Confederation had ordered a negotiated settlement. Anger welled up again in the brigadier's breast.
Half the Confederation Council was in St. Cyr's pocket; no
wonder they voted to spare the bastard. All those good men
dead, and for what? Worst of all, every man in the 34th FIST
knew what was going on. Gunny Bass was only saying what he
himself was thinking.

Dinner, served after Charlie Bass had consumed eight more
glasses of Wanderjahr Katzenwasser '36 than were good for
him, started as a minor disaster and went downhill quickly
thereafter. The Marines were seated opposite and a few places
down the table from Ambassador J. Wellington-Humphreys.
Sitting directly opposite Bass was none other than Professor
Jere Benjamin, whom Bass had seen around headquarters and
knew by reputation. In a too-loud voice he began a conversation with the academic about the operation of the Straight Arrow
antitank rocket.

When the sautéed tenderloin tidbits in creamy Bernaise
sauce were served, Bass looked down at his plate in alarm and
said, in a voice loud enough that J. Wellington-Humphreys
heard him clearly, "Jesus Muhammad, Skipper, looks like some
bastard blew his nose on this shit!"

The croissants had been served, vanden Hoyt was enjoying
his enormously and Bass was working on still another glass of
Katzenwasser '36, when the lights suddenly went out. At first
there was shocked silence in the dining hall as the 150 guests
contemplated sitting in the pitch-darkness, then a few nervous
laughs and someone shouted, "Who didn't pay the light bill this
month?" followed by more laughter.

Vanden Hoyt leaped from his seat onto the table, scattering
food and tableware as he went, and jumped down between Ambassador Wellington-Humphreys and Degs Momyer. He put
his arms around the startled woman and dragged her away from
the table before she could even scream. "Dean! Mac! To me! To
me!" he shouted. The two enlisted men, orienting themselves
on the sound of vanden Hoyt's voice, followed their officer noisily
across the table top. Vanden Hoyt whispered into Wellington-

Humphreys's ear, "Don't make a sound, Madame! This is a kidnapping attempt. We're going to get you out of here." Vanden Hoyt silently prayed that he was right, otherwise he'd probably be spending the rest of his career counting rations on a supply ship.

A few other people around the huge table had produced glowballs and there was now a dim light in the hall, just enough illumination to see the outlines of people's figures.

"Remember how to get out of here?" vanden Hoyt asked the two enlisted men.

"Sure," MacIlargie said.

"Then you and Dean run interference for me, because we're getting this lady the hell out of here."

"Just a moment," Degs Momyer said, laying a restraining hand on vanden Hoyt's shoulder. Vanden Hoyt threw a punch in the direction of Momyer's voice. His fist connected solidly and sent Momyer thudding to the floor, incidentally saving the Minister of Finance's life. At that very moment, the wall a few meters down from where they were standing suddenly blew inward with a brilliant flash. Someone had detonated an implosion device, so the tremendous force of the blast was not accompanied by much noise, which left the survivors able to hear. Debris followed by a terrific blast wave swept into the hall, tossing body parts across the table and into the people sitting on the opposite side. Armed men dressed in black charged through the gaping hole the blast had left, coming straight at the Ambassador's little group, firing blasters up and down the table as they went.

Bass lay in the debris underneath the table. He felt around and armed himself with the only weapon he could find, a metal serving tray still smeared with a sweet chocolatey substance. He skittered out from under the table and began swinging.

Dragging and pushing the Ambassador, vanden Hoyt and the two enlisted men ran through the semidarkness of the dining hall. Hell reigned behind them as the attackers, evidently frustrated when they found the ambassador's position at the table empty and unable to spot her in the pandemonium, began firing aimlessly into the crowd. Plasma bolts cracked and hissed throughout the great hall. Dignitaries, reduced to terrorized animals, trampled one another in an effort to escape the blaster bolts.

MacIlargie led them into a corridor off the main hall. It was pitch-dark. Cautiously they felt their way along the walls. "What's going on?" Wellington-Humphreys asked.

"St. Cyr's attempting to kidnap you, ma'am," vanden Hoyt answered. "Looks like they knew just where you'd be sitting and came through the wall to get you. They set the charge far enough down the outside of the building so it wouldn't kill you when it went off." He stopped to get his breath.

"Who the hell are you?" vanden Hoyt asked suddenly as a figure came sliding into the corridor.

"Benjamin," the figure wheezed.

"The professor?" vanden Hoyt exclaimed.

"Yes. I just followed you. I figured you knew how to get out of here."

"Okay, Professor. Just stay calm and follow us." They walked cautiously down the corridor.

"Door," Dean whispered ahead of them. He shoved it gently. "It's locked or jammed, sir." MacIlargie joined Dean and they put their shoulders to the door and pushed.

Vanden Hoyt added his own weight. "What the fuck?" he muttered, and then, "Oh, excuse me, ma'am."

"Those were my sentiments exactly, Lieutenant Vanderman," the Ambassador replied dryly.

"Ensign vanden Hoyt, not Lieutenant, ma'am."

"We could stay in here until help comes," Wellington-Humphreys suggested.

Vanden Hoyt thought about that possibility for a moment. His mind was made up by a blaster bolt that caromed off the ceiling and slagged the marble behind them. "On three, we all hit the door as hard as we can," he said. "One, two, three!" The Marines slammed into the door with all their weight. It shook but still held. "Again!" They assaulted the door a second time. It still held.

"Goddamnit!" MacIlargie shouted, braced himself on one leg and slammed the other into the door.

Cool night air engulfed them as the door came off the frame and hung by its hinges.

"Good thing you had me along, eh, Mr. Vee?" MacIlargie said. He held the broken door aside as he went through, and the others followed him down the steps into the darkness outside.

"Good thing this is one of those old-fashioned doors and not a pneumatic one," Dean muttered as he followed the others.

Suddenly, brilliant light illuminated the quintet, freezing them on the stairway like feral animals caught in the hunter's sights. Marston St. Cyr, surrounded by dozens of heavily armed men, stood smiling in the street outside, a tiny radio-tracking device held in one hand.

" 'Welcome to my lair,' said the spider to the flies." St. Cyr smirked.

CHAPTER
TWENTY-NINE

The foothills of the Chrystoberyl mountain range began their gentle rise from the Pryhrotite salt flats some thirty kilometers north of New Kimberly. Some of the peaks reached in excess of four thousand meters, and the residents of New Kimberly were treated to spectacular sunrises over their perpetually snow-capped tops every morning. But that mountain range was far more to the people of New Kimberly and Diamunde than a beautiful example of the planet's ancient tectonic activity.

Generations of miners had made their living exploiting the mineral deposits that lay under the mountains, and Diamunde had become wealthy on the ores and gems they brought out of the rock down there. The range was honeycombed with shafts, chambers, and thousands of kilometers of tunnels. So extensive and so deep had the excavations gone over the centuries that no one really knew anymore where they all led. Once a vein or deposit was used up, it was sealed off and the miners moved on. Over the years, as companies went out of business or were absorbed in mergers, many site maps and plans were misplaced or deleted from databases, and when operations moved on from one sector to another, nobody spent the money or the time needed to go back and remap the excavated areas.

So the chambers, some of them hundreds of meters high, lay dark, silent and unknown, forever hidden from the sunlight. Rumors and legends grew up around the abandoned works: they were haunted by miners' ghosts; strange creatures native to Diamunde and never seen by humans had taken up their abode down there. The rumors were handed down from one genera-

tion to the next, each embellishing the stories as they passed
them on, and they had become so wild over time that eventually
no one gave them any credence—while aboveground, that is.

But Diamundean miners never ventured far from their current operations; miners' lives in the active excavations were
dangerous enough without them taking risks wandering around
in the abandoned diggings. To most of Diamunde's hard-
working people, the abandoned mines became places of mys-
tery and potential danger, and no one cared to go into them
anymore. Until Marston St. Cyr came along, that is.

Completely immobilized, unable even to speak, the hostages
were aware only of constant motion that seemed now to have
been going on for hours. Dean tried to calculate the passage of
time and the direction in which they were being taken, but that
proved impossible. In the first few minutes of their capture, just
after they were injected with immobilizing drugs, he had thought
they were being taken north. Now he had no idea where they
were. The way the engine noise seemed to echo around him, it
seemed most of the trip was in a tunnel.

And then the vehicle stopped and Dean lay in total darkness,
listening. He heard men dismount, then loud metallic noises as
doors slammed somewhere. All was quiet for a moment, and
then it seemed the bottom of the world fell out from under him
as he plunged rapidly downward. After a moment of panic, he
assumed the vehicle had been loaded into a high-speed elevator
of some kind. After what he judged was a good two minutes, it
began to slow and then stopped. More doors clanged, and then
he could hear men talking and walking very near where he lay.
He was lifted into the air, and from the way the body pod in
which he was encased moved, he knew he was being carried
somewhere.

Wham! He was dropped on a solid surface. *Wham!* Someone
else was dropped onto a solid surface. *Wham! Wham! Wham!*
The chamber in which they were being unloaded echoed loudly
as each hostage's pod was unceremoniously deposited on the
floor.

The men who unloaded the hostages walked off. All was total silence for a long time. Dean lay there in the darkness, working on his vocal cords, but no sound would come out of them; he could only get a sibilant wheezing noise to emerge from his lips. A tingling sensation in his left little finger indicated that the immobilizing drug was beginning to wear off.

"M-Mac . . ." Dean croaked. He could feel his feet now. He tried again, "M-Mac . . . !" He coughed. "MacIlargie!" he rasped. He could move his left leg a little now. He kicked the container lid weakly.

"Dean! MacIlargie! It's wearing off! Can you hear me?" Ensign vanden Hoyt whispered hoarsely.

Dean still had not recovered enough to answer fully, so he kicked the lid several times again instead.

"Madame Ambassador?" vanden Hoyt said, his voice stronger now. "Madame Wellington-Humphreys? Are you all right?" No answer. "Professor—er, uh . . ." A muffled response from one of the pods was all he got.

"I'm gonna kick somebody's ass when I get out of here!" MacIlargie shouted in an almost normal voice. Dean smiled despite himself. Hey! He had the use of his facial muscles!

"Lieutenant—Lieutenant Vanderpool . . . ?" It was Madame Wellington-Humphreys.

"Vanden Hoyt, ma'am, Ensign vanden Hoyt. How are you?"

"It's Benjamin, Ensign," Professor Benjamin said.

"Sorry, sir. Good to know you're okay, ma'am. Good to know you're okay too, Professor."

"Call me Jere, Ensign."

After a few more minutes the five were carrying on a spirited conversation.

"Silence!" a powerful voice roared. They could hear many men moving about around them now. The fastenings on their pods were unsnapped and bright artificial light flooded in upon them as the lids were torn off. The hostages blinked in the light as strong arms lifted them out of the pods.

They were in a large cavern. Several corridors led off in different directions. In one wall was the elevator. Its doors were closed. They were surrounded by at least two dozen armed men in battle-dress uniforms.

Still too weak to stand or move by themselves, they were held up as someone applied manacles to their wrists. Black hoods were then placed over their heads and they were carried and shoved in different directions. Dean and MacIlargie were taken down one corridor, vanden Hoyt another, the Ambassador and Professor Benjamin a third.

The two enlisted men were taken to a chamber just off the elevator shaft, and as they stood before an iron door set into the solid rock, their hoods and manacles were removed. Their escort shoved them roughly through the door and it was locked behind them. They found themselves in a room three meters wide by about four deep. The ceiling was perhaps five meters above them. It was lighted indirectly from an undetermined source. Bunks lined the walls, which had been faced with wood, and crude toilet facilities occupied one corner. Judging from the lockers and cabinets built into the walls, the place evidently had been someone's living quarters at one time.

MacIlargie collapsed on one of the bunks. To his surprise, he found it comfortable. He was still too weak to move about much. Dean flopped on the other bunk. "I am gonna kick some ass when we get out of here," MacIlargie growled.

"Silence!" a loud voice boomed from somewhere up near the ceiling. The two Marines were surprised at first, and then MacIlargie broke forth in a stream of profanity.

"Eavesdropping on us, you son of a bitch?" MacIlargie shouted. "I'll give you an earful, you shitduk!"

The voice demanded silence again. Both MacIlargie and Dean cursed back at it. The lights went out suddenly. In total darkness they screamed obscenities at the voice until they ran out of fresh insults. Eventually the lights came back on, but the voice did not bother them again.

"How are my guests?" St. Cyr asked as Stauffer entered his well-appointed office suite. While he had never anticipated he would be defeated so soundly when he grabbed power on

Diamunde, Marston St. Cyr always had a fallback position. This complex and the hostages were his tickets to freedom.

"They are fine, sir. The Ambassador is outraged; the professor is curious; the ensign is threatening us; and the two enlisted Marines, well, they are acting like enlisted men." He shrugged.

"Fine, fine. Pour yourself some refreshment." He waved to a well-stocked bar in a corner. "Come, sit down with me, Clouse, and we will discuss our future." The Woo that had been crouching in one corner got up and limped after Stauffer, hoping perhaps to get a handout from the bar. It was limping because St. Cyr had broken one of its feet in a rage the night before.

"Back to your place!" St. Cyr shouted. Clouse jumped involuntarily and the Woo scuttled back to its corner. St. Cyr grinned. The Woo trembled in fear. "Throw the damned thing a cracker," St. Cyr commanded. Stauffer selected a heavily salted cracker from a basket on the bar and tossed it to the Woo. The creature snatched it adroitly in the two fingerlike talons at the end of its only arm and stuffed it into the slot in its torso that served as a mouth. It stared back at Stauffer with its large, round, wet eyes as if offering thanks for the cracker, then folded its five good legs under itself and turned a glistening brown, the sign that it was digesting, its pain and fear apparently forgotten for the moment.

The Woo was the highest life-form humans had ever found on Diamunde. The early colonists, surrounded by packs of Woos bobbing, weaving, murmuring, and staring at the newcomers and gesticulating menacingly with the talons on the ends of their arms, had killed them by the thousands, thinking they were some form of predator that took a while to make up its mind to attack. Eventually the colonists recognized the creatures' seemingly natural affinity for the company of humans, and in time the Woos began attaching themselves to anyone who would have them. Since they reproduced by sporing, the early decline of the Woo population was soon made up.

They were moderately intelligent creatures. In time, most could understand enough English to respond to simple commands. How intelligent they really were, compared for instance with Terran canines, was a matter of debate, however. But for the majority of Diamundeans who owned one, the creatures were affectionate, obedient, and useful animal companions.

As a boy, Stauffer had owned several Woos—their normal life span was only about five human years—and he had lavished affection on the strange little things. But since becoming St. Cyr's man, he had never owned another. Stauffer treated St. Cyr's Woos with a compassion he never felt for his master's human victims. You could, often should, hate humans, Stauffer rationalized, but Woos, after all, are only animals. Now, with everything lost in this ruinous war, and as a hunted man hiding underground, Clouse Stauffer began to realize what it must be like to be a Woo under the feet of Marston St. Cyr.

"My dear boy," St. Cyr said as Stauffer took a seat beside his desk, "you think all is over with us, don't you?"

"Uh, well, sir, things look mighty grim from where I'm sitting."

"They'll look up again, and soon, Clouse. These hostages are our ticket to freedom and ease for the rest of our lives. We lost the big prize, Clouse, but we're not finished yet, not by a long shot."

"Sir, something I don't understand . . ." Stauffer hesitated but when St. Cyr nodded he rushed on. "Well, why didn't you accept the offer to negotiate with the Confederation? Then we could have avoided, well, this . . ." He gestured helplessly at the living rock that surrounded them.

St. Cyr smiled. "That is not my 'style,' as they say. As you know, Clouse, we have many friends in the Confederation Council. Why otherwise did the Confederation stop short of annihilating us?" He laughed bitterly. "Many of the delegates themselves are shareholders in our company. They fought against this war in the first place, and of course they didn't want us destroyed. But you know what the Confederation was going to offer me? A comfortable exile somewhere out of the way, in exchange for my giving up all the power I worked so hard to achieve here. No! I'm going out on my own terms, Clouse, not like a Woo with its legs dragging behind it. No, no, no! I commanded armies larger and more powerful than any Napoleon ever led. I ruled a planet, Clouse, a whole world! Nobody's going to exile me to some deep-space Elba."

"Sir, do you think that's what the Council would've done, had you negotiated with Wellington-Humphreys?"

St. Cyr shrugged. "Same thing, Clouse. Clipped my wings. Now I have the upper hand, and you, my boy, will play a vital role henceforth."

"Me, sir? How?" Stauffer was not sure he wanted any more "vital roles" in St. Cyr's plans.

"Clouse, you will deliver my demands to the Confederation forces. I have a little business to clear up with the hostages, and then you will proceed to New Kimberly. Deliver a message to Brigadier Theodosius Sturgeon, commanding the 34th FIST, Confederation Marine Corps."

"Brigadier . . . ? But sir, won't you deal with the Fleet Admiral himself? Why a mere brigadier?"

St. Cyr laughed. "Because I have his people, Clouse. And it was his job to protect the Ambassador; the Marines we captured with the Ambassador are his. He failed to protect her. I don't know the man, have never met him, in fact, but it was his troops who spearheaded the breakout at Oppalia, and they did us a lot of harm. I'm going to rub the fellow's nose in this business. Oh, don't worry, Clouse, he'll get the word to the admiral. But we start with him, my boy, and you have the honor of being my messenger."

Stauffer did not understand St. Cyr's line of reasoning, but he knew St. Cyr well enough not to question him further about it.

St. Cyr paused for a moment. "I have contacts on any of a dozen worlds who owe me, and we will be welcomed there." He paused again and looked reflectively into his glass. "It was a great war, wasn't it?" he whispered. "We almost had them. We gave those boys a run for their money, didn't we?" Clouse nodded, but in the back of his mind he was horrified. The war had cost tens of thousands of lives. He would never forget the destruction he'd seen, the terror he'd felt, and the cries of the wounded and dying.

Privately, he doubted anyone would give St. Cyr safe passage to their home world. That would be like inviting a ravening beast into your family's bosom. Never before had he doubted his master's ability to get what he wanted. Something had happened to Clouse Stauffer during these last weeks, but nothing, apparently, had changed for Marston St. Cyr.

"Yes, yes, I had it all, everything—I took everything," St. Cyr continued. Clouse was horrified when he realized St. Cyr was talking aloud to himself. "All right, Clouse," St. Cyr said, getting a grip on himself and jumping up energetically, "time to interview our guests!"

Despite St. Cyr's optimism that he could pry concessions out of the Confederation by using the hostages as pawns, Stauffer could not shake off a profound sense of depression. Except for the two enlisted Marines, the hostages were being held in separate cells and, for the most part, treated decently. St. Cyr needed them in good condition. So far he had made no overtures to the Confederation. When Stauffer asked him what his plans were, he only smiled and told him to be patient.

So Stauffer became friends with Professor Benjamin. The professor indicated he understood Stauffer's position and sympathized with him. He gave the impression he did not hold any resentment against either himself or St. Cyr for what they had done. He was just curious about how St. Cyr had commanded his armies and made the strategic and tactical decisions that led to his ruin. Stauffer believed the professor was already plotting the book he would write about the war once he was released.

"You know, Professor, General St. Cyr was once a student at M'Jumba University," Stauffer remarked one day. "He says he remembers you."

Benjamin raised an eyebrow. "I don't remember him."

"He says he once took a course from you. He was in the engineering school there but he had to take some humanities courses to get his degree, so he took one of yours on twentieth-century warfare. Some survey course."

Benjamin shrugged. He could not remember anyone like Marston St. Cyr in any of his classes. He would've remembered a student like that. "But Clouse, let's talk about you. Why don't you give up? What St. Cyr has done is madness. Get out of this while you can. The Confederation will never negotiate with your master purely on his own terms."

Stauffer did not reply at once. "No, Professor, I am General St. Cyr's man. Where he goes, I go. I must share his fate."

"You can be so devoted to a man like him?" Benjamin couldn't believe that. He sensed that underneath his facade, Clouse Stauffer was human after all. Why couldn't he see how twisted and evil his master was? He said as much.

Suddenly, the earth trembled under their feet as a shock wave passed through the rock around them. From far, far below where they stood they could hear a muted rumbling. Benjamin glanced at Stauffer in alarm. "Cave-ins," Stauffer shrugged. "They happen all the time. It's the tunnels and shafts from old mining operations collapsing after being abandoned for hundreds of years. That's one reason we didn't go deeper. You can't trust those old structures anymore. Still, we're pretty safe here, and we're still plenty deep to keep you from being rescued."

The door burst open and St. Cyr stepped in. He signaled to two men behind him and they dragged Ambassador Wellington-Humphreys, bound and gagged, into the room, dumped her on the floor and left.

"This is outrageous!" Benjamin shouted, and moved to help Wellington-Humphreys.

St. Cyr drew his pistol and pointed it at him. "Sit. She is here for a special reason. Clouse, we have waited long enough. Now we shall open negotiations with the Confederation. But first, Professor, you really think I am 'twisted and evil,' I believe those were your words. That's what you told Clouse here when you were trying to suborn him."

"H-How did you—"

"Sir, he's an old fool," Stauffer said, trying to intervene. A look had come over St. Cyr's face that was all too familiar to Stauffer, and he did not like it.

"I took a course from you at the university, and you really don't remember me, Professor?" Benjamin shook his head; he really did not. "Well, let me refresh your memory. The course, as the colonel noted, was on twentieth-century warfare. I wrote my term paper on the United States in Vietnam. My thesis was that had the U.S. applied the right amount of military pressure on the communists early enough in the war and kept it on, they would have won. The war was lost because of their cowardly politicians."

Benjamin remembered the course, but still could remember neither St. Cyr nor his paper.

"You gave me a C, Professor, the only mark I ever got under an A during my studies, and you wrote on my paper in big red letters, 'The U.S. lost in Vietnam because they were fighting an ideal, the ideal of liberty. Decent people realized this and brought pressure on the American government to withdraw.' That's vomit, pure vomit, you silly little twit! Wars are won by killing. The Americans folded because they couldn't take the casualties. The communists won because they could. Pure and simple. 'Ideal!' Your ideals aren't worth spit unless they're backed up by guns. It was North Vietnamese tanks that ended the war, Professor, not idealists preaching freedom. That lesson was not lost on me."

"The accepted analysis of that war is that the communists had the moral high ground—"

St. Cyr stepped forward and smashed his pistol across the side of Professor Benjamin's face. The professor gasped and fell back on his cot, blood seeping out from beneath the hand he clapped to his jaw. St. Cyr, breathing heavily, controlled himself with effort. "Camera!" he yelled. Somewhere within his hideout a technician made sure that what was to follow would be recorded.

"Sir!" Stauffer protested, "I must—"

"Shut up! Clouse, stand up against that wall and keep your goddamned hole buttoned up or I will kill you!" Stauffer stumbled back against the wall as ordered. He sensed what was coming but he never considered drawing his own side arm.

"Academics!" St. Cyr sneered. "Historians, philosophers, librarians, you are parasites." He spit the words out. "You sit around, spinning your theories, and you think you really know something! You worthless carcass. You've spent your whole life studying what real men do, and now you propose to tell me why wars are lost? Are you watching this?" he screamed at Ambassador Wellington-Humphreys. He turned back to the professor, who looked up at him, unafraid.

"You lost because you are a stupid megalomaniac," Professor Benjamin said evenly. "You lost because brave men were willing to pay the price to crush you like the ugly insect you are. And I had a hand in your defeat, so I must be good for something. And you are about to lose again because the Confederation will never negotiate with a madman like you."

"We'll edit those remarks out," St. Cyr replied as if talking to himself. "Well, Professor, here's your chance to be a hero." He pressed the firing lever on his pistol, sending a bolt sizzling through Professor Benjamin's left calf.

The professor at first just sat there, mouth gaping open, a look of profound horror on his face. The room immediately was filled with the sharp stench of vaporized flesh. The bolt passed through Benjamin's leg and slagged the floor beneath his cot, which began to smolder from the intense heat beneath it.

Then Professor Benjamin screamed. St. Cyr fired another bolt, this time into his right leg. His scream intensified to a keening shriek. His mattress burst into flame as he writhed on it. "Are you enjoying this?" St. Cyr screamed at Wellington-Humphreys. She had closed her eyes and was shaking her head back and forth. St. Cyr stepped over to her and shook her violently. "Watch, you bitch, watch! This is what I will do to you if I don't get my way!" He released her, and against her will she watched as St. Cyr stepped back to where Benjamin was, his body wrapped in flame on the burning bed, put the muzzle of his pistol close to the professor's chest and depressed the firing lever a third time. The bolt burned its way entirely through his chest and Benjamin's body went limp.

St. Cyr stepped to the door and threw it open. "Get in here!" he shouted to the guards. "Put that out!" He pointed to Benjamin's smoldering corpse. He turned to Stauffer, who stood trembling and perspiring against the wall. "I have a special job for you, my boy," St. Cyr whispered. He shouted to the guards:

"Drag that bitch along with us." Then he turned back to Stauffer. "Come with me, Clouse. We are going to visit Ensign vanden Hoyt, and you will see how I negotiate with my enemies."

CHAPTER THIRTY

Clouse Stauffer, his face an expressionless mask, stood rigidly at attention before Brigadier Sturgeon's desk. "General St. Cyr commissioned me to bring you these," he said, and gestured at two hermetically sealed containers now resting on the brigadier's desk. "And here," he handed over a microdisk, "are his terms, to be delivered to the President of the Confederation Council at once."

Stauffer had come to Sturgeon's command post in New Kimberly under a flag of truce. To avoid being tracked, he would return to the hideout by a circuitous route through various checkpoints where he would be screened for hidden tracking devices and ambushes would be laid in case he was being followed.

"Admiral Wimbush speaks for the Confederation Council in this quadrant of Human Space," Brigadier Sturgeon answered stiffly. He fingered the disk and then looked apprehensively at the containers. They were too small for bombs and too big for . . . what? A peace offering? "Where is the ambassador? Where are my people and Professor Benjamin?"

"Everything is on the disk, Brigadier," Clouse said, avoiding a direct answer.

Brigadier Sturgeon pressed the latches on the containers and opened them.

A grim-faced Commander Van Winkle was waiting for Captain Conorado, First Sergeant Myer, and Gunnery Sergeant Bass of Company L at the battalion command post. The commander's face was deeply lined with fatigue. "The Old Man

wants us, and it's something very bad," was all he would tell
Conorado. They engaged in desultory small talk as they walked
together to the brigadier's headquarters. Captain Conorado was
sure the meeting had to do with the hostages—everyone assumed the Ambassador and her party had been taken hostage
and were still alive, although St. Cyr had not as yet announced
that he was holding them, and every effort to find them had
come to nothing so far.

An aide showed them into Brigadier Sturgeon's office.

The brigadier stood behind his desk, his face drawn and pale.
Stauffer, who had been sitting off to one side, sprang to attention when Commander Van Winkle came through the door and
remained that way without moving a muscle or showing any
emotion.

"Come over here," Brigadier Sturgeon said, waiving military
formality. "There is something you must see." Captain Conorado felt a terrible cold knot forming in the pit of his stomach.
The men gathered about his desk. The brigadier pressed a
button on one of the containers and the lid popped open. Inside
lay the severed head of Professor Jere Benjamin. He opened the
other container. Ensign vanden Hoyt's head slowly rose out of
the container on a pedestal, its glazed, lifeless eyes staring
straight at the Marines.

A dead silence enveloped the men in the room. "The man
standing over there is St. Cyr's messenger, his chief of staff,
Colonel Stauffer," the brigadier said. Stauffer offered no acknowledgment, just stared straight ahead at a point on the opposite wall. "Colonel Stauffer has also delivered a recorded message
I will pass on to Admiral Wimbush. It contains St. Cyr's demands for the freedom of the Ambassador and the two enlisted
Marines he continues to hold. I want you to see that message."
He pressed a button on a console and Ambassador Wellington-
Humphreys's image appeared on a flatvid screen off to one side
of his desk.

The Ambassador's eyes were swollen and red and her deeply
lined face was puffy. "Madame President," she began, as she
had been told to by St. Cyr, although she knew Admiral Wimbush, as the Confederation's primary representative in this

quadrant of Human Space, would act in the President's stead if there were to be negotiations with St. Cyr, "in exchange for my life and the lives of the two enlisted Marines who are also being held here with me, Major General Marston St. Cyr demands that he and a small contingent of supporters be given safe conduct to an as yet unspecified destination. They will be allowed to pass through the Fleet now blockading Diamunde and into hyperspace without being followed. Furthermore, no attempt will be made subsequently to locate him and no retribution for anything he has done is ever to be attempted." She delivered this speech in a monotone, glancing occasionally to her left.

Marston St. Cyr's face now appeared on the screen. He made a mock bow to the camera, smirked, then said, "You have heard my demands, Madame President. They are simple. They will be easy to meet. To the Confederation armed forces now in possession of Diamunde, who I am sure will watch this before it is transmitted to the Council, any attempt to locate me, any attempt to free the remaining hostages, will result in their immediate and terrible deaths. If you do not believe me, please watch the following." He bowed again, and for the next three minutes the horrified Marines watched Professor Benjamin and Ensign vanden Hoyt being tortured to death. The file ran out on vanden Hoyt's death scream.

For what seemed an eternity after the tape quit running, none of the Marines seemed able to breathe. Then so quickly nobody could stop him, Bass leaped upon Stauffer, grabbed him by the throat and slammed him to the floor, smashing him into his chair on the way down, shattering it and sending a steel rod from one of its arms deeply into Stauffer's own right biceps. Stauffer made no move to defend himself. His eyes bulged and he gasped for breath, and by the time the officers were able to pull Bass off the hapless messenger, Stauffer's face had already begun to turn purple. He lay choking and gasping on the floor. The wound in his arm bled profusely. While Captain Conorado and Commander Van Winkle held Bass's arms, Top Myer put himself between the platoon sergeant and his victim, but nobody made a move to assist Stauffer. Bass said not a word, just clenched his teeth and breathed heavily.

Stauffer gasped as he tried to get air into his lungs. He rolled onto his side, got his legs underneath him, and using his overturned chair as a prop, managed to stagger to his feet. He stood there, swaying and wheezing loudly. "I—I—under-understand how you feel, Sergeant," he managed to say at last. "I wish you had killed me," he whispered mournfully. Already his throat was beginning to turn red from the bruises Bass's fingers had left there.

"I wish he had too, mister," Top Myer raged. "Vanden Hoyt was Charlie Bass's platoon commander, and a finer young officer we'll never see in this life again, you miserable sack of shit!"

An aide stuck his head in the door and looked inquiringly at the brigadier. "Put this man under guard and get him over to the FIST surgeon, Lieutenant—"

Stauffer shook his head and waved his hands. "Not yet, Brigadier," he rasped. "I have something more for you to hear."

"What?" Sturgeon snapped.

"I—I know—I know where they are."

"What?"

"I can tell you how to get there." The Marines stared at Stauffer unbelievingly. "I will tell you how to find your people," he went on, speaking in a nearly steady voice. He nodded. "I will show you."

"And what the fuck do you want in exchange?" Bass roared.

Stauffer shook his head. "Nothing. Nothing. I'll tell you how to find St. Cyr, and then I will go back to him. That is all I want."

Again the Marines stared at Stauffer. "Lieutenant," Sturgeon said to his aide, "take this man to the surgeon. Keep him under tight guard. Don't let anything happen to him. Colonel Stauffer," he said, more gently now, "go with the lieutenant. You will be well cared for. We'll talk later, when I have an answer for—your boss."

After Stauffer was gone, Sturgeon turned to Bass. "Feeling better now, Charlie?"

"Sorry, sir. I—vanden Hoyt was—" He shrugged. "Sir, if this bastard can lead us to St. Cyr, I want to go along with the rescue party."

"No," Commander Van Winkle said.

"Charlie—" Top Myer began.

Bass shook his head. "I want to go along," he repeated. "I am responsible for them getting taken the night of the reception. If I hadn't had my head up my ass I'd have been more alert. And Dean and MacIlargie are my men, sir. I want to go along. Please."

Captain Conorado said nothing, but he nodded in agreement.

Brigadier Sturgeon was silent for a moment. "Charlie, you aren't responsible for what happened that night. But I'll think about letting you go. Meanwhile, let's get over to General Aguinaldo's headquarters."

"Sir, I'll take those," Bass said. He carefully picked up the containers with their grisly contents.

General Aguinaldo did not bother to watch the tape all the way through. He did not bother either to inform the army commander what was going on. "This is Marine business," he said. "We are responsible for the Ambassador, and Dean and MacIlargie are our men. If the army gets involved in this, they'll only screw it up. Let's go see the admiral."

Admiral Wimbush could not sit through the whole tape. "This is monstrous, monstrous," he whispered when it got to the part where St. Cyr began shooting plasma bolts into vanden Hoyt's legs. "Shut if off!" He sat for a moment, nervously running a hand through his thinning hair. He had been made physically ill by what was on the tape, and it was only with considerable effort that he was able to keep from vomiting. Part of his reaction was the grisly nature of what he had just seen, but part of it was because now the buck was squarely on his shoulders. He could not bargain with St. Cyr after what St. Cyr had done to the peace negotiations, and certainly not after what he'd just seen on the tape. But if the rescue attempt went awry, he'd have the Ambassador's blood on his hands. After Oppalia, Wimbush wanted no more failures. He had the authority to act, since it would take weeks to ask for and receive instructions from the Confederation that would relieve him of the responsibility. They had to act quickly too because as unstable as St. Cyr appeared to be, he might just kill the hostages at any time.

"All right," he said at last. "We try to rescue them. Let me call for a council of war—"

"Sir," General Aguinaldo interjected, "excuse me. I mean no disrespect. We don't have time to discuss this, and if the army gets involved they'll only fuck this up. It'll be Oppalia all over again. I want to handle this operation."

Admiral Wimbush twisted nervously in his chair. Oppalia had been a nightmare, and all Han's doing. The bastard had not delivered, and Wimbush knew it reflected badly on him, because he'd supported Han.

"Well . . ." The admiral hesitated.

Brigadier Sturgeon spoke up quietly. "Sir, this man, Stauffer, I think we can trust him. He has nothing to gain by misleading us. But we must act quickly. My men are ready. Let's put an end to all this right now."

Admiral Wimbush regarded the two Marines carefully. "Very well, gentlemen, you are authorized to proceed with your rescue plan, and you may execute on General Aguinaldo's order. Keep me informed. Good luck. I shall prepare an answer agreeing to his terms. You have this Stauffer character deliver it to St. Cyr." In Fleet Admiral Wilber Wimbush's long and very carefully planned, virtually risk-free naval career, it was the most independent and risky decision he had ever made. It was also his best.

Commander Fil Rhys-Topak, the FIST surgeon, stood next to Commander Sparks, the FIST signals officer, in the small lab adjacent to Commander Rhys-Topak's infirmary. He was showing Brigadier Sturgeon a small piece of tissue the doctor had removed from Clouse Stauffer's arm earlier in the day, when he debrided the wound made there.

"Amazing device, this thing, sir, even though it is older technology," Sparks said, holding up the piece of tissue with a pair of tweezers. Inside, Sturgeon could just make out a black dot with his naked eye. "It's a body-heat-powered transmitter. I did a full-body scan on him when he was brought in," Sparks continued. "He's an enemy alien, after all, and I wanted to see if he was carrying any eavesdropping devices. Fil here dug it out of him. It's inert now. It only transmits when heated to body temperature. That means it would've been transmitting from the time it was put in there until Doc here took it out. Old as it is, the thing still has virtually unlimited range and life span."

"When I saw what it was," Rhys-Topak said, "I popped it into a cryotube tube and called Sparky, sir. It was embedded just under the skin, under what looks like an old vaccination scar. I suspect that's how it was introduced, and small as it is, he probably never knew it was there. I don't know how long it was in that arm, probably a long time, according to Sparky. I'm afraid—"

"That St. Cyr knows what Stauffer told me in my headquarters," the brigadier finished the sentence.

"Yessir," Sparks answered. "Sir, Fil sedated him, and while he was out I took the liberty of scanning him for other devices. I'm sure this was the only one."

"Well, the bastard knows Stauffer is gonna spill the beans." The Brigadier sighed. "Okay, I'll take it from here. If St. Cyr was listening in or recording what went on in my HQ, maybe he'll think the transmitter just got dislodged or broken in the fight."

"Sir," Sparks said, "maybe it was broken. I haven't tested this thing to see if it'll work."

"Don't," Sturgeon answered. "Let's hope he doesn't know that we know. Is Stauffer awake now?"

"Yessir."

"Okay, take me to him. Bring that damned transmitter along."

Stauffer was lying comfortably in bed. Brigadier Sturgeon came straight to the point. "Colonel, I believe St. Cyr knows you have betrayed him." He held up the tiny transmitter, still encased in clotted flesh but safely preserved in a tiny refrigerated specimen baguette. "This is a radio transmitter, Colonel. My surgeon took it out of your arm. It's been there a long time. St. Cyr was using it to eavesdrop on you."

Bad as Stauffer was, as much havoc as St. Cyr's chief of staff

had caused all those years, Sturgeon still believed he deserved
to know what he was getting into. "There is still a slight chance
the thing was damaged when Bass attacked you. We don't
know. We must assume it wasn't. As soon as we have a plan, we
will attack. There's no reason why you should return there. The
tribunal will no doubt take into consideration the help you are
going to give us."

Stauffer looked at the foot of his bed. "No, Brigadier, I must
go back," he said slowly. "None of this surprises me," he went
on conversationally. "That St. Cyr would spy on me? I guess he
had that thing put into me when I was in the hospital, oh,
twenty-five years ago now." He shrugged philosophically. "He
knew about everything I did and said for the past twenty-five
years." He shook his head. "Long ago I realized Marston St. Cyr
has no human emotions, Brigadier. He favored me, advanced
me, made me a rich man because I was useful to him, not because he liked me. And I was satisfied with that. Now I have to
pay the price for having been so accommodating. But let me
tell you this, Brigadier, you may not have to deal with Marston
St. Cyr once I get back."

"You are going to kill him?"

"I am going to try."

Brigadier Sturgeon regarded Stauffer for a moment, then
stuck out his hand. "Good luck, then, Colonel." They shook
on it.

Clouse Stauffer seemed a different man as he stood in the
FIST operations center, briefing the rescue team on St. Cyr's
hideout. "He has only about a hundred men with him down
there," he said. "He doesn't need any more than that, and those
men will die defending him. Do not expect to take any prisoners.

"Although there are several approaches to his lair, getting
into them and then making it through the maze of old shafts and
tunnels to where he is would take forever, unless you knew the
precise route. They are all monitored by electronic means, and
mined. Even if you got by the checkpoints—" He pointed them
out on a schematic he had drawn, which was now projected into
the flatvid screen. "—you would need to know the precise

twistings and turnings of the hundreds of tunnels that branch off the main ones to get to him. And all along the routes are video monitors and command-detonated explosive charges capable of blocking them completely once an intruder is spotted. You'd need heavy machinery to get through after that, and by the time you did, he'd be gone."

Stauffer pressed a button on his console and a close-up of a rugged mountain peak came into view. "This is Mount Amethyst, one of the highest peaks in the Chrystoberyls. Look here." He pointed to an outcropping just below the snowline. "This is St. Cyr's escape route. There is a shaft under the outcropping—actually, it's a cleverly concealed plug that blocks the opening—under which is a launch site for a Bomac 36 V starship."

That information caused eyebrows to rise. The Bomac 36 V was capable of both atmospheric and hyperspace flight, which eliminated the need for a shuttle. It had never been adapted to military use because its payload was so small, but commercial and nonmilitary governmental agencies had found the craft very suitable for their requirements. The Bomac Corporation called the 36 V its "interstellar VIP ship."

"That shaft is the only one in the complex that, for obvious reasons, is not mined," Stauffer continued, pausing significantly as a murmur ran through the assembled staff. "This is your way in, gentlemen." He paused again. "The entrance is three thousand meters above sea level, and the shaft itself goes 4,500 meters deep. At the bottom is a completely computerized launch facility. It is inspected twice daily, at dawn and just after sunset. Between those hours it is unoccupied.

"As soon as you breach the launch shaft, St. Cyr will know you're coming through that way. You must get to the bottom as quickly as possible. If you do, you'll have a chance to fight off any reaction force. The tunnels inside the complex itself are not booby-trapped. Once outside the launch facility, you will find a bewildering array of tunnels leading in every direction under the mountain. Let me tell you now, not even the men who live down there with St. Cyr, not even I, could navigate around that place without help. That is provided by markings painted on the walls at intervals. These markings give off faint signatures that

should be visible through your infra screens. They are coded."
A hand-drawn chart of the directional symbols appeared on the
vidscreens. Each one marked the direction to a different area
or level, and beside each symbol Stauffer had printed the facility to be found at that destination. The headquarters complex,
where the hostages were being kept, was indicated by $Q>$.

"You all realize that while St. Cyr only knows I offered to
lead you to his hideout, he does not know you have accepted. I
will try to convince him that it was just a ploy to get you to lay
off me. That's to your advantage. He does not know your actual
plan of attack either. Also to your advantage. He cannot risk
damage to the launch facility because it is his only way out. Big
advantage to you. But he may have assumed you did accept,
and shifted the hostages or even killed them. Or he may just
load up the 36 V and take off ten minutes from now, counting
that you won't open fire because you think the Ambassador
might be on board. I have known Marston St. Cyr for forty years.
All I can tell you is that he won't panic and he will do what you
least expect him to do." He paused. "And you must act at once."
With a small bow he walked out of the room, leaving the staff to
start planning the raid.

"My only question," Captain Conorado asked after Stauffer
was gone, "is how the hell do we get down that shaft?"

"Well, we could free-fall using back-pack puddle jumpers,"
the FIST operations officer suggested. "I haven't done the
math, but it would probably take more than half a minute or so
to get all the way down, providing nobody bounced off the shaft
wall on the way."

"We could get an Essay in there, sir," another staff officer
suggested.

"Anyone here ever free-fall in a puddle jumper?" Brigadier
Sturgeon asked. Nobody responded. "How about maneuver an
Essay straight down a shaft 4,500 meters, land it at the bottom,
and fight off anybody waiting there? And what happens if the
coxswain makes a tiny mistake and she slams into the wall on
the way down?" Again nobody responded. "The problem with
going in through that shaft is it's a shooting gallery if you don't

get to the bottom in seconds after we blow the lid. Puddle jumpers seem the only way, but damn, it's chancy." Brigadier Sturgeon frowned and ran a hand through his hair.

"We could do a few practice jumps from hoppers right outside town, sir," the ops officer suggested.

"That might give the whole thing away," Captain Conorado interjected. It had been decided that he would lead the rescue attempt with men from his own company. Gunnery Sergeant Bass would go along. "Sir, may I make a suggestion?"

Brigadier Sturgeon nodded.

"Well, remember how the Persians defeated the Greeks at Thermopylae?"

"They found a way to get behind them," the intelligence officer said. "Found a local man who knew a path through the hills."

"Right. Maybe there's somebody here in New Kimberly who might know another way in, some old miner. Maybe not all the maps have been lost. Not that I don't trust Stauffer, but he's not a miner, he's probably never been in those works up there that much."

Brigadier Sturgeon snapped his fingers. "Maps! Charts, plans, goddamn! I know just where to start!"

"Marines? Here? I didn't know you boys could read," Joachim Banarjee Poste croaked as Brigadier Sturgeon and his staff walked into the Free Library of New Kimberly. "Just a friendly jest!" he said as he saw the expression on the men's faces. "Welcome to FLONK. We don't have much here in the way of girlie books, gentlemen—just a friendly jest, just jesting!"

Brigadier Sturgeon quickly explained what they wanted while Gunnery Sergeant Bass glowered silently at the librarian. "Maps of the old diggings? Hmmm." Poste rubbed his chin, punched some keys on his console. Now here was legitimate research. He warmed instantly to the visitors. "Yes, we do have 'em. Most of the companies who worked in there did make plans of their sites, and many of them are in our collection. I'll check our digitized database first and then the catalog of our paper holdings."

"You actually have paper copies of these maps?" Captain Conorado asked.

Poste nodded happily. "Yes, yes we do. Very precious, those are. Not much call for these things, and I've been a librarian here for the last eighty years. The companies aren't interested in 'em, just a few old independent diggers trying to make a living gleaning what the big boys missed years ago. Worked a few years in the mines myself, when I was young." When he was young? Sturgeon raised an eyebrow at Bass. He shook his head. Nobody felt like asking how old he was. "Why are you gents interested in 'em? Going to do a little prospecting while you're here?"

"Yeah," Bass answered, "we're tired of getting killed protecting shits like you for nothing. Thought we'd look for some gems, supplement our pay. We usually do that by looting."

"Touché," Poste said, punching some more keys.

The maps Poste produced for them proved very complicated and hard to read. The problem was, there were so many of them it was difficult to relate one to the other. Often the excavations of one company started where another left off, so there was little continuity between one chart and another. Trying to read them was like looking at a blowup of a single map quadrant without any reference to its neighbors. "Is there anyone who can make sense out of these things?" Captain Conorado asked at last.

"Certainly. Hard Rocks Viola."

"Hard . . . ? Where can we find this guy?" Bass asked.

"I'll call him. If he's not out prospecting, he'll come right over."

Fifteen minutes later a short, stocky, bandy-legged man with flaming red hair entered the library and introduced himself. "I'm Hard Rocks. What can I do for you fellas?"

For the next three hours they pored over the old maps, Poste happily punching graphics up on his screen or scurrying into the stacks to bring out huge atlases stuffed with moldering map sheets. "Got a hernia when I was younger, lifting all these atlases," he remarked to no one in particular. During the whole time, not a single patron came into the library.

"This is it," Hard Rocks said at last, putting a broken fingernail on a ragged blue line that snaked along a section of one of the old maps.

"How the hell do you know?" Bass asked, completely bewildered.

"I just know, Charlie," Hard Rocks answered. Almost from the start Bass and Viola had decided to be on a first-name basis. And, of course, the Marines had quickly discarded the fiction as to why they needed the maps and advice. "That 4,500-meter shaft is new, but the tunnels under it aren't. I've been in there, maybe thirty years ago, and man, you go down into those places and you don't come out unless you've got every nook and cranny memorized. But look: none of *this* construction is new. St. Cyr just moved into the old diggings and renovated the place. Another thing. The miners used to live down there in those days. The spot marked 'headquarters' is actually their old living area. You can get into this parallel corridor right here"— he put his finger onto the blue line again—"and blast through into the main tunnel. There's maybe two meters of rock between them. That'll bring you out seventy-five meters from where this, ah, launch pad is located. Then you're only a hundred meters down this other tunnel to the headquarters complex."

"We blow the lid on the shaft first, make 'em think we're coming in that way, then go in here, and we'll catch any reaction force by surprise!" Brigadier Sturgeon said. "Mike Company will be the diversionary force and Lima will go in here."

"You'll have to go with us, Hard Rocks," Captain Conorado said.

Viola shrugged. "In all the years I been freelance prospecting up there, the big companies never bothered me much, but you know, I never liked any of 'em, and this bastard, St. Cyr, he's ruined everything here for everybody. If you boys can nail him, count me in."

Bass clapped Viola on the shoulder. "I'll be right there beside you, Hard Rocks," he said.

"Yeah, that's the only thing that worries me." Viola laughed.

"Mr. Poste, kindly get your personal things, you're coming with us," the brigadier said.

"But closing time isn't until—"

Bass gently lifted the librarian out of his seat and pushed him toward the door.

"You are going to be a guest of Fleet Admiral Wimbush until this operation is over, Mr. Poste. We can't chance it that somebody might want to find out what we've been doing in here all afternoon."

"Oh," Poste said in a small voice as Bass escorted him outside. "Brigadier, how are the accommodations on the admiral's flagship?"

"The finest, Mr. Poste. The food is excellent."

Captain Conorado gently nudged the brigadier and whispered, "Now, sir, that was really unkind."

CHAPTER
THIRTY-ONE

After the first hour in their cell, Dean and MacIlargie discovered and disabled the surveillance device that allowed St. Cyr's jailers to monitor them. No one seemed to care, because it was never fixed. Subsequently, the door would slide open at intervals and food and drink would be unceremoniously thrust inside. They searched their cell carefully but found nothing of interest and no other way out except through the metal sliding door, which was locked from the outside and apparently impossible to open from the inside.

Inside one of the empty lockers, peeling from the steel, they found a pinup, a computer-generated holo hardcopy of a young woman dressed in a hundred-year-old style smiling happily at the two Marines, now prisoners in her husband's—boyfriend's? lover's?—former living quarters.

The hours passed slowly. The two whiled away the time napping and reminiscing about home and comrades and the adventures they'd had in the Corps.

"Why did you join up?" Dean asked MacIlargie at last, getting around to the inevitable question that came up in every extended conversation Marines have ever had among themselves.

"I was stupid, loved guns, and needed the money," MacIlargie said quickly, giving the stock reply. "I suppose for the same reasons everybody does," he went on after a few moments. "I wasn't going anywhere back home. Couldn't see spending the rest of my life working to support a family, like my dad and mom did. Wasn't connected well enough to get into the Merchant Marine, and shit, being a colonist somewhere's no way to see the universe either. So I went down to the recruiter's office one day, saw the snazzy dress reds those guys were wearing, and here I am. How about you?"

Dean told him about his father's army experiences and the desire he'd always had to be a military man too. He also described some of his own experience at the recruiting office, and they both laughed. "What about your family?" he asked MacIlargie.

MacIlargie shrugged. "You know," he answered vaguely. Dean understood he didn't want to talk about his family. "I had a girl . . ." Dean waited for him to continue. "I was pretty serious about her," MacIlargie went on. He stood up, walked over to the old locker and stood there looking pensively at the faded pinup. Then he punched the metal door—hard. "We would of been married," he said, his voice tense with tightly controlled emotion. Dean did not ask him why he didn't marry, or anything else about the girl. MacIlargie returned to his bunk and sat down again. The reminiscences were over for a while.

The subject of MacIlargie's aborted marriage made Dean think of Hway, back on Wanderjahr. He wondered what she was doing, whether she ever thought of him. Would they ever see each other again? Thinking of her aroused him physically. He forced himself to control the emotion. He had far more important things to worry about, like survival. Yet try as hard as he could, it was a long time before the unbidden image of the young woman so far away in time and space faded at last from behind his eyelids.

The hours continued to pass slowly for the two Marines. No one had bothered them, questioned them, or even looked in on them, except at meal times. Both understood it was the Ambassador whom St. Cyr wanted, and that they were just pawns in his plan.

They had just finished breakfast on the morning of what they judged to be their third day in captivity when MacIlargie remarked, as he had after every previous meal they'd been served, "That was really lousy chow, but good, but good! I didn't realize how hungry I was."

Dean nodded, mopping up the last traces of a glutinous gravy substance with a stale chunk of bread. MacIlargie farted. "You bastard!" Dean shouted.

"So long's you can still do that, Deano, yer still alive 'n' kickin'," MacIlargie responded, unconcerned.

"You know, Mac," Dean said after the air had cleared, "it's too bad about those reds the admiral had made for us." The dress red uniforms they'd been wearing at the reception were specially tailored for them since they didn't have their own uniforms along on this operation. Now those new reds were soiled and torn. Somewhere, Dean had lost the marksmanship badge and campaign medals someone had found for him to wear. "I wonder if the Corps will replace these uniforms free of charge."

"Sure," MacIlargie said, masticating a piece of stringy meatlike substance. "Fair wear and tear, combat loss, somethin' like that. Long as we don't tell them they weren't our issue reds."

"What a hell of a way to end this miserable deployment," Dean said with sudden bitterness. He threw his metal plate into a corner and cursed violently. "We survived all that fighting, only to be . . ." He gestured helplessly. "And here I am, worrying about new uniforms, and all those guys—all those Marines . . ." He made another helpless gesture.

"Easy, Deano. You can't bring any of 'em back. We gotta worry about the here and now. I figure from the time we were knocked out to now, we've been in captivity three days. That means the guys are due to get us out of here any minute now." It was a commonly accepted myth that no captured Marine ever remained a prisoner for more than seventy-two hours.

"Mac, we're stuck down here. It was the Ambassador they wanted in the first place, not us. Soon as they don't need us anymore, *pfffttt.*" He drew a finger across his throat. "Nobody's gonna—"

From far above them there came a distant *cra-a-a-ak*, and then a muffled rumble.

Dean paused and glanced apprehensively at the ceiling. "Another cave-in?" They had heard several deep rumblings before and assumed they came from old tunnels collapsing far below.

MacIlargie held up his hand. "Listen."

"I don't hear—"

"Listen!" he shouted, then more quietly, "Listen." The rumbling seemed to go on for a long time, getting louder as every second passed. "It's them! It's them!" MacIlargie shouted. The rumbling ended in a tremendous crash, as if a heavy object had just fallen a long way, and the rock underneath them shook with the impact. Outside they could hear shouting and men running. "Gimme a hand!" MacIlargie shouted as he began tearing the mattress off his cot. The cot was constructed of tubular pieces of metal, and together they pried off two metal legs. He hefted one experimentally, "Oughta do," he said, smacking it into the palm of his hand.

"Hold it behind your right leg," Dean said. MacIlargie looked questioningly at him. "It's how the cops do it. On Wanderjahr," he added. "Bring it around in an arc, real quick," he said. MacIlargie shrugged and shifted the heavy metal tube to a position behind his right leg.

Someone outside fumbled with the lock. MacIlargie braced himself and stood facing the opening panel, feigning a look of surprise on his face. In his left hand he held the tin plate his breakfast had been served on, as if finishing the morsels still clinging there. Dean flattened himself to one side of the panel, his tube raised over his head.

The panel slid open and one of the guards stepped in. All he saw at first was MacIlargie, staring at him in surprise from the middle of the room.

MacIlargie brought the tube down in a huge overhand arc squarely on the top of the man's head. It hit a few inches behind the tip, somewhat dissipating the force of the blow, but with a solid *bonk*. Stunned, the man went to his knees. Mac could feel the blow all the way down his arm. On the way down the guard grabbed MacIlargie by the legs. MacIlargie staggered backward to get away from him and gain room to swing the tube again. The man held on in a daze, so, holding the tube in both hands, MacIlargie brought one end straight down on the top of the guard's head with all his strength.

The guard's partner jumped through the door, to the rescue, at the same time Dean's tube caught him on the bridge of his nose with a sharp crack. Blood flew everywhere. Dean grabbed the man with his left arm and jerked him inside. The other guard smashed into his partner, and under his added weight the two of them toppled onto the floor with MacIlargie on the bottom. Dean slid the door closed and attacked the two guards with his bloody metal pipe, holding it in both hands and raining blows with all his strength onto their heads and necks.

When the guards ceased moving, Dean stood there, breathing heavily, his face and uniform flecked with blood. In the corridor outside, pandemonium reigned as groups of men pounded by and officers shouted orders, but nobody bothered to look into their room.

"Get them off me," MacIlargie mumbled from beneath the inert bodies. Dean rolled the two men aside and held out his hand to MacIlargie. "Get their weapons," MacIlargie said as he got to his feet. Much to their disappointment, the Marines found the guards unarmed. "Ah, smart fuckers, of course they wouldn't come in here with weapons on them," MacIlargie muttered.

"Let's change clothes with them," Dean whispered, still out of breath from the adrenaline rush, "and find out where the others are."

"Good idea. Use the sheets to wipe the blood off your face and hands, Deano. You look like a butcher."

Quickly, they shed the remnants of their dress reds and started putting on the guards' battle-dress uniforms. One leg inside a pair of trousers MacIlargie paused. "Hey, Deano, you know, these poor bastards made one big mistake."

"What was that?"

"They thought they could handle Marines one-on-one."

"My dear Clouse," St. Cyr said, smiling and rising from behind his desk. "What is the word from the Confederation?"

"They accept your terms, sir," Stauffer answered. He held out the microdiskette Admiral Wimbush had given him. From far above them came a sharp crack followed by a rumbling noise.

"Ah," St. Cyr said, "right on time, my dear boy. Yes." He smiled again and drew a pistol. "I know you betrayed me, Clouse. I knew you would. Fortunately, I prepared an alternate plan."

"No!"

A huge crash thundered through the complex, shaking the rock underneath them. It was the remnant of the rock outcropping that hid the escape shaft falling onto the launch pad only 150 meters away.

"Ah, yes, you did, my dear boy, you did. You were going to say it was all a ruse to get them to leave you alone, weren't you?" He shook his head sadly. "Maybe it was, Clouse," he said reasonably, "but alas, I cannot take that chance. Time to go now." He raised a blaster in his right hand. Without hesitation he shot a bolt into Clouse Stauffer's chest. Stauffer staggered back into a chair and fell heavily to the floor, his torso a steaming mass of liquefied flesh and organs. St. Cyr came around the desk and stared down at his dying chief of staff. "We came a long way together, my boy, but I always knew it would end this way."

Stauffer felt no pain, just a massive lethargy. The light in the room about him was slowly fading. He thought, If this is death, it's not so bad after all. From far away he could hear St. Cyr saying something. Who cares what that bastard has to say anymore? I should have drawn and fired first. Ah, well, at least the Marines are here, he thought just before losing consciousness.

"Clouse," St. Cyr was saying, "you may be wondering why I didn't flee as soon as I knew you were going to betray me." He kicked Stauffer's inert body. Getting no response, he shrugged. "Very well, die then, if that's what you want to do." He turned to the Woo crouching in the corner and shook his finger at it. "It's not my style to go slinking off like a Woo, Woo. Life's only worth living if you run just ahead of the wave."

The Woo moaned in fear and scuttled toward the door. St. Cyr kicked at it absently. His foot connected solidly with the creature's midsection, sending it tumbling into the wall, a mass of jiggling appendages.

The sergeant of the guard stuck his head in the door. "Sir, a rescue party is attempting to come down the launch shaft. A reaction force is on the way to stop them. What shall I do with the prisoners?" He glanced briefly at Clouse Stauffer's body on the floor and decided not to get curious.

"Nothing, Sergeant. I shall take care of the woman. Give me the pass card to her cell. Kill the two enlisted men. Delay the rescue party as long as you can and then join me in Section Que Slant." Section Q\ led into a series of tunnels equipped with escape vehicles which his men had been told they could take to the surface in an emergency. None of the men now with him had been involved in renovating the old mines. If any of them survived the first engagement with the rescuers and did manage to flee into Section Q\ they would all perish, the survivors and their pursuers, because the escape tunnels were mined.

St. Cyr had his own way out, known only to him. The 36 V on its launch pad was only a diversion.

"Now for my hole card," St. Cyr said to the cringing Woo.

As soon as St. Cyr departed, the Woo painfully got to its legs and limped toward the door. It paused by Stauffer's body, examining it briefly and moaning sadly to itself, then followed St. Cyr out the door and down the corridor.

Under the cover of a battalion-size search mission, the men of Company L had infiltrated onto the mountain slopes the night before. When the battalion withdrew after dark, Company L was left behind. Such missions had been conducted frequently over the last days as the Confederation ground forces mopped up small pockets of St. Cyr's army that had refused to surrender. Now Conorado and his Marines crouched close to the solid rock walls fifty meters from where the explosive charges had been set. Third platoon, advancing by fire teams, would lead the way in once an opening had been made. They would go in firing and advance to their objective fifty meters down the main tunnel toward the branch leading up to headquarters area, where they would establish a position until the rest of the company was inside.

"You ready for this?" Captain Conorado said to Hard Rocks, crouching by his side. The old miner had become the company mascot in the brief time he'd been with them, but he was going along as their guide, if things got confusing next door.

"You know it, Captain. Boy, these rigs you got are really fantastic!" The old prospector had been given some instruction on how to use the infras and communications devices built into the issue helmet, and he was enjoying himself enormously. "Wisht I'd a had one of these things in my younger days," he whispered. He made a mental note to ask for one when the operation was finally over.

From far above them came a sharp crack. "Heads up!" Conorado said over the company net. He started counting the seconds, his thumb on the detonator. When the detritus from the blown outcropping 4,500 meters above impacted on the launching pad, the ground under them shook violently. "Steady, steady," Captain Conorado said over the net, foregoing communications procedures. "Platoon commanders, get ready. Charlie? You ready?"

"Aye, sir," Bass answered. He was commanding third platoon now, since there'd been no time to replace Ensign vanden Hoyt.

Three minutes ticked slowly by. "Fire in the hole!" Conorado shouted and pressed the detonator switch. A brilliant flash engulfed the waiting men—at the same time, there was a dull *thump!* as the shaped charges stove in the tunnel wall.

Bass was the first man up. The tunnel was full of dust, so thick he could hardly see. He fired plasma bolts to the left and the right as he came through the jagged hole and took up a position facing toward the headquarters complex. The first fire team came in right behind him, adding their weapons to his. Firing steadily, they advanced fifty meters into the choking dust and took up a defensive position. The second fire team proceeded directly to the launch pad, to secure whatever was left down there.

As the dust dissipated, St. Cyr's men came running at the first fire team positioned just down the tunnel, evidently unaware the Marines were in their way. The team cut them down as they emerged out of the dusty gloom. The company radio net came alive with commands and reports. The launch pad was in ruins but unoccupied. Conorado ran to the first fire team, Hard Rocks by his side, and ordered the rest of first platoon up the tunnel after him.

They came to a branch. "This way!" Hard Rocks shouted.

With his infra screens down, Conorado clearly saw the symbol pointing its way toward the headquarters. A grenadier fired several explosive bolts down the tunnel. Second platoon, acting according to plan, continued on down the main tunnel. A hundred meters farther on they would take another branch and come into the headquarters area a different way, hopefully taking any defenders in the rear by surprise and cross fire. First platoon sent two fire teams after the second, and the rest joined Bass and their company commander.

Seventy-five meters into the branch tunnel they met heavy resistance. Plasma bolts cracked and hissed around in the confined space. The air danced with the concussions of explosive bolts that disintegrated solid rock and tore men to pieces. The platoon sergeant acting for the second platoon's commander, who was wounded, reported he was fighting his way through a similar ambush. Lying in the narrow tunnels, the men could do little else but fire back at the defenders' muzzle flashes and inch their way along on their bellies, relying on their deflective screens to protect them from the plasma bolts being fired in their direction. Marines crawled up over the bodies of dead and wounded men or fired over them, and when return fire became too intense, they used the dead as shields and kept on firing.

Each man knew he was there to rescue his comrades and put an end to Marston St. Cyr, and each was determined to do that or die trying. Many did.

The firing stopped suddenly. In the eerie quiet, broken only by the moans of the wounded, Captain Conorado ordered his men cautiously forward. St. Cyr's guards had disappeared. Second platoon reported the same thing in the tunnel where they'd been ambushed. Conorado ordered them forward too. Moving slowly, looking for booby traps and ambushes, the Marines advanced along the tunnel to where it opened out into a huge gallery. A lightly wounded guard was dragooned into accompanying them.

"They told us the general fled," the man informed Captain Conorado, "so our sergeant said we should leave too. That was when I was wounded."

"Where'd they go?" Conorado asked. The man pointed down a tunnel branching off from the gallery. "There's an escape route up there leading to the surface," he said.

"The general?"

The man shrugged; he didn't know where St. Cyr might have gone.

Captain Conorado motioned to Sergeant Hyakowa. "Take your squad and go up that way," he said, pointing up the tunnel where the guards had gone. "Be careful. Meanwhile, we'll look for the hostages." He had little doubt they were already gone, but he had to be sure first. "How do we get into these rooms?" he asked the guard.

The guard held up a metal card. Bass snatched it from him. "I'll handle this, Skipper," he said.

Captain Conorado informed Brigadier Sturgeon that the hideout was secure but St. Cyr had apparently fled along with the remaining hostages. Company L had lost seven men killed and six wounded. He did not know how many of the guards had survived, but as soon as the headquarters area was searched, he would take the rest of Lima Company up the escape tunnel. Meanwhile, Mike Company was alerted to block any escape attempt at the surface.

A tremendous explosion roared down the tunnel into which Hyakowa and his men had just disappeared. Conorado swore and ran toward the billowing cloud of dust that rolled out into the gallery. Before he could get there, the Marines began stumbling back out, covered with rock dust and coughing.

"I'm okay, I'm okay!" Hyakowa gasped as he staggered back into the gallery. "We're okay! The goddamned thing went off too far down to get us. I don't think we're going very far down there, though." He wiped dust off his face with the back of his hand.

Bass ran up to where they stood. "They were being kept in cells down that tunnel." He pointed behind him. "I found this in one." He held up a soiled and torn dress uniform blouse. "It belonged to MacIlargie. There were two dead guards in the cell, all beat to hell, Skipper, and minus their own clothing." Despite himself, Bass grinned.

For the first time that day, Captain Conorado smiled.

Then another explosion rumbled up from the tunnel where Bass had just emerged. This one came from much farther down in the mines, but still the passageway filled with dust. Cursing again, Captain Conorado muttered, "This is getting to be a bad habit with me," and ran into the tunnel, followed by Bass and a dozen other Marines.

The light source inside was dim to begin with but worse now, with dust floating in the air. The tunnel sloped gradually downward. After a hundred meters the artificial light source that illuminated the rest of the complex ended and the party proceeded by the glimmer of glowballs. Warily, weapons at the ready, they went forward. Two hundred meters from the gallery they were stopped by a solid rockfall.

"Somebody doesn't want us to go any farther. Hard Rocks?" The old miner had been by the captain's side all the way.

"Captain, best I remember, this tunnel goes on for a long ways, but if you follow it down far enough, it ends in a geothermal pond just beside an underground river. I think it flows eventually into the Carnelian."

"Can we get around this somehow?"

"I don't know. Lemme see those charts again. I never spent much time down in that area."

They stood there in the semidarkness. Captain Conorado thought for a moment. His instincts told him this was the way St. Cyr had escaped. "Goddamn it to hell," Conorado swore. "Get some goddamned men down here with the equipment to move this shit." He gestured at the rock fall blocking the tunnel in front of them. "I'll be damned if I'm gonna sit on my ass while that bastard gets away."

The corridor outside their cell was empty when the two Marines emerged. MacIlargie carefully slid the door panel shut and it locked with a snap. He fingered the digitized metal card in the dead guard's uniform pocket. "I wonder where else this thing can get us into?"

They were just down a side tunnel from a huge, brightly lighted gallery. Large groups of guards were running through it toward the sound of a violent firefight going on somewhere ahead. Dean's pulse began to race. "We're behind them," he whispered, meaning the defenders.

"Yeah, but no weapons!" MacIlargie whispered back.

"Then let's get some."

A door panel slammed open behind them. Not ten meters away, farther back down the corridor where they stood, was Marston St. Cyr himself with the Ambassador. One of her eyes was almost swollen shut and a thin rivulet of blood seeped out a corner of her mouth. Her hands were secured behind her with plasticuffs.

"What are you two doing there?" St. Cyr shouted.

"We-we're here to, uh, get the two enlisted Marines, sir," MacIlargie said, suddenly inspired.

St. Cyr nodded. "Drag them out and kill them. Then join the others. I have business with this woman here." Yanking her roughly by one arm, he started down the corridor, away from the gallery and into the shadows. As Ambassador Wellington-Humphreys turned to stagger after her captor she took in the Marines at a glance and an expression of recognition came over her face, but she said nothing. The pair disappeared rapidly out of sight down the tunnel.

"What the hell are you two doing down there?" a voice yelled suddenly from the gallery. A big man stood at the tunnel entrance framed in the light from the gallery, one arm akimbo on his right hip, the other cradling his weapon.

"We're escorting General St. Cyr and his prisoner, sir!" Dean answered.

"What?" the figure's arm fell to his side and he lowered his weapon.

"We're going after the general," MacIlargie said, pointing on down the corridor into the dark shadows. MacIlargie thought to himself, If the bastard comes five meters closer, I can get that weapon away from him.

"What!" the man shouted again. He swore violently and looked over his shoulder. Then he muttered something that sounded like "running out on us," turned and ran out into the gallery.

"Now what?" Dean asked. MacIlargie didn't answer. They were fugitives surrounded by heavily armed soldiers who would not hesitate to shoot them. And those soldiers stood between them and the Marines who were coming to their rescue. If they stayed right where they were, they would survive.

"Well . . ." MacIlargie shrugged and nodded down the dark corridor in the direction St. Cyr had disappeared. "We were told to be her shadow."

"Right," Dean replied, and unarmed, with no idea where they were headed, the two started off after St. Cyr and Ambassador Wellington-Humphreys.

CHAPTER THIRTY-TWO

Holding a glowball in his left hand, St. Cyr shoved Wellington-Humphreys, her wrists bound tightly behind her back, along with his right, catching her every few steps as she stumbled in the near darkness.

"Pick up your feet," he ordered. Then, abruptly, he stopped. Wellington-Humphreys gasped for breath, grateful for the chance to rest. She was also grateful now that one of the guards had given her a battle dress uniform to replace the formal dinner dress she'd had on when abducted. "Quiet," St. Cyr ordered. "Breathe through your goddamned nose." He shook her violently, then stood there listening. Aside from their own breathing, total silence enveloped the tunnel around them. "Good, good," he whispered. "Now to make sure we're not being followed." He let go of her for a moment, fished in a cargo pocket and took out a tiny black object. "Detonator," he said with pride, holding up the little black square.

Wellington-Humphreys gasped. Those two Marines! Somehow they'd managed to escape, and she felt sure they must be following. She couldn't let St. Cyr detonate that charge. Suddenly energized, she lunged at him. Caught off guard, St. Cyr lost his balance when the woman smashed into him, and they both fell to the floor with a crash. The detonator flew out of his hand and skidded off into the darkness. Recovering quickly, St. Cyr delivered several hard blows to the side of the Ambassador's head. Hands fastened behind her, she could not defend herself. She lay on the floor, dazed, as St. Cyr scrambled on his knees after the detonator. He retrieved it and pressed the firing

317

switch. A dull thud sounded up the tunnel from where they'd just come, and then the concussion buffeted them as it passed down the tunnel. A thick cloud of pulverized rock dust engulfed them, temporarily reducing the light from the glowball to a tiny dull spark. They both coughed in the dust.

"You bitch!" St. Cyr gasped. Wellington-Humphreys lay on the floor, all hope gone now, the fight completely taken out of her. In her long and successful career as a diplomat, she had never really cared about the people she represented in her negotiations. Now she could only think of those two Marines, buried under the tons of rock behind them. They had sacrificed their lives for *her*.

Gradually the dust settled. "That, my dear, is insurance we won't be followed." St. Cyr tossed the tiny black box aside. He held the glowball close to Wellington-Humphreys's face. It was streaked with tears. "You are not a bad specimen," he said, bending close and running his tongue along her jawline. A terrible rage suddenly welled up inside her and she turned and bit him on the neck.

"Goddamn!" he shouted, and punched her in the head with his balled fist. She staggered back into the wall and collapsed. As she fell hard on her side, at last she understood how someone could kill another person with a knife. The glowball rolled on the floor, eerily illuminating St. Cyr's legs. "Try that again, and I'll break your arm," he shouted.

"Put your filthy tongue on me again, you bastard, and I'll bite your fucking throat out!" Wellington-Humphreys screamed back.

St. Cyr reached down with one arm and hauled her upright. "Any more biting around here, and I'll do it," he hissed. "When I get you to where we're going, Madame Ambassador, I'll have my way with you until I'm done with you." With a nasty laugh he shoved her hard on down the tunnel.

"Where are you taking me?" she asked.

"To my bower." St. Cyr laughed. He felt expansive and confident now. He was still ahead of the wave. "There is an underground river about a kilometer farther down this tunnel. Its channel runs in an old shaft the miners dug two hundred years ago. It flows into the Carnelian Sea. I have a small watercraft just ahead that will take us to the river's delta. From there it's a short walk to where I have hidden a 36 V spacecraft. You figure out the rest of the plot."

A brilliant flash followed immediately by a rush of hot air threw the two Marines head first along the tunnel they'd been trying to negotiate in the almost total darkness. From far ahead they could just make out the tiny speck of light that was St. Cyr's glowball. Now they lay stunned on the rocky floor as tons of debris crashed down upon the spot where they'd been shuffling along only minutes before.

"Mac!" Dean shouted. His ears were ringing loudly from the blast. At first he was afraid he'd lost his hearing completely.

"Here," MacIlargie answered from somewhere in front. They had both been picked up by the force of the explosion and hurled down the tunnel. Dean felt wetness on one side of his face. He wiped at it and then put his fingers to his lips. Blood. He began crawling in the direction of MacIlargie's voice and found him by touch. "Are you okay?"

"Yeah. Stunned, is all. Well, Shadow, we're really in the shit now, aren't we?"

"Yeah—" Suddenly Dean screamed. "Something's in here with us! It touched me!"

A small, blue-green light began to glow beside Dean's leg. Quickly it formed the outline of a Woo.

"Ee, gods," Dean whispered, "one o' them whatchamacallits!"

"Yeah, yeah!" MacIlargie exclaimed. "Never seen one before. But it must be a Woo. They're harmless," he added. "And look, it can generate light!" With that, the Woo glowed even more intensely, as if showing the Marines what it could do. "Stop it, you idiot! He'll see us!" MacIlargie whispered, and the Woo suddenly stopped glowing. "It understands English," he exclaimed.

Dean did not believe that, but grateful for the source of light, he decided not to chance insulting the creature, so he kept quiet.

The huge eyes mounted on either side of the Woo's long

narrow head gazed silently at the pair. Then it nodded down the tunnel in the direction St. Cyr had departed. When they did not respond, it nodded again. Then it scuttled down the tunnel a short distance, and beckoned them on with its one armlike appendage.

"It's gonna guide us, Deano, the little bugger is going to guide us!"

Cautiously, they picked their way along behind the creature, which now scurried down the tunnel in short dashes, emitting just enough light to guide them but not enough to give their presence away.

St. Cyr pushed Wellington-Humphreys into a small gallery out of which led several passages. He put an infra device to his eye and shoved her across the gallery into a branching tunnel. "Half a kilometer down this tunnel we will skirt a geothermal spring that bubbles up through a fissure. It is boiling, so don't fall in. The path around is negotiable even with your arms tied behind you. Once on the other side, we crawl up a steep slope and we are there." He smiled voraciously and pushed her onward.

A minute later the Woo, followed closely by the two Marines, skittered through the gallery and unerringly picked the tunnel down which St. Cyr had just disappeared. The Woo increased its pace and the Marines scrambled to keep up with it.

Suddenly, the tunnel began to broaden, and just ahead they could see the faint glow of light and hear voices, one of them clearly that of a woman. The temperature had gradually increased and the air inside the tunnel had turned humid. The Woo had stopped generating light and now squatted at the mouth of the tunnel. The three crouched in the darkness and peered out across a steaming pool of water at St. Cyr, clearly silhouetted by the glowball in his hand as he inched carefully along a rock ledge just above the steamy surface of the water. The sound of running water came to them clearly on the humid air.

Dean put his ear close to MacIlargie's. "That must be how he's going to get away. There's a river somewhere nearby. We've gotta stop him now, before it's too late!"

"How? We don't have any weapons!"

The Woo reached up to Dean, and between the fingerlike talons that served it as a hand, it clutched a large rock. Dean's expression changed as he got the idea. MacIlargie caught on almost as fast and groped on the floor of the tunnel for rocks of his own. When the Woo saw that each Marine was ready with a rock in each hand, it began to generate a brilliant orange light that rapidly swelled to illuminate the entire chamber like daylight.

Dean threw his rock with all his might. It narrowly missed St. Cyr's head and bounced off the wall and into the pool, where it disappeared with a splash and a cloud of steam. MacIlargie's rock hit St. Cyr on the shoulder and caused him to wince. He pulled the Ambassador closer to him to use her as a shield, and stepped off the ledge onto a gradual rock-strewn slope. Holding her tightly with one arm, he drew his blaster and leveled it at the two Marines, who were now clearly visible on the other side of the bubbling pool. At the last instant, Wellington-Humphreys shoved him, and the bolt spattered harmlessly into the rock vault above the pool. St. Cyr smashed the blaster barrel across the bridge of her nose and shoved her away from him, up the slope. Then, turning back toward the Marines and using two hands to hold the blaster, he planted his legs firmly about ten centimeters apart and took careful aim.

The Woo's light went out and everything plunged back into darkness. St. Cyr hesitated to shoot, and at that instant Wellington-Humphreys smashed into him with all her weight behind her shoulder. St. Cyr staggered forward and plunged head first into the pool. He went fully under, popped quickly to the surface, screaming. The Woo's light came back on, and Dean stepped onto the ledge and began inching his way toward where Ambassador Wellington-Humphreys lay dazed, her head only a few inches from the bubbling pool.

St. Cyr screamed and thrashed about in the boiling water. He reached for the ledge on which Dean stood and tried to pull himself up. Dean stamped hard on his fingers. The nails and flesh shredded off under the boot, but still screaming, St. Cyr clung to the rock. Dean stamped on his head and a large patch of his hair sloughed off. Balancing himself precariously on the slippery rock, Dean ground his heel on St. Cyr's fingers and then kicked him again in the head, and this time he slipped back into the water. Afraid that St. Cyr would come back and get a grip on one of his legs, Dean dashed the rest of the way across.

Meanwhile, MacIlargie stood on the other side of the pool and tossed rocks at St. Cyr as he splashed about in the pool, his screams increasing in intensity as the boiling water cooked him alive. MacIlargie tried to silence him with a blow to the head, but the rocks just thudded into his swelling flesh without effect.

Dean crouched beside Ambassador Wellington-Humphreys. "Are you all right, ma'am?" He helped her to her feet. She nodded that she was, although blood still flowed freely from her broken nose. "I can't get this damned fastening off your wrist," Dean complained as he tried to loosen it. "I'm afraid we'll have to go back along that ledge. Can you make it?"

"Yes. Can you shut him up?" she asked, nodding at St. Cyr, who now had drifted to the middle of the pool and floated there with only his head and shoulders above the water, trying to keep the burning liquid out of his nose and mouth.

Once on the other side, the two Marines gathered rocks and began pelting St. Cyr with all their strength, not for revenge or punishment, but in an effort to silence his terrible screaming, which gradually weakened into a high-pitched keening. The man who had fancied himself a greater conqueror than Napoleon Bonaparte, the man who had conquered a whole world, was reduced to a screaming mound of stewed flesh twisting in the boiling water. The rocks bounced off his head and face, crushing his bones and teeth, but still he kept up the keening. At last he sank beneath the water and the grotto became silent, except for the Marines' heavy breathing and Wellington-Humphreys's retching.

With a forearm, Dean wiped perspiration off his brow and sat down inside the mouth of the tunnel. MacIlargie and Ambassador Wellington-Humphreys joined him. The three sat in silence for a few moments, catching their breath. The Woo diminished his light so they would no longer have to see St. Cyr's lifeless, obscenely swollen body floating like an overdone sausage in the steaming pool.

"I thought I recognized you when St. Cyr dragged me out of my cell, but it was just too good to believe you'd gotten free," Wellington-Humphreys told the Marines. In turn, MacIlargie explained what had happened to them. "I've heard of daring rescues before," she replied, "but what you did beats everything."

"Hell, ma'am, it was you who saved our asses—er, saved us when you knocked that bastard off into the pool," MacIlargie said. "We were just following orders the skipper gave us the night of the reception, to stick, uh, close by your side."

"Do you know what happened to Professor Benjamin and your ensign?" she asked. Then she told them what St. Cyr had done.

Both men were silent for a moment. "Woo," MacIlargie said, his voice choked with anger, "please turn the lights back on!" and for several minutes he and Dean pelted St. Cyr's floating corpse with more rocks.

"Now what do we do? The tunnel behind us is blocked." Dean said as the trio sat disconsolately by the pool.

"He had a boat of some kind stored at the river over there," the Ambassador said. "We could find it and escape to the sea."

"How far is that?" MacIlargie asked.

Wellington-Humphreys shrugged her shoulders. "I wish you could untie these bonds, I'm beginning to lose feeling in my hands." While the Woo gave them light to see by, they examined the cords that bound her hands behind her, but there was no way they could break them or cut them without tools.

"Let's see if we can manage to get your arms in front of you," Dean suggested. She sat down, and with Dean pushing her legs onto her chest while MacIlargie pulled her arms out over her butt, they managed to push and shove until her arms came around in front. They worked the bonds as best they could to relieve the pressure on her wrists, and gradually some feeling came back into her fingers. "At least this way you'll be able to keep your balance better," Dean said.

"Shall we take the boat?" MacIlargie asked. Before he could answer, the Woo scrambled back up the tunnel a meter from where they were sitting and beckoned for them to follow.

"Well, Mac, looks like he has another plan. What do you say?"

"The little shit's done okay by us so far; let's go. Besides, I don't much like boats." They helped Wellington-Humphreys to her feet and followed the Woo back up the tunnel.

"Still afraid of Woos?" MacIlargie asked, draping an arm around Dean's shoulders as they trudged through the tunnel.

"Hell no!" Dean answered, and added, without thinking, "Why, if he had tits on his back I'd marry him!" Ambassador Wellington-Humphreys smiled in the dark behind him.

A crew of miners had been flown in from New Kimberly and set to work clearing the debris out of the tunnel. "This'll take us about an hour," the foreman told Captain Conorado.

Conorado had set up a command post in the gallery, and from there he coordinated the search parties he'd dispatched throughout the complex, to find a way around the collapsed tunnel. General Aguinaldo had mobilized his entire division and, with help from the army, a thorough search and surveillance operation encompassing all the territory within a hundred-kilometer radius of Mount Amethyst was mounted. St. Cyr had to come out somewhere, and when he did, the Confederation forces would be there—they hoped.

Captain Conorado was pouring over the chart of the tunnel complex with Hard Rocks Viola when a distinctly feminine voice behind him said, "Captain, would you do me a slight favor, sir?" He turned around and his mouth fell open. There stood Ambassador Wellington-Humphreys in a thoroughly bedraggled battle-dress uniform, her face covered in blood. Behind her stood Dean and MacIlargie, grinning like fools. The Woo, glowing a satisfied pink, sat on Dean's shoulder.

"Madame Ambassador, how? Well, where the hell did you come from?" was all Conorado could think to say.

"The Woo knew a way out. Now, sir, could you get these fucking goddamned cords off my wrists?"

As the FIST surgeon attended to Wellington-Humphreys's broken nose, Dean and MacIlargie told their story.

"Mighty smart of you boys to take that Woo along with you," Hard Rocks commented when they'd finished. "Little buggers have an unerring sense of direction and they generate their own light source. Never come down here myself without one or two of 'em along."

"We didn't bring him along, he brought us along," MacIlargie said. They stared at the Woo for a moment.

"And Captain," Dean said, "I want to take him back to Camp Ellis with me. Can I do that, sir?"

Captain Conorado laughed. "Well, okay, Marine, but have Mr. Viola here show you how to take care of the thing. And Lance Corporal, you take him back, *you* will be responsible for him." Dean grinned and the Woo glowed a dull pink. The Captain turned back to the others. "Men, you can thank Mr. Viola here for getting us into this place. And what's more, he stuck right by me during the worst of the fighting."

"I was hiding behind him, actually," Viola said, "nowhere else to go."

"You know," Captain Conorado said contemplatively, "you should get something out of this besides satisfaction, Hard Rocks. I know where there's a Bomac 36 V starship nobody's got a claim on anymore. Interested?"

Hard Rocks was silent for a moment. "Well, Skipper, a 36 V is a bit out of my class, but thanks very much for the offer. You know, if you're in the mood to give things away, how about one of these helmets you boys wear?"

Captain Conorado laughed and clapped Viola on his shoulder. "Done!"

"Captain," Wellington-Humphreys said, rising from the litter where the surgeon had been working on her, "since you're giving away rewards, these two Marines of yours saved my life down there. I'll see to it that the President knows about it, but until then I have an 'interim' award for them." With that, she walked over to each man, hugged him tightly and kissed him on the cheek.

"Thing about kisses, ma'am?" MacIlargie said. "You get one, and right away you want another."

CHAPTER
THIRTY-THREE

Fleet Admiral Wilber Wimbush, despite his faults as an officer and a man, was a traditionalist who believed in the value of military ceremony. He was the only commander in the Confederation naval forces who maintained a special unit of bandsmen for banging and tootling on real musical instruments at every official occasion he hosted. The formal surrender of Diamunde's military forces lent itself perfectly to this indulgence. It would be, in fact, the grandest and most ostentatious ritual the admiral had ever held. His long-suffering staff planned every aspect down to the smallest detail, and Wimbush personally, after long and careful consideration, selected the most suitable marches and airs for the bandsmen to play. A weary wag on his staff had remarked to a colleague that if the admiral had planned his Diamundean campaign half so carefully, the war would've been over in twenty-four hours.

Admiral Wimbush selected the 34th FIST as the guard of honor for the ceremony. He did this not in recognition of its fine combat record, but just to make them stand in the hot sun all day. Privately, he blamed them for letting Ambassador Wellington-Humphreys get kidnapped. So far he had not been able to foist any of the blame for that off on the Marines, but he'd tried. The fact that the Marines had then gone in and rescued her did not help his case. The kidnapping—and frankly, the spectacular rescue—had only added to the admiral's embarrassment over the army's failure to reinforce the Marines on the planethead at Oppalia, and his less than perfect performance as

Fleet commander. So far it appeared that the army had taken the fall for that fiasco.

General Aguinaldo, as acting ground-force commander, was to receive the formal surrender. His appointment to Assistant Commandant, the Confederation Marine Corps' second highest position, had just been announced, to the great annoyance of the Fleet commander. Aguinaldo had been nominated for the gold nova of his new rank before deployment to Diamunde. Evidently, his conduct during the fighting had not diminished his standing on the promotion list, further galling evidence to Wimbush that the Marines, at least, were going to come out of this with their fighting reputation unscathed.

The admiral, accompanied by Ambassador Wellington-Humphreys, the civilian appointees of the new government—who would be announced afterward—and the army commanders, would occupy a raised platform at the surrender site. The Ambassador and the military commanders would sign the actual surrender document, while the dignitaries witnessed the signing. The ceremony was to take place just a few kilometers outside New Kimberly, on a flat plain that could accommodate the thousands of civilian and military onlookers that were expected. Not only would St. Cyr's remaining forces surrender, marking the formal end of hostilities, but Ambassador Wellington-Humphreys would present the new coalition government of Diamunde, thereby abolishing in an instant the monopoly the Hefestus Conglomerate and Tubalcain Enterprises had had on the planet's economy for years, and removing the main reason for the internecine conflicts that had threatened the planet's peace and stability for generations.

Best of all, from Admiral Wimbush's point of view, now that the war on Diamunde was ending on such a high note of success for his forces, when the naval representative to the Combined Chiefs of Staff retired—any day now, according to Fleet scuttlebutt—his chances of being appointed to fill that vacancy would be excellent.

The day of the ceremony dawned hot and still. It was dead summer in that part of Diamunde, and the thousands of people gathered on Surrender Plain, as it was already being called, perspired in the sun as they waited anxiously for the ceremony to begin. Video units had been set up so those not close enough to see the ceremonies might watch them on the huge vidscreens strategically placed throughout the vast crowd.

Ambassador Wellington-Humphreys, Admiral Wimbush and his party, and the dignitaries, sat silently under the canopy that had been stretched over the high platform where the surrender would be consummated. The terms had been written out on a large sheet of the fine parchment called treaty paper, by a member of Wellington-Humphreys's staff, who was also an expert calligrapher. The text had been drawn up in the flowery language of the late twentieth century. Old-fashioned styluses stuck out of genuine glass inkwells strategically placed on a felt-covered table, behind which sat the signatories. The Diplomatic Corps had its own distinct but, of course, refined flair for ritual.

From far off toward the Chrystoberyl Mountains came a steady rumbling. The crowds hushed and all eyes turned in that direction. Soon a huge cloud of dust appeared on the horizon, and then the earth beneath their feet began to tremble as the remaining armored battalions of St. Cyr's forces rolled out of the shimmering haze. All the tanks had their cannons pointed to the rear, the ancient traditional symbol of surrender. Slowly, with ponderous dignity, engines roaring, tracks *skreek*ing in the hot, quiet air, the behemoths ground to a halt in precise ranks only a few yards from where Admiral Wimbush and his delegation sat waiting.

Admiral Wimbush sat flanked by Ambassador Wellington-Humphreys and General Aguinaldo on his right, and the two army Corps commanders on his left. Just behind the Ambassador stood two enlisted Marines—Dean and MacIlargie—at stiff attention, their dress red uniforms brilliant even in the shade of the canopy. Since the dress uniforms they'd been issued for the reception had been ruined, the admiral had paid a local tailor to make the new uniforms for the men, and best of all, they could keep them! That had really galled Wimbush, because he'd never wanted the enlisted men there. When he protested their presence at such an important function, Ambassador Wellington-Humphreys replied, "Admiral, you might not like it, but those two lads are going to be standing right there behind me. *None* of this would be happening if it hadn't been for those two infantrymen." Wimbush backed down instantly. And he paid for the goddamned uniforms out of his own pocket. Damnit, you couldn't have flag officers in their mess dress sitting out there with two scroungy enlisted men in battle dress—especially those confounded chameleons—bringing up the rear!

A few paces behind their tableau, the provisional government of Diamunde sat, waiting to be announced.

"Hope these guys are serious about giving up," MacIlargie whispered out of the corner of his mouth to Dean.

Dean tried to ignore a rivulet of perspiration creeping down inside his high stock collar. He twisted his lips in MacIlargie's direction and whispered, "What I wouldn't give for an ice cold liter of Reindeer Ale."

MacIlargie smiled. Let's get this over with, he thought. The Marines were looking forward to returning to Thorsfinni's World and the long stand-down that awaited them there. For those men who did not get home leave, that would mean a pleasantly reduced training schedule and lots of liberty in New Oslo. Even Big Barb's, with all its noise and smoke and spilled beer, seemed attractive to him. God, home, he thought. His heart raced with anticipation. He liked Ambassador Wellington-Humphreys a lot, but the surrender ceremony was all dukshit. He didn't see any special honor involved in standing up there like an idiot. If he had to be there at all, he'd rather be sweating in ranks with the other men of third platoon.

He thought about home again. If he didn't get leave this time around, he'd get it next time. Top Myer kept a roster of eligibles and sooner or later his turn would come up. And when I get home leave, he thought with sudden inspiration, I'll invite good old Deano to come with me, and boy, will we ever tie one on!

He turned his attention to the tanks, all moving up into neat rows. All I need now is some Straight Arrows for good old Eagle's Cry! he thought.

The tanks, light and heavy, and their support vehicles—fuel tankers, retrievers—sat ominously silent in ranks for several minutes, the crews waiting until the dust clouds generated by their arrival had dissipated. At a prearranged signal, hatches popped open and the crewmen dismounted. Each crew stood at attention before its vehicle.

A profound silence descended over Surrender Field. It was broken by a tank hatch clanging open. People standing a kilometer away heard it, and those closer started at the sharp crack of metal upon metal. Slowly, a figure dressed in dirty tanker's overalls climbed out of the lead vehicle. He jumped lightly to the ground and strode alone and purposefully toward the assembled delegation at the tables. The man was unarmed, but he wore a thick black leather belt about his waist from which flapped an empty side-arm holster; the belt was secured by a rich gold buckle embossed with a spread-eagle device. The highly polished leather belt and its brilliant buckle contrasted sharply with the dirty, oil-stained coveralls the approaching man was wearing over his uniform. On his shoulders glittered four silver stars.

It was General Naseby Namur.

As soon as news of St. Cyr's death reached Namur, he proceeded directly to army headquarters, bypassing his divisional and Corps commanders. He took his brigade, reduced now to the size of a mere battalion, with him. During the cease-fire, before St. Cyr kidnapped the Ambassador, Namur had done his best to restore some morale among his troops. Orders had been issued from army headquarters to refurbish and rearm, in case the negotiations broke down. When it was announced that St. Cyr had kidnapped the Ambassador, all units were ordered to make preparations to resume fighting. But no one gave the actual order to attack because none of the several army commanders dared act on his own, since none wanted to take upon himself the responsibility for restarting the war they had already lost.

The army commander, Brigadier General Newt Lott, was in conference with his staff when Namur broke in.

"Who gave that order to prepare to attack?" Namur demanded without preamble.

"What the hell . . . ?" Lott exclaimed. "Colonel, you're out of line busting in here like this!"

"Who gave the order?" Namur gritted through clenched teeth. A lieutenant, two sergeants, and a dozen more enlisted men, all armed, crowded in behind their commander.

Lott sputtered, "Well, if you must know, Colonel, they were issued as sealed orders before we began the campaign. Now go back to your unit before I have you court-martialed!"

Namur spat on the floor. "General, you are relieved. As of now I command this army, and in a few minutes I'm taking over command of what's left of Diamunde's forces. This war is over, and I'm gonna see to it some idiot doesn't start shooting again. Anyone disagree with that?" The other officers stared in disbelief at Namur.

Namur's reputation was well-known in the army. Every officer present knew the colonel was quick on the trigger. After a brief moment of hesitation, Lott sighed and nodded his acquiescence. "Colonel," he said wearily, "what are your orders?"

"Contact all other army commanders and tell them that I am arranging our surrender. Oh, yes, one more thing. I am now General Namur. And General, thanks for your cooperation. You are now Lieutenant General Lott and my deputy."

Faced with Namur's determination, the other army commanders quickly caved in and Namur lost no time putting on his new insignia of rank: four silver stars.

As General Namur approached the stairs leading to the platform where the surrender table stood, the band struck up a lively tune. "What is that?" Wellington-Humphreys asked Admiral Wimbush in a low voice.

"It's called 'The World Turned Upside Down,' ma'am. Very ancient," he whispered, smiling broadly. "They used it at another surrender ceremony, not as important as this one, though, oh, years and years ago," he added proudly.

"Well, I guess it is turned upside down, from their standpoint," she replied.

As the music began, Brigadier Sturgeon shouted, "THIRTY-FOURTH FI-I-IST . . . !"

All down the line his subordinates prepared for the next order: "BATTALIONNNNNN . . . ! Companeeeeee . . . ! Platoooooon . . . !"

"A-ten-SHUN!" the brigadier commanded, and the ranks snapped smartly from parade rest to the position of attention.

Slowly, with great dignity, Namur mounted the stairs. The surrender delegation stood as Namur approached to within a few paces of the table, where he saluted Admiral Wimbush. The admiral returned the salute. Namur made a slight bow toward Ambassador Wellington-Humphreys and then slowly, ceremoniously, unbuckled his belt and handed it over to General Aguinaldo. A great cheer arose from the assembled crowd. A soldier brought a chair, and Namur was invited to seat himself before the delegation. Aguinaldo handed the belt to an aide who had rushed up to receive it. Admiral Wimbush offered Namur the surrender document, which Namur read and signed with a flourish. Then each of the delegation signed in turn. Wellington-Humphreys, as the Confederation President's personal representative, signed last.

"These proceedings," Wimbush announced ponderously, happily plagiarizing the remarks of a renowned warrior from the distant past, "are now ended." The crowd burst into wild cheering and dancing. Quietly, Admiral Wimbush, his generals, and Naseby Namur, arose, stepped back from the table, and took up places on the far side of the platform, next to the dignitaries. To that point every move had been carefully choreographed, even Namur's noisy emergence from his command tank and his dirty uniform, to emphasize the fact that his side had lost.

Wellington-Humphreys now stood and waited patiently for the crowd to quiet down.

"Ladies and gentlemen," she began, and the crowd roared again. She made several more starts. Gradually the multitude began to quiet. "Ladies and gentlemen," she said, "I am now going to introduce you to the provisional government of Diamunde." She gestured at the dignitaries sitting behind her. "I shall call each person's name and appointment, and each will join me here so you can see them all. With help from the Confederation, they will maintain peace and economic stability on this world, and then—" Here she paused. "—the Confederation will assure elections, so for the first time in your planet's history your government will represent you, and not some corporate entity."

At first these remarks were greeted by a long silence, but as their import began to sink in, first scattered applause and then gradually a roar of approval rose from the thousands of throats. Astonished at the reaction, Wellington-Humphreys smiled, and as the crescendo swept over the platform like a palpable wave of sound, for the first time in her career as a diplomat she was sincerely moved by her own words—a very rare thing for any diplomat—and deeply embarrassed as unbidden and unfamiliar tears formed at the sides of her eyes.

Wellington-Humphreys's staff had done their work thoroughly. From among the survivors of the Hefestus, Tubalcain, and the smaller consortia management staffs, they had selected individuals who had the knowledge and technical skills required to form a government that could work.

After the introductions, Wellington-Humphreys stood flanked by six men and four women, the nucleus of the new government of Diamunde. Only a president was needed now, and her work would be completed. He had been contacted several days before and had agreed to the appointment only after a long meeting with Wellington-Humphreys. "Ladies and gentlemen," she intoned, "I give you your new president, a brave man who has the moral courage, the leadership, and the fortitude to lead Diamunde back into its rightful place in the Confederation of Worlds." She paused.

Admiral Wimbush looked quizzically at General Aguinaldo, who shrugged. Only the military men remained seated. Everyone else was standing beside the Ambassador. The military, because government was none of their business, had not been included in any of the civilian rigmarole. Wimbush was anxious to return to his flagship and see how the five stars of a marshal of the Fleet would look on his collars.

"Ladies and gentlemen," Wellington-Humphreys announced, "I give you Mr. President Naseby Namur."

Back in his quarters onboard the *Ogie*, Admiral Wimbush relaxed with a stiff drink in his hand, going over a stack of dispatches and reports. An aide, a full commander, entered and stood waiting for the admiral to recognize his presence. After a long moment Wimbush looked up inquiringly.

"Sir, a hyperspace drone from the Combined Chiefs has just delivered a dispatch. It's Eyes Only for you, sir." Wimbush's heart raced. The Combined Chiefs—this was it! Eagerly he snatched the cassette and popped it into his decoder. In seconds a message leaped out at him from the vidscreen. Wimbush blinked. Then he just stared at the screen for a long time. The aide quietly took a pace forward from where he stood and leaned forward slightly so he could surreptitiously read the message over the admiral's shoulder. Wimbush never noticed. The commander straightened up, a tiny smile twitching at the corners of his mouth. After waiting several minutes for the admiral to dismiss him, the commander shrugged and quietly let himself out of the admiral's quarters.

Wimbush continued to stare at the vidscreen. No Combined Chiefs, not even another operational command. Fleet Admiral Wilber "Wimpy" Wimbush was to be the next Commandant of the Naval War College. Preposterous; no one went there. Even naval officers preferred to attend other service schools. Why, even ICAF figured higher on most officers' dream sheets. He'd be rubbing shoulders with people like—like—Professor Benjamin. He was being told to retire. All he could think of was how he'd like to murder General Han.

In the companionway outside, the aide whistled softly to himself as he headed for the wardroom. There really is a

God, and He loves us! he thought. The wonderful news would spread like wildfire throughout the Fleet—and he would be the messenger.

EPILOGUE

When the weary men of the 34th FIST returned to Thors-finni's World, the unit began a reduced training schedule while each eligible man was afforded a chance to go on leave. Refitting, replacements, and the necessary personnel reorganizations required because of combat losses, would be taken care of during the training stand-down, and there would be plenty of liberty for everyone.

Selected from company rosters by their first sergeants, those Marines would go to their home worlds, where friends and family eagerly waited for them. A few of the eligibles opted to spend their time between New Oslo and Bronny, soaking up the beer and 'Finni hospitality. Dean was one of them. He'd gone to the top of the home leave list when his mother died, but he'd asked Top Myer to give him a few days to think it over. Claypoole and MacIlargie both invited Dean to help them drink up all the beer in Bronny. But not even that appealed to him very much. He found himself at loose ends. His only reason to return to Earth would be to visit Fred McNeal's family and his own mother's grave. McNeal had been killed on Elneal, Dean's first deployment. For their part, his friends in third platoon understood how he felt, so they did not press him to join in the revels.

So in the end Dean remained most nights in the barracks at Camp Ellis, wandering through the nearly empty hallways. "Make up your mind, Dean," Top Myer had told him. "If you don't want to go somewhere, I'll give your allocation to somebody else, but I won't hold it open forever."

Then Captain Conorado called him into his office.

"Dean, you need to get out of here for a while. You need to unwind. Don't you have anybody at home you'd like to see?"

"No, sir, I don't. My mom died while we were coming back from Elneal, and my dad's been dead for years. I don't have any brothers or sisters. I was never close to my aunts and uncles or their kids. My friends are all here in the 34th. I was gonna stop in on a buddy's family and see them, but that'd take only a few hours."

"McNeal's folks?" Conorado asked. Dean nodded. The captain understood. "Well, Dean, I've got some company business to finish up here and then I'm off for New Oslo." The married officers and senior NCOs kept their families at New Oslo. "Look, if you stay around here, come on out and spend a few days with us."

Dean was flabbergasted. His company commander was opening his home to him? He didn't know what to say except thanks. But he knew he just could never be at ease in a situation like that. On the other hand, he was flattered.

Dean's long flight back to Earth was not scheduled to depart for two days. He went into Bronny, but the beer tasted flat and neither Claypoole nor MacIlargie's clowning around could relieve his depression. And to make matters worse, both were scheduled to depart on leave soon themselves, so if Dean did stay behind, things would get even lonelier. Gunny Bass was not around to lend a hand; he had gone on leave in New Oslo, keeping the promise he'd made to Katrina. Dean left early that night.

Back in the barracks, he lay on his bunk and tried to read. No good. The room was a mess and would stay that way until the other members of his fire team returned. There'd be few inspections in the 34th until the stand-down was over. From way down the hall a door slammed, sending a sharp echo throughout the whole building. He thought he might go see who it was.

Then he sat bolt upright, stunned by another thought: He didn't *have* to return to Earth, he could go anywhere he wanted to in Human Space. Okay, he would go back to Wanderjahr! He might be able to see Hway. Oh, she'd be busy with the details of running her mother's state, Morgenluft, and it might be hard to get in to see her, but he could try. Hell, he thought, sure she'll see me! Just thinking about her aroused him. And he'd made friends with the police officers in Brosigville, so he'd always have a welcome there. And if nothing else, he could sit in the cafés, smoke thule and drink beer and sing songs with the bar girls for two months. But it was Hway he wanted to see; if only for five minutes, the trip would be worth it.

During the night he dreamed of combat. St. Cyr's tanks were rolling down on him again, just like that first night at Oppalia, and he crouched with a Straight Arrow over his shoulder, the ground shaking underneath him, men screaming orders all around and the darkness split by the vivid flashes of tank cannons and exploding shells and rockets. He awoke with a start, bathed in perspiration.

He lay awake in the empty, darkened room for a long time, then turned his face to the wall and let the tears run down his cheeks.

STARFIST

by David Sherman and Dan Cragg

Book I
First to Fight

Stranded in the desert on a distant planet, stripped of their strategic systems and supporting arms, carrying only a day's water ration, and surrounded by a well-armed enemy, Marine Staff Sergeant Charlie Bass and his seven-man team face a grim future seventy-five light-years from home.

Book II
School of Fire

Deployed to assist the oligarchs of Wanderjahr in putting down a rebellion that threatens the planet's political and ecomonic stability, the Marines must fight two wars at the same time . . . one against the resourceful, well-led guerrillas and another with the entrenched police bureaucracy.

Published by Del Rey Books.
Available at bookstores everywhere.

**Visit www.delreybooks.com—
the portal to all the
information and resources
available from Del Rey Online.**

• Read sample chapters of every new book,
special features on selected authors and
books, news and announcements, readers'
reviews, browse Del Rey's complete
online catalog and more.

• Sign up for the Del Rey Internet Newsletter
(DRIN), a free monthly publication e-mailed to
subscribers, featuring descriptions of new
and upcoming books, essays and interviews
with authors and editors, announcements
and news, special promotional offers,
signing/convention calendar for our authors
and editors, and much more.

To subscribe to the DRIN: send a blank e-mail to
sub_Drin-dist@info.randomhouse.com or you can
sign up at www.delreybooks.com

Questions? E-mail us
at delrey@randomhouse.com

www.delreybooks.com